PHOENIX SOUL

Tarren Guy

Books by Tarren Guy

Veritas Rerum Novels
Power of Will

Written in the Stars Novels
The Earth Beneath Us
The Stars Above Us

Novels From Earth
Hail Atlantis

Sword of the Immortal Novels
Summoner Mage

Trigger Warning

I have used Phoenix as both singular and plural.
Also, this novel has been written in Australian English, and the spelling,
terminology, grammar, and slang have all been edited accordingly.

Prologue

Thick snow crunched beneath my feet. Each step, a battle against both the numbness that claimed my legs and a trembling will to survive. I hadn't felt anything below my knees for what felt like an eternity, and my fingers were mere icicles, unresponsive to the misty breath I tried to warm them with. A chill seeped into my bones causing my head to grow foggy, my eyes taking longer to open after each blink. The only anchor holding my soul to this fragile existence was a faltering willpower I didn't know I had.

As the wind howled through the forest, its mournful cry echoed the despair that grasped my heart. Snowflakes danced around me, swirling in maddening patterns that obscured my vision and harassed my senses. I stumbled, my balance precarious, as the world tilted ominously. The trees, once green and vibrant, now stood as skeletal sentinels, their branches etched against the grey sky like bony fingers.

Memories flooded my mind as I trudged through the snow. Memories of warmth and laughter that now seemed like distant dreams. I recalled the faces of my parents; their features etched in my mind as they pushed me through the small hole in the wooden wall surrounding our village. The wall did well to keep out wolves and bears, but not raiders who attacked to the sound of multiple, deep thrummed, horns. Not ravagers, who brought destruction upon us and the village we called home. My dad, wearing wolf furs, scooped me up in his arms, his beard scratching the side of my head as we ran. My mother followed close behind, her fiery curls trailing behind her like a banner of defiance, reminiscent of a blazing fire. As my dad shoved me through the hole, my mother pushed through her warm jacket, the last act of love in a moment of chaos.

I remembered the sound of warning bells and the cry of my dad as an arrow pierced my brother's skull, the tip poking through the eye socket to fall with him. My mother had looked at me in that moment. Her face filled my vision and cradled my innocence so I couldn't witness the destruction behind her.

"I love you, my darling girl. Be strong." The last words my mother spoke etched themselves in my mind as if in stone. She smiled tenderly, before a sword pierced her chest. Pain ripped through my mother, locking her in a silent scream before she tumbled over, coughing blood.

My mind pleaded with me to run, and I never looked back. At 5, I was too young to know any better, too young to form some sort of bravado and race back in to die in a futile battle. Fear owned my heart, my legs moving on instinct.

Now, as I rubbed my exposed arms, I wished I'd picked up my mother's jacket. Maybe the added warmth would have been enough. Or maybe my torment would have been drawn out long into the night. In the late afternoon, a southerly chill brought the temperature down to unfathomable depths and soon, could drain the life from anyone caught out in the open.

A sudden bout of dizziness caused me to stumble to my hands and knees. Darkness began to take me as my arms shook with the added pressure of holding myself up. Or was I just that cold and didn't realize my body was trembling? It didn't matter anymore. I slumped to the snow, my eyes catching the last of the sun's rays in the minute space between the layer of clouds, the horizon, and the canopy of tall Fir trees. I smiled gently, witnessing the beauty in my final moments.

As my vision began to blur, I focused on what I thought was a hallucination, a pair of strong legs standing in the snow beside me. They seemed solid, but I couldn't trust my senses with my mind so muddled and groggy. I had no energy to turn my head and see if the person I imagined was as naked as those legs. Such a ridiculous notion, I knew, but my mind couldn't offer me truth.

Yet, as I gazed at those legs, a sense of peace washed over me. A conjured image to keep me company in my death throes. My final thought lingered on whether anyone would ever find me, whether anyone would know that Elara of Three Pine Village existed. Darkness flooded me, and my body turned weightless, feeling as though it floated away.

As I drifted into the void, I felt a gentle touch on my shoulder, a warmth that seemed to seep into my bones. A fleeting sensation and one I couldn't grasp, but it was there. A moment of connection in the cold, dark vastness of this frozen world.

Chapter 1

A mist shimmered at the edges of my vision, always just out of focus. As I tried to look closer, it shifted with my gaze, taunting me with its elusiveness. Each step I took felt weightless, as if my body was a mere spectre. My heart pounded in my chest, and my arms tingled beneath the dark, long-sleeved dress I wore for my duties. Something was terribly wrong.

Stumbling towards the nearest window in the long stone hallway, I leaned out into the crisp morning air. The distant mountains, their peaks capped with a layer of snow, glowed softly as the sun rose over them. Yet no warmth reached my cheeks; instead, my body shivered in a cold sweat, my head growing light. With each breath, my lungs burned, but I forced myself to inhale deeply, trying to push through the pain.

Suddenly, a dread clarity sparked in my mind. I was having an asthma attack, but this time, it was while I slept. My mind was awake in this dream world, a place I often created in my subconscious. It was always hard to tell when it was happening, as my mind crafted familiar surroundings like this very hallway. The challenge now was to wake myself up. No one would enter my room until an hour after dawn, when my absence from my maid duties would be noticed. By then, it would be too late.

I looked around the hallway, desperate for anything that might jolt my body into waking but there was nothing familiar. Only a winding stairwell at one end and a large iron door at the other. Telveria Keep, the base of operations for the Telverian Army, was vast, and I'd only explored its public areas during my youth, after the accident that brought me here. It was surprising that my mind could recreate even the restricted areas.

Needing to act, I stumbled towards the iron door. There was a better chance of finding someone inside. If not, I would throw myself from a window, a desperate measure, but I hesitated only because of the slight chance this might be real. I tried the handle, and the metallic click as it opened was a stark contrast to the numbness of my dream body. Pushing through, a horrible sense of disconnection from my physical form began to grow.

Inside, the room was dark, lit only by torches set evenly around an octagonal space, their flames dancing in dark iron sconces. A large oak wood table dominated the centre, surrounded by high-backed chairs. Seated at the table were General Suniel and eight commanders of the war council.

"This is the war room," I thought, realizing with a jolt that I definitely shouldn't be here. Or at least, no one should be able to see me. Yet Commander Walan was staring straight at me, his eyes wide in surprise.

The misty haze began to close in tighter, stealing more of my sight with each passing moment. My eyes pulsed with each heartbeat, and my head swirled. It must be getting worse in the real world. I had to wake up soon, or I might never wake.

As the General rose to his feet, a chair was pushed back scraping across the floor. I remembered him as a grey-bearded man with icy blue eyes, clad in a crimson cape over shining armour. Now, all I could see was a dark shimmer moving at the head of the table. My eyes were failing.

"Then it's settled," General Suniel said, his words barely audible. "The 24 new Souls will be informed immediately and set out for the North."

"General, I have one more name I'd like to put forward," Commander Walan interjected, his form more defined as he spoke closer to me.

"There is no space for another," Suniel replied. "The warriors have been named."

"This is a special case," Walan countered. "She is not a warrior, but on this occasion, she may fill the perpetually empty spaces for a mage."

General Suniel's brow rose, curiosity etched on his face. "Name your candidate."

A sudden surge of energy coursed through my dream body as Walan turned to look directly into my eyes once more. His features became clear, and as he spoke, the single word ripped through my soul, forcing me from this dream prison.

"Elara," he said simply.

Transitioning back into my body was agony. I sat bolt upright gasping, each breath a ragged battle against the constriction in my chest. It felt like trying to inhale through a cloth pressed hard against my mouth. Desperate, I scrabbled for my pipe and the precious Lemna Raja Leaves. They were the only thing that could relax my airways when an attack hit this hard. The smoke soothed the tight muscles in my throat, promising the life-giving air I craved.

But my haste betrayed me. As I fumbled to pack the leaves into the pipe, it slipped from my trembling fingers, skittering across the cold, stone floor. It might as well have landed a mile away as I was at my limit. Rolling off the bed, I dragged myself across the room, my sight blurring at the edges, until my strength gave out and my head thudded against the unforgiving stone.

Then, a presence. A hand lifting my head and the cool metal of a pipe pressed between my lips. A flame flickered before my unfocused eyes as a deep voice, laced with command, ordered, "Breathe."

At first, only desperate rasps of air filled my lungs, each one a painful reminder of what I was missing. Slowly, the smoke from the pipe worked its magic, easing the pressure on my throat. I managed to sit up, leaning back against my rescuer, my eyes squeezed shut against the world. Trembling, I inhaled deeply, again and again, until my strength returned and my body began to settle.

Relief washed over me, and I finally looked up at the man who'd saved me. He was a guard. One I'd seen around the keep, usually assigned to the commanders. It was odd to find him down here, and even more so in my quarters. With him was another guard who stood awkwardly by the door. Heat flooded my cheeks as I remembered I was still half-naked, clad only in an oversized tunic. I tugged at the fabric, trying to cover myself.

"What are you doing here?" I demanded, my voice sharper than intended.

"Elara, Commander Walan sent..." the guard began, his voice hesitant.

"What the bloody hell is going on here!" Baras's voice boomed down the hall, and I couldn't help but smile as the guards snapped to attention. He wasn't due back from patrol for another day or two. The Keep always felt a little emptier without him.

The two guards saluted. "Commander Walan requests Elara's presence, Captain."

Baras's eyes narrowed, his gaze flicking between the guards. "And how long do you expect this... Request to take?"

Leggero, the guard who helped me, shifted uncomfortably. "That's above my station, Captain."

"I've been called to a meeting by the commanders," Baras stated, his tone leaving no room for argument. "I'll be needing Elara to prepare a bath for me beforehand."

"Our orders are..."

"Your orders can wait." Baras cut him off, his voice dangerously low. "The Commander wants his chamber pot emptied? There are plenty of maids for that task. If he truly requires Elara, he can wait half an hour while she prepares my bath."

"The commander said this was urgent."

"The commander can wait," Baras repeated, stepping closer to the older guard. "Or would you prefer to take responsibility for my tardiness? Elara is my maid, and I require her assistance." He was close

11

enough now that I could see the steel in his eyes, the unspoken threat that brooked no argument.

The guard's shoulders slumped. "Don't keep her long, Baras. This summons is... more important than you know." His gaze shifted to me, a strange flicker of warning in his eyes, before he nodded curtly. "Consider that favour I owed you repaid."

Baras's eyes narrowed, but he simply nodded as the guards turned and left.

"Thank you," I called after Leggero, but he didn't acknowledge me. It was odd for them to come for me personally and even more so, that what was happening in the physical world seemed to echo my dreams. A problem for later. Right now, Baras was here and I was filled with a giddy warmth.

"Did they harm you?" Baras asked, his furrowed brow showing concern.

"They saved me, actually. My asthma spiked while asleep. You may have been able to reach me with time to bring me back, but it would have been a close thing."

His jaw tightened. "I felt the temperature plummeting near the Tenebrou borders. I knew it wouldn't be long before it hit here. I was worried."

I tilted my head, studying his face. "Am I that fragile?"

A playful glint sparked in his eyes. "You dress too scantily for this time of year," he teased, tugging playfully at the edge of my shirt before I swatted his hand away with a laugh. "And I swear, every year, mid-autumn, you have a horrible asthma attack. You need to take better care of yourself. You should take the day off. Catch your breath..."

"And I thought you needed me in a bath," I retorted, a playful smile tugging at my lips. The light flirting between us was a familiar dance, but I longed for something more. I wanted to feel his strength, to be held aloft against a wall with only him for support. To know that he desired me as much as I desired him, but Baras was too honourable, too protective and I was still just his maid.

"I need you to run the bath," he corrected, his voice suddenly cautious. "You can rest afterwards. I'll make sure of it. I fear there isn't time for you to join me."

"Because I've been summoned?"

"Ignore that," he dismissed. "It's probably just some soldier with a bee in his bonnet about his laundry. I'll take care of it when I see the commander."

"Thanks, Baras. You always have my back," I said softly. The full day

12

off would be wonderful, but I'd never let him down. "Shall we?"

"Sorry, I need to run to cool down after my mornings exercise. 15 minutes around the grounds will do."

I pouted but relented. "I'll make sure the bath is perfect and set out a change of clothes too."

Leaning in Baras, kissed my forehead, sending a shiver down my spine and a flush to my cheeks. "It's why I only ever come to you. You know me too well. I'll see you shortly."

"Enjoy," I said, watching him stride down the hall, my gaze lingering on the way his leather pants moulded to his firm arse cheeks.

I closed the door, pulling the oversized shirt from my now naked body. In the bronze mirror, I studied my reflection. My dark hair cascaded over my shoulders, framing my face but as always, my soft green eyes were drawn to the dark, swirling scar that ran from my shoulder, between my breasts, and across my stomach. Frostbite from my childhood, the doctors said, but it felt like so much more. It felt like a brand.

I quickly donned the dark, long-sleeved, maid's uniform. The heavy fabric a stark contrast to the lingering warmth of Baras's kiss. With one last glance in the mirror, I headed to Baras's quarters.

The halls and courtyard were more chaotic than usual, even for when a war party returned. Lost in a sea of soldiers and servants, I had to dodge and weave until I was skimming the outer walls to avoid being trampled. A wave of chatter washed over me, almost overwhelming. As I neared Baras's room, snatches of conversation caught my ear.

"The Phoenix Souls have fallen."

Souls? Just like in my dream. A shiver ran down my spine.

"All but Enzo Sinclair? Rumour says he wasn't in the area. Left them for dead, he did. He returned to the field from a completely different front. No one questioned him though, cos it looked like he'd been through hell and back himself."

"Did they say what happened?"

"Just scraps of rumour from some soldiers. Nothing substantial."

"We're going to be in real trouble if the Western Tribes decide to revolt now."

"What are Phoenix Souls?" I blurted out before I could stop myself, my eyes widening in dismay as I realized what I'd done. I hurried into Baras's room, hoping to disappear. What was I thinking? The last thing I wanted was more attention.

Ignoring the usual routine of heating the water, I began to fill the bath. I'd learned long ago that a cool bath was the best way to recover after a hard run, especially for Baras. The colder, the better. But with the chill in the air, I tempered it to the temperature of the old well.

Baras strode in, taking in the lack of steam with a raised eyebrow. His gaze met mine and I held it hoping he would complain, hoping I could reprimand him for the way he loathed the cold.

"It's why you always choose me, right?"

"Damned if I understand why. Maybe I should hire someone who doesn't have my best interest at heart. You know, the ones with the large rumps," he laughed and shot me a wink. I was relieved to break the tension.

"Take your clothes off," I said, my eyes craving the show that was to come.

"You know we don't have time for that." Baras began to disrobe.

"Tch," I said snapping my fingers at him. "Get in the bath. I'll get your clothes. Anything in mind?"

As Baras stripped down to his undergarments, the dim light of the room danced across his physique, accentuating the scars that mapped his body like a testament to his service. I couldn't help but feel a flutter in my chest, a familiar sensation that grew more pronounced over the years. Our history was woven with moments like these, carefree days spent skinny dipping in the great lakes, followed by nights huddled around a roaring fire, our laughter mingling with the crackling flames. Yet, despite our closeness, there was an unspoken boundary between us, one I never dared to cross.

"Officer attire minus the armour," he said, his voice a gentle reminder of the task at hand.

I nodded, my gaze lingering on him for a moment longer before I turned to the tall set of drawers. The officer clothing was neatly folded in the top drawer, a testament to Baras's meticulous nature. As I retrieved the uniform, my thoughts drifted to his upcoming meeting and the dream that had been plaguing me. The words of the two soldiers outside echoed in my mind: *"Phoenix Souls."*

"Baras... can I ask you something?" I said, my voice barely above a whisper.

He paused, water dripping from his hair as he turned to face me. For a moment, I thought he was about to make a quip, but something in my expression must have caught his attention. His eyes narrowed, and he said, "Ask."

I hesitated, the words feeling like lead on my tongue. "What is a Phoenix Soul?" The question hung in the air, heavy with unspoken meaning.

14

Baras's expression shifted, a flicker of concern crossing his face before he masked it with a neutral tone. "Where did you hear that term?" His voice was abrupt, not harsh, but it was enough to make me realize I touched a sensitive topic.

"It's hard to explain," I admitted, feeling a flush rise to my cheeks.

"Try me," he encouraged, his eyes never leaving mine.

I took a deep breath, the memory of the dream flooding back. "Two soldiers mentioned it outside. And then there was this dream... I was in the War Room, and they were discussing names for new Souls. Twenty-four names in all."

Baras's laughter was brief, a momentary lapse in his composure. "Twenty-four is too large a number for Souls. And what did the soldiers say exactly?"

I swallowed hard, recalling the fear that gripped me. "All the Phoenix Souls except Enzo had died."

Baras's reaction was immediate and intense. His eyes flared, and he demanded to know which soldiers had spoken. Before I could answer, he was out of the bath, water dripping from his body as he strode to the window. I pointed out the soldiers, and he rushed to the door, his urgency palpable. I tossed him a towel, and he wrapped it around his waist, his expression grim.

When he returned, his eyes held a dread so deep that only someone who knew him as well as I did could see. His voice was low and serious. "A Phoenix Soul is one of our highest ranked soldiers. We choose six candidates to replace a lost Soul, but..."

I laughed, the sound feeling hollow. "Twenty-four is a far cry from six."

"We've lost four of the five. There will be twenty-four candidates to cover the gap."

Baras's gaze drifted to the Bone Reaper armour mounted on a stand in the corner. The suit was a macabre assembly of gnarled skulls, ribs, and other bones, a showcase of the harsh realities of his world. "If they've summoned me to a meeting after calling me home early, I don't think I'll be wearing the official uniform," he said, his hand resting on the ribbed chest plate. "Those chosen as Phoenix Souls leave immediately with only what they hold. It's as much a test of strength as it is of character and flexibility."

I felt a shiver run down my spine as he whispered, "The Bone Reaper."

"Are you sure?" I asked, my voice barely above a whisper.

"Help me dress," he replied, his eyes locked on the armour.

As I assisted him, a realization dawned on me. "They summoned me too," I said, remembering the dream. "Maybe they want me to be a

Soul."

Baras's expression turned sombre, his words laced with a harsh reality. "You're too weak. They'll be reassigning you once I'm gone."

His words cut deep, but I knew he wasn't trying to be cruel. This was the harsh truth of their world, one where strength and duty were paramount. I nodded; my heart heavy with the knowledge of what lay ahead.

My heart grew weary. I'd dressed Baras in his bone armour, each plate cool and smooth beneath my trembling fingers. He stood silently, staring at a single point on the wall, lost in a world I couldn't reach. His silence was a heavy cloak on a morning usually filled with our boisterous laughter. As I secured the last strap, Baras drew me into an embrace, the bone of his armour digging into me. I tried to ignore the pain, but a chilling premonition gripped me, this was goodbye.

"When I leave, head back to your room. Rest. Gather your strength."

He still wouldn't meet my gaze. A cold knot tightened in my stomach. "Tell me what's going on, Baras."

Baras sighed, a sound heavy with unspoken words. Finally, he looked at me, his eyes filled with a sorrow that mirrored my own. "I'm going to miss you, Elara."

He leaned down, his lips brushing mine in a kiss that was both tender and heartbreakingly final. It was our first true kiss, and the sadness of it threatened to overwhelm me.

As it ended, so did our time together. Baras walked out without another word, leaving me with a hollow ache in my chest. The thought of my empty room, of facing prying eyes, was unbearable. I needed to be alone. To breathe. I headed for the rooftop, hoping the autumn breeze might offer some solace, even if it brought on a cough from my asthma.

Reaching the rooftop, I was grateful for the absence of the morning chill. The sun was a warm balm on my skin. I chose a spot overlooking the courtyard gates, where I could bask and sulk in equal measure. Gazing at the growing town to the east and countryside beyond the walls, memories flickered through my mind, picnics by the great lakes of the east, walks through the western forests, the majestic Firebird Ranges to the north, where my birth home lay beyond. Little information ever made it back from that harsh, sparsely populated land within Telverian territory.

Time blurred. The sun climbed higher into the sky and a sudden roar from the courtyard jolted me back to the present. Two armoured men strode out to stand before the gates, the crowds continuing to cheer. I hadn't even realized so many people had gathered. Then came another cheer, this time for a woman in ranger clothing, a bow slung across her back.

One by one, more men and women, warriors and fighters, emerged from the keep. Each was greeted with thunderous applause. Only the previously chosen Souls remained silent, their faces stoic as they watched. When the seventeenth candidate appeared, laughter rippled through the crowd. A man, completely naked, strode out, confirming Baras's words: a Phoenix Soul leaves with nothing, but what they wear.

Twenty-three now filled the area, and hope flickered within me. Perhaps Baras had been mistaken. Perhaps I could keep him here, share another kiss beneath the crescent moon.

Then, the crowd roared again and my heart plummeted. There was no mistaking that armour. Baras walked to the front of the group asserting his dominance.

Minutes ticked by, heavy with anticipation. Baras said there would be twenty-four candidates. I would have expected them to leave immediately. General Suniel said so in the dream... General Suniel said... A wave of dizziness washed over me. Were they waiting for me? Me, sitting here dressed in a maid's uniform? Was I about to be named and sent on a trek with nothing but these dark, worn clothes?

I stumbled to my feet, heading for the stairwell, desperate to reach my room and prepare for the inevitable. Desperate to get anything more than the rags this Keep clothed me in.

"Good morning, Elara."

The voice, warm and silken, sent a jolt of fear through my entire being. I hadn't heard it since my dream this morning. And rarely before that.

"Good morning... Walan," I managed, my voice betraying my anxiety. My chest constricted, as if Death himself was reaching for me. "What brings you to the roof?"

"I would have thought you'd already know." He stepped in beside me, his gaze sweeping over the gathering below.

My mind screamed obscenities as I continued to try and hold a calm outward demeanour. "I can't say I do."

His lips curled into a smile that sent shivers down my spine. "When I noticed you floating around the meeting room, I thought there might be more to you than just tidying and cleaning. Hidden talents, perhaps, that would be more useful as a Soul. That's why I put your name up. How are you feeling, by the way? You weren't looking to well. My guards were sent to your room to check up on you, but it seems they missed you."

My mind began to race trying to make sense of his words. "No. That was a dream," I said.

Understanding dawned in Walan's eyes. "You don't know what you are. I thought it odd you'd seek to travel in your work outfit, but now it makes sense. You're a Drifter, Elara."

The word echoed in my mind, a hollow sound. "I've never heard the term. Not outside of those that roam from land to land."

"Someone along your family line would have the same ability. To leave your body at will. To fly the lands without restriction or fear. It may even come to pass you find other abilities as well. Many will never notice what you can do but I'm special. I am similar to you. I can *see* and *cast* myself into my immediate surroundings."

'Many people can see," the words running over my head in a torrent too fast to catch.

"Not like me. If you come to know the Phoenix and are accepted, you will find your innate abilities will be amplified tenfold."

"Drifters? Phoenix? Powers? What are you talking about, Walan? You're giving me a death sentence unless I become something I'm not. You've killed me, Walan." Tears welled in my eyes, my chin trembling.

"Look at the people below," Walan commanded, his voice sharp. "Each one is the same as you. Skin, muscle, blood, organs. Each fragile, with their own weaknesses and strengths."

"And what are *my* strengths, Walan? I can barely walk to the fields without collapsing. I can't wield a weapon. Even cleaning wears me out. What fucking strengths?" My anger broke free. Normally, I'd never curse, but this felt like the perfect occasion.

Walan simply smiled, his gaze sweeping over the assembled Souls. Finally, his eyes settled on me.

"Elara. I name you Soul. From this moment forward, that is your title. You will leave this village with what you currently have on you. Only beyond these walls may you gather what you deem useful for your new life. You will follow this path until your life is bonded with a Phoenix and you become Phoenix Soul, or it fades into the nesting grounds to bolster future reincarnations."

The words washed over me, meaningless down to the last syllable. "You've killed me, Walan."

"Then let me give you a parting gift. Nothing physical, mind you. See ol' Jermaine down there watching the exits to all these buildings."

I nodded, apprehension prickling my skin. "I see him."

"Commander Jermaine would not normally mingle with the villagers from around the keep. He would only bring himself so *low* when he believes it necessary."

"It's not for the Souls? What's so important that he remains out here?" I asked the question but feared the response.

"He seeks to kill you." Walan kept his voice even.

"He *what*?!" this was far beyond what I was expecting.

Walan stared into the distance as if in thought a moment then looked back at me. "It was 5 years ago. A young lad, barely old enough to go to war, was named Soul. At the time Jermaine protested the choice, thinking he would die on the side of the road or worse, taint the name of Phoenix Soul should he actually succeed and be chosen. Enzo proved himself in the trials and on the field, but Jermaine still sees him as a black mark against the Phoenix Souls. He believes you will be the same."

"Why wouldn't he? Look at me!" I gestured to my threadbare clothes. "Even I didn't believe I'd make the mountains. Now, I won't even make the gates."

"I named Enzo. I named you. My word carries weight. If I back someone, there's a reason, even if others can't see it."

"And now I won't have the chance to live up to it."

"You need only parry his attack. The outcome might surprise you."

"I'll never manage that."

Walan laughed, a dispiriting sound that made my stomach churn. He stepped close, his thumb jabbing up beneath my chin into the soft flesh by my jaw. Pain shot through me. Gasping, I tried to pull away but his other hand gripped the back of my head, holding me fast. He pressed harder still before releasing me and I stumbled back, rubbing my throbbing jaw.

"That's Jermaine's favourite move. Right-handed, a ten-inch stiletto straight into the brain. You'll drop silently. He'll step in as if greeting you and attack without hesitation. All you need to do is bat it away."

Incredulous, I stared at him. "Bat it away? Just like that?"

"Just like that. I'll show you once. Then we'll reenact it three more times. Each time faster than before. After that, you leave this village and face your destiny. Yes?"

"And if I refuse?"

"As the one who named you, I kill you here and now. I will take your soul to lands of the Phoenix and feed the soil with your energy. Your essence will create stronger Phoenix. Honestly, though, I could do without the trip."

"As could I." I looked into his eyes, searching for any sign of doubt. All I saw was sincerity, perhaps even... belief? It didn't sit right, but he was my only hope. I nodded.

Walan sighed in relief. "Good. Step back and approach me, stabbing

19

for my chin with your right hand. Don't try to be accurate; that's my job. Just move slowly and watch me."

I did as he instructed. Walan scratched his stomach with his left hand like he hadn't a care in the world. As I thrust, he moved in perfect synchronization.

"Your left hand, already on the inside of the attack after scratching your stomach, blocks with an open palm here." Walan placed his hand on my forearm, directly on the elbow. "Immediately, your right hand strikes here." He tapped my wrist. "The force will divert the dagger by inches."

"And how do inches help? He's far stronger."

I flinched as Walan raised his thumb to my chin, bracing myself for the pain. Instead, he gently turned my face. His thumb traced the tender point where the knife would enter, then he took an inch step to the edge of my jawbone.

"One," he murmured, his voice barely audible. His thumb then stepped another inch to glide up the side of my cheek. "Two. Two inches. The knife misses completely, and you live."

"He'll just get another shot."

"That remains to be seen." Walan retreated. "Ready?"

Hesitation gnawed at me, but I nodded. "Let's get this over with."

"Then start scratching. And make it look natural."

My mind raced, trying to recall the movements. Adrenaline surged as I watched Walan's arm begin to move, twice as fast as I'd managed. Reacting instinctively, I clumsily followed the motions, hitting close to the marks and shoving. It didn't feel quite right, but I manage to move his arm away.

"Leverage, Elara. Not strength. You disrupt his arm's natural movement by applying pressure to the right points. Again."

Elated by my success, I nodded. But this time, I focused on how I'd done it, and Walan came at me even faster. My timing was off, my hand placement sloppy. His thumb glanced off my jawbone, scratching the skin but not drawing blood.

"Don't dwell on past successes. Focus on the here and now. Your life depends on it." Walan's voice was sharp. "Even that blow would have glanced away and to only leave a scar. This time, I'll attack with full force. Be ready, because Jermaine won't hold back.... Focus."

He was right. Jermaine wouldn't give me a chance. He would attack with everything he had. A commander has the right to eliminate anyone they deem a threat to the nation's security, even if others disagree.

I stepped back, scratching my stomach. Walan charged. My body tensed, then, at the last instant, relaxed as instinct took over. I hit the marks, shifting the thrust past my face by millimetres. A glint of steel caught my eye. Looking at Walan's hand, I froze.

I must have turned ghostly pale, because a flicker of concern crossed Walan's face.

"You used a real knife." My voice was barely a whisper.

"My thumb wasn't long enough to simulate a blade. Besides," he shrugged, "better to die now, without fear, than later, consumed by it."

"I'd prefer not to die at all." A tremor shook me.

"It's time to join the others." Walan gestured toward the stairwell.

I met his gaze, a surge of indignation flooding through me. "Can't have the others waiting all day." Sarcasm dripped like the words from my mouth. Turning, I headed for the stairs.

"I trust you know to go straight to the meeting point," Walan called after me.

I waved a dismissive hand. Of course I knew. The naked guy was a clear indication, but then, a wave of longing washed over me. The dagger Baras gave me, my comfortable shoes, better clothes, my warm jacket...

"Ah, fuck!" I swore, realizing I was also without my Lemna Raja leaves. Checking my pockets, I found only enough for two, maybe three, strong doses. Weighing my options, I knew better than to break the rules. There would most likely be guards by my room anyway.

So, out into the courtyard I went, the crowd pressing in around me, the weight of my fate crushing me. Everyone cheered but kept a respectable distance... except for one figure striding towards me. Jermaine! In feeling sorry for myself, I'd forgotten about him. Eyeballing the distance, I had maybe eight seconds... Seven seconds to prepare.

Without wasting a moment, I shifted my weight, planting my feet firmly on the ground. Seven seconds to prepare was seven seconds more than I had before. The initial shock of the encounter with Walan on the rooftop faded and I stared into Jermaine's eyes. They were filled with hate. The hate of a thousand suns burning into me saying I had no right to be alive. I had no right to be a Soul. The hate of one who had never failed before.

Five seconds.

He moved with a deceptive speed that belied his size. As he drew closer, I noticed a subtle shift in his posture, a slight angling of his body that foretold his intent. Walan's words echoed in my mind: *"Right-handed, ten-inch stiletto, straight into the brain."*

At three seconds I remembered to bring my left arm to my stomach.

"Elara, I would like to wish," Jermaine started with the pleasantries trying to cover his assault.

The words were a blur humming in the air. My focus snapped tight, locked on Jermaine's eyes, but my awareness stretched, a spiderweb of tension reaching for any flicker of movement. When it came it was like I watched the attack from outside my body. Call it adrenaline or instinct but my body moved in time with the commander. Even then, it was too close to call. My hands snapped up, deflecting the worst of the blow, but the speed of his attack still carved a shallow gash across my chin. The dagger hissed past my ear, a whisper of steel on skin.

This was all I knew. React. Survive.

Jermaine, shock momentarily paralysing his features, needed only to reset his mind and bring the blade around again. Or aim for my stomach. I'd heard the stories. Slow, agonizing deaths. Was this Walan's plan? To keep me alive just long enough to begin some pointless journey so he wouldn't be obliged to cart me across half the country?

A heartbeat stretched into an eternity. Jermaine, a soldier honed by strategy and years of combat, recovered with terrifying speed. I saw a glint of steel and the practiced thrust of the dagger aimed at my gut. My breath hitched, and I braced myself for the searing pain, squeezing my eyes shut against the inevitable.

Then, a jarring impact. An arm slammed into Jermaine's elbow, deflecting the killing blow as the dagger scraped harmlessly against the thicker parts in my maid's uniform. I risked a glance. An older guard, the one from my room earlier, stood between us, his face grim. Defiance like this meant the noose for him.

"I demand you release me! This is my right!" Jermaine's voice, tight with fury, cracked on the last word.

The guard didn't answer. He simply twisted Jermaine's arm with brutal efficiency. A sickening crack of bone echoing in the sudden silence. The dagger clattered to the cobblestones.

"She has been named by Walan," the guard stated, his voice ringing with conviction. "You have committed the highest treason, attacking a Soul."

I saw the blood drain from Jermaine's face, leaving his skin ashen. His dark eyes widened, reflecting a primal terror. The implications of Walan's naming hadn't fully registered for me yet, lost as I was in the fight. Walan, though, understood. It was why he'd only drilled me on deflecting that single, initial attack. Now, Jermaine had signed his own death warrant, and the guards would see it carried out.

But the commander was quick, dangerously so. With a sudden, violent twist, he broke free of the guard's grasp and bolted toward the gathering crowd, hoping to lose himself in the throng. He counted on the townsfolk's indifference, their refusal to aid the guards, the soldiers, even the Souls. To them, we were all cogs in a system that ground them into poverty, our taxes fuelling the armies that kept them suppressed.

This time, however, his gamble backfired spectacularly. The townsfolk surged forward, a mass of bodies and barely restrained rage. They dragged Jermaine down. A snarling, kicking mass of limbs swallowed by the mob. A glint of metal flashed, followed by a wet, gurgling sound, and then crimson sprayed against the grey stones. The blood was the only evidence of Jermaine's ending. Their grim task complete, they turned as one and faced me, their hands pressed to their hearts, heads bowed in reverence.

"Soul," they said, the word coming out in a low, resonant hum.

No one received this kind of respect from the townsfolk. The unexpected display of reverence sent a tremor through me, a strange mixture of awe and disbelief. I fought back the urge to weep, forcing myself to remain composed.

Walking towards the group of waiting Souls, I took my place in the small space beside the naked man.

He leaned in, his voice a low murmur. "It's because they see you as one of them. A servant of the Keep, just like them."

I glanced at him, giving a curt nod to the man who now accepted his lack of attire. My attention remained fixed on the crowd.

"Some reflexes you've got there," he continued, his eyes crinkling at the corners. "Most wouldn't have seen that attack coming, let alone blocked it. No wonder you were chosen. Fitzroy...Fitz." He offered a hand.

I took it, a flicker of amusement dancing in my eyes. I wouldn't correct him. "Elara."

"Elara!" Baras's voice cracked like thunder, cutting through the murmur of the crowd. He finally turned back as his impatience started to get the better of him. Seeing me his expression changed to a mask of fury and disbelief. "You can't be here. This is for Souls only. I know you wanted to say goodbye, but you need to leave now." He grabbed my arm, his grip tight, and began to pull me away.

"She has as much right to be here as you do, *Captain Boner*. She has been named," Fitz said, stepping between us and placing a hand on Baras's chest, his expression challenging. Fitz was new to the Keep and he thought he was saving me. He had no idea the history between Baras and I.

Baras's anger was a tangible thing, radiating from him in waves. He

23

slowly turned his gaze to me, his eyes narrowed. "You? They named *you*, Elara?" He let out a harsh, grating laugh, devoid of humour. "That is an insult to all the Souls who were chosen before you." He glared at me. "You will stay behind when we leave." Spinning on Fitz, his face contorted further into rage. "Were it not for your service record, I would have ordered you to do the same, Fitzroy."

There it was. The overprotective, arrogant side of Baras that I both resented and, on some level, expected. Fitz squared his shoulders, meeting Baras's gaze, the air crackling with unspoken threats. I placed a hand on Fitz's arm, grounding him, and slowly, he stepped back.

"The choice has been made for me," I said, my voice steady despite the tremor in my hands. "I become what I have been named, or they kill me and toss my body into the wilds beyond the mountains. I will walk the path to the Phoenix."

"You will die," Baras spat, the words laced with venom. I saw Fitz flinch, mistaking it for a threat, but I knew Baras's words were born of a twisted concern.

"Long before I reach the foot of the mountains, I suspect. That is my right and my choice. I accept my fate."

"You will *not* come," Baras insisted, as if that settled the matter.

"And what would you have me do instead?" I countered, my voice rising, fuelled by a sudden, unfamiliar anger. I was sick of everyone dictating my life, of being treated like a pawn in their games.

Baras's face hardened, becoming a mask of stone. "You will do what you've always done. What you're good for. You will maintain the upkeep of these halls," he said, gesturing dismissively to Telveria Keep.

His words crystallized the truth, the bitter reality of Baras's perception of me. I was his maid. Nothing more. "You are a stubborn ass, Baras. I have been named."

"You are not a Soul. You possess neither the tactical insight nor the fighting ability required. You cannot be here, Elara."

"Does it offend you so deeply that I am now your equal?" I asked, my voice dripping with scorn. "I pity the boy you are." I knew what was coming. Baras could be predictable, especially when his pride was wounded. I braced myself, both physically and emotionally.

The blow was brutal, a sweeping backhand that sent me sprawling across the cobblestones. He'd never struck me before, but I had witnessed his violence directed at others. And I'd never pushed him this far.

"You will *never* be my equal. You are nothing, Elara. I can't believe you would try to take this from me," Baras snarled, his face contorted with rage.

Pain pulsed through the right side of my face. A searing, throbbing agony. There was a high-pitched ringing in my ears, and I tasted blood where my teeth bit into my cheek, but I would not give him the satisfaction of seeing me break. Pushing myself into a sitting position, I slowly turned my head to face him, a manic smile twisting my lips. Blood trickled from the corner of my mouth, staining my chin. I focused my gaze, deliberately injecting a hint of pleasure into my eyes, pushing him, daring him to react.

I saw the flicker of doubt in his eyes, a hint of regret creeping into his expression as his anger began to subside. Even Fitz, who instinctively moved to intervene, hesitated, stepping back.

A glint of metal caught my eye, and I looked up to find the guard, Tomin, the one who saved me from Jermaine's attack, offering me the hilt of Jermaine's dagger.

"You dropped your dagger, Miss Elara," Tomin said, his voice respectful.

I hesitated, surprised both by his offer and by the unfamiliar title *"Miss"*. No one ever addressed me that way. It was going to take some getting used to.

"Elara doesn't own that dagger. She cannot take it. Stop encouraging her and return to your post, Tomin," Baras snapped, his voice laced with annoyance.

To my astonishment, Tomin didn't move, didn't even acknowledge Baras's command. He simply continued to extend the dagger. I realized with a jolt that he was treating me as an equal. Another adjustment I would have to make.

"She cannot take it, Tomin," Baras repeated, his patience wearing thin. He grabbed Tomin's arm, yanking him back.

"With all due respect, sir," Tomin said, his voice firm. "She has every right to take her dagger. Myself, the other guards, and all the townsfolk here," he gestured to the crowd, his arm sweeping across the sea of faces. I saw Baras finally acknowledge them, his eyes widening as he took in their determined, almost outraged expressions. "We all witnessed the dagger being used when Jermaine was killed."

It was almost comical, watching the realisation dawn on Baras's face. He'd been so consumed by his own anger and ego that he'd been oblivious to the events unfolding mere feet away.

"Jermaine is dead?" Baras asked, his voice stunned. "Who killed him?"

Tomin's brow furrowed, a hint of impatience in his eyes. "Elara did. Didn't you see the fight? Jermaine attacked her as she stepped from the keep. Without hesitation, she deflected his blow, and moments later, Jermaine was dead. Her dagger was knocked away in the struggle, and she left it behind, assuming she wasn't entitled to it anymore. A misconception and not how this works. The dagger is hers." Tomin's words were twisting and stretching the truth with great skill.

"Elara killed the commander?" Baras asked, incredulous.

Tomin simply gestured behind him, and the crowd parted, revealing Jermaine's lifeless body lying in the dirt. "His body lies where she left him. No one will touch the corpse of a traitor who attacked a Soul. The dogs can feed on him later. The dagger is Elara's."

He extended the hilt to me once more, and I, throwing caution to the wind, reached out and took it, my fingers closing around the worn leather. My eyes locked with Baras's, a silent challenge passing between us. "Thank you, Tomin."

Watching Baras's gaze dart between Tomin, Jermaine's body, and myself, I felt a surge of satisfaction. He was losing control, his carefully constructed world crumbling around him. He grunted, turning away and stalking towards the front of the group, where two other figures joined him. Captain Baras was losing his grip on the top rung of the ladder, and, after the way he treated me, I found I no longer cared so much. He could have protected me, kept me by his side, but no. He chose to belittle me.

Turning back to the crowd, I placed a hand over my heart and bowed my head in thanks. Many of the villagers returned the gesture, while others simply smiled or nodded. I felt their respect, their admiration, a tangible weight pressing on me. I took my place beside Fitz at the rear of the group, the weight of the Commander's knife heavy in my hand.

"I was going to kill you when we left the gates," Fitz said quietly, his voice devoid of emotion.

I raised an eyebrow, my expression a mixture of surprise and amusement. "Oh."

Fitz laughed, shaking his head. "See, that right there," he said, his eyes glinting with something akin to awe. "When you stepped from the keep and it was made clear you were a Soul, I thought, 'Perfect. She looks weak. Those clothes will keep me warm, if a little uncomfortable.' But *that* right there. Your casual dismissal of my confession. And after everything else this morning... Well, you fucking scare me, Elara."

His words made a twisted kind of sense. He was a survivor, opportunistic and ruthless. Of course, he would have been planning his next move, assessing the value of each member of the group. Now, a series of seemingly random events had thrust me into a position of power I didn't understand or earned. I couldn't help but laugh, a hollow, almost hysterical sound. Some unseen force, God or Demon, was clearly enjoying this, and for lack of anything better to do, I laughed along with them.

As we stepped beyond the gates, Fitz gestured towards my newly acquired dagger. I tilted my head, questioning. He smiled, a flash of white teeth against his sun-weathered skin. With a smirk, I reversed the blade, offering it to him hilt-first. "I think I've made a friend," I said, and he took the knife, his fingers closing around the worn leather.

The casual precision with which he moved, the deadly grace he displayed as he stalked one of the rangers, was unnerving. Even knowing his intent, I couldn't hear a single footfall or detect any sign of his assault. A moment later, the ranger was dead, his throat slit with swift, brutal efficiency. The man's death as silent as the attack.

Baras glanced back for a moment, his expression unreadable, before shaking his head and continuing on.

Waiting beside Fitz, I watched as the rest of the group continued up the road, their pace relentless. They clearly didn't care whether we kept up or not. Fine. I had no illusions about their loyalty.

"Think you're gunna need a sheath for that," Fitz said, handing me the ranger's belt, complete with a sturdy leather sheath. My dagger now rested snugly within. He looked far more the part in ranger's garbs. The ranger's cloak billowing behind him. A bow and quiver held inside.

"I think I do," I said, accepting the gift and strapping the belt around my waist, the rough leather a stark contrast against the coarse fabric of my maid's uniform.

Chapter 2

The pressure started again, a familiar weight sitting on my lungs, making each breath a struggle through what felt like a constricted pipe. Telveria Keep was only half a day's walk behind, but I'd already burned through a dose of my Lemna Raja leaves. Panic clawed at me. At this rate, I'll be dead on the side of the road long before doing anything adventurous.

The group ahead started to pull away, their figures blurring into the distance. Twenty-five we were when we left. An unusually large number of Souls. I grimaced. But then again, it's not every day four Phoenix Souls die. My condition meant Fitz and I were bringing up the rear, a fact that gnawed at my pride.

Waiting for a break in the grip my asthma held over me, I used the momentary lull to excuse myself. Coughing wracked my body, leaving my voice a raspy mess. "Just... need to clear my throat," I managed to croak, hoping to hide the true extent of my weakness, for now.

Ducking into the tree line, I pulled out the last of my leaves. One more dose. Enough to get my lungs working for another hour, maybe two. I started jamming the leaves into my pipe, the bitter smell of breaking the leaf playing in my nose. After that, I'll need to call an early camp, and pray Fitzroy decides to stick around.

The man was brilliant. He could see the fine webs in nature that held everything together. Rotting carcasses returning to the earth as nutrients, the role of dung beetles and flies clearing waste, he saw it all. And when he got really excited, he'd punctuate his stories with leaps and cartwheels, his dark, shoulder-length hair flying in every direction. If all I get out of this is meeting this man, I'll be happy. In another life, he'd be an incredible friend.

As I leaned against the nearest tree, two broad hands slowly wrapped around my neck, their firm grasp holding me in place. I tried to wrench away, but the lack of oxygen made my movements sluggish.

"Calm, Elara. You need to relax," Fitz said, and I felt his thumbs start to work on the muscles near the top of my neck. "Deep, slow breaths. I know it's hard right now but trust me and allow your body to let its fear and distress fall away."

Fitz finally knew me well enough not to be scared of creeping up on me. His words were soothing, and after the initial shock, I realized I wasn't breathing at all. Closing my eyes, I tried to breathe as slowly and deeply as my lungs would allow. It wasn't much to begin with, my body screaming for more air with every breath. It was actually a terrible struggle of willpower and I almost lost. Alone, I would have given in, but Fitzroy's soothing words and the deep muscle massage kept me sane enough to push through. After a few minutes, I felt a small pocket of space open in my lungs. Fitz moved his massage to my shoulders and lower neck, relieving the tension, and I felt myself melt into the relief.

"Your hands are a gift, Fitz. They could make much more of a difference healing rather than taking lives," I said, my breathing finally stabilizing. I couldn't believe a simple massage could help so much.

"My father was a healer, and soldiers killed him anyway. My mother was a healer, and bandits killed her anyway. I learned enough to make a career of it if I wanted to, but I also learned that no matter whether you're helping someone or fighting someone, that someone will more than likely kill you anyway."

Now that's a simple, straightforward, yet deeply philosophical view on why this man is who he is. I would think if I'd been so close to my parents, if I could even remember them, maybe I too would have chosen a similar path.

"Lemna Raja leaves?"

I nodded.

"I could smell it when you returned after the last bout. Not many would have picked up on the unique smell of the burnt leaves. Just those who've smelled it enough times to remember."

"You too?"

"Not me. My dad. The cabin we lived at always smelled of it. After a while, you'll build a tolerance to its healing strength and will find you need more and more to stop the fits. It'll start to become a morning-to-night type of fix until you decide to help someone with an exceptionally time-consuming wound and have a coughing fit in their face."

"I seem to remind you of less happy times."

"All I'm saying is there are better ways to train your body. Yes, there will be times a puff or two is necessary, but on the most part, you'll get through more days than not without an attack."

That sounded like a dream, yet he'd already gotten me through one bout that I couldn't have managed on my own. "Teach me what I need to know."

"Only if you do something for me," Fitz said.

"If you're about to ask me to wash and dry your clothes..." There was little more I could think of that my body might be useful to him for, but I decided the moment I left the gates this morning I would never cater to anyone again...

Fitz considered me a moment, looking me up and down. A little too long, I thought, and then he shot me a wink.

"If I must," I said hesitantly, and Fitz laughed long and loud. The sound was so joyful and full of life.

"To that, you are safe."

"Then what? Those were the only two options I could think of: my body or my previous skills."

"Just don't kill me in my sleep," Fitz said, with no hint of sarcasm.

"Now, why would I do that? You're one person I actually like in this world."

"Because, I have this kick-ass, wind-resistant, very warm cloak." He spun around, the fabric swirling as he did. "Come nightfall, when this is all that's between the cold air and those delicate lungs, you'll definitely be considering it."

I grinned a wicked little grin. "Tell you what. If such a temptation finds its way into my waking mind, I promise to try and share in its warmth with you first. If that doesn't work out... well, I can't make any promises after that." And did I feel clever and empowered for those words. Sure, there were far better sentences and references I could have made to sound tough, most of them entering my mind moments after speaking, but to a girl who had always done what she was told and never rubbed against the grain, it sounded pretty damn fantastic.

"I think I can accept those terms," Fitz said and started moving down the road again. He was walking half-speed until I reached his side, and we continued battling the ever-growing distance from the others. "All over the body are thousands of points that control the flow of energy. Block the correct paths, and you could destroy a man in minutes. Open those paths of energy that are starting to falter, and you could bring someone back from the brink of death. Each point looks after different places on or inside the body."

"Inside?" I asked, trying to slow the conversation to get a grasp on what he was saying. Energy lines through the body were a hard concept to swallow.

"Take your lungs, for example. The places I massaged on your neck and shoulders are an easy way to relax the lungs and open the airways. These places also..." Fitz reached over and slowly touched points at my knees, my elbows, and then points in the fleshy part of my hand between the thumb and pointer finger. "That last one is easiest for you to massage and will mean longer time between attacks from strenuous activity. That includes walking the countryside and climbing mountains. We will need to restock the Lemna Raja though. The base of the mountain in the shadow of the cliffs is your best bet."

"Why are you doing this for me? I haven't done anything for you."

"You let me borrow your knife. My life expectancy rose from 30 to 90% after that."

I shook my head. "Such an insignificant thing. Why were you naked anyway? Got a cute little thing back home?" I could see the storm clouds rolling in up North. Not a significant threat right now, but if the winds were to change and they started heading even slightly South, we were going to need to find some better shelter than a shared cloak. Fitz was right, though. That cloak was looking mighty tempting.

"Nothing like that," Fitz said. He seemed almost too embarrassed to tell me, but after a moment, he found the words. "An idiot friend heard before I did that, I was to be a named Soul. He found me and dared me to salute the General's quarters from the main square buck naked for half an hour. Long enough to be found and named. Thought it would be funny, he did."

I stifled a laugh behind a hand. "And if the General looked from his window?"

"Well, I knew he was in a war meeting, didn't I? The risk was minor. The prestige, great."

"Boys," I said simply. Many of the soldiers would have known about the meeting. When the head disappears for a time, the body will always notice. Then thoughts of the Phoenix Souls entered my mind. I still had no idea what I was supposed to do if I became a fully-fledged Phoenix Soul, and that worried me. "Fitz?" I asked, leaving it open to emphasize my need.

He turned to me, one eyebrow raised. "Ellie?"

The name was starting to catch, but I was still unsure of it. Even Baras was too formal to use a nickname. "What is a Phoenix Soul? I mean, what do we need to do?"

He kept staring for a moment, trying to decide in what context, and I started to grow embarrassed, my cheeks glowing red.

"Why don't we start with what you do know," Fitz said. An easy place to begin.

"A Phoenix Soul is the highest rank a soldier... or mage," I added, thinking back to the dream. "Can achieve. You outrank even a General. When one dies, six are chosen to replace them. We then go on a journey until someone is chosen as the replacement, and the rest are left to die."

"Mage?"

"There are provisions for a Mage to be chosen. It was how I was chosen. Walan put forward my name after the 24 warrior names were determined," I said, finding it strange I was now teaching Fitz.

31

"And how do you know what happened in the war meeting?"

Not wanting to give away all my secrets, I just kept a neutral expression. "Mage... apparently," I said, raising a hand.

Fitz narrowed his eyes on me. "So, you can use magi..." he shook his head. "No, not going there. What would you like to know? Specifically?"

"How can we get chosen?" I asked. I wanted to know about the road ahead too, but I guessed if I only worried about that, then I'd be sorry at the end.

"It's the birds that choose. Nothing really to do with us?" Fitz said in an offhanded manner.

"They leave the fate of those who could very well run the army to... birds?" I asked, incredulous. The concept sounded like a fault in the system.

Fitz considered me. "Firebirds. The Phoenix choose who will ride them. Nothing we can do."

"Phoenix!?" I thought it was just a title. To have the miracle birds of myth and flame choose me to ride them? It sounded magical, like the old legends.

Fitz's eyes went wide, and he grinned. "Oh, Ellie, you have a lot to learn. To put it simply, Phoenix riders are called Phoenix Souls. They ground the Firebirds to this plane, and when the bird dies, the soul of those that ride them return to the earth and are reborn with the Phoenix in their ancestral home. The Phoenix grows and learns with each death. We are then sent as Soul candidates. We climb the mountain and travel a harsh land. On average, 4 of each group die. The rest reach the birds who then choose the one they want to succeed their last rider."

A picture formed in my head. It was broken and unclear, like a story passed down through the ages. Orange flame fanning out from the feathers of a large bird. Darkness swirled around the image, but it looked to be encased in ice or crystal.

"How do the flames not burn you?" I asked, intrigued.

"They burn everything but those they allow close."

"What's in it for us, then? I mean, they get all this benefit. What do we get out of it? I wouldn't think the General would send out his best warriors to die or serve these birds."

Fitz laughed. "You are so innocent, Ellie. The Phoenix will serve us in our war movements. Also, they grant abilities to those who become Phoenix Souls. Things akin to pyromancy. I have worked to this goal since I was a child, listening to the stories of the Phoenix."

"It's a lot to take in," I said. I remembered Walan said the birds might just unlock some of my dormant abilities. Still, I felt a little disheartened by the fact that it was solely up to the Firebirds. I was too weak to beat trained warriors.

We continued to walk in silence for a while. Fitz could see I was deep in thought and a little disturbed by the new information.

The rest of the afternoon became a gruelling test of endurance, each step a battle against the fading light and the relentless pursuit of the main group. Fitz, with his superior tracking skills, managed to keep us on course, but the terrain and the weather seemed determined to wear us down. By the time we finally stumbled upon the campsite, nestled against a shallow, curving rockface, the sun had long since surrendered to the horizon, and the trees thrashed wildly under the assault of a fierce wind. The rain, a constant sight throughout the afternoon, shifted and intensified, transforming the world into a blurry, grey canvas. The cave, barely more than an alcove, offered a welcome respite from the elements. An unspoken promise of dryness and protection in a world consumed by moisture.

Inside, the scene was a study in contrasts. A large central fire cast dancing shadows on the rock face, radiating warmth and light that pushed back against the encroaching cold. Two smaller cooking fires flickered nearby, illuminating separate groups of Souls huddled together, their faces etched with exhaustion. Most sat with their backs pressed against the damp rock, cloaks pulled tight, seeking solace in shared body heat.

Fitz and I gravitated towards a quieter corner, away from the dense clusters of people. The rain, driven by the gale-force winds, formed a shimmering curtain just beyond the alcove's opening, a stark reminder of the inhospitable world outside. I breathed a sigh of relief, grateful for the unexpected sanctuary, knowing I wouldn't have lasted the night exposed to the elements. Glancing at Fitz, a playful smirk tugged at my lips.

"I'm already regretting the promise to let you live," I said, injecting a light-hearted tone into my voice. "That cloak is looking mighty warm right now."

My jest drew a genuine laugh from Fitz, the sound echoing through the camp. "I'll need you to hold onto it for a while, at least," he replied, his eyes twinkling with amusement.

"Don't go giving me the cloak while you freeze. I don't need your sympathy. I'm a big girl. I can snuggle without taking advantage of you."

Another laugh escaped Fitz, the sound warm and comforting in the chill air. "You hungry?"

33

I nodded, my stomach rumbling in response to the tantalizing aroma of stews that drifted down from the cooking fires. A fragrant invitation that was hard to resist.

"Then I'll need to hunt. No one here will be willing to part with their rations."

"You're going out in that?" I squeaked and my eyes widened in disbelief. "I can go a night or two without food. Maybe the storm will settle, and there will be a lull in the rain. Don't go out there just for me."

He ruffled my hair, a familiar gesture that softened his rugged features. "You think too highly of yourself. This is what I do. I was a scout, remember? I've spent nights like this out on the trail, keeping a lookout for enemies."

"Then keep the cloak. You need it more."

"I won't be long. I noticed a rabbit warren close by. Besides, I'll need something dry when I get back, and my clothes are drying by the fire." With a swift motion, he unclasped the cloak and tossed it to me. The warmth trapped within its fibres enveloped me, a comforting embrace against the biting cold. I found a spot to sit near the cliff face, promising to keep the cloak warm as Fitz disappeared.

As Fitz vanished into the downpour, a different kind of shadow fell over me. A dark silhouette materialized against the flickering firelight, its form vaguely familiar, yet undeniably imposing. The glint of bone, unmistakable even in shadow, gave away his identity.

"What do you want, Baras?" I asked, my voice flat, unwilling to deal with his issues at that moment.

"Can I sit?" Baras asked, gesturing to the space beside me.

"Spot's taken," I replied, holding his gaze, refusing to yield. Baras glanced around, his expression a mixture of frustration and resignation.

"Friends with shadows now?"

"They've been better friends than some."

I saw his eyes flicker with vulnerability, his shoulders slumping slightly, as if the weight of the world had suddenly settled upon him.

"Listen, Elara, I'm sorry. I've had plenty of time to think on the road. This was no more your choice than it was mine, or anyone else here for that matter."

For a fleeting moment, I saw the boy I once knew, the one who would sneak out of his window to watch the falling spring stars with me. He knew how much I loved that yearly spectacle, and he always made sure I didn't have to experience it alone.

"I should have listened to my dream and prepared better. Given myself a chance at getting a glimpse over that mountain range. Instead, I just sat on the roof, watching everyone gather in the courtyard. It happened so seldom that I never paid it much attention the few times I was at the keep when candidate Souls were sent out."

A grunt, laced with amusement, escaped Baras. "Ain't no man alive that would have guessed you'd be named, nor that it would have stuck. Dream or no."

"Ain't that the truth," I said, a genuine smile gracing my lips. I felt the walls I had erected around my heart beginning to crumble, succumbing to the familiar pull of my childhood friend.

"I'm glad we can agree on something. So, what's next for you? Tenebrou, maybe?"

"Tenebrou?" I asked, confusion clouding my features.

"Or Poltaveri. They have even temperatures all year long. It'll do wonders for your asthma," Baras said, his voice laced with a strange mixture of concern and resignation. He almost looked like he was considering it himself.

"What are you implying, Baras?" I asked, my eyes narrowing. A sense of weariness settled over me.

"We both know your asthma's worse in the cooler climates."

"I'm going north, over the mountain, with the rest of you," I growled, my voice harsher than I intended.

"But you just said..." Baras stammered, taken aback by my vehemence.

"Said what? That no man alive would ever guess I'd be named? I did say that. But I was named, Baras. This is my life now."

"You'll die, Elara. I don't want to see that happen." Baras's voice began to rise, his frustration bubbling to the surface.

"The moment Walan told me I was a Soul, I was dead. Whether it's here, halfway up the mountain, or halfway across the fucking country in the presence of those damned birds, I'm already dead. But I'll be damned if I ever go back to cleaning up people's shit after someone believed in me."

"You're not a Soul! In the morning, you will gather your things and disappear. To everyone else, you will be dead." Baras yelled, his voice echoing from the stone. The other occupants, those who hadn't already been eavesdropping, turned to stare, their expressions ranging from indifference to morbid curiosity. Most shrugged and went back to their own affairs, seemingly agreeing with Baras's assessment. The rest remained, intrigued by my impending reaction.

I glared at him, my eyes burning with dark indignation, a torrent of violent fantasies flooding my mind. What was I supposed to say? 'Yes, I am,' like a scared child trying to deny the inevitable? That wasn't going

35

to cut it. Here was a soldier asserting his dominance, and I needed something drastic to stand my ground. Walan's words on the rooftop echoed in my mind, and a reckless idea began to take shape. Stupid and foolhardy, perhaps, but undeniably viable.

Shrugging the cloak from my shoulders, I let it fall to the dirt, the sudden loss of warmth sending a shiver through my body. Even as a sharp rush of cool air assaulted my skin, I maintained fierce eye contact with Baras. Next came the belt around my waist, the one holding my dagger. I had to look down for a moment to undo the strap, but my eyes snapped back up as the dagger landed with a soft thud.

"Elara, what are you doing?" Baras asked, his voice hushed, laced with a hint of panic. I didn't give him the satisfaction of an answer.

I continued, my fingers working on the laces and buttons that held my dark, maid's outfit in place. The movements were ingrained in my muscle memory, a testament to years of servitude. As the dress loosened, ready to fall, I felt Baras grab my arm.

"Elara, what are you doing? Stop this!" he demanded, his grip tightening.

"You will let me go, Baras Vongaries," I said, my voice resonating with a newfound strength, my eyes blazing with fury. Baras hesitated for a moment, then took a step back, releasing me.

I let the dress fall to the ground, a dark heap around my feet. A small loincloth and some strapping around my breasts were all that remained, barely preserving my modesty. The cold air was a brutal assault on my exposed skin, my muscles instinctively tightening and I could feel my lungs beginning to complain. The large, hauntingly dark frostbite scar that marred my body stood out in stark contrast to my pale skin.

Whoops and whistles erupted from the camp as my cheeks burned with a mixture of defiance and embarrassment under the weight of everyone's gaze. Baras, however, remained impassive, his face a mask of grim concern.

"Can you see me, Baras? Do your eyes have the capacity to take in the person in front of you?"

He nodded slowly; his expression unreadable.

"I have the same flesh and bone, muscle and tissue, as you. I have the same flaws, the same weaknesses. If a stone gives way partway up the mountain and you slip, if those damned Firebirds decide your misogynistic views on the frailty of women are distasteful and deny you, you are just as dead as I am."

Baras pursed his lips, his anger barely contained.

"Don't think yourself so special just because you hide behind the bones of dead beasts. I am your equal, and I am a Soul."

He opened his mouth to speak, but I held up a hand, silencing him. "If the next words out of your mouth are not an apology and acceptance of my status, I don't want to waste my time listening to you."

I already knew the answer. Baras's jaw tightened, his eyes hardening, and he stormed off, slumping down at the far end of the camp.

The rain eased slightly, but the temperature continued to plummet. It was impossible to tell if I was shaking from the cold or the adrenaline coursing through my veins, but my chest was constricting in protest. It wouldn't be long before I couldn't breathe. Quickly donning my dress and the thick cloak, I pulled the pre-packed pipe with my Lemna Raja leaves from a pocket and placed it in my mouth. Setting flame to dry leaves, I inhaled deeply. The soothing smoke easing the tension in my muscles, opening my airways. I continued to puff on the pipe as I drew warmth from the cloak, a temporary shield against the encroaching cold. "I need to get my own cloak," I muttered to myself, glancing at the other Souls, many of whom were staring back, their expressions a mixture of curiosity and speculation. I quickly averted my gaze, suddenly self-conscious.

Moments later, three figures stood before me. I hesitated, then looked up to see a male swordsman and a pair of rangers, one female, one... ambiguous, smiling down at me. The situation was awkward, but I didn't feel threatened.

"We've seen you around the keep and honestly thought Baras was trying to pull a swifty, bringing his maid along for the journey, but you say you're a... Soul?" The female spoke, her voice light and whimsical, like a melody. Her hood was pulled back, revealing golden blond hair that cascaded over her left shoulder. The soft cheeks and lightly freckled face gave her a youthful appearance, making me wonder if she was truly as experienced as she seemed.

"Yeah, how did you pull that off? The twenty-four were chosen." The other ranger's voice was gruff, leaving no doubt about his gender, despite his clean-shaven face and androgynous features. His build, too, seemed to straddle the line between masculine and feminine.

I remained silent, unused to the casual banter of these warriors. My eyes darted to the ground, voice barely a whisper. "They said... they said there was room for a Mage," I stuttered, tripping over my tongue.

"Hey, Caeli, this one can do magic and the like," the gruff ranger said, nudging his companion.

Caeli's eyes widened, sparkling with wonder. "Is it true?" she asked, her voice filled with childlike excitement.

"I don't really know. I've had a dream or two that seemed to show me the future, but other than that..." I shook my head, my self-doubt creeping back in.

"You impressed someone, somewhere. That's all that matters. Once you're a true Soul, the world will open up for you. I'm Caeli, by the way," she said, squatting down to meet my gaze. "My friend here is Dustin, and the quiet one beside us is Korr. He's always judging people."

"Korribubugungalah," Korr said, his voice deep and resonant, tinged with the lilting accents of the southern islands. His dark features and intense gaze made him appear intimidating, but I had little experience with Southerners to know for sure. The complimenting, dark hair was tied at the back, and he wore no chest armour or clothing of any sort. It was as if the cold weather had no effect on him at all. Korr's chest was covered in tribal tattoos signifying his warrior status.

"And that's why we call him Korr," Caeli said with a laugh.

"Elara," I replied, my eyes dropping away once more, unable to maintain their unwavering gaze.

Caeli reached out and gently cupped my chin, lifting my head until our eyes met. "You'll never get to know any of us if you keep studying the ground like that. Your role in this world requires a little more confidence now."

"And allies," Dustin added, flashing a friendly smile.

"You're right. Truth be told, I don't know what I'm doing or how I'm supposed to act. Until this morning, I didn't even know what a Phoenix Soul was, or that the Firebirds even existed outside of legends. It's true what Baras said. I don't have the capacity to be a warrior. I can't be a So..." I stopped abruptly, realizing that a finger had gently pressed against my lips, silencing the word before it could escape. I looked up to see Korr's dark eyes fixed on mine, his expression unreadable in the shadows.

"Sometime, it least likely person that make biggest difference. You no waste time on Baras denial. You no waste time on you denial. Elara Soul," he said, his broken English and thick accent making his words difficult to decipher. But as my mind pieced together his meaning, tears welled in my eyes.

I raised a hand to his finger, gently pulling it from my lips. "Thank you, Kooribugan...gal."

"Korribubugungalah," he corrected slowly, a rare smile illuminating his face and revealing a dazzling row of white teeth in the shadows.

I nodded, a genuine smile spreading across my face. "Thank you, Korribubugungalah. I will not forget the name a second time." I turned to face the three warriors; my heart filled with a mixture of gratitude and bewilderment. "Why?"

"Hmm?" Caeli asked, tilting her head in confusion.

"You're all being so nice to me. What if I become a Phoenix Soul, and one of you is left to die?"

Caeli smiled, her eyes crinkling at the corners. "Sure, most people here would probably try to kill each other in their sleep if it meant they had a better shot at getting a Phoenix to choose them but we believe that forging alliances, even friendships, gives us a better chance at surviving beyond the mountains to reach the birds. If we die on the way, we won't be chosen anyway but that doesn't really answer your question, does it? Why you? What importance could a maid have to our survival?"

Dustin cut in, his voice brimming with enthusiasm. "Just look at what you've accomplished today. Titled a Mage. The only one who would have judged that is Walan, and he doesn't make mistakes. He's a mage himself, you know. Titled a Soul. The General and Commanders had to agree on that, even knowing you were a maid. And they chose well. All but Jermaine, and we all know what you did to him. You have the balls to stand up to Baras. You scared Fitz, the 'Night Crawler,' enough to already ally with you. And quite frankly, when your ally goes shopping for some new clothes for you, we don't want to be on the shopping list. Not to mention, Korr spoke more than a word to you. How many have you gotten from him, Caeli?"

She held up three fingers. "Three good sentences."

"And I've gotten two from him. You're in a unique position, Elara, and we see the potential in you."

"What's happening here?" Fitz yelled, his voice sharp and demanding, cutting through the comfortable atmosphere.

We all turned to see a hazy figure emerge from the rain, dropping something substantial to the damp floor with a heavy thud. His movements were unnervingly swift, and before Dustin or Korr could react, Caeli had a knife pressed against her throat.

"Causing issues for my girl here, Caeli?" Fitz's voice was low and menacing, sending a shiver down my spine.

"Fitz, it's okay. They offered me an alliance. I've accepted."

Fitz's eyes narrowed; his gaze intense as he scrutinized Caeli's face. "What's your angle?"

"She stood up to Baras only moments ago. She has spark, and she intrigues me. It's a feeling more than anything, just like you had."

Fitz hesitated for a moment, the dagger remaining at her throat, before finally sheathing it with a sigh. Only then did I notice Caeli's dagger, barely visible, pressed against Fitz's stomach.

"Well, I'm glad to hear that. A young deer wandered across my path, possibly separated from its mother. You can help prepare it."

"Venison?" Dustin said, rubbing his hands together in anticipation. He turned to me, offering his hand. "This alliance is already paying off. Come on, Elara, let's shift over to our fire. We have a stew waiting, as well."

I took his hand and, as I rose to my feet, turned back to face Fitz, who was returning to the deer carcass. "I'll warm the insides of the cloak by the fire," I said with a smile, one that he returned with genuine warmth.

The sky was slowly warming with predawn light, and I yearned to reach out and touch it. I glanced back at the other warriors in the camp beneath the cliff face, surprised that none of them had risen yet. Typically, they would be up and going by now, engaging in training exercises and drills around the Keep. Perhaps, with no obligations for the day, they had decided to sleep in for once.

A moment later, movement caught my eye, and I wasn't surprised to see Baras jogging into the campsite. The man had never missed training a day in his life. It was only because I wasn't specifically looking for him that I hadn't noticed his absence earlier.

I looked down to where Fitz still slept, my body cradled in his arms. A small glint of white from his eyelids suggested he was awake as well, but he remained still, allowing me to rest. I froze, realising I was watching myself sleep. My hands came to my mouth, and I shook my head.

"No, no, no," I whispered, crouching beside myself to scan for signs of an asthma attack. My breathing appeared fluid and smooth, my chest rising and falling steadily. There was no concern in my features, and with a background like Fitz's, he didn't seem worried either. Maybe this *drift* wasn't triggered by an attack after all.

I turned my gaze back to the sky. Flight shouldn't be out of the question if this is my spirit. Jumping, gravity pulled me back to the earth, and I fell to the dirt. It was astonishing that gravity even existed in this place, and soon I wondered if it was my own creation. A link to normality that I chained myself to.

Closing my eyes, I willed myself upwards. My body and muscles pushed skyward, but there was no rush of air or the familiar motion of movement. There was nothing.

My eyes opened again, and a small scream escaped my lips. It was an eerie feeling, hanging in mid-air without a fear of falling, but rather being stuck at this point high in the sky. The view was breathtaking, though. All the lands of Telveria to the south of the Mountains stretched out before me. The Keep we had left yesterday looked tiny from this vantage point, like a wooden piece on one of those little war maps the commanders use. A large fire was burning on the southwestern borders of the country, but thankfully, that wasn't the direction we were heading.

Turning back, I gazed at the might of the imposing Shatterstone Mountain. The large rocky mass burst high from the range that divided north from south, its fractured web of nooks and crannies giving birth to its name. And I would need to climb that in a day or two.

As the sun hit the snowy caps, sparkling at the peak of the mountain, my longing to be in the light once more propelled me forward. Focusing like before, I tried to move myself with my eyes open this time. The sight was surprising. It wasn't how I imagined flying to be. The feeling of movement through the sky, or any movement at all, was absent. The world below me seemed to roll and pan as I remained in place until I reached my desired destination. It almost made me feel sick, knowing I was moving without motion, but that wasn't a feeling my spirit form needed to accept or endure.

At the summit, a large rock shelf overlooked the cold lands to the north. And on this shelf sat a man, casually gazing out over the lands as he threaded rope and whistled an enchanting tune. Dark leather armour covered most of his body, except for his arms. Strong, toned arms, tattooed with intricate archaic designs, worked the ropes. Those arms could easily sweep me off my feet. A tender warmth ran through me like nothing I'd felt in this form before, and I moved in closer to get a better view of him.

His eyes were dark amber with flecks of brown and gold shimmering as the new sun danced within. A subtle breeze whipped his dark, stormy hair to curl around his face. Raising a hand, he brushed a lock from his eyes. The strong jawline promoted strength, and the scar that ran in a jagged curve just below his left ear suggested he'd had to defend himself. There was no doubt in my mind that this man could fight, and I wondered what it would be like to be pinned beneath him... or for that matter, tied up by those ropes.

In a place where temperature shouldn't exist, it was suddenly getting extremely hot, and my cheeks began to blush.

The whistled tune shifted into a full ballad sung out across the waking land. His voice was deep and resonant, drawing me in, and I came to sit beside him, lost in the words and sound. Echoes of a time beyond my memory called to me. It was like gravity, and he was the earth. I shifted closer, my hand hesitant to touch his arm as he worked, hovering just over the skin.

Light, like the sun, burst into life to the northeast. It rose in the air and, as the song died away, shot towards us like a furious meteor. My eyes locked onto the phenomenon, and as the distance grew short, I realized exactly what it was.

"A Phoenix!" I tried to shout at the man, but he seemed blissfully unaware. All I could do was watch as he tied the rope off and threw it over the side of the cliff in random places.

The Firebird, however, didn't attack the man as I thought it would. Instead, it flew past him and stopped itself in the air, its wings outstretched, all momentum halted. The burning eyes were focused on me, and I realized it had formed a barrier before this man. It sought to protect him... from me.

"Enzo," I mouthed, my voice barely a whisper.

The Phoenix, flames glowing brighter and fiercer, let forth a shrill cry that pierced my spirit and forced me back to my body.

I woke with a start, feeling the warmth of Fitz against me and a reassuring hand rubbing my back.

"Shh. Just a dream, lass," he said.

Chapter 3

It was an odd feeling having friends. Real friends, not just people who were nice to me because I was their maid. I shot a glare at Baras's back as we continued walking. These were genuine, quirky people. I had already learned so many things about them, and it was getting hard to keep track. Dustin had a thing for Caeli, a big thing, yet Caeli never seemed to notice, nor did Dustin push the point. There might have been something in their past, but it was almost heartbreaking to watch.

Caeli transformed in open fields, always on guard, carrying her bow as if enemies were hidden behind every blade of grass. And Korr... Well, Korr was just Korr. Quiet, watchful, and always in balance. It made me more comfortable knowing he had my back.

Watching Fitz interact with the others was always fun. I got the feeling they all knew each other well, especially after getting back on the road. Fitz was continually playing pranks on them. Often pulling them off with peals of laughter, but sometimes he got caught and had them turned back on him. In these times he was like a child, walking off to sulk on his own.

And they all made me feel so comfortable. It felt like I'd finally found a real home among these people. A first for me, as my memories of family were fractured or incomplete. My last memory of them was of a great beast dragging my parents away as my older sister hid me in a tree. She, too, fell to the creatures.

I shook my head, dispelling the memories.

"So, who are we going to kill to dress our little Elara back there?" I heard Fitz saying. He was leaning close to Caeli, much to Dustin's distress, and scanning the forward group. "Fifi is an option. No one will miss her."

"Nah, Miss Fiorefalli has too much in the trunk. The pants will give Ellie too much grief up the mountain," Dustin said, trying to gain traction in the conversation.

"Geldan's rather feminine. About the right size too," Caeli giggled over her own comment.

"I can see another about Caeli's size," Fitz said, eyeing Caeli up and down.

"Oh, uhuh," Caeli said, putting up a finger. "No one gets into these clothes but me."

"You should swap. I could definitely see you pulling off the dark, maid dress while hunting down your foes. Can't you, Dustin?" Fitz called over his shoulder, and I could already see Dustin was thinking about it, his face going bright red.

A deep and heady laughter came from Korr, and Caeli turned as if insulted. "You too, Korr," she squealed.

"Guys, it's okay. We don't need to kill anyone on my behalf."

"Not after Caeli swaps anyway," Fitz threw in, and Caeli just spun with a clear, defining "Hmph."

"All good, Ellie. After we round this next corner, we can get what we need at the nearby town." Fitz continued, enjoying the state Caeli was in.

"Town?" I said, cocking an ear, trying to hear the comings and goings of normal town life, but nothing reached me. "You sure we're that close."

"Valaos is just..." He leaned forward to look past some shrubbery. "There," he said, pointing.

I bounded forward, excited at seeing my first new town in years, only to pause in the middle of the path. There was no one around. No workers in the fields or horse and cart carrying goods. It was quiet, as if it had been abandoned for years.

"They're there," Caeli said, as if reading my thoughts. "They don't like new Souls coming into town. We take what we want, be it parts, goods, or, as some have in the past, people, and there is nothing that can be done. They've learned to hide away when we're close and let us pass through quickly."

"That's sad," I replied. It was the first time I began to think negatively of my acquired position. We should be protecting the people, not scaring them to the point they need to hide away from us.

Walking into town was like entering a true ghost town. It was like the stories I'd heard of where villages were ravaged by disease to the point no one survived or remained to keep the town alive. The town itself was in good condition. Patchworks on rooves had been carried out. It was clean and tidy with freshwater in the barrels around most doorways. It was actually set up fairly well, so it surprised me that even the stables were empty. I soon realised the horses were highly valuable to such a community and their absence made sense. If they were taken, it would be a big blow for months to come. Especially with winter on the horizon.

"So, how do we do this?" I asked. I could see a number of Souls already entering different premises and returning with extra supplies.

"I demand the leadership of this village attend me?" A voice boomed out over the town. It was coming from the centre square, and I recognized it instantly. Baras.

"That's definitely not the way to get it done," Fitz said, beginning a light jog towards the centre of town.

I followed to find Baras standing up on a raised dais the town used for announcements and the like. He seemed annoyed by the town's ignorance. Joining him were two other warriors with shifty statures. They looked more like the type of people who wanted to use someone more than take equipment.

"Baras, get down from there. Demanding attendance won't get you anywhere," Fitz said, remaining calm.

"It isn't right. We're Souls. We deserve respect," Baras grunted back, looking down on Fitz as if the man was something stuck to the bottom of his boot.

I let out a laugh, long and loud. "Respect?" I scoffed. "You don't even know what respect is. I was friends with you because I believed you respected me, but you only saw me as a maid. Anyone you deem below you, you see as a servant. These are people with lives just as important as yours. You provide them protection; they provide you with clothing, food, and other goods. That's called mutual respect. So why don't you get down off your high horse and treat these people with the respect they deserve? Better yet, go collect your own equipment and leave them in peace. You have done nothing to earn their respect. Only their contempt, as you have mine."

Baras was glaring at me after my outburst. He looked ready to explode. As a Captain, he wasn't used to people disobeying him, and it showed. The warriors at his side jumped down from the dais and made to confront me and Fitz, but I was in no mood.

"Oh, sit down, little puppy," I growled at him. "Your master hasn't barked his commands for you to move yet. Heel!"

"You Bitch!" the man's eyes bulged, affected by my slight. Baras had tried to calm him, but the man was too far gone. Fitz seemed to already have his hands full with the second one, so this was on me.

As he approached, a short sword appeared in his hand. With enough time to get a hand on my dagger but no further, I was completely unprotected. As the sword came up to land a slashing cut, an arrow appeared through his wrist, and the sword fell to the ground. The man let out a rolling yelp as he doubled over, clutching at his wrist.

Looking around, I spotted Caeli on a nearby rooftop, bow in hand. She waved at me, and I nodded back with a smile, noting Dustin was casually sitting beside her. Taking my own dagger, I struck the man across the back of the head with the hilt, and he dropped silently.

Dispatching his opponent in an arc of crimson, Fitz joined me. He looked at the still breathing form at my feet and lent down, dragging a knife across the assailant's throat.

My eyes widened. "You didn't have to do that. He was already out."

45

"He was scum. I couldn't stand him as a soldier, and I will not risk him becoming a Phoenix Soul."

"You've fallen far, Elara," Baras said, just shaking his head.

Anger stirred in my chest, pounding to get free, but I held it back. Baras would only bite back if threatened.

"As a person, I am still far beyond where you seem capable of reaching. Stop acting like a spoiled brat. Earn your place and earn these people's respect. There is no rank here, only hard work and dedication..." My expression grew soft, and I looked up at Baras in pity. "It won't matter in the end anyway. No Phoenix will want to carry around a blubbering child for a lifetime."

I left him with that thought and wandered off, ignoring his calls. Fitz followed close behind, and as we rounded a corner, he caught my arm.

"Hold a moment, Ellie. Let the past few minutes catch up to you," he said.

I could already feel my hands trembling. My breath shallow. I almost died. The thought began to consume me as the adrenaline started to leave my system. My whole body began to shake.

A light slap brought me back as Fitz drew my attention. "Breathe, Ellie. Deep breaths. Let your body recover. Don't think of what could've been. Tell me what outfit you want to travel in? You look like a heavy armour type of girl."

The thought was so absurd I scoffed as the image of me in full plate armour came to mind. The distraction was working, nonetheless. "As much as she won't trade, I do very much like Caeli's outfit."

"And a pity too. She would totally suit the maid look," Fitz said.

"Are we still on about that?" Caeli asked, dropping from the rooftops, Dustin close behind.

"Ellie's just been picturing you out of your clothes," Fitz said, and I squealed.

"No. I was picturing myself in your clothes." Which didn't help my situation. I could feel my cheeks starting to warm.

Caeli smiled and traced a finger seductively down my cheek and under my chin. "There isn't enough room for you to fit in my clothes, but I'm sure I could get into yours with you. It'll be a *snug* fit."

There was such a sexual aura coming from her eyes that I turned away, my face burning red. I felt her lips gently on my cheek, the kiss lingering a moment. Then she stepped away.

"Clothing store's this way," she called, walking to a nearby doorway. It took a moment before my senses could reboot, and I followed.

If anyone could turn me...

"Let's let them have this one," Fitz said to a still wide-eyed Dustin.

Following Caeli into the building, I was surprised to find it as desolate as the streets. Shelves were empty, and cupboards were bare. The only stock available was piled on the countertop and clearly had already been gone through. Caeli was standing by this pile, shaking her head in disgust.

"None of these will do at all," she said, studying a thin cloak.

"Psst," came a voice to my side, and I looked across to see an elderly man motioning for me to come into the next room. He had a finger to his lips and kept glancing at Caeli. Without a word, I did as I was bid, and the man closed the door behind me.

"I saw how you stood up to that brute out in the street, and I'm sorry you got caught up with a band of Souls heading through. Just bad timing. My name is Fletcher. I run this store. Was there something from our true stock I could assist you with?" Fletcher opened his arms, and for the first time, I noticed the shelving and racks full of items. Most looked to have been thrown in here haphazardly when word came of the Souls approaching.

I gave a sad smile.

"Are the Souls so bad you need to go to such lengths?" I asked.

Fletcher considered the question. "The ones who are Phoenix Souls are not so bad. They can cover great distances quickly, and anything they require, they can get from the army. Normally, they treat villagers with respect. It is a new Soul, drunk on their newly appointed rank and power, who cause the most grief. Because our village is close to the mountains, new Souls travel through here. They usually have what they need, and those that don't are content with what is left out. I'm glad it's only rare we need to deal with them."

"Me too." I hesitated a moment. "Before we continue, I need to come clean with you."

"You're traveling with them? You're helping them? I assure you that won't be a problem."

"I am them. I was named yesterday."

"But you're..." The man went quiet, contemplating the situation. He glanced at me a number of times before he finally spoke again. "Where did you get that outfit?"

"I was a maid at the keep. This was my uniform. When they named me, I had to leave with what I had on."

"You didn't take it from a maid along the way? Steal it from someone's washing maybe?"

I shook my head and smiled. "I am no soldier, ranger, or scout, or any

47

other titled rank connected to the armies of Telveria. I was named due to some innate ability seen in me, but I have no idea what I'm really doing."

The man considered me for a time, looking deep in my eyes. Finally, he relaxed. "And what would you do if I told you to leave?"

"She would invoke her right as a Soul to take as she pleases," Caeli said, entering the room, a stern look on her face.

I held up a hand. "I would leave this room. Choose a more travel-appropriate outfit from what had been left aside for us and depart without another word. I will not steal your livelihood."

"It's not stealing, Ellie. It is a vital role," Caeli said, ignoring the man's glare.

"No, Caeli. The army has provided for you everything you needed the moment you entered their ranks. You may have skipped a meal on the road but when the very items we are taking could mean survival through the harsh winter for these people... I cannot take that from them."

"Enough," the man said, looking at Caeli. "As you are acquainted and seem to be looking out for this one's best interest, you may remain. Just close the door in case others wander in."

Caeli did as she was bid and stood just inside the closed doorway.

The man turned back to me. "I would like to give you a gift for your travels," he said, extending his arm to his wares. My eyes widened, having believed I was about to be thrown out.

"Oh, I couldn't possibly."

"Which is exactly why I want to. You understand the average person. It is you I put my hopes in to become a Phoenix Soul."

The sentiment was heartfelt, and I felt a lump in my throat. "Thank you," I stammered.

"If you don't mind," Caeli called, "let me pick out the items. I have an eye for these things."

"Please," I said, and the man stood back.

Caeli walked around the room, gathering this and that as she went. They were similar to her ranger's garb in greens and browns.

"Can you use a bow?" Caeli asked, and I shook my head. Placing the bow back, she picked up two short swords and tested them for weight and balance. Perfect. The edge was sharp too. "Great blacksmith in this town," she commented before taking up a nice hunter's dagger also.

Giving me the pile of clothes and weapons, she smiled. "This will be everything you need except for..." She scanned the room, her eyes coming alight when she spotted a cloak. "May I get that cloak, Sir?"

Nodding, Fletcher brought over the cloak. It was a deep blue that shimmered like the ocean. I loved it instantly.

After Caeli helped me dress and put on my weapons, I looked at myself in the mirror. Apart from the colour of hair and cloak, Caeli and I could have almost passed as twins. I didn't recognize myself in the slightest, but it felt so comfortable.

"This is too much, umm?" I looked at the man feeling awkward having lost his name.

"Fletcher," he offered.

"This is too much, Fletcher. I couldn't possibly accept all this."

"For me, it lightens my heart that I may help you live a little longer," he said with a bow.

"Thank you," I whispered, then noticed the blade of Jermaine. As I had a proper trail dagger, I wouldn't need this one anymore. I held it out before me. "Here. This was a commander's dagger. I'm sure it could be sold for a fraction of what your gift was."

Fletcher's eyes went wide as he recognized the blade. "More than a fraction. This blade is from a master craftsman. The metal is mined in only one place on earth. This is going to cover your outfit three times over. I couldn't."

"For your kindness towards a Soul," I said with a smile. "And if you can do anything with my maid's dress, I won't be needing it anymore. Use any excess money to help the rest of the villagers if you don't feel worthy of it all."

Hesitantly, Fletcher took the dagger, stashing it away. He pulled a small box from the cupboard and took something from it. Taking the front of my cloak, he placed a silver broach in place of the default steel one. "It was my daughter's. She passed a few years back."

I looked at the Silver Phoenix broach in the mirror, and my eyes teared. "I will make her proud."

"I know you will. Anything more I can do for you"

Caeli stepped in. "Five sets of climbing gear out of the question?"

Fletcher laughed. "Oh, but you are a Soul," he said shaking his head and retrieving the required equipment.

After a few more minutes, we finally came back out into the street. The climbing gear was hidden away in our cloaks.

Baras spied us and noted my outfit. "I didn't see any of that before," he said.

"I found a small amount of respect," I replied with a smile.

Baras just snorted and walked off.

My heart pounded with every step, each beat reverberating in my ears like a drum. Butterflies churned in my stomach, their frantic fluttering making me feel as though I might retch at any moment. It wasn't the height that unnerved me but rather it was the climb itself. Shatterstone Mountain's winding trail was manageable for most of its ascent, but the final quarter was a sheer cliff face. Ordinary travellers would have taken the pass a day west, but as a Soul, my path led to the summit where Enzo waited. That was where the true journey began.

Leaning against a jagged boulder, I gazed out over the vast lands below. Valaos appeared deceptively close, its creek winding like a silver thread through the terrain. Fletcher's cloak had been a gift of foresight; it shielded me from last night's biting cold, and I silently thanked him for it. Telveria Keep was now just a faint speck on the horizon, a reminder of how far I'd come despite being woefully unprepared. The kindness of those who had helped me along the way fuelled my resolve to prove myself worthy of their faith.

On the distant horizon, the smoke from my dream lingered ominously. It had spread further now, blanketing more land than before. A late-season bushfire wasn't unusual, but this one seemed unchecked. Likely smouldering on the border where neither nation dared intervene for fear of igniting war. It was tragic how greed and pride kept nations from cooperation. Negotiations always failed when one ruler demanded more than the other could concede, conflict inevitably following. And here I was, climbing this mountain to become yet another weapon in their endless struggle.

"Fuck them all," I muttered under my breath.

A voice startled me from my thoughts. "Sounds like a plan," said a woman who had rounded the corner and stopped close to me. "You're the Phoenix Maid, aren't you? Where's your little posse?"

I turned to face her, instinctively wary. She was a soldier by her attire. A short-handled mace was strapped to her side and chainmail glinted beneath crimson hair that fell loosely over her shoulders. But it was her scar that caught my attention: jagged and stark white, it stretched across her left cheek as though her flesh had once been torn away.

"They'll catch up soon enough," I replied evenly, though I cursed myself for waking early to get a head start. Her gaze unsettled me. "I'll meet them at the base of the cliff."

"It's a treacherous climb," she remarked, her tone laced with doubt. "Think you're up for it?"

I narrowed my eyes at her and scanned her gear, or lack thereof. No ropes or climbing equipment. She wanted mine.

"That's a nasty little look you're giving me," she said with a smirk, shifting her stance to appear more dominant.

I needed control of this situation, now. Rising to my feet, I reached for one of my short swords and drew it. The unexpected weight threw me off balance. My attempt to recover with my off hand resulted in an embarrassing fumble. I ended up launching the sword at the woman, the blade clattering harmlessly against her armour before falling to the dirt.

I froze in place, mortified by my own ineptitude.

Scarface stared at the fallen sword for what felt like an eternity before bursting into laughter, a deep, rumbling sound that echoed off the mountain walls. But her mirth vanished as quickly as it had come.

"That's going to cost you, Bitch," she snarled before slamming her armoured fist into my eye socket with brutal force.

Pain exploded in my skull as I crumpled to the ground. A booted foot crashed into my ribs next, and though I prayed Fletcher's cloak or the ranger leathers would cushion the blow, they offered little relief. My vision blurred as darkness overtook me.

When consciousness fled, my spirit rose, a strange detachment overtaking me as I stood outside my own body. The pain was gone now, but watching Scarface deliver blow after blow to my limp form filled me with helpless fury. Then she found it: my climbing equipment hidden beneath the cloak.

I screamed silently at her retreating figure as she walked away with everything I needed to ascend Shatterstone Mountain. My spirit lingered over my broken body until Fitz arrived, laughing and running with Dustin close behind him.

He froze when he saw me sprawled on the ground; Dustin colliding into him from behind, sending them both tumbling into the dirt.

"Ellie!" Fitz scrambled up first and rushed to check my pulse, relief washing over his face when he found it steady but weak.

Korr arrived moments later with Caeli trailing behind him. "You've had more medic training than I," Fitz said urgently to Korr. "Can you check her"

Korr nodded. With a quick study of my body, he was confident to move me. I watched him pick up my body like it was nothing and laid me gently on a softer patch of earth. While he studied me, Caeli stood of to one side concerned.

"Who did this, Fitz?" She asked and Fitz just shrugged.

"There was no one here when we arrived. It could only have been a Soul, though," he said with concern.

Caeli just reflected the look as they waited for the diagnosis from Korr.

"No broke. Only bruise," he said as he stood. "She not wake."

Though his words reassured them all, I remained trapped outside myself, unable to return until Caeli knelt beside me with a vial in hand. She broke its seal and held it beneath my nose; its pungent aroma pierced through even my incorporeal state like daggers of fire.

My soul fled back into my body with a jolt and agony erupted anew as consciousness returned.

"Don't move," Caeli instructed firmly but gently, holding me still with comforting hands.

Tears spilled down my cheeks unbidden, humiliation mingling with pain as emotions overwhelmed me entirely.

Caeli pulled me close and stroked my hair soothingly. "Shh... It'll be all right," she whispered softly.

"I couldn't stop her," I choked out between sobs and gasps for air that sent fresh waves of pain through my battered ribs.

"Take your time," Caeli said rubbing my back. "Speak when you're ready."

I was still having trouble breathing but there was an urgency in the situation. "She stole climbing gear. 20 minutes ago. Scarred face, red hair."

"Bitch!" Caeli exclaimed. "It's Kymberlin."

Fitz nodded and took off up the trail followed closely by Dustin. Caeli sat down next to me, her hand still on my back, as Korr stood watch, arms crossed.

"Why did you leave us this morning?" Caeli asked after a long moment.

The question hung in the air, inevitable yet unbearable. I knew it was coming, but now that it was here, I couldn't face it. My pride had led me to this moment, beaten down, broken on the side of the road, all because I wanted to seem stronger than I truly was. The storm inside me swirled until it overwhelmed me, and I crumpled into a heap of tears and sobs that shook my entire body.

Caeli knelt beside me, her arms wrapping around me like a shield against the world. She didn't speak; she just held me until my sobs softened into shaky breaths. "Hey," she whispered gently, tilting my chin up to meet her gaze. Her fingers brushed away the streaks of tears on my cheeks before she used a scrap of cloth to clean my face. "There we go. Can't let the boys see you like this."

I managed a weak smile through the lingering ache in my chest. "He likes you, you know," I said, my voice raw but steady enough now to form words. The pain hadn't disappeared, it lingered like tiny daggers, but breathing through it helped.

Caeli's expression shifted, distant and tinged with sadness. "Dustin? I know," she replied softly.

52

"Sorry," I said quickly, regretting my words. "I didn't mean to open whatever box that was."

"It's okay." She paused, her gaze fixed on some unseen point in the distance. "It's obvious enough, anyway, but it's not meant to be." Her voice faltered as she continued, each word heavy with unspoken emotion. "We had something once, young, passionate, reckless, but then... I met his dad... My dad," she clarified, her voice barely above a whisper.

Her words hit me like a thunderclap. My eyes widened in shock. "You mean...?"

She nodded slowly. "I'd only met him once before when I was little, but when I saw him again... everything changed. Dustin and I, we couldn't go back after that."

"I'm so sorry," I murmured, my heart aching for her. "That's a cruel twist of fate. You didn't try to... pretend," I said, trying to look for the right word.

Caeli shook her head with a faint smile that didn't reach her eyes. "Once you know the truth, it's always there," she said quietly.

Desperate to shift the conversation away from her pain, I blurted out, "I left early this morning because I didn't want to slow you down getting to the climb. I thought if I got a head start, we could all climb together."

She gave me a weak smile that mirrored my earlier expression. "A slow stroll up the mountain wouldn't be so bad," she said thoughtfully. "The summit is the last place where all the remaining Souls need to gather before they can move forward into the Phoenix lands and find their own way. We could take another week here and they'd be stuck waiting for us at the top."

I frowned at this revelation. "So, if one soul travelled to Poltaveri before reaching that point, no one could proceed?"

She nodded gravely. "The Phoenix sense all Souls within their domain. If even one is elsewhere outside its lands, the others are barred from entering Phoenix territory. Anyone who tries would face its scorching flames."

The thought made me laugh, a sharp sound that turned into a gagging cough as pain flared in my side again. Caeli watched me with an odd expression as if trying to decipher something hidden within me.

"Baras wanted me gone," I said suddenly, the memory surfacing unbidden. "He wanted me to leave, to escape to another country and live as someone else but if I had've done that..." My voice trailed off as realisation struck me like lightning.

"He'd never have gotten what he wanted," Caeli finished for me, her tone laced with understanding.

I nodded slowly. "Did he know about this rule?"

"Of course," Caeli replied with a bitter laugh. "Baras would've been thoroughly informed about every step in the path to becoming a Phoenix Soul years ago."

"The argument at the cave," I muttered under my breath as pieces fell into place.

Caeli snorted softly at the revelation, shaking her head in disbelief. "The bastard really tried to save you at everyone else's expense. You two must have been close."

"Like sib...lings. Sorry," I said moments before realising I shouldn't even make anything of it. "I'm just going to drop that line of conversation," I said and Caeli nodded.

There was a soft breeze entering the halls of my mind shifting away the beginnings of the darkness over Baras and my friendship but before I could respond further, Fitz and Dustin returned empty-handed.

"She got away," Fitz announced grimly as he approached us. "Kymberlin was halfway up the cliff face by the time we spotted her. I didn't have an angle with my bow."

Dustin handed me my fallen sword with a quiet nod before adding pointedly, "You took off early this morning."

"Already covered," Caeli cut in smoothly before I could respond, a welcome relief from having to explain myself again. "She was trying to lighten the burden Elara thought she was."

"Really, a nice slow walk up the mountain wouldn't have been the worst thing in the world," Dustin replied. They must have spent a lot of time together having almost replied the same way as his sister. Looking at him now, I could see the similarities. It was so blatantly obvious when you know where to look.

"We could have taken in all the scenery along the way," Fitz said. "We're going to need to share some gear around to even us all out. Even then it's going to be a slow climb."

The group began preparing for the climb ahead when Korr tossed his climbing gear at my feet with an unapologetic shrug.

"Korr no need ropes. Korr no use rope," he said simply in his rough accent. "Korr strong. Korr climb like goat."

I couldn't help but laugh despite myself as Fitz clapped Korr on the shoulder approvingly.

As we moved toward the cliff face together, I leaned closer to Fitz and asked with genuine curiosity: "Do goats really climb?"

Fitz grinned broadly and chuckled under his breath as he replied cryptically: "You'll see, Ellie."

I moved cautiously along the path toward the base of the cliffs, each step deliberate. The bruises and sore muscles from my clash with Kymberlin slowed me, but it wasn't just the pain, I couldn't risk triggering another asthma attack. Fitz's energy point massage techniques were working wonders, yet I still longed for the reassurance of my medicine.

"You said there were Lemna Raja leaves near the base of the cliff?" I asked Fitz, breaking the silence.

He froze, his eyes widening before darting to meet mine. "Oh no," he muttered. "When I said 'base,' I meant..." His gaze shifted back down the path.

A sinking feeling settled in my stomach as I followed his eyes. A cheeky laugh echoed from behind us, and I turned back to Fitz, my expression darkening. "Where are they?"

"Close to the cliff face," he admitted with a smirk. "Not far off the path. I scouted them earlier when chasing Kymberlin." He arched an eyebrow at me. "No sense of humour?"

"Humour when it's deserved," I replied, swatting his arm lightly. "Can I ask you a favour, Fitz?"

"Anything within my power, Ellie," he said, his tone turning serious.

"If I make it up this cliff."

"When you do," he corrected firmly.

I smiled faintly at his confidence. "When I do... I need help with my sword work."

"That's doable. What level are you at now?"

"I can unsheathe it and... throw it at an opponent."

Fitz blinked before chuckling softly. "Right. We'll start with the basics and build from there."

"Thanks, Fitz," I said quietly, appreciating his unwavering support.

The path opened up ahead, revealing the imposing cliff in all its monstrous glory. It loomed over us, its summit swallowed by thick clouds that obscured just how far we'd have to climb. My breath hitched as memories of falling from an apple orchard tree as a child resurfaced, the sharp crack of my collarbone breaking still vivid in my mind. Baras had forbidden me from climbing ever again after that.

A shiver ran through me as I whispered, "Now that I see it... I don't know if I can do this."

Fitz placed a reassuring hand on my shoulder. "We'll get through this together."

Before his words could fully settle, a piercing shriek echoed down the cliff, followed by a soldier's lifeless body crashing to the ground below with a sickening thud. My eyes widened in horror as panic surged through me. I turned to flee.

Fitz's arm shot out, pulling me back into the clearing. "Don't let Indres's quick descent scare you off," he said calmly. "He wasn't great at climbing to begin with. And climbing without gear? Foolish. Not to mention the dagger in his back didn't help matters."

I hesitated before glancing at Indres's body and nodding grimly. "Promise me, Fitz," I whispered. "Promise me I won't end up like him."

"You've got three good climbers and Korr on your side," he replied with a shrug. "I promise you'll see the lands of the Phoenix."

"That's all I ask."

Fitz led me up the track to a bush brimming with Lemna Raja leaves. Its abundance was staggering. Enough to last me a year if harvested carefully. I made certain to leave the purple flowers untouched. They were coated with a clear poison that was absorbed through the skin on touch and could cause horrific bouts of vomiting and diarrhea. I learned that the hard way.

"This'll do nicely," I said gratefully.

With my medicine restocked, we returned to where our group was preparing for the climb. Korr stretched and squatted nearby while Caeli and Dustin meticulously checked ropes and pulleys. Dustin took my gear for inspection before showing me a few pointers.

"We climb in pairs," Caeli announced as she surveyed the cliff face. "Dustin and I will lead; Fitz and Ellie will follow. Stick to the best handholds and footholds, no risks. If trouble arises, call out immediately."

Korr grunted in response, earning a smile from Caeli. "The goat will probably just run up the side," she added wryly.

Korr puffed out his chest proudly at that remark, eliciting chuckles from all of us.

As Dustin handed back my gear, he tied my asthma pipe securely to a loop near my chest. "Lose this or get stuck without access to it up there," he warned, "and we won't reach you in time."

"Thanks," I said warmly, appreciating his foresight.

Suddenly, Caeli shoved me aside as something heavy crashed into the ground where Dustin had been standing moments earlier, a bundle of bone armour tangled in rope.

"Baras..." The name escaped me softly as I scanned above for any sign of him.

Fitz knelt beside the bundle and shook his head grimly. "He must've removed his armour for an easier climb but was forced to cut it free when it snagged. Smart move." He glanced at me pointedly. "Let this be your first lesson: better to let something go than risk your life trying to save it."

I nodded slowly but couldn't help asking softly, "Do you think we could... recover it?"

"No," Fitz said firmly before softening slightly. "Why would you want to? He hasn't exactly been kind to you on this journey."

"I owe him... for old times' sake." My voice faltered as Caeli gave me an encouraging smile.

Fitz sighed heavily but relented when Korr hefted the bundle without hesitation.

"Cutting things away includes unnecessary emotions. Come on," Fitz said briskly, turning back toward me. "Let's review climbing techniques one last time."

He walked me through grips and holds again, how best to use gear and avoid slipping on ropes, all while instilling confidence with every word. Finally, he slipped fingerless gloves onto my hands.

"These will protect against rope burn while keeping your fingertips free for precision," he explained.

I stared up at the towering cliff once more as fear churned within me, a small ripple threatening to become a tidal wave.

"Don't look up or down once we start," Fitz advised gently. "Keep your focus on what's right in front of you."

I nodded resolutely and murmured, "Let's do this."

Korr let out an excited bellow before charging up the cliff face as if gravity was merely a suggestion.

"Is he fighting the cliff or celebrating it?" Dustin quipped with a laugh as he and Caeli began their ascent.

Fitz followed next, leaving me tethered behind him. My first attempt at gripping a handhold failed miserably. I slipped back onto solid ground with an embarrassed huff.

Fitz glanced over his shoulder but didn't say anything; his calm gaze was enough encouragement for me to try again and this time, I held firm.

It was a hard crawl up the cliff face. Within minutes, my arms screamed in protest, and my resting times grew longer and longer. Fitz displayed incredible patience in matching my snail's pace. I knew it must have been trying for him. Gradually, Caeli and Dustin traversed further across the rock face, creating a longer climb but with a glance, even I could see the handholds and footholds were more pronounced on their chosen path. It would be a longer climb, but a significantly easier one.

Another body plummeted from the clouds overhead, a scream abruptly silenced by a sickening thud. I shot a worried glance at Fitz, then noticed the absence of Caeli and Dustin.

"The clouds can make the stone slick. Easy to lose your footing up there," Fitz said. "Come on. A few more metres, and we can rest."

I watched Fitz disappear over an invisible ledge. The rope remained taut, but uneasiness crept in. I felt isolated, the sole occupant of this vertical world. Strength was fading fast, and I didn't know how much longer I could push on. Rushing the last few holds, my feet slipped out from under me, one hand losing its grip. My remaining arm locked in a crack as my eyes fixed on the dizzying drop below. Panic threatened to overwhelm me as I flailed, desperately trying to regain purchase.

"Ellie... Ellie! Hey, Ellie. Calm down. Breathe," Caeli's soothing voice cut through my rising panic. "Fitz has you. You're not going to fall. Stop moving, and we'll pull you up. There's only a metre left."

Her words cut through the fear, grounding me. I stilled my movements, allowing the rope to take my weight. Scrambling over the ledge, I collapsed against the cliff face. Pressing my fingers into the pressure points on my hands, trying to calm my ragged breathing, I tried to arrest the asthma attack. When that proved futile, I reached for my pipe, my trembling hands fumbling with it and without the rope, would have lost it over the edge. I glanced at Dustin, gratitude plain on my face, as I recovered my pipe. Filling it with fresh leaves, I inhaled deeply, the smoke soothing my aching lungs.

"How's Korr doing?" I asked, finally finding my voice.

Dustin simply looked past me, then pointed. I followed his gaze.

"Maaaaaah."

"Ah, shit!" I exclaimed, startled to find myself face to face with a goat. "How?" I scanned around it, trying to discern its path, searching for purchase it could be standing on. Its hooves barely grazed millimetres of rock, yet it stood there, calmly chewing a tuft of grass as if on level ground. I turned to the others, baffled.

"Goats," Dustin shrugged, as if it explained everything.

I stared back at the goat, still perplexed, while Caeli distributed dried meat and cheese. My stomach growled, and I devoured the food, feeling energy flood back into my weary limbs.

"How much further to the top, do you think?" I asked, already shifting my weight back and forth, trying to keep my muscles from seizing up.

"The clouds are thick, but I've noticed a few thinner patches where the sun is shining through. I'd guess about 20 more metres to the top of the clouds, then another 15 to the summit," Fitz replied.

"It couldn't be that close," I said, my voice rising in surprise.

"Take a quick peek over the edge," Caeli suggested.

"Fitz said..."

"Just a quick look," Fitz said.

Peering over the edge, a sudden wave of vertigo washed over me as I fully comprehended the height we had gained. Fitz was right; focusing on what was directly ahead of me had kept me from realizing just how far we'd come.

The next words from my mouth surprised even me. "Shall we finish the climb, then?"

The others merely smiled. Without a word, we resumed our ascent, disappearing into the cloud cover. Visibility dropped drastically. I could feel a thin film of moisture coating the rock and understood the need for bare fingertips now; the extra sensitivity was essential to maintaining my grip.

A roar, almost a battle cry, echoed through the thinning clouds.

"It's Korr!" Caeli shouted, quickening her pace, Dustin close behind.

I could feel Fitz's eagerness to join them, but he held back, matching my speed. I pushed myself to climb faster, but I couldn't hurry.

When we finally broke through the cloud cover, the scene that greeted us was both terrifying and absurd.

We were almost 70 metres from where we would have emerged had we climbed straight up the cliff. Three soldiers were battling Korr on the cliff face. A normal climber would have struggled against such odds, accounting for the number of Souls who had already fallen but Korr seemed to have the upper hand. His movements were swift, his arms unburdened by climbing gear. And then my eyes widened in disbelief. Korr launched himself from the cliff face, swinging the bundle of bone armour like a flail, dislodging one of the soldiers on impact. He caught a handhold, then swung the armour again, smashing it into the skull of another soldier, sending him plummeting. The third turned and fled towards the summit, Caeli and Dustin still too far away to intercept. Like a beast, Korr bounded up the mountainside, tackling the last soldier. Holding onto the cliff with one arm, he stretched the man out from the cliff face with the other. He said something... witty, I hoped, before releasing him. The man's scream echoed into silence far below.

I spotted Kymberlin standing at the summit's edge, staring down at me. Her expression was one of pure disgust before she turned and walked away. I couldn't help but feel the warriors had been stationed there to prevent me from reaching the top.

Following Fitz's lead, I scrambled up the last 10 metres and hauled myself over the summit. Gasping for breath, I focused on controlling my breathing, determined to do it without the aid of my pipe. I sat with my feet dangling over the edge, taking long, steady breaths, allowing my body to relax while rubbing pressure points. It was a relief to know the hardest part of this journey was over, even though we still needed to cross the harsh lands beyond, filled with what children called monsters and demons.

I glanced across and saw Korr holding out the bundle of armour to Baras, who, in turn, looked at me stunned. Korr wouldn't have brought it up the cliff on his own accord; Baras knew exactly who had requested it. I looked away as he began to approach. A moment later, an arm wrapped around me as Baras sat beside me.

"Thank you, Elara," Baras said softly. "I'm glad you made it up the mountain."

A soft blush warmed my cheeks at his sincere words. "Thanks for putting me before becoming a Soul."

He nodded, and we sat in comfortable silence for a while. Glancing over my shoulder, I saw Fitz standing behind us, arms crossed, dagger in hand. He was watching Baras intently, and I burst out laughing.

Looking back at Baras, I smiled. "Friends?" I asked.

"Friends," he replied, before we both stood.

I smiled as I saw Fitz finally undoing the rope that had connected us. Even though I knew Baras, Fitz had made sure Baras wouldn't be throwing me from the clifftop, possibly out of jealousy, I theorized.

All the Souls gathered on the precipice I had dreamt of two nights prior, waiting for the Phoenix to arrive and grant permission to cross into the lands of rebirth. Looking over the group, I was surprised to find that we had already lost eleven Souls, Fitz and Korr responsible for over half the deaths. I was even more surprised that I was one of the few that made it.

A cheer erupted as a fiery glow appeared deep in the lands beyond. The Souls arranged themselves in two straight lines on the ledge, which was barely wide enough for more than three people to stand side by side. An empty space the size of a person clear down the centre. I took an empty position second from the back and looked around. Fitz and Caeli stood at the rear. Korr was beside and Dustin ahead of me. To my surprise, Baras stood across from Dustin, effectively boxing me in. I noted Kymberlin near the front, standing with seven other Souls whose names I had yet to learn.

The Phoenix swooped in, landing on the edge of the ledge in a ball of flames and embers. The swirling fire played around the legs of the foremost Souls, causing several to fidget, trying to avoid the intense heat. Feathers shimmered and danced in oranges, yellows and reds. The small flames all over the body was mesmerizing. To think, someone could ride that ball of fire and live.

And then, suddenly, he was standing between the two rows of Souls. He was taller than I had realized in my dream, but my skin still burned as if ignited by the Phoenix itself. If only I could get those tattooed arms on me. To play rough with me. I'd take anything that man could throw my way...

A scream pierced my daydream, and I watched a Soul plummet from the edge of the precipice in wide-eyed fear. My heart transitioned from an innocent flutter to a terrified pounding as I watched Enzo scanning the Souls while walking before throwing another warrior from the ledge.

He's weeding out the weaker Souls, the thought came unbidden to my mind as his amber eyes came to rest on me, leaning out further than the other Souls in the line. There was shock in his eyes as he assessed me.

My body stepped back on its own as Enzo began marching towards me, intent in his eyes. Korr's hand came up to halt his approach as Fitz stepped out of place to stand beside me. Dustin and Caeli seemed tense as if they could pounce at any moment. Even Baras rested a hand on Enzo's shoulder, His face stern.

Enzo's dark, Amber eyes swirled like flames as he held mine before speaking. The deep, sultry, almost husky voice resonating deep within my soul. I found it odd to be sexual attracted to a man intent on killing me.

"Move back to your positions or my Phoenix will set this whole rock shelf alight, and we start this process again with a new set of Souls," Enzo said. When no one moved he looked down at his side. "Talon," he called what must have been his Phoenix's name.

"Wait!" I said. "I know you're all trying to protect me but if you all die for me, how will I feel in my role to protect you. This is my battle. Stand down."

It took a moment longer, but my friends finally stepped back. Enzo's eyes remained on me as a shiver ran down my spine.

"Throwing me from the ledge?" I asked looking over the side. A smile crept to my lips. "Don't think I can't die just as easily out on the plains?"

His leather-bound chest paused inches from my face forcing me to look up at him. If there was any other way to die, I couldn't think of it.

Damn, his smell was intoxicating and the heat that pulsed from his body chased away the chills at this altitude.

"Who named you Soul?"

"Same man who named you." I was so happy my voice remained even as I checked his gaze with my own. Enzo's left eyebrow rose.

"Walan? That's a surprise. He rarely names anyone."

"Named me a Mage. I can already see you know I'm no warrior."

He just scoffed. A hand came up to grab the side of my face. It was rough and strong. I hesitated in trying to remove it, feeling the large palm upon my skin. "Even as a Mage, you're unworthy." His hand tensed and I readied myself for what was to come.

A piercing screech filled the air and everyone, but Enzo reached for their ears. Enzo only looked back at Talon, glaring.

"She is not yours to kill. Her death belongs to another," the whimsical voice of the Firebird said.

I felt Enzo's body tense, and he slowly turned back to look at me as if for the first time. There was something different in his eyes. Real, undeniable shock. The hand upon my head slid down and latched onto the scuff of my cloak. Dragging the collar aside, he revealed the black scar of my frostbite.

"Elara?" His voice barely above a whisper.

My eyes narrowed on his. "Enz..." I began.

There was a deadly shift in his features as if even saying his name was painful. A strong hand reached up to grab me by the hair and before I had time to react, Enzo threw me from the cliff.

The world tumbled sporadically as I tried to keep my bearings. My hand lashed out to catch at empty air but finally on the third attempt I caught the thin rope dangling from the ledge I'd spied earlier while talking. My body righted itself, swinging round to slam into the rock face. Pain erupted through my side, but I had mind enough to catch a handhold with my other hand and plant my feet.

My face went deathly pale as I realised there was barely a hands breadth of rope left below where I caught. I'd fallen... three metres, I judged looking up and around. Giving myself a moment longer to get my head straight, I tied a loop into the bottom of the rope and fed my hand through it. At least if I was to fall again, I'd have a safety.

"Get back in line," I heard Enzo call as Caeli gave a quick glance over the edge, her face awash with relief.

Determined for answers, I began dragging myself up the cliff once more, anger fuelling my muscles. Enzo knew me, was angered by me, yet there were barely a few years in my younger childhood that he could have met me without me remembering. He was going to need to explain. And the damned bird too. Who the hell wanted me dead?

Pulling myself over the edge to the relief of those closest to me, I walked to the centre of everyone and faced Enzo. Maybe I wanted to ask how is it he knew me, or maybe I needed to know who it was that wanted me dead. My determination would ensure I got both answers.

"How is me dead?" I demanded of him, stamping a foot.

A confused look broke his steady gaze, and he just shook his head turning to look back at Talon. With a nod the Phoenix took to the skies leaving Enzo with the group.

"Now you will know hell," he said to the group, his voice booming over everyone. "As you can see, frailty will get you killed. Live past my sentence and gain yourself another day. I will always be watching. Leave!"

Enzo walked past the other Souls who had begun moving to the slopes of the mountain into the valley far below. Without a second glance, he passed me as if I was nothing.

"Answer me!" I screamed at his back before a hand rested on my head.

"I don't think anyone knows how to answer that," Dustin said and my mind played the words back through my head, embarrassment erupting across my face.

"Glad you're alive," Caeli said cutting in with a hug.

Chapter 4

As I gazed out over the lands of my birth, a shiver ran down my spine. The experience was in some ways more overwhelming than when Enzo had thrown me off the cliff. The eastern side of the valley was hemmed in by a sharp, thin cliff that was not easily traversable. There were small pockmarks along the cliff face that could only be caves. An icy, slow-moving river flowed along the base of the cliff until it snaked its way across the valley, evident by the dense following of trees.

Dark clouds in the North were dropping the first snowfall of the year, earlier than usual. Already, the land was falling into shades of whites and pale blues. The weather was going to be harsh on the lungs.

The only place untouched by snow was in the far Northwest, exactly where Talon had risen from in my dream state. I was willing to bet that would be our destination and was already looking forward to the warmth.

"So, what do you think?" Caeli asked, walking up beside me.

I pointed out the area where I believed the Phoenix to be. "That's our destination. The easiest route would be through the middle, cutting back at the last quarter," I said, moving my hand with an open palm to carve out the path. The western borders were too hilly and thick with forests, stretching most of the way to the horizon.

"Only if you want to run afoul of trolls and drakes," Dustin cut in. "Plenty of nasties down there to give us trouble."

I pointed at a different path.

"Centaur," Dustin shrugged.

I changed again.

"Imps."

"Those little devil looking things with the funny looking wings. That wouldn't be so bad," I said

"Powerful magic wielders that begin eating even if you're only partially immobilized. Small bites. Long torturous pain."

My eyes went wide, and I pointed at the harder western landscape. "How about the West?"

"Nah," Dustin shook his head. "There's talk of a Lich that stalks the forests leading to the handful of villages in the area. I'd risk the Imps over that demon."

"Okay, so we have monsters over most of the area. We can either go along the base of the eastern cliff..."

"Chimera and Harpies," Fitz called from where he had been arguing with Baras for the last half hour.

My brow furrowed. "Weee... hire a boat and come in from the North?"

Caeli pursed her lips, and Dustin just looked away.

"Oh, what? Giant sharks destroying boats."

"That's just silly, Ellie," Dustin replied. "The sirens and large squid-like creatures don't allow sharks in the bay. Or boats for that matter."

"What's the point of this conversation?" I asked, becoming frustrated.

"Mark trail," Korr joined in. His hand carved a path like I had originally. "Through middle, cut across."

"Good plan, Korr. What I was thinking," Caeli said, smiling.

"Yeah, it's the path I was heading for," Dustin said.

"Excuse me?" I demanded. "What about all the monsters?"

"We're just messing with you, Ellie," Caeli said. "There are monsters everywhere. The most direct path is as good as any."

I just puffed out my cheeks at them.

"It's why all the villages are found to the West."

"In fact, the only village that ever thrived in the valley below was destroyed by humans more than three centuries ago. Three Pines, I believe it was called and even then, it was still along the western edge."

The name stirred long forgotten memories, but I couldn't quite grasp them enough to recall their secrets. Just a feeling and a glimpse of snow. "I can't say for sure I'd heard of it. Maybe."

"I guess living in Telveria Keep would leave you open to hearing about a lot of places and things you can't always file away in your mind," Fitz said with a smile.

"Elara's first few years were spent in one of the villages to the West. The name Three Pines Village could be from bedtime stories," Baras said, walking up behind Fitz. There was a dark expression across his features, and I could tell he was angry, guessing he lost the argument.

"Is that true? No wonder your resolve is so high," Fitz said, surprised.

"I don't remember much of the time. Mostly just the death of my family in the woods." It was a sore subject, and I was happier letting it fade away. "What have you two been arguing about, anyway? You've been at it for a while."

"We were discussing the merits of who would be best teaching you the sword," Baras replied.

I didn't like the sound of this. I asked Fitz. I didn't want my life to be determined by others. Especially Baras, who had been trying to determine a lot lately.

"Yeah. We decided I'd be best," Fitz almost smirked. "I'm better with short swords and daggers. You wouldn't be able to wield what Baras is proficient in."

"Yes, but I'm still going to watch and make sure he does it right," Baras said stubbornly, staring down Fitz.

"No," I said, anger rising in my chest. Baras glanced back at me.

"Sorry, what?" He asked.

"Fitz knows what he's doing. I asked him. *I*... asked him to teach me, and that's all there is to it. You are too close to me to allow me to grow without arguing with Fitz every five minutes out of jealousy and wanting the bigger dick."

"Elara, I..." Baras stammered.

"Friends, yes, but I need to find my own path to grow, to become stronger. I can't do that with people looking over my shoulder. The others don't get involved out of respect. I know you only do because you've protected me most of my life. I need to make my own decisions now."

"Fine," Baras said and walked to where Caeli and Dustin stood on the cliff's edge. He scanned the valley. "I propose through the centre."

"That's troll and drake territory," Dustin said.

Baras took a moment to consider and chose another path.

"Centaur," Caeli shrugged.

I smiled, riding the déjà vu of the conversation. Walking back to Fitz, I punched him in the arm. "When you consider arguing over my life again, include me, okay?"

"Next time you can stand right next to me. I was just having too much fun."

"And go easy on him. All he knows is soldiering. He didn't give much time to the written word or the teachers his father hired."

"I can see that," Fitz said, watching Korr give his choice of path and seeing Baras begin to arc up.

I smiled again. "At heart, he is a good man. Trustworthy under pressure. I will vouch for him."

"I know, Ellie. We've already accepted him. Now shall we start your first lesson?"

I was confused for a moment, then my eyes shot open. "Swords? Now?" I squealed.

"The first step in becoming stronger is always the hardest," he replied.

"Unless it's forced upon you and you have no choice but to partake," I said, smiling. I was thinking about the moment Walan sent me on this journey. There had been very little time to think, and just this short amount of time had seen me grow.

"Then let me be the force that makes you grow. Now, show me how you unsheathe your short sword," Fitz said.

I tried to look as dangerous as possible as I reached for the sword. I wanted to try and get that warrior essence into it. Taking hold of the pommel, I pulled it from the sheath, but as I reached the first point where my arm began to bend around, the sword swung as if on an axis. I watched as the blade carved a path in the air, ever bending back towards my shoulder. It took Fitz to lunge with his own sword to block and prevent any wounds my arm may have taken.

"Okay, thank you, Ellie. My assessment is complete," Fitz said.

"Assessment? I thought you were going to teach me first," I said. I clearly failed whatever that test was.

"I can't teach you properly if I don't know where to begin. I could show you all the finer points of gutting a man from hip to ear, but if you can't even retrieve your sword, you will never protect yourself."

Understanding dawned on me, and I gave a sheepish little nod. The next half hour was learning a proper grip on the hilt and different stances I needed to take. I'd never realized just how complicated sword fighting could be, and I hadn't even swung a weapon yet.

When Fitz was satisfied with my hand and footwork, he showed me a series of thrusts, parries, and slashing motions to practice. It was to give me muscle memory of the motions to use, and I was to sheathe and unsheathe the weapon at the beginning and end of each movement. He wanted me to do this slowly, getting a feel for the correct posture rather than trying to put any force into it. Fitz corrected me from time to time, emphasizing the need for accuracy and fluidity over chaos and strength.

"Enough," he finally called and Caeli walked up to us with a midday... I looked at the sun, afternoon meal.

"You have promise," Caeli said. "I'm glad that Fitz is starting you out on the right foot. My first instructor ran me through complicated drills long before I even knew what end was the pointy one."

My face blushed in a soft pink at her compliment. "You're so good now, though," I said.

"Yeah. My first instructor threw me from his ranks after a couple of weeks. Sure, I could do the manoeuvres he wanted, but they weren't perfect, and I had trouble besting many fighters. When I found my next instructor, he was shocked and appalled at my level and skill. He kept saying how my last instructor needed a running through with a sword while pointing to the tip as if I needed to know. Riall had to tear down everything I knew and rebuild me from the ground up. It was terribly hard forgetting what I'd previously learned, but it paid off."

Sitting quietly, I listened in awe to Caeli's story, envious of her skill. I began to wonder if Fitz had a similar story or if he was lucky straight up.

"What was your teacher like, Fitz?" I asked.

"He was a dancer, and when I wasn't learning the sword, I was learning to dance," Fitz replied evenly.

I heard Baras scoff. "No wonder you like to prance around the field. I'm surprised you're even still alive. I bet he liked to stick you with his other sword too."

My brow furrowed as I heard Baras's words. Sure, I'd heard plenty of soldiers cuss and talk with such foul language around the Keep, but this was aimed at a friend. I was about to move forward in protest when Fitz stuck out a hand.

"The art of dancing is the art of keeping one's body always in balance, no matter the height or angle you perceive to flow. I would argue that apart from luck, it is one of the most valuable skills a fighter could have. And for your other comment, I wouldn't let Tarantio hear that. Sure, his tastes were rather masculine, but he never touched a student."

There was a sudden shift in Baras. "Tarantio? As in, Master Swordsman, turned the tides of the Allurian Wars, Tarantio?"

Fitz just raised an eyebrow, and Baras turned his attention back to the view. It was amusing, and I laughed loudly.

"I'm guessing he's famous?" I asked.

Caeli just smiled. "I forget you're not of our world. Kings and Princes, knights and the elite, have all approached him for training and rarely been accepted. Even Baras would have dreamed of being trained at the hands of Tarantio. I'm surprised Fitz was a student."

"He saved me from some thugs when I was young. I was protecting the honour of a girl. Took the beating myself. He offered me lessons for the honour and integrity I showed."

"Wrong place at the right time. Depending on the outcome of our journey, your choices that day may very well define the future of this realm."

Fitz scoffed. "Come on, we should get on the road."

Fitz began to move, and one by one, we all slowly followed. This side of the mountain was going to be a far easier descent. There was an even slope that ran into the valley. Few trees spotted the hillside, and a small path wound up to the precipice at the top. It definitely wasn't made by the few Souls that ever got to walk this path. It must have been worn in by the people who lived north of the range, those who got past the Lich, at least. I glanced at Dustin.

As we reached the flats, I noted there was only forest ahead after a small clearing. I bid the mountains goodbye and stepped out into the valley.

A buzzing began ringing in my ears, droning through my mind and sending my immediate thoughts scattering. There was a pulse running between my mind and the grass, throbbing in my body until a pain bit into my flesh. Letting out a small scream, I fell to the unforgiving earth, unconscious.

The world around me grew hazy as I caught sight of my body lying on the grass. Caeli was immediately by my side, checking my vitals, while the others prepared as if for battle. From the trees, small shadowy figures resembling dogs, emerged and the group formed a defensive circle around me. The physical realm began to blur as I struggled to maintain focus on the unfolding battle. Soon, I could only make out the moving wisps of cloud where my friends once stood.

Energy lines started to glow across the land, swirling in yellows and reds that consistently flowed back to the northwest, toward the Phoenix nests. It became clear that the Phoenix truly fed on energy, building their power year after year to ensure their rebirth. When Walan said he would feed my soul to the Phoenix if I didn't comply... I shook my head. Best not to think about that.

Among these intense lines, another energy path emerged, a cinder like, stormy blue that snaked beneath the surface. Small tendrils leeched energy from the Phoenix's lines to feed this darker path. It seemed harsh and angry, as if the world was against it, and it would gladly watch the lands burn. The only creature that came to mind that fit was the Lich, another semi-immortal being though very different from the Phoenix. But if the Lich's power came from the Phoenix themselves, who then had the strength to end this creature?

I realized, as if for the first time, that my body lay atop the blue-grey energy line. My sensitive nature must have detected the draining tendril and shifted into its spirit form to investigate. I tried to move the line away from my body, but each time I touched it, pain flared through my soul. I needed to explore deeper into the ephemeral realm to find a way to break the connection.

Focusing my will, I drifted along the energy line, disgusted by how much energy it was stealing from the Phoenix. There were hundreds of tiny syphons buried deep into the red and yellow hues, but none seemed weak enough to sever. I couldn't find a way to shut down the dark blue line without risking harm to the warm red and yellows, and I fell into despair.

A screech, much like Talon's, echoed from the north, and I couldn't help but understand the danger nearby. I felt the dread terror approaching from the west, a small distance from the Phoenix nests. The feeling grew with paralysing speed, and in an instant, a wispy blue mist, much the same as the energy line I'd been following, engulfed my vision ahead. The terror I felt sent me fleeing the field, and my soul forced its way back into my body on instinct, waking me to the physical realm.

I drew in a sharp, exasperated breath as I took in the chaotic scene around me. Terrifying creatures lay scattered across the clearing, but my friends were still locked in battle with the remaining hounds. Even Caeli had abandoned my side, her bow a blur as arrows flew relentlessly. Dustin and Fitz fought back-to-back, while Korr and Baras were each consumed by a fierce battle rage, their greatswords cleaving through the ranks of the Terror Hounds with brutal efficiency.

Suddenly, one of the creatures broke through the line and charged straight at me. No one could afford to turn away from the pressing horde to help. Their tactic was clear: distract the fighters while one slipped away with the weakest prey, me.

I staggered to my feet, facing down the snarling beast. Its mouth was a grotesque maw of jagged, gnarly teeth, dripping with excessive saliva. Its lips were peeled back, revealing hard, black gums. There was no nose, only two large slits opening and closing as it breathed. They matched its blood-red eyes, slit-like and devoid of any human iris. The creature's body was lean and muscular, covered in ragged tufts of fur clumped much like that of a stray, street dog.

My heart froze, but I forced myself to draw a sword and level it at the beast, now mere feet away. I was never going to be a fighter as the person I was. Closing my eyes to whatever fate awaited, I thrust my short sword forward with all my strength. But it met no resistance; my body stumbled on, only for my foot to snag on a large mound and crash to the ground again.

Dazed, I looked up and realized the mound was the very Terror Hound I faced, motionless, a thrown dagger lodged deep in its temple.

That didn't feel right. The small victory leaving a bitter taste in my mouth. How many more times would my friends need to save me, risking their lives while I remained a liability? Anger surged within me. As another hound lunged, I lashed out with my forearm, striking it across the face.

A shockwave of icy force pulsed through me and into the creature. To my astonishment, its face crystallized into an ice sculpture before shattering into thousands of shards on the hard earth. The beast wouldn't rise again.

I twisted my arm in the fading blue light, stunned by the cold, dreadful power I'd just wielded. It reminded me of the blue energy from my spirit walk, the same harsh, biting force. A theory formed in my mind: if the Lich could steal power from the Phoenix, could I, in turn, draw from the Lich? I had lingered on that energy line for some time. It was the only explanation that made sense.

Glancing at my friends, I saw the Terror Hounds retreating, clearly wary of my newfound power. The one thing worse than a nightmare creature hunting you by instinct was one with cunning intelligence but at least they now recognized our strength.

"What did you do?" Baras asked cautiously, nodding toward the shattered hound. He approached as if I might suddenly sprout horns and a tail. The others looked at me with a mixture of awe and suspicion.

I shrugged. "I don't know. There's powerful energy in these lands. Overwhelming energy. I think I tapped into it. I just acted on instinct."

Baras frowned. "You don't just 'act on instinct' like this."

Fitz was quicker to recover, perhaps out of trust, or rivalry with Baras. "Apparently, she does. She wasn't named a Mage Soul for her looks alone," he said, stepping past Baras to study me. "You okay?"

"It was touch and go. Did you take down the first hound?"

Fitz shook his head. "No, that one got through at the worst moment. I feared you were lost." He bent to retrieve the dagger lodged in the hound's temple, examining it closely.

"Dustin? Caeli? Surely one of you?" I asked, glancing between them.

Both shook their heads.

"This knife isn't from any of the Keep's weaponry. I haven't seen anything like it from the surrounding nations either," Fitz said, tossing the dagger gently to me. I fumbled it, the blade flying back toward him. With a swift twist, he caught it where his belly had just been.

"Sorry," I murmured, shuddering.

Fitz smiled. "Watch the hilt and let it come to you. If you fumble it at that point, you will more likely subdue its momentum rather than add to it. Think of flipping a feather duster, maybe. It's similar."

"Except this one has two sharp blades ready to carve me up," I muttered, rolling my eyes.

He threw the dagger again, and this time I tracked its spin, catching the hilt cleanly before dropping it to the ground.

"Better," Baras said. "Next time, close your hand just before it lands. It corrects the mistiming you perceive and will improve your overall timing."

"Thanks, Baras. I'll try that," I said, bending to pick it up. The intricate handle felt oddly familiar, though I couldn't grasp why.

"Oh, while I was out of it, I travelled the land's energy lines," I added. "There's something harsh and cold near the Phoenix den. The energy was intense. We need to avoid it."

"Where exactly?" Dustin asked, intrigued by the idea of spirit travel.

"Near where you said the Lich might be. From the power I sensed, it could be the Lich itself."

Dustin and Caeli exchanged worried looks.

"What is it?" I pressed.

"There are many beasts and ghouls in this region," Dustin began, hesitating. Caeli took over.

"When we talked about danger earlier, half of it was dramatic exaggeration. There hasn't been word of a creature as powerful as a Lich in this kingdom for centuries. Millenia even. If one existed, it wouldn't stay in one place."

I frowned, relieved to hear my friends had overstated the risks but what I'd seen and felt told a different story. "There's something strong in those woods, and it's not friendly," I said, my concern deepening.

Korr stepped forward, tilting his head. "Korr watch. Keep monsters at bay."

I smiled. "Thanks, Korr. I'll feel safer at night knowing you're here."

As I spoke, a dark shadow slipped from the tree line. Humanoid in shape, it seemed to have been watching us all along. A thought struck me that perhaps this was the owner of the dagger... or the Terror Hounds. Either way, I kept the sighting to myself.

An enchanting glimmer danced along the edge of the blade. Under the firelight, the metal seemed to come alive, sparkling and swirling like stars scattered across the night sky. As I swished it from side to side, orange arcs traced the air briefly before fading back into the steel. It was magical, and more than that, it called to me.

Deep within the recesses of my mind, something stirred, trying to surface. It was something far beyond the dark depths I'd ever dared to explore, sending a shiver down my spine each time it pushed forward. Each attempt to reach the light left me fumbling, unable to grasp it firmly. A tightness pressed at my throat, my body tingling as if awakening a memory before my waking mind could even process it. I focused on the feeling, desperate to bring it forward, but no matter how hard I tried, I could only catch a fleeting glimpse of a hazy, cold backdrop tinged with a faint warmth.

Flipping the blade, I caught it subconsciously, watching the bands of orange and gold twirl into the air before settling back into my palm. I repeated the motion twice more, my peripheral vision narrowing until all I saw was the blade. I shook my head, trying to clear the haze but the scene that returned wasn't the campfire we'd set up earlier that afternoon, nor the rucksacks and friends resting nearby. Instead, it was a terrible snowstorm in the dying light of day. A boy, dressed only in shorts, stood close by, watching me as he flipped this very dagger. I had no memory of when it was, if it was even a memory at all. There was a chance it was simply the stirring of deep emotions embedded in the blade.

A heavy weight pressed upon me, like a pile of fur rugs, holding me down, keeping me warm. But as quickly as it came, it vanished, and I was back by the fire, still flipping the dagger. Seemingly, no one noticed my brief departure.

Korr sat beside me, bare-chested as he had been since we began this journey. He glanced around to ensure everyone was asleep, then reached out with his large, dark hand and gently took the dagger. His fingers caressed the blade delicately, sparks flickering where he touched. It was beautiful yet tinged with a sadness that ran deep in his eyes. He handed the knife back.

"Thank you," he said, his voice heavy with yearning.

"You know what this is, don't you?" I asked.

"Boulder of stars fell from sky on island. Ancestors name it Dura Kunga... Heaven's Gift. Make daggers from. Gift to BrongTa, Fire Dancers. Korr BrongTa. Korr no honoured. No give dagger Korr."

I pieced together the fragments of his story, sensing a tradition from his homeland. "Why did no one honour you with a dagger?"

"Korr flame small. Father no honour weak flame."

"Is the flame a fire you build?"

Korr smiled, then held out his arm. Flames licked around his fingers, swirling and dancing along the length of his arm. I shifted back a few paces on hands and feet, eyes wide. After a moment, I shook my head and settled back down. I knew Korr would never hurt me.

"Flame keep Korr warm, help in battle. Flame gift, but Korr flame no light kiln for dagger."

An ache burned in my heart for my friend. I offered him the dagger, but Korr shook his head.

"Dagger link to BrongTa. Korr no have."

My heart sank further. The dagger was bound to a BrongTa already and would never accept him.

"Why do you hide it?" I asked, curious. It was clearly an asset in battle.

"Many hunt BrongTa. Abomination, no natural. My village keep hidden. Not know who friend or foe."

I nodded. "A harsh reality we all face, hunted by demons, whether of this world or of our own making." I placed a hand on his shoulder for comfort, but he immediately stood, sword in hand. A figure had entered the clearing, and as they approached the fire, I recognized Enzo.

"Why here, Phoenix Soul?" Korr said, sword still ready.

Enzo opened his arms and paused at the edge of the fire's reach. "I seek an audience with the Mage. She and I have things to discuss."

Korr stepped in front of me, glaring.

"By my honour, I do not seek to harm her. She earned this day when she saved herself. Tomorrow, I'll try again if I feel so inclined."

"Speak," Korr said, levelling his sword at Enzo.

"She will join me in the woods," Enzo replied, unfazed by the threat.

I saw Korr was about to press the point further, so I rested a hand close to his shoulder.

"I will go. There are things I need to work out about myself, and I don't believe he'll harm me. I can't be as open as I need to be with everyone around."

Korr's eyes narrowed on me.

"Please, Korr. Promise me, no matter what, you'll stay in camp and keep the others from following."

Korr remained hesitant.

"You have your heritage. Things you wish you could change. I believe this may be about mine. Empty echoes where memories once stood. I need to know." Our eyes met, and finally, he nodded, looking away.

"Thanks, Korr," I whispered, smiling as I followed the steely man into the dark, private woods. Had I pushed the heritage excuse too hard? Sure. Would I have ended up stalking him on one of my dream walks? Definitely. I knew nothing could happen between us with him wanting to kill me, but those hands around my throat carried a mischievous air. It surprised me how badly I wanted a shadow daddy.

I found myself staring at those curved buttocks with a desire I barely hid. At a moment of his choosing, Enzo suddenly turned around. He smiled as I squeaked, my eyes darting anywhere but below... Like those strong, broad shoulders.

I chastised my wandering mind.

"Thanks for trusting me enough to come out here," Enzo said.

"As you said, I won this day. You'll have plenty of time to take me out tomorrow." I was glad my voice remained steady, feigning nonchalance.

He didn't seem to care. "Firstly..." He circled me until I was trapped between him and a tree, with little room to retreat. "I would like my dagger back." Enzo leaned over me, one hand braced against the tree, the other extended expectantly.

"What dagger..." I furrowed my brow, then realization dawned. I pulled the BrongTa dagger from within my cloak. "You're a Fire Dancer?"

His eyes narrowed, as if confused by my words.

"It shouldn't be such a surprise. Didn't you find my attire odd the day we met?"

Something in his voice felt off, like he was testing me. But I couldn't recall the day we met. Enzo was an enigma. His impatience grew as his eyes bore into mine.

The thought of a boy flipping the dagger came to mind. "Shorts in a snowstorm," I said, and his expression softened, the dark edge evaporating.

"The flames of my birth keep my soul and body burning. No natural cold can pierce that veil. It's why I'm drawn to you, Elara. You are my forbidden fruit. My taboo, if you will." Enzo leaned in closer, his breath grazing my cheek, sending goosebumps across my skin. But what did he mean?

"Excuse me. Your forbidden fruit? You didn't even recogni..." I started to protest, but a finger danced over my lips.

"Shh. Let's not fight tonight. Not after all this time. Let us just, be," Enzo whispered before leaning in to kiss me. His lips were warm against mine.

My eyes shot open for just a moment as my mind struggled to register what was happening. Enzo's hand threaded through my hair, holding the back of my head, and I melted into his embrace. My hands slid up his back, lost in the passion of the kiss. Suddenly, he lifted me off the ground, pressing me against the rough bark of the tree.

My hand caught the front of his shirt and tore it away, fingers grazing the hard muscles of his chest. As he pulled clothes from me, our tongues collided in a desperate dance, each craving to be closer. I didn't know who this girl was he knew but I would gladly be her for this moment.

Enzo broke the kiss, trailing tingling nibbles and bites down my neck and collarbone. His mouth found my breast, taking my firm nipple between his lips. His tongue curled around it, suckling gently, sending sparks racing through my body. My whole being ignited in that moment, and I moaned deep and long into the trees above, my hands clutching the trunk for support.

Leaning back, I wrapped my legs around this godlike man and then felt his burning weapon, between my legs, at the gates of heaven. This god wanted home. Who was I to deny him? My breath came out with raspy steam.

"Fuck me, Enzo. Make me scream," I moaned, my body already consumed by desire and lust.

Without a word, he thrust his cock deep inside me, my defences no match for this engorged wand of ecstasy. My velvet walls squeezing him tight as he began to move. His cock coming right to the very tip of its existence to plunge deep in me once more. I struggled to release even the moans as waves of pleasure rolled through me.

Wrapping my arms around Enzo's neck, I took control and used his shoulders to pull myself up, only to impale myself once more. He didn't get to walk away from this being the only one to enjoy it. For this moment, he was mine and I attacked that gorgeous cock with all the strength I could muster.

"Elara," Enzo moaned in my ear, sending shockwaves throughout my entire being.

"More," I demanded between thrusts. "Say my name more." And he obeyed.

"Fuck, Elara. Oh my God, Elara, your body is incredible. El ar raaa." His words stoked the fire inside me. My vaginal walls tingled and clenched tighter with every thrust. I knew I wouldn't last long.

"Enzo, you're going to make me cum... I can't hold back."

"Me too, Elara. I'm..." I felt him clench, holding back for the last few fragile seconds, and I thrust down hard one final time.

"Enzo, I'm cumming!" I screamed as he released with a grunt, his cock exploding deep inside me. The warmth pushed me over the edge, my soft walls clenching fiercely around him as my body convulsed. My mouth locked in a silent moan, eyes clenched tight, holding him close as the waves of ecstasy crashed over me.

Slowly, my senses returned, my breathing ragged and uneven. I struggled to comprehend what had just happened. All I knew was that it was one of the best moments of my life.

Leaning in, Enzo kissed me one last time before lowering me to the ground. A small aftershock rippled through me as our lips met again, tremors causing me to bite my lip as I pulled away.

"I've missed you terribly, Elara. I knew you still loved me after everything," he said, his voice a low rumble that left my mind too dazed to respond clearly.

"I think I've missed you my whole life, Enzo," I whispered, voice trembling. I would have gladly scrubbed the Keep from top to bottom if this was the man I'd find in my chambers each night.

He laughed softly. "Ain't that the truth. I'll see you again before the Phoenix." Then he helped me gather my clothes. "I've cloaked you in warmth for the next five minutes. Get dressed and get back to the fire."

"You're leaving?" A hollow ache formed deep in my soul at the thought of this night ending.

"You're strong, Elara. I know you'll make it. Five minutes." And with that, he vanished back into the darkness leaving me alone in the dark of the woods.

I wasted a minute just staring into the emptiness, my face burning red thinking about what I'd just done. Dressing, I walked back through the forest, surprised and embarrassed by how short the path actually was. No doubt Korr had heard everything. I just hoped the others were asleep deep enough to remain undisturbed.

A deep blush set alight my cheeks when I saw Korr had moved to the far end of the camp and ignored my returned. I made a beeline for the spot where I'd prepared to sleep and curled on my side, wrapping my cloak tightly around me.

Glancing at Caeli across from me, I was met with two wide eyes staring back, her face almost as red as mine. They definitely heard it.

"Who?" she whispered, though no clarification was needed.

I hesitated; mouth slightly open. "Enzo," I finally said softly.

"Even after he threw you off the cliff?"

I shrugged coyly, nodding at the same time. Caeli's grin grew wide, her eyes shining with pride.

"You fucking go, girl."

My blush burned anew.

All in all, I got away with last night's tryst lightly. Caeli and I had a rather awkward girl talk consisting of me describing some of the more prominent features of Enzo and her talking about her greatest love and the promiscuities they got up to. Though she didn't mention a name, there was no doubt that Dustin was playing through her mind.

The others had been politely quiet about it all. I could see it was playing on all their minds in some of the conversations and actions towards me, though. This was especially true with Baras. I wondered if he even realized I was a girl or could use my gifts with such effect. He'd become awkward with how he acted around me. His actions becoming over embellished as he tried to come to terms with what he heard.

The events had left me with some vivid and breathtaking memories, but I was still left with more questions than answers. Enzo was an enigma I couldn't break through.

"Anything we need to know about, Ellie?" Fitz asked, finally bringing the topic to air. We had been training for over an hour and were now sitting down to our morning meal. His training was tough on the body, but he was really good at it too. He would slow his movements just right to show me places I could disable an opponent, maim, or even kill them. He would point to places like the Achilles tendon, wrist, elbow, legs, neck and organ placement. He would always show me the points to hit and how to do so, allowing me to run through them all a few times before testing me on each, randomly. Still, I was now glad we had been training away from the others, or this would have been really uncomfortable.

"Nothing overly important," I said trying to close the topic quickly.

His eyes narrowed on me a moment before he looked away, taking a bite of the dark bread and cheese. "I see. In other news, be weary of leaving the campgrounds at night. There was some strange creature out there last night. Sounded like it was dying."

Offended, my eyes locked to his. "Thanks," I said, rich in sarcasm before I saw his grin.

"You didn't want to attack the subject directly. I thought maybe some light banter might help things along."

A pout teased my lips but was settled as I scoffed. "What would you like to know? Clearly, you don't care about the *dying animals*."

"What is his agenda?"

"I don't, exactly, know," I admitted honestly.

"Why did he single you out last night?"

"Am I being interrogated?"

Fitz smiled. "Interrogation comes with fun tools. I'm only collecting facts to determine risks moving ahead."

I scoffed again. "Enzo wanted to see me last night. He also wanted his dagger back."

"Makes sense why I didn't recognize the blade of a Phoenix Soul. Doesn't make sense him saving you after throwing you off a cliff."

No, that didn't make sense and I chastised myself for not asking Enzo that very question. The little information he did give, didn't make sense to me. Still, we didn't have much time for talking. "Enzo seems to know me from before all this."

"Know you how?"

"That's where it gets fuzzy. He knows my name for one. And he believes we first met while he was still a child. I only have a memory from the dagger, but I can't be sure if it was mine or just a strong feeling the dagger had attached to it. The event could have happened. It was correct for when I lived this side of the mountains. My only memory of that age was my family dying and being stuck in a tree. Maybe he helped me and got me to the Keep."

Fitz seemed concerned but he held his thoughts. "Have you had any run ins with him after that?"

"As far as my memories are aware, I have never seen that man in person until the cliff top. I remember my time at the Keep. Most of it was bundled together with Baras."

"And he... forced himself?"

My lower lip came up to overlap my upper lip, and I just shook my head trying not to make eye contact. "Nooo... I wanted it."

"Caeli assures me she would have as well," Fitz said shaking his head in return. "Spontaneous?"

A flutter of jealousy crossed my mind thinking of Caeli in Enzo's arms, but it passed quickly knowing the alternative was Dustin. "Again, fuzzy. He was saying how he missed me. His actions spoke as though we had more than a single meeting. I just didn't go against the grain, so to say. It was only because I saw the memory from the dagger that I got that far to begin with."

"An opportunist," Fitz laughed. "Just a one-off adventure special, then?"

"Maybe two one-offs," I said with a cheeky grin. "He said he would see me again before the Phoenix."

Fitz just laughed and got up. "Come on. We got daylight burning. And the closer we get to the Phoenix the more *opportunity* you may have."

"Oh shush," I said walking after him. "You're just jealous you don't have a cute little thing stalking you in the woods."

"When you put it like that," he rolled his eyes.

I chased Fitz back into the deconstructing camp and from that point on everything seemed to come back into alignment with everyone. Except Baras of course. Clearly everyone else had talked about it before Fitz approached me. They were happy to fall back on his assessment. Baras on the other hand didn't work well with others and needed to come to grips with things on his own.

The morning rolled by uneventful right into the afternoon. We stopped when we needed and fed when we were hungry. Every so often, Fitz would call a halt and shuffle us off the road. At times like these there would be some sort of creature bounding down the path, usually timid and harmless, but at the times we witnessed the creatures like the black bear or a smaller pack of Terror Hounds, I was grateful my friend was so cautious.

Every now and again we would come across other Souls wandering the woods. Not that they knew we were nearby, sitting in hiding, but it was a gentle reminder we weren't alone. Two Souls had blood on their armour, one sporting a nasty gash on his arm. I began to watch the bushes wondering if a predator may lay in wait nearby, hidden, as we were when others passed us. This simple walk was an eye opener to what the warriors of the realm must go through every campaign.

The one thing I never got tired of seeing was the Phoenix flying overhead. It was majestic and graceful as it glided along the wind currents, trails of flame swirling off to fade into nothing. I couldn't help but think of Enzo in these moments, my skin heating up thinking he may be close by. At any moment he could burst from the brush and sweep me up in those arms once more. I let out a soft sigh. Any time apart, now, was too much. I needed more of his heat and his body. A small... large taster wasn't enough.

And even with all the excitement passing by, I couldn't help but get bored. It gave me an opportunity to try out something I'd been contemplating with my spirit walks. Walan mentioned I may be able to do this while awake. If I could get a grasp on it, it would really make a difference. I could even keep watch and let Fitz know what was coming.

I took note of who was close and grabbed at Dustin's sleeve. "Let me use you a bit," I said.

He considered me a moment. "We all know how that turns out. Flattered, but I don't need Enzo chasing me down in a jealous rage." Dustin just grinned a cheeky smile.

My eyes narrowed on him. "Ooo, the things I could say to you right now," I said shaking my head slowly. "Let me hold your sleeve for support. I may stumble for a bit."

He instantly turned serious. "You ok?"

"Yeah, just trying some Mage stuff. Trying to be better."

"We all feel that way sometimes. Hold as much as you want," Dustin replied.

"Thanks." I paused a moment. "How quick are your reflexes?

"Lighting has nothing on me."

I scoffed. "If I fall unconscious, please don't let me face plant."

"I'll keep watch. How likely is it."

"Fairly. I'm trying to spirit walk while awake. I have only ever done so asleep or unconscious."

Dustin seemed impressed but didn't know what to say from there. "Good luck," he managed.

Keeping pace with Dustin, I tried to bloke out the rest of the world.

The feeling of transitioning was becoming familiar but to be able to recreate it at will was going to be hard. Drawing on that feeling, I tried to emanate in my mind the process of flowing out into the world. It almost felt correct until I found myself within my body and Dustin holding me aloft, his arm under my chest. And after that, two more times I found myself in the same position.

"Thank you," I said with a coy smile. "This may be a lot harder than it sounds."

"You're trying to imitate the state in which you have been in before? This was unconscious or asleep?" Dustin asked, his brow furrowed as if thinking.

"It's the only experience I've had with this ability," I replied.

"Then maybe you're doing it wrong. You're trying to step away from your body completely. If you do that who will be here to keep your body functioning?"

"I don't follow."

"Think of a horse and cart where your body is the cart and your soul is the horse..."

"'Scuse you," I cut in, smacking his arm.

"If the horse is detached from the cart, the cart ceases to function."

The concept itself made such simplistic sense and I pondered the implications. "What would you have me do? By your thoughts, I shouldn't be able to spirit walk while awake."

"You need to learn to do both at once. That's the ideal outcome. Maybe you only allow part of your spirit to leave or maybe you tether some type of lifeline like the rope on the cliff. Something to keep you grounded to your body and still give you control."

My eyes unfocused as I considered the possibilities. It all sounded possible but still felt like it was more advanced for the level I was at. I just wanted to become more useful to the group. "You know, you're a lot smarter than I gave you credit for."

Dustin's head tilted sideways. "Thanks?"

"Most welcome," I grinned.

"One more thing."

"Hmm?" I raised an eyebrow.

"Maybe practice at camp or with a different lackey. The eyes burning into the back of my head doesn't bode well for my future."

I glanced back to see Caeli walking behind, her eyes focused on Dustin. As she saw me her eyes shifted away only to come back to us moments later. I quickly let go of Dustin's sleeve and dropped back to walk beside her.

"You two are becoming close," Caeli said. She tried to remain neutral, but I already knew what I was looking for. The deep well of sadness just below the surface.

"I would love to call you sister, Caeli, but I would never come between you to do so. I was just using him a moment."

Her eyes came up to study mine, seeking any sign of deceit but all she found was true and honest emotion. For a moment, I saw past Caeli's defences. A moment she almost broke but that moment was quickly seized and packed away to whence it came.

"We all know how that turns out," she said with a sudden grin.

I stuck a finger up. "No. No. I fuck one man in the woods in a moment of hot and steamy pleasure. That's not me." I suddenly laughed. "But you two are so alike."

"Who? Me and Enzo?" A sly grin curled the edge of Caeli's mouth.

"Forget about the stigma society puts on it. When we leave this world none of that will truly matter and you will be sadder for listening to them over your heart and the love you can't let go of."

It was as if Caeli shrunk into the background, becoming withdrawn. When she finally spoke, her voice was barely a whisper. "I can't."

"We have been named Souls. From today to the end of days, death will stalk us. Could you face him without regret?" I asked, pausing to let the words sink in. "Seize the moment and free yourself from the shackles you've placed upon your soul. You have every right to love and be loved in return."

There was no reply.

The rest of the day became a quiet trek across the wilderness.

The night had been just as quiet as the afternoon. Baras tried to talk to me, sprouted a few sentences how the weather seemed to be smelling nice and the few rabbits on the fire were getting cold before he turned on his heel and stalked across the camp.

Korr was content in keeping watch around the boundary and I believe I'd made things more awkward for Caeli and Dustin. Dustin believed Caeli was blowing off some steam for his interactions with me while Caeli was sitting off to the side continually glancing at Dustin.

Fitz was the only one seemingly having fun. He was teasing Baras over one thing or another, whatever boys like to get rowdy about, and Baras was taking the bait as normal. I smiled at their bromance. They were becoming closer through their rivalry without even realizing.

The thought struck me that it was the perfect time to practice my abilities. I bounced around excitedly and got myself comfortable in a sitting position. There was a lot of fidgeting as I tried to find the best position. Often times, I'd get some phantom itch and feel it wasn't the right position to be in. Once that thought poisoned my mind, there was no shaking it. Finally, I settled on cross legged.

It was another 20 minutes before I even attempted my first try. I was still trying to get my head around how I could possibly be in and out of my body at the same time. It came to a head when I decided to just try it. My first try had me walking the campsite in spirit. I was so elated by the fact I succeeded without outside help that I didn't realise my body had slumped face first into the dirt. Turning I found myself in the awkward position and my shoulders slumped. It was a win but not the victory I was after.

It took a lot longer to work out how to re-enter my body. It's one thing to sever the links holding me to the physical plane. It was a whole other thing to reforge those links and having me wake. For all the effort I put in to reforging the links, it took a moment of stopping and sitting in my body to merge back into it. I was finally beginning to understand the inner workings of this ability.

Scrunching my sore nose and rubbing the dirt from my face, I looked up to find Dustin standing over me. There was a massive grin on his face as he studied me.

"The rabbit not to your liking?" He asked and I raised an eyebrow in question. "The mud pies. A delicacy as a kid but you must have been rather desperate to try again now that you've grown."

"I made some progress in what we were discussing earlier and if you don't mind, I'm busy."

"Touchy," he laughed aloud. "I'll leave you to your meal."

"Tch," I sounded, shooing him with my hands and he skittered away.

This time, I laid back on the ground to further practice my skills. It was easier now that I had broken through the barrier of planes. I found shifting back and forwards between physical and spirit forms were now as easy as breathing. I started jumping back and forward between blinks, a euphoria spreading over me at my achievement. It was a wonderful feeling to be so powerful and as I blinked into the spiritual, I suddenly froze, eyes wide in fear.

A green ephemeral glow began to grow in the woods beyond. There was a powerful, though mostly docile, energy pushing towards us. A tingling ran through me like my sensory system, my whole spirit, was reacting to this as a threat. Steeling myself, I drifted forward. I needed to know what was coming so I could warn the others. It might be docile now but that could change if it found prey.

I noted the Phoenix lines of energy all around the woods, integrated into every tree and shrub, rock and patch of dirt. Also, I registered the ever potent and terrible power of the Lich lurking below. This new energy was different. Automated and instinctual as if it moved to the rhythm of the world with no true intelligence.

Along the ground began to spread arms of this green power, stretching forwards like the path of lightning arcing down from the sky. Almost 60 feet wide, I followed these arms back to a single glowing point of brilliant green yet there was no creature. Behind this point a large canyon took shape that wasn't present earlier. It was as if the ground had fallen in along a set path, uprooting trees and crumbling stone.

It made no sense until more of the earth fell away and the large rear end of a tunnelling bug-type creature was shown to be below the earth. It was burrowing fast, but it wasn't an aggressive creature. It was just doing what was natural to it.

Smiling, I floated into the air to view the natural destruction. Passing the canopy of trees, I was amazed as the clear night sky opened out before me. A river of sparkling diamonds stretched from horizon to horizon with a soft crescent moon just peaking above the nearby mountain range. The majestic brilliance more vibrant now that we had travelled far from the nightly fires of the Keep. It was such a wonderful feeling to be so free, the world at my fingertips.

Pivoting around, my eyes took in the destruction of the tunnelling bug. I traced its tunnel back for miles and could see where it moved Terror Hounds followed, feasting on any of the creatures unlucky enough to get caught up in the destruction. Glancing to the East I noted the bug would need to shift its course or tunnel right beneath the vast cliffs.

And then I noticed our camp. The green arms of this creature's energy already encompassed the space where we chose for the night and despair gripped my soul. How could I be so stupid, I thought as I raced to where my body lay, lines of energy all around me. I could see the vibration beginning in the earth below.

Entering my body, I sat bolt upright.

"Flee the area. The ground is about to fall away," I called. There was already a growing worry upon my friends faces at the tremors in the earth but with no more questioning their soldiering instincts kicked in. Without wasting energy on gathering unnecessary objects, they began to scatter left and right as the trees fell away near the edge of the clearing. Near where Caeli sat away from the others.

Too slow to react, the ground began to tremble and crack all around her. I watched as Caeli stumbled along the breaking ground before

Dustin circled back and held her to stabilize the retreat. He held her around the waist, and they slowly made their way from the epicentre.

A large crack echoed through the clearing. I lurched forward as the ground tore apart all around us, carving up the campsite as if it was nothing.

"DUSTIN!" Caeli squealed.

It all happened so quickly that I didn't properly see what occurred, but Caeli had been pushed forward to the ground while Dustin was nowhere in sight. Tears were rolling down Caeli's face as she stared screaming into the churned and mangled ground, a large gully splitting the earth. I could only surmise that Dustin had been engulfed in the destruction with no way to recover.

Tremors continued as Korr pulled Caeli away. It was still unstable in the area, and they needed to get out quickly. I felt terrible and even worse for Caeli with what she must be going through losing her brother but as they were on the other side of the ever-increasing gulley there was now no way to comfort her. The trench met with a smooth cliff face, successfully splitting the group in two.

"Keep heading North and East. We will try to find a way to swing around and get back you," Fitz called.

Korr nodded and pulled Caeli into the woods. They weren't going to get too far ahead of us with Caeli as she was.

I turned to look at the others, my face pale and bottom lip quivering. We probably weren't going to catch up to them the way I was either and blinked rapidly trying to clear the growing tears. Fitz was looking concerned, but Baras had already forged a path ahead. An anger over Baras's lack of sympathy burned in my stomach overriding the sadness. I focused the daggers in my eyes on him and surged past Fitz, leaving him hanging with an offered hug.

Chapter 5

I couldn't guess to the hours of sleep I was able to get last night. I was too tired to even hazard a guess. We spent hours finding our way around the turmoil and broken land the tunnelling bug created, a small cave allowed access past the cliff and back onto level ground connecting to Korr and Caeli.

To top off the lack of sleep, Fitz still had me up an hour before dawn to work on my sword skills. The lessons were beginning to bare fruit at least with dexterity and muscle memory. I was still a little sceptical about application in real life but that was, hopefully, still a time off.

After a cold meal and a puff of the Lemna Raja leaves for my burning lungs, we were back on the road, stumbling in my case. Fitz mentioned a number of signs to keep watch for that Caeli should have set up. Etchings in tree trunks, bent and broken stems, Markings in the dirt. Things that seemed rather irrelevant under normal circumstances but to those looking for it, it was everything. Fitz noticed a marking an hour earlier but since then the trail had gone cold.

After coming across a frozen creek snaking along the Eastern, mountainous border. We began to follow this; Fitz was convinced it would be the best point to find them should Korr and Caeli come across it. Baras though remained sceptical. You would think they could at least try to get along under the circumstances, but they seemed more worried about seeing who had the bigger cock, bickering back and forward over everything and anything all morning.

It was disconcerting that everyone was still acting like we hadn't lost a friend in the night, like we hadn't just walked hours to find the remaining friends who were currently lost to the party. I was having a hard time deep down. My mind was filled with thoughts of Dustin's death and the few days I got to know him. He was a bit of a mischief maker but...

"Damn," I said aloud and the others stopped. Tears welled in my eyes uncontrollably as I buried my face in the cleft of my elbow. My whole body was trembling in an effort to hold back, to bury these powerful feelings but it was all for naught. Great sobs burst from my mouth as tears rolled down my face. I felt an arm around my back, hands I had known for years, and I turned into Baras's chest, crying unashamedly. The bone armour had been uncomfortable, but it was a mute issue against the death of a friend.

"Why?" I said, my body beginning to calm. I couldn't tell you just how long I was lost to the world, but I could swear the shadows around me had changed angle.

"Death comes for all of us, lass," Baras said, a loss for anything real. "There is no reason."

"No!" I shout pushing him back. He doesn't seem angered or confused by this. There is just a soft understanding. "Why are you and Fitz so calm about it? Why are you laughing and acting like it's just another day?"

"It is just another day, Elara," Baras said softly and the words burned into my soul.

"Dustin was our friend! Our Ally! Why are you so cold?"

"Because we are soldiers, Ellie," Fitz spoke up when the heat in the words cut into Baras. There was an underlying flow of anger and regret in his words. "The life of a soldier is the life of death. Too many times I have been having breakfast with those I considered brother in the morning only to be burying them in the afternoon. On more than one occasion due to an error of my own. Baras is the same. There isn't a soldier alive who hasn't experienced the pain you've felt today. Do you think we don't? We feel it right here," Fitz said tapping his chest with all five finger points. A single tear marred his cheek. "We honour our friends by living the life they deserved. We honour them through, smiles, and laughter, and comradery because that's what their sacrifice gives us... Life. Do not think we are so heartless." Turning on his heel, Fitz moved further along the edge of the frozen creek.

Words were lost to me after that. The emotion and physical anguish present in his words put my life into perspective. In fact, it tore it down completely. My easy, sheltered life was won on the life and death struggles of the soldiers I chose to ignore. He was right, though. Dustin would have never wanted his death to bring sadness.

Baras had moved past me to follow Fitz once more and I followed close behind. My embarrassment holding me back from breaking the ice with them just yet. Maybe it was something for when we settled down again tonight.

Half an hour down the road and we came to a halt. A terrible, blood curdling, roar had sounded close by in the trees. There could barely be 50 metres between us and the creature, and my heart was pounding like crazy. Unlike an asthma attack, anxiety had me holding my breath, not wanting my breathing to make even the slightest noise. I stood listening intently for what could be out there. A sharp cracking echoed around us as a tree was uprooted.

"Weapons," Baras called and both Fitz and I unsheathed our weapons. Fitz went with a bow. Probably the better choice for how large the creature sounded. Whatever it was, it was close and heading towards us.

A few tense moments passed, the sword trembling in my hand. And suddenly, there was movement. My heart stopped at the terrible sight. Caeli and Korr burst from the tree line at a full sprint followed by another Soul I didn't recognize and... My heart pounded rapidly. Enzo! He was bringing up the rear in a fighting retreat against something I couldn't quite see yet.

"Caelie, Korr, this way," I called only to see the added despair on our friends faces.

"Caves. Now," Korr yelled pointing to the small openings in the cliff face just passed the river. Neither stopped running.

I turned to see Enzo craft a wall of flames as tall as the trees before following the others. It did little to hinder the creature other than mask a few seconds of the retreat. From the flames came a reptilian being with a shimmering, scaly skin. Razor sharp teeth lined its mouth in the hundreds, and wickedly curved claws sent a shiver down my spine as flames licked and played upon its scales.

Warmth fled my cheeks as the blood drained from my face and for a moment, I couldn't move. The beast was massive. Standing on its hind legs, it almost cleared the canopy. It's tail still lost back in the brush and its arms dangled close to the ground.

The creature looked around and as its slitted, yellow eyes turned to focus on me a large fireball hit the side of its head, the shockwave turning it away to face the other Soul I didn't recognize.

"Run, you pot-bellied sow," Baras yelled at me before pushing me out in front of him. My legs began to work again and I started running harder than I had ever done before. There was nothing in front of me but my friends and the cave mouth that felt as though it was miles away.

A scream sounded from the other Soul.

"Don't look back." I heard Baras shout and I fought myself to not view what must be a horrific scene. The rather audible crunching and snapping of bones painted a terrifying image in my mind. As we slipped along on the sheet of ice, my mind got the better of me and I glanced around. The creature was bearing down on Baras and I, blood smeared across its face. Of course, one human couldn't satisfy such a beast. I saw as it got its speed up it was using its knuckles to keep upright in a horrific loping motion.

A sudden crack and the creature fell through the ice at a mere 10 metres away. The creek was deep enough that it sunk to its knees, all momentum crashing to a halt as it navigated the icy waters. It let out a tormented roar as we made the shoreline and were racing away to the cave and sanctuary in the small opening.

I let out a soft squeak as I was swept off my feet. Baras had become too impatient with my running abilities and decided to carry me. This proved to be a gut-wrenching choice for me as it gave me opportunity to look back. The creature was ashore and picking up speed once more. Its mouth was wide open now and with nothing more to do I trembled in fear.

"Baras..." I tugged at his clothes.

"I know," He replied.

"Baras!" My voice raised as the creature got closer.

"I know!" He growled.

I watched the creature take a running dive at us, arms outstretched, mouth wide, and saliva drooling from the rows of fangs.

I screamed as it descended on us. The only thing louder was a large booming, crack of what seemed to be thunder, when the creature crashed face first into the cliffside inches from us. Baras continued to move as the rock walls rumbled and the entrance caved in.

Breath seemed to come back to me, surprised that I had been holding it so long and I took in trembling mouthfuls of air, trying to calm my nerves with adrenaline rich in my veins.

"Thank you, Baras," I managed to say and he placed me down, keeping an arm on me until I was steady.

"Against that little thing. Don't mention it," he said with a grin lit up by the newly crafted flame of Enzo's. It was such a light hearted comment that everything seemed to rush in on me and all I could do was laugh. Laughter for the death of my friend. Laughter for the fear and anxiety in the flight across the creek. Laughter for being stuck in this cave without knowledge of an exit. Laughter for life.

A slap echoed through the tunnels and my cheek caught aflame. The stinging pain sent a shockwave through my body. Caeli stood before me, eyes bleary and red rimmed as if she had been crying for hours. Her right hand was by her left hip after following the arc of the slap and she was breathing heavy.

"You're laughing? Dustin died. We all almost die and you're laughing about it."

My heart sank. Here I was only an hour before, reprimanding Baras and Fitz over the exact same thing and now I had gone and done just that to Caeli of all people. Sure, she was a soldier too but this was her brother and greatest love. Of course she was going to feel this one.

"I meant no disrespect. Dustin was a friend of mine too."

"Then why did you let him die?"

"Wha... I didn't," I said, confusion setting in.

"Liar!" Caeli screamed. "I know you can see things. I know you saw the attack and his death. Don't patronize me with your fake bullshit."

"I can't, Caeli. It doesn't work like..."

A fist cracked into the side of my face sending me to the dirt. I looked up at Caeli standing over me as I held my cheek.

"If you two are quite done," Enzo called. "We need to keep moving." With that he turned and began to head down the passageway, the light close behind.

"Oh, we're done," Caeli said, the words deadly calm. The shadows playing across her face gave an almost demonic look as she turned to follow Enzo.

Baras helped me to my feet and we began after the others. Fitz gave a compassionate smile and I could see he was about to say something when I held up a hand.

"I know. She's heartbroken and I'm the easiest target. I can take the pain if it means she will continue forward."

"I was only going to say the cheek will swell but let's pretend that was going to be my advice," Fitz replied. Already he was trying to lighten the mood. I shook my head and kept moving.

"Where exit?" Korr asked and Enzo turned to the big man with a shrug.

"Dunno but do you feel the sticky, almost clingy, sensation on the walls and floor?"

Korr nodded.

"Its web. This is a spider den and if there is one thing that spiders are good for its exits." He turned back to us, knowing we all heard. "Don't stray from the light. The spiders are fearful of fire. There won't be any issues behind us for the moment. As we begin to pass small passageways and offshoots, watch every quarter."

"What could a little spider do, anyway?" Baras asked.

"They made this tunnel," Enzo replied before turning back to facing forwards.

"Spiders made this?" My eyes bulged as I looked around. It was evident that many of us were thinking the same thing. How fucking big were they?

Everyone was quiet, eyes darting left and right around them as we made our way through the tunnels. With every footstep, I winced from the noise echoing back and forward along the walls. It was a small thing as I knew the spiders would already be aware of our presence, messages running along each disturbed web. I could only hope the fire would keep us protected long enough to see daylight again.

Enzo paused up ahead peering out into an opening. His eyebrows furrowed and he turned back to us.

"There are three ahead. One above to the right and two either side. They are all in separate tunnels waiting for us. I cannot say how many may be beyond but I'd prepare for a long battle," Enzo warned us.

"Why not ask our *Mage* to tell you what's waiting for us," Caeli said, her voice dripping with malice. "Better yet, why not have her describe just how you are going to die, life slowly drained away while paralysed in some web."

Enzo's eyes fell on me. "Is it true? Do you have the sight?"

My knees became weak under his gaze. Those arms, those lips, that... I shook my head. There would be no chance in this den of spiders. "It's only new to me," I replied after a moment, my mind needing to reply his words two more times.

Enzo pursed his lips and his eyes narrowed as if I had said something wrong. He considered me a moment longer before replying. "Sure," he said slowly. "It would definitely explain a lot. Let me know how many spiders there are in close vicinity."

There he goes again treating me like some long-lost puppy he'd found again after years apart. There could be nothing to explain. Ignoring his comments, I sat against the wall and let my soul free. One day soon I hoped to master the ability of shifting forms while awake.

I couldn't help myself floating close to Enzo. Now that I could see the aura of living beings around me, I desired to know what colours surrounded Enzo. A soft, passionate red, or cute, electric blue, maybe. Opening my eyes to take in his hue, I wrinkled my nose. It was an uninspiring orange much like the clay vases forged at a potter's kiln. A sparkle caught my eye as I turned to look away, bringing my attention back to him once more. Drifting closer, I saw deep in the dull colour below the surface as if smothered, was a galaxy of diamonds sparkling in an array of colours. A fiery strand connected deep into the inner essence of Enzo, and I recognised it as the bond to his Phoenix. Where it connected the orange had formed an opening in his aura almost as if it didn't want to touch the Phoenix bond lest it taint it. The beauty of it all was alluring and I found my fingers reaching out to caress the colours.

As they dipped through the orange, moving to the energies of this sultry, desirable man, a jolt of electricity made me recoil. It was painful and terrifying even in this form. Enzo suddenly turned sharply to look me in the eyes. No, he was definitely looking through me, but I knew he could feel me. With a quick flick of his head, I got the message loud and clear. I was on mission.

Gliding into the large chamber, I spied the threat Enzo spoke of. Their large, hairy, multi legged forms glowing a soft purple. A cold shiver ran through my being as I spied the massive fangs tucked in close to their bodies, salivating with poison. The next few moments were going to be torture. Scouting through and behind the arachnids, there was no evidence of any others waiting to reinforce their friends.

"All clear," I said, giving a thumbs up as I merged back into my body. "There's only the three you mentioned."

Nodding, Enzo turned back to the chamber. "This will make things easier. I'll burn the one above. I need you to break into two groups to take out the others. Don't allow them to draw you into the parameter of their legs or they will take you out instantly. Pair off and circle either way. As it follows one of you the other should take out a leg or two. I shouldn't need to tell you what to do from there. Ready?"

"Yes sir," those of us who were soldiers spoke in unison.

"Uh, Ye, Yes," I stuttered after the others.

"Move," Enzo said and they burst into the room like a raging tsunami. Each fighter flowing off in every direction. I was mesmerized by the chaotic efficiency in every move they made.

Enzo made the first move, arms raised over head. A large ball of fire manifested in a roaring swirling mass to speed off straight up at the now moving spider. The ball engulfed the creature, its body disappearing into the dense mass of flame.

The other two spiders were already out and battling. Their front legs up and lashing out trying to knock down and bundle up any one unlucky enough to get caught. The first went down easily to Caeli and Fitz. Fitz took the attention while Caeli danced in and out taking down three legs before the first even buckled. Fitz plunged his sword into the falling spider's head and it stilled instantly.

The final spider seemed more capable. The two times Baras attacked it picked its leg up, the sword passing harmlessly below. Korr feinted in and tacked away at the last moment drawing the Spiders attention in chase. Giving Baras a chance, he charged only for the spider to instantly shift back at him. The trick enough to bring Baras directly below it.

The fangs unfurled before it with venom dripping to the floor. Lowering its body, Baras became pinned while it positioned itself to bite him. Korr didn't wait for this to happen and charged in, a small ball of fire burning in his palm. With the fangs snapping down Korr twisted and pushed the fire into the spider's small head. There was a moment of nothing before its body began to spasm in pain and it curled up into a ball of death. Dragging himself from below the carcass Baras turned to thank Korr but froze.

Staggering a few, uneasy steps, Korr fell to his knees. A hand barely kept him stable before his eyes rolled into the back of his head, his body slumping to the floor.

"No!" Baras yelled and rushed to Korr. There was a gash down the side of his chest where a fang must have grazed. Venom was all over Korr's chest, easily entering the wound. "It's poison."

Enzo approached inspecting the body of the spider. "It's a Demon Back," he said dismissing any urgency. No one showed any recollection of the name and Enzo grunted. "The venom will knock him out for 8 hours. He will come back to consciousness with a massive adrenaline rush that'll heighten all his movements and abilities for a time. After that everything will balance out and he'll be groggy. We'll make camp at the entrance to the pathway we came from. We know it's secure from the rear."

"What? Not killing him for his weakness," I said. It wasn't a serious recommendation. More, just feeling slighted for being targeted when I stood wrong.

"Oh, I'm sure you'd love that," Caeli said. "Why not just kill him yourself. Easy when they're unconscious. You may enjoy it more."

Another slap and I was surprised to find my hand stinging, my body moving on its own. Her hand was holding her cheek more from the unexpected assault than any real pain. Her eyes levelled on me and I knew in that moment I was about to die. That was until Fitz stepped in at the last moment pulling Caeli away, giving her some stern words.

"You really need to provoke the girl?" Enzo asked walking up beside me but kept talking before I could reply. "We could have used your skills back there. Next time don't leave us hanging."

I looked around. Baras was dragging Korr back to the security of our camp and Fitz was still talking directly to Caeli who was now looking away.

"Felt I'd get in the way," I finally said not wanting to admit I was too stunned by everyone's efficiency to move. I didn't even have the sense to react when Korr fell, too mesmerized by the battle.

"You can make up for it with the small task I have for you. Come to me when you're ready to settle for the night," Enzo said, before moving to the head of the pathway setting a large, fiery door across the entrance and sitting before it as if in meditation.

My face burned bright red just thinking about how I could attend this man but there was one more thing I needed to do. Not an easy thing but

I needed to say my part. I walked over to where Caeli had sat apart from everyone in a small alcove. It was protected from sudden attacks with no other way than through the group to get to her.

"I'm sorry for slapping you, Caeli. I can't see glimpses of the future. Only what is in this moment. Yes. I saw the creature tunnelling nearby but believed it not to be a threat. It was only in the last moments that I found out my mistake. I lost us 20... 30 seconds to prepare and flee. It was my inexperience. It was my fault and his death is on my hands. It was never my intention."

"Rot in hell," Caeli said and turned away.

Letting out a soft sigh, I left it at that. There was no point pushing any further. I'd already become the relief for Caeli's anguish. If it helped, it was all that mattered.

Walking back to where Enzo waited, I sat behind him, back against his. It sent tingles across my skin when he leaned back into me as if it was completely natural. I realized just how wrong it was to flaunt this closeness in front of Caeli but I couldn't hold back. This man set my heart a flutter and my world alight.

"How may I service you this evening?" I grinned as I felt him tense with the use of my words, the flames flickering a moment.

"I need you to travel the tunnels. We need a clear way out of here with as little risk as possible," Enzo said, his voice deep and resonant.

That made more sense than risking our flame barrier for a little fun. Still rather disheartening.

"I'll scout around," I said. "Just keep me stable."

Enzo scoffed.

Entering the spirit world, I travelled the twists and turns of all the paths that a person could easily traverse. Always did I try to steer clear from a vibrant purple light coming from a Northern route. Always did I find a dead end or large barriers of thick web holding the soft purple light of spiders bigger than the ones we just fought. In the end I found there was no other route to take than towards what I could only imaging was a great threat.

Drifting into the room, I saw it had two other exits leading away. All around the walls were spiders as tall as my knees. The numbers themselves were intimidating though it was easy to conclude these were still babies when compared to their larger counter parts. They were feasting on two large wrapped creatures I concluded without a doubt were tunnelling bugs. Another fresh carcass hanging from the ceiling. Its insides slowly melting into the sludge these spiders eat.

A small movement caught my eye behind it and I shifted focus. The roof was a vast funnel of webs with small black... I looked closely at them thinking they were stones somehow caught up in the web.

I backed away wide eyed seeing one move again. They were the tips of a spider's legs and as I cautiously drifted below, I found It to be almost as large as the reptilian beast outside. Its body so big it couldn't fit through the opening above anymore. It now relied on these tunnelling bugs to cross its path.

A deep fear set my soul trembling as it was inevitable we would need to pass this way.

I picked a path. One easily determined by a large white, triangular gash in the stone. I found little resistance along this path and if we kept straight with only one left turn at a T-section, we'd be out into the light of day... Or stars as it was now. I could see the makings of the suns first rays licking at the Eastern horizon and was surprised by the passing of time in these tunnels. It would be a quick rest for us tonight before pushing forward.

Phasing back into my body, I relayed everything to Enzo as he sat and listened, a stern expression on his brow.

"It's never easy in this valley," he muttered before making himself comfortable leaning into me. "Get some sleep. It'll be a harsh trek through the caves."

With this warm, strong man at my back, I had my doubts there'd be any sleep but I closed my eyes anyway and relaxed into him.

"Come on, princess, time to wake up."

My left eye spasmed open as I chewed subconsciously with my mouth. It took a moment to realise I was slumped over as a stream of drool rolled off my knee. Wiping my mouth and chin, I looked up to find Fitz standing before me, two swords in hand.

"Now? In here?" I whined.

"Everywhere, Ellie. I can't let a day go by without training," he said offering one of the short swords.

I groaned and reached for the blade before staggering to my feet. My head began to split apart and I held it forcing the pain back inside. I needed more sleep and water.

"Ready?"

"No," I said and Fitz laughed.

Without waiting for more, Fitz dashed in with a quick lunging thrust. My body acted more on instinct because clearly my mind wasn't awake in this moment. Parrying the blade with a cross-body block, I rolled my wrist and brought the blade around to rest against his throat. I yawned.

When I looked again, Fitz was wide eyed, his head leaning away from the sword edge. He was surprised by the move so much he forgot to react. Slowly moving the sword from his throat, I lowered it.

A deep and throaty laugh pierced the passageway and we both looked to Enzo. He'd been watching our bout with undisguised interest.

"It'll be a cold day in hell before you beat her," Enzo said to Fitz before leaning in close, lowering his voice. "Don't worry it took me two years before I could best her but I do see the intrigue in learning under her."

Fitz looked at me, eyebrow raised. I just shrugged.

"Mind if I step in?" Enzo asked before taking the sword from Fitz who then stepped back, curious to what was about to happen.

This wasn't going to be good. For a man who kills over weakness and me now squaring up to show how uncoordinated I was, I couldn't say I was long for this world. The only thing in my favour was this insane link Enzo insisted we had.

My eyes drank in the view. Enzo removed his leather chest plate and was going through a series of stretches and manoeuvres getting ready as if he was going to be fighting a life and death battle. His life. My death. He flexed his chest one last time and I knew at least, I'd be happy at the end.

The only indication the fight was beginning was a flicker in the fire barrier as Enzo's focus shifted to me. The speed and agility he showed in moving towards me was incredible and as he darted in, dodged from side to side. I could barely follow him with my eyes and feeling insecure, brought my sword up, instinctively moving as Fitz had taught me. It was just in time too. Enzo's sword glanced off my own and he jumped back.

"You've always had a good eye," he said, a daring grin crossing his face. "Let's see if you..."

Without finishing he was moving again and my eyes shot open seeking a glimpse of his blur. There was nothing until I felt my arm pulled up hard behind my back, a sword at my throat. Normally uncomfortable, all I felt was his *figure* pressed into my butt cheeks. I melted into him tilting my head back.

"Are you taking this serious?" Enzo asked, an eyebrow raised.

"Which one are you going to stab me with?" I asked, trying to lace a seductive tone through my voice.

"Tch." Enzo pushed me away and circled once more. "Take this seriously and I'll take you later."

I purred then shook my head giving up the façade. "I am taking it seriously," I said softly, lowering my guard.

He just raised an eyebrow in question.

96

"I haven't touched a sword before the last few days. Fitz has been training me. Anything you have witnessed this morning has been luck and happenstance. For all intents and purposes, I have been a maid all my life."

Enzo's expression grew serious. Darting in he cut a sweeping left, arcing over to stop upon my neck, the blade opening a slight cut. I reacted too slow, bringing my arm up and effectively disarming myself upon his arm when my sword was twisted out of my hand.

He grunted, his nose wrinkling as he kept those deadly eyes on mine. "Where has all your skill gone?"

A dark hand gently pushed the blade from my throat and I looked up to find Korr awake and moving. Smiling, I nodded my thanks before turning back to Enzo.

"You sensed it on the cliff top. I'm no warrior. I am a mage and a lousy one at that. You even went against Talon's wishes of keeping me alive."

I noticed that piqued his interest as his eyes narrowed. "Only a paired Phoenix Soul can hear a Phoenix's words with the exception of you. I don't know what game you're playing, Elara. If you threaten the Phoenix, I will kill you without hesitation."

Storming off, Enzo swiped his hand over the protective flames. They swirled around him as he stepped through before dissipating completely. "Anyone who wants to be left in the dark stay behind."

"I don't think he's a morning person," I said to Korr before attempting to hug him. Baras beat me too it, though. Racing in, he embraced the man slapping him on the back a few times.

"Thank you, brother. Anything you need within my power I will grant you," Baras said.

"Korr help. Korr happy," Korr said.

"If ever something comes up, you ask. Baras be happy too."

Korr considered Baras a moment, likely deciding if he was being mocked. That's when Fitz stepped in.

"Come on. The light is fading," he said.

Caeli had already followed after Enzo when the man stalked off. Korr left without another word and I just shook my head at Baras when he glanced my way.

"What?" he asked and turned to follow the others when I didn't answer.

Fitz filed in beside me as I brought up the rear.

"The Phoenix spoke?" He asked

"You didn't hear it? Damn thing was loud," I replied.

"It was screeching like most birds do."

"Ha?" I said, as if this was news to me.

"What did it say?"

"It told Enzo that my death belonged to someone else and he had no right to kill me. It was at that moment Enzo recognized me. It doesn't make sense."

"Little of this does. Enzo spoke of knowing you for years. It didn't sound like it was a small thing either but you never spent any such time with him?"

I was about 5 when I was brought to the Keep. Baras has been the only person I really interacted with all that time. Well, that wasn't demanding of my services, of course. He'll vouch for that."

"The man is psychotic. He's making up his own backstories for us. Maybe these birds have a deeper influence over their bonded Souls then we've been led to believe."

"Might be why Enzo survived. He was influenced to leave the battle where the others were destroyed. Someone needed to make sure the new Souls reached the nest and bonded."

"Stay on your guard, Ellie. I think we are only scratching the surface of something much deeper. I fear your part in it has still yet to come to light."

This didn't sit well with me, being manipulated for reasons unknown. Putting it out of my mind, I focused on the tunnels ahead. I needed to survive the spiders before I worried about the Firebirds. My breathing became deeper as I tried to calm my nerves. I couldn't have anything distracting me for this next fight.

"You okay?" Fitz asked noticing the difference in my demeanour.

"I searched the tunnels last night and informed Enzo on the way out. He will be leading us there."

"That's good news, isn't it?"

"There is a section of cave that will lead us through the centre of the spider's den. It can't be avoided. Mostly, there are spiders as tall as my knee and the sheer numbers of those are going to be hard enough but sitting above the room is a massive spider. The reptilian creature chasing us earlier would have had a hard time battling this thing."

Fitz went quiet a moment considering the information. "Let's hope we can get through the room before it can react."

"Maybe," I said but doubted even the small chance we had to get through without a fight.

Remaining quiet as we wound our way through the maze of tunnels, I was surprised Enzo hadn't needed anymore guidance than the small amount of information I provided him the night before. Soon, we were standing outside the entry to the main chamber with Enzo and the others assessing the area.

I got a glimpse through the doorway as I came up behind them and my heart sank. The amount of activity from the smaller ones indicated they knew we were coming. Even the giant spider had his legs further out of the funnel as if he was ready to pounce at a moment's notice. I was already starting to gauge Enzo's strength with the flame and knew instinctually this room would be too much for him alone.

"I really don't like spiders," Baras said peeking out through the opening.

"Korr protect," Korr said and Baras's shoulders slumped.

"No, Korr, not this time. Have my back but I'll also have yours. I'll not have a friend die for me again."

This statement surprised me. It took no time at all for him to integrate into this group but it was unlike him to use terms like friends. It was always comrade. I guess Korr putting himself out for Baras touched him deeper than I originally saw.

"Which door, Elara," Enzo said looking back at me. I walked forward to stand by him tentatively. Even with this small chasm between us I could feel the warmth of his body. The smell was intoxicating and I forgot just what was asked.

"Is your memory so bad you forget which door?"

I glanced inside and pointed to the door with the triangular mark. "Fairly straight run if we can get through."

Scanning the room, I noticed Enzo scrunch his nose a moment. "They aren't going to make it easy. These ones are smart. They understand it's our best chance out and are guarding that door more than the other. I'm guessing the big one is directing them."

"So, what's the plan?" Caeli pushed in between us.

I could see what she was doing and it wasn't going to work. Just because she was angry with me about what happened to Dustin didn't give her the right to try and get between me and Enzo. I glanced at Enzo who looked annoyed and I smiled. Whatever hold those damned birds had on this man wasn't going to let little miss short and boobs get between us. My eyes grew wide when I saw that line of thought come to fruition.

Enzo reached up and with his full palm grabbed Caeli's face and pushed her back out of the way. This caused Caeli to stumble backwards and the darkness that grew in her eyes was terrifying. I stepped in front of Enzo.

"That was too far. Caeli is just as eager to get out of this hole as everyone else is," I said. Caeli probably deserved it but didn't deserve it from him. I turned and offered my hand to her but she batted it away as she got up. There was a softness in her eyes that wasn't there before.

"I'm strategizing for the battle. I don't need her getting up in my face, blocking my source of information," Enzo replied coldly. He turned to face the others. "I'll let you choose your opponent. I can either send a tornado of flames around the room destroying the spiderlings and in turn blocking our exits for a time. This will mean your battle is with the big guy up there." He pointed to the funnel of webs on the ceiling. "Otherwise, I use my fire to keep the big guy busy while you take out the smaller ones."

"And the positive is we can make a fighting retreat all the way to the exit," Fitz added. "My vote is our fastest way out."

Everyone else agreed and we stood ready to move at Enzo's word. It was almost exhilarating but for the certain death I was about to experience. I pulled my sword from its sheath and waited with the others. My heart was pounding out of my chest and I tried to keep my breathing steady but they were coming through shaky at best.

"Move," Enzo said and stepped out into the middle of the room and raised his arms. A firestorm began to form above our heads as we ran out.

I saw the larger spider come part way out before backtracking a few feet as the flames became too intense all around it. For anyone that said a little fear goes a long way had never felt a fear so all-consuming that it motivated a person to do anything needed to never come face to face with that eight-legged monster.

The next few minutes became a blur. It was as if a barbaric rage took over and I was cutting and slashing my way through the waves of spiderlings trying to overwhelm us. Blue blood splattered over the walls and my clothing as I let my sword dance through their ranks. 10 little beady eyes popped up in front of me and before I even had a moment to think it was halved to two sets of five and I was moving towards the next one.

A scream echoed around the room and I turned to see Caeli was on her arse once more swinging her sword at a steadily increasing rank of enemies. Enzo was beside her but was too busy holding the flames in place. If Caeli was to fall then Enzo was going to be next releasing the real enemy.

"Korr," I called but he was too caught up with his own horde to help. Small flames popping from his hands as he fought.

I looked around desperate and found Fitz and Baras to be just as tied down as Korr. It was as if the spiderlings were trying to overwhelm us while one was down.

"No. No. No," the whimpering voice of Caeli caught my ear. She was beginning to struggle, still not getting a moment to reach her feet.

"Argh fuck," I swore before shifting my path towards her. There was no way I was going to get to her in time as a larger mass of spiderlings moved to block my path. I wasn't going to make it.

A thrilling battle cry echoed around the walls and a figure came running from the third exit to the room. That someone else was down here was incredible. They must have been doing it rough, sneaking around a spider's den with webs...

"Oh my god. Dustin!" I cried. May not have been the best thing to call out as the distraction almost cost Caeli everything but as she saw that it was indeed her brother running in, she got a second wind. Her sword play became like the wind flowing and carving. As the spiders didn't account for another fighter, Dustin was by her side in moments. Helping her to her feet, they fought back the horde of spiders around them saving Enzo in turn.

This miracle was going to have to wait. It seemed the giant spider had finally begun to push the limits of Enzo's flames. Poking the barrier with one then the other of its front most legs, I saw emptiness swirling in the flames before filling back in. Both legs popped through the flames and didn't rescind, the flames not seeming to worry it so much anymore. I looked to Enzo and could see he was in pain. Sweat was rolling down his face as his brow furrowed in concentration. He was about to break.

"We need to get out of here... Now!" I almost screamed. I could see the large dark eyes shimmering in the swirling flames. Fitz had made it to the doorway and was doing what he could to keep it clear. Korr made it to his side while Baras reinforced Dustin and Caeli as they remained to guard Enzo. And now I was torn. Fear compelled me to run, to leave this cave behind me and leave this valley of death. It was my friends and yes, Enzo, who made me hesitate. They were enough to get me through the fear controlling me.

The flames died back until there was only enough light to navigate the room left and Enzo stumbled a moment. My eyes shot up and all I saw was fangs and legs descending to the stone floor from a string of web. A shrill squeal escaped my lips and as the dripping fangs came down upon me, power flowed through my limbs. I grabbed the fangs even as they flexed above me.

The spider's movements slowed to nothing as I felt it once more. The line of blue energy like in my spirit walk must be somewhere below my feet. The power of the Lich, feeding me, pushing me to do things I never dreamed of and as I stared into the spider's hollow eyes, I watched his limbs freeze over into solid ice. The cold, dark power destroying this centuries old being as if it was insignificant under the boot of this power's owner. The spider ceased to move, its solid and lifeless form, now only a statue of worship and wonder. Sensing they're leader's demise the spiderlings backed away down holes and other routes leaving us to flee.

A strong hand grabbed my arm and dragged me from the spider.

"Are you trying to kill him?!" Enzo yelled at me, fury in his voice. I couldn't understand what I did wrong.

"He needed to die." I replied, my brow furrowed as I tried to make sense of his words. The spider couldn't be that important to him. There was no reason.

"Get out now before I ram my sword so far up your gut you'll be spewing blood," the words were delivered so quietly so calmly that it was impossible not to hear them. The tremors I felt through his arm told me he was trying desperately to restrain himself and it was time to go.

I took lead having been the only one to have navigated these tunnels and within a matter of about 3 hours we were free. The fresh air was blissful and sweet having never fully realized just how rank the cave system was. It was great to be free and alive once more.

"Speaking of alive," I turned to Dustin finally having a moment to speak. Everyone followed suit, all staring at the man, the unasked question heavy in the air. How are you alive?

With a large grin crossing his face, Dustin made some fancy moves as if he was about to do a big reveal. Before he got the chance, Caeli ran in and pounced on him, wrapping Dustin in her arms to never let go...

Caeli backed away gagging and spluttering. She was half bent over dry reaching into the air, her face turned away from Dustin who was now looking embarrassed. Approaching cautiously, I sniffed the air around him and immediately held my nose. Everyone burst out laughing.

"What is that, Dustin?" I asked. "You smell like something Baras leaves in his chamber pot each morning."

"Hey," Baras called in protest and the laughter just doubled.

Helping Caeli to her feet, we fled the general proximity, and I tried brushing some of the dirty marks from Caeli's attire.

As Dustin made to approach, I stuck a finger up. "You're fine right where you are, thank you very much."

Caeli also held up a hand. "Not another step until you've rinsed off in the stream." She pointed to the icy river.

"But I..." Dustin complained.

"Now!" Caeli and I said in unison.

Defeated, Dustin's shoulders slumped, and he moved to the nearby riverbank to begin removing his clothes. I smiled as I watched Caeli's eyes. They never once left Dustin as a red hue began to colour her cheeks. It was as if the whole world faded away for her as she watched her man. It warmed my heart to see her genuinely smile once more.

"It's fucking cold," Dustin squealed. His voice climbing far higher than normal.

"Hey Dustin, gunna be a while before you find those nuts again. They're climbing right up inside," Fitz called, and Caeli gave a soft giggle.

Leaning down close to Caeli's ear I whispered. "You're drooling."

Caeli's eyes grew wide and she began pawing at the edges of her mouth as she tried to wipe away the metaphorical saliva. Turning back to me, she gave me a quick shove. "Don't tease. I can't help myself sometimes."

"Especially after just getting him back," I said and she shook her head.

"Any time he gets that cock out..."

I scoffed then started to giggle. I wasn't expecting something so personal from Caeli just yet and when I settled, I could see she'd turned serious.

"I'm sorry," Caeli said. The words came out almost as a whisper and I shook my head, hands up, suggesting she didn't need to. Grabbing my hands, Caeli pushed her point. "I am sorry, Ellie. I've treated you so bad even after you warned us of the coming danger. Without you we all would have stood around assessing long enough to be engulfed by the earth."

I brought my hands to the outside of hers and held Caeli. "You were grieving. We all grieve differently. I understood your anger and devastation and made sure to provoke your feelings. Draw them my way because I understood and I could take it. I made sure you targeted me, Caeli."

"Why?" She asked, tears welling in her eyes.

"Because there was so much emotion within you spiralling out of control. You needed release. It wouldn't have been good for you to bottle it up."

Pulling me into an embrace, Caeli's tears dampened the front of my attire. "Thank you, Ellie. I truly don't deserve a friend such as you."

Giving into the hug, I remained like that a moment before opening my eyes, my head tilted down. The sight I was privy to at this angle caught the breath in my throat.

"I see what you mean... And this is the cold version," I told Caeli my cheeks turning crimson.

Caeli looked around and found Dustin's Cock swinging freely between us. "Oi, put that away and get dressed. You're shivering."

His clothes in one arm and his other rubbing up and down his sides trying to stimulate blood flow, Dustin was dancing from foot to foot as he shivered.

"I... Need... Fire," Dustin said through chattering teeth. "Clothes will become... damp if I... put on."

I fireball tore through the empty air of the clearing to explode in the hollow of a fallen tree trunk. Flames licked along the dry wood catching easily and growing in intensity as it ravaged the tree. I looked up to see Enzo, arm extended with a dirty look on his face. He looked me dead in the eye, shook his head and walked out of the clearing and into the dark forest.

"What's his problem?" Caeli asked, her attention once more on Dustin by the growing flames.

"I think he's jealous," I replied. I couldn't be sure. It was just a feeling I got from the way he looked at me. "I don't think I'll be getting another chance to be alone." There was a tone of sadness and hunger in my voice and I was surprised to find, I meant it.

"Sorry, girl, Dustin can be intimidating to other males," Caeli said with a smirk. She seemed rather proud.

"Enzo wouldn't have been intimidated," I flared my eyebrows. "I'm sure it was just straight up jealousy."

"Rather possessive, don't you think?"

"I don't mind being possessed." I smiled, watching the empty space where Enzo stood.

Laughter rang out from the boys. "No way. Hey, Caeli. Ellie. You gotta hear this," Fitz called, the guys had congregated around the fire listening to Dustin. "Dustin followed the tunnelling bug all the way from our camp to the spider den. His close proximity behind the bug meant it continuously shat on him."

"That explains a lot," Caeli said, eyes coming alive. "Let's go listen."

A sudden and odd sadness came upon me as I watched Caeli and Dustin. Catching Caeli by the arm, I drew her back into a deep kiss. I couldn't explain what it was in my mind that decided this was the best course of action or that I was definitely going to act as such. I just couldn't stand by anymore.

Caeli's eyes went wide, the kiss surprising her, before she gave in to the moment and threw her arms around my neck. When the kiss died away and our lips parted, the warmth of our breath came out as wispy steam.

"What...?" Caeli asked, her voice husky.

"I've never kissed a girl before. I've heard maids talking of the intimacy between girls as opposed to the brutish nature of men. When we meet the Phoenix tomorrow, will I regret the things I haven't done as they leave me behind to die alone. You need to tell him tonight."

"Tell. Him?" Caeli repeated slowly, her eyes still lost in our kiss when her brain clicked over. A look of fear crossed her brow. "I can't, Ellie. It's not done."

"Says who. Don't waste another moment living for others. Listen to your own heart. We can never be sure what tomorrow will bring. Live the moment. Choose love." I could see she wasn't convinced. "Just think about it. If you were to lose him again, could you live with your choice?"

Offering a soft smile, I moved closer to the fire.

Footsteps in the night brought me awake with a start. I opened my eyes to see Dustin and Caeli sneaking off into the privacy of the trees, hand in hand. Rolling over, I closed my eyes once more, a large grin crossing my face.

Chapter 6

I felt trapped in my mind. Phoenix had enclosed me into a circle and with claw and beak, tore long strips of skin and flesh from my body. Talon stalked around the edges watching the others before he stood before me, his eyes aflame, radiating hatred. With a final screeching protest from Talon for the life I held, I felt the Phoenix tear me apart and awoke in a panic. Breathing was hard and I could feel my lungs burning in pain as they struggled to draw oxygen past my contracting windpipes. I scrabbled for my pipe and supply of medicinal herbs.

With the woody smoke filling my lungs once more, I looked around. My body was still trembling from the Phoenix attack, and I took a moment to steady myself. A thick frost was upon the ground and over my cloak attributing to the asthma attack. Baras was already building a small fire and Korr was standing by ready to light it.

"How's the Asthma?" Fitz asked squatting beside me, a look of concern on his face.

"For a morning such as this I would be surprised to get through without an attack. Otherwise, the techniques you taught me have done wonders to keep the worst of it at bay. I thank you again, Fitz, for this gift."

Resting a hand on my shoulder, he nodded before his brows furrowed. "Are you cold? Your body's trembling," Fitz said.

"This morning, I had a dream. It didn't quite feel like a spirit walk, but it felt so real I can't deny the possibility."

"Tell me about it."

"The Phoenix were angry with me. They tore my body apart, feeding on my flesh, making sure it was slow and painful. I'm scared for today. I know I won't be chosen. The Firebirds have sentenced me to death, and I don't know why."

"Then we will ask them together," Fitz said.

Reaching up, I rested my hand on his. With a gentle smile, I shook my head. "I don't want you involved this time."

"But..."

"Not this time," I said reinforcing my decision. "I know there is a growing conspiracy with the Phoenix but anyone that isn't chosen will die, their soul feeding the land around us. I don't want you to do anything that will risk your chances. Siding with me is the same as asking for my punishment. We don't know for sure what they want with me. If, somehow, I do live and you die for me, I will be heartbroken. As

106

least this way we already have an idea of my fate and I don't doubt they will be fighting to choose you."

"I'm starting to question the worth of being chosen," Fitz said, forcing a weak smile.

"The worth is in saving hundreds of innocents over countless battles. You will be saving these people for yourself and for me. Please, Fitz, promise me you'll stay out of this conspiracy surrounding me."

His mouth twitched and he seemed conflicted in agreeing to my demands.

"Promise me."

"Ok, ok," he said dropping his head in defeat. "I promise, Ellie. Are we still training?"

"Every day." A soft underlying tone was all that announced the sadness in my heart, hidden deep below the surface.

"Good because I have something to talk to you about," Fitz said motioning to the sword at my side. I unsheathed it with practiced efficiency before taking up a stance before him.

"What would you like to talk about?" I asked intrigued.

"In training you show promise..."

"Well, it's not that hard swirling a piece of metal around," I said, and smiled as he baulked at the comment but didn't take the bait.

"Your still green and awkward with the sword but on occasion, when you're not all there," Fitz pointed to my head indicating my mind. "Or when your instincts kick in like when your fear was growing in the spider cave, you show a deeper skill. It's like you've been training for years."

"How could that be possible?" I asked blocking a slow overhead blow. Parrying, we both stepped back circling once more.

"What did you feel fighting the spiders?" Fitz charged, stepping one side to the next before switching blade hands and thrusting with the left. He'd tried this move at least once each training round and at this point, I was blocking it from muscle memory without need to think.

"You need to switch up your moves sometimes. I'm going to get so use to that move, I won't expect anything more from a real attacker. Come at me with all you got."

"I like that move," Fitz said with a feigned pout. Without changing face, he darted in faster than I expected and I had trouble keeping track of the sword. Blocking one swift cut, he instantly swung again. Halting the attack, I shivered with the edge of the blade kissing my neck.

"You've come a long way in just a few days, Ellie. The you from the top of the cliff wouldn't have been able to follow the first slice let alone block it. Best you could've done was throw your sword at me."

I scoffed and lobbed the sword at him sideways to land harmlessly against his chest. He laughed and I leaned over to scoop up the blade once more.

"When I was in the cave and all the spiders were around me, it was like the world melted away. There was both an emptiness and a rage that took over, fuelling my mind and taking over my actions. It was almost like I wasn't in control anymore. Like death was meaningless and fear was insignificant."

Fitz simply nodded with a knowing grin. "There are those on the battlefield with whom you stick to like glue. You watch their back and trust that they will watch yours and keep you safe. They are your Sword Brothers and Sisters. And then there are people like you. You put them out on the field and give them a wide berth."

"Are you saying I can't be trusted. That my lack of skills makes me dangerous to allies."

"Yes and no," Fitz replied, and I gave him a dirty look. "It's more complicated than that. You are what soldiers call a Berserker. On the battlefield, fear drives you, opens your mind and quietens your thought. Your moves become almost intuitive, and you fight in a frenzy where death and pain are no longer relevant."

"The description sounds familiar. I can't remember the first few kills. Any memories I do have, it's like I was watching from within my mind. I still had control enough to influence movement. What does it mean for me?"

"It means you're harder to kill, like a wounded wolf trapped at a dead end. Your instincts kick in and anything around you should flee or die. Where a single skilled warrior could take down any other soldier, it normally takes about 3 to 5 warriors to bring a berserker down and even then, they should expect casualties."

"I never knew this...?"

"Let's call it rage."

"I never knew this *rage* lay dormant inside me."

"No one ever does. It normally takes a life and death battle to realize it. Though, maybe, Enzo saw this trait in you and had expected you to use it with him in your sparring match. You mentioned he met you as a child. You may not remember but there was possibly a fight where he witnessed you go into a berserker rage. It would only take a moment."

I considered this, hand rubbing at my chin. It definitely made sense. "It may explain the few comments in the cave. There is far more he's said that doesn't make sense, though."

108

"Was just a thought."

The rest of the training was done as we normally do. A number of sparring matches where Fitz would pull me up on certain errors and technical mishaps. He would then make obvious his movements and point out parts to attack at any given moment. We would run through attack and retaliation until the movements felt natural and I could attack open defences on instinct. I'd come to enjoy the morning training immensely. It got my endorphins running, waking me up and giving me a head start into the day ahead. It even felt like this constant training was strengthening my lungs.

Towelling the sweat from my body, I looked to my friend. Rarely would he break a sweat in our matches, always in balance and fluid like water. A dancer of such terrifying skill. I was so happy to have met him.

"Thank you, Fitzroy," I said before walking over and kissing him gently on the cheek. "You brightened my world."

"Don't be speaking like we won't see each other again. You're getting through today like you made it through the rest of the journey. Have a little faith."

A smile touched my lips but was too weak to influence the rest of my face. I could only nod having no more words. I wandered back to the fire and sat beside Baras.

"Not putting the bone armour on?" I asked seeing the armour left in a neat pile where he slept.

"The armour was the dream of a self-centred child. He was selfish and rude, conducting himself in questionable ways. He wasn't a hero."

"These people are getting to you, aren't they? You learn a lot about yourself when you begin to rely on others and make friends."

"I'm sorry I ever doubted you, Ellie," Baras said with deep sincerity, using my nickname for the first time. "I felt you were going to ruin this dream for me, holding me down like an anchor dragging on a boat. And I am truly sorry for striking you."

I shook my head. "I have no recollection of that. There was a self-centred boy at the keep who had a little temper tantrum when he didn't get his way on our departure. There wasn't the man I see before me and therefore no reason he should be apologizing."

Baras just scoffed and stood up. "Come on, the day is getting on. We have a meeting with some Firebirds and shouldn't keep them waiting."

Taking a deep, calming breath, I prepared myself for the road ahead. I didn't have the heart to tell Baras my meeting wasn't with the Phoenix but with Death himself. At least there was still a few hours left to smell the flowers and drink in the beauty of life.

But of course, the walk could never be long enough. Mostly, it was uneventful, save for another small skirmish from the Terror Hounds. As the distance to our destination grew short the weather and landscape began to change. The temperature plummeted to below freezing. It was at a point even Korr would rub his arms to gain a little extra warmth. Snow fell around the breaks in the canopy above and even with the sun at its apex for the day, it seemed to grow increasingly dark as if a storm was brewing in the world above the forest's canopy.

"You'd think the Firebirds would want a warmer climate to nest in," Caeli said offhand. Her teeth were chattering with each word, and Dustin drew her in to share body warmth. I smiled as she melted instantly into her man.

"Phoenix burn, cold tame fire," Korr said and we looked at him quizzically. "Comfortable," he said and I understood.

"The Phoenix are Firebirds. The colder climate is more a neutral temperature for them than our warmer climates." I could understand why Korr realized this. His body had a constant flame keeping him warm. I don't doubt in the warmer climates he'd be uncomfortable.

Soon there grew a light through the trees. It was a deep orange glow as if a fire burned ahead just out of site. That description proved more accurate than I could guess as whisps and swirls of flame became visible the further we moved through the forest until finally we stepped past some charred trees into what should have been a large clearing. A few metres from the trees stood a massive fiery dome, swirling around the area keeping both us and any other creature of the woods from approaching closer. There was no doubt the flaming barrier spanned the entirety of the clearing.

"I guess we wait until invited then," Fitz said taking a seat against a tree and allowing himself to nod off to sleep.

"Why do soldiers do that?" I asked Caeli motioning to Fitz.

"Soldiers take sleep when they can. You never know when the next attack might come so staying rested is vital," came a voice to the far right.

All heads turned to see Kymberlin walking around the barrier, coming into view. Baras stepped in front of me, sword drawn and Kymberlin laughed.

"Still need your little, pet soldier to save the day, Miss Maid. I'm surprised and disappointed you even got this far."

I could see Baras's knuckles whiten, his anger growing over the comments and I placed a hand on his shoulder to calm him.

"Her words have no power here, pet," I purred in Baras's ear sending a shiver down his spine. "Let her waste her breath while we amuse ourselves with much more salacious past times." I kept face so well even when Baras's knees buckled threatening to give way. My eyes remained on Kymberlin the whole time playing her little game and showing her I had my pet under control.

Kymberlin just scoffed and moved to a tree near Fitz. "They're waiting for the remaining Souls to either arrive or die," she said before her head lulled and she was asleep.

Dark eyes turned on me and I just laughed.

"Don't do that again. You're like a sister to me," Baras said.

I glanced at Caeli and the look on her face dared me to even try and say anything. I bit my tongue. Without looking from her, I spoke. "Guess you better hold me like a brother would. Keep me warm while we wait."

Caeli just shook her head as she rolled her eyes and walked to where Dustin sat. "Hold me and don't let me go," she said before getting comfortable in his arms.

I did the same with Baras. Though there was never anything to happen between us, the extra warmth was a blessing.

Korr stood apart looking from one couple to the next before glancing at Kymberlin. As if sensing the eyes on her, she tilted her head to the side and looked up at the big man.

"Don't even think about it," she said before closing her eyes again.

"Bring it in, big guy," Fitz said holding out his arms and Korr grinned, bouncing across to him. The big guy became the little spoon much to our amusement and Kymberlin's disgust.

The two hours we spent waiting for the last of the Souls to arrive were some of the hardest of my life. The dread feeling to the west began to eat into my soul making any attempt at sleep impossible. It was only that Baras held me protectively in his arms that I didn't go crazy with anxiety and fear. The power was calling to me, pulling me towards the west. I dare not even investigate in my spirit form as the Lich seemed to be able to sense me last time. Who knew what he could do to me in that form.

My heart shuddered as a crack of sound and movement came from the West. I let out a trembling breath as I saw two more Souls enter the area. They looked at the barrier, then at us before resting against a tree without a word. It just didn't seem necessary to break the silent vigil.

There was a synchronicity about the two new Souls that suggested they had been brothers in arms for a long time. I was glad to find that under the dark and twisted realm of war such strong bonds could still be formed.

There were no pyrotechnics or marvellous wonders when the barrier came down. It was late into the afternoon as the sun began to sink into the canopy of trees when the final Soul died somewhere out in the wilderness. The flames that once held us from our goal, simply thinned away into nothingness opening a pathway to our fate. A fate we'd been moving towards since leaving the Keep. This is what it was all about and I became suddenly terrified to move forward.

Kymberlin was the first to move towards a small opening, like a portal in the inner ring of trees. It was as though the trees had grown to weave and knot themselves together creating a tight knit barrier with just this one entrance. The two unnamed Souls were close behind her.

"Trust Pythia and Kiarrl to follow in Kymberlin's footsteps," Dustin said. I guess they weren't so unnamed after all.

Slowly the rest of us gathered ourselves, stretching as we stood. Everyone seemed so serious in this moment and I needed to lighten the mood else I would never walk into the area at all.

"Odds are at least one of us will become a Phoenix Soul," I said realizing how much of a downer I sounded in that moment. "Let's all make a pact. Cheer those who are chosen with love in our hearts. Those remaining will work together to defy our fates. I'm not dying for some birds. Agreed."

"Agreed," everyone said in unison.

It was my footsteps that led everyone into the small, dark tunnel, the dim light at the end gaining strength and size with each following footfall. Walking into the soft, warm light, I found myself standing in a dome of trees. Their broad leaves, a dark pink hue that gave the whole area a magical atmosphere. A large opening was present high in the rear where the branches of the trees had curled outward. This gave the Phoenix access to their nesting grounds.

Immediately, I felt the weight each gaze from the five Phoenix. Their eyes burning into me like the flames leaping from their tales and riding across their feathers. There was such hatred in those beady, little eyes, just like from my dream, I knew where my fate lay. Each sat in a nest of intertwined tree limbs, and I was surprised their flames had no effect on the wood.

Seeing Kymberlin and the others standing in the makings of a line, significant space between each other, I moved to continue the trend. It just made sense, given these Firebirds were supposed to assess and pick from us while they sat on their wooden thrones. Dustin came up beside me, then Fitz, Baras, Caeli and Korr. I smiled at my friends. If anything, they were the best things to have happened to me in this lifetime.

"That's the thief," a whispered voice caught my ears and I remained still, not turning my head.

"We should take her now," another voice said.

"Make her pay."

By now, I knew for sure it was the Phoenix whispering amongst themselves.

"Chicklings," Talon screeched and I almost burst into laughter with what could only have been a bird insult. "She can hear us. Stick to the plan."

My brow furrowed as I turned to face my judges. They accuse me of stealing from them when before a week ago I hadn't even heard of them. Could it be my family heritage that now had me in this awkward situation. A smell or recognition of my blood. I shook my head and locked eyes with Talon who returned the gaze with ferocious intensity.

Distracted I looked away to see Enzo entering the clearing from a separate entrance to the West. The trees swayed open away from him to come back together as he passed. It was almost as if they were afraid of his touch. Though, the power of his eyes was found lacking in comparison to the flames swirling within the Phoenix eyes, there was still such a harsh aura around them. Their focus solely on me. It was beginning to get on my nerves and so I flipped him the bird in front of everyone causing the first genuine smile I'd seen on the man's face in days. This was something I could die happily seeing and I settled in for the show.

"You have all been named Soul for your skills and abilities in matters of war and armed combat. After today, four of you will gain the highest honour of becoming Phoenix Soul. You are to defend the lands and the realms of men from any enemy that seek to threaten it, be it from other nations or within," Enzo said. The last words gained a few worried looks but it was mostly decided this to mean traitors. "My Phoenix is Talon. The Phoenix who will choose from you are Flint, Ember, Ash and Haze." Each Phoenix bowed their head as their names were called. "If you are chosen, a Phoenix will approach you and bow his head. You are to place your forehead against theirs creating a bond. From that moment you will mount and leave this nesting ground."

"To what end?" Either Pythia or Kiarrl asked. I still wasn't sure which was which.

"To whatever end you choose. Now, if there are no more questions?" Enzo glanced up and down the line. "Good. Ember, will you do the honours?"

113

"Ember got to choose first last time," Flint whined.

Talon turned on him. "The last to return to ash is the first to choose. If you wish for the honour next time, do better."

"There were only moments between us. When the Chi..." Flint began.

A high-pitched screech filled the air causing everyone, even Enzo, to hold their ears.

"We don't speak of what has been," Talon hissed before turning to Ember. "I will depart. You may proceed."

With that Enzo stepped up to Talon and mounted him. As the Firebird took to the sky, it's body became like flames and Enzo seemed to melt into them, almost losing form, before a single beat of those burning wings sent them out of the clearing like a meteor across the sky. Everyone stood in awe of the display, their impatience growing for the chance to fly like Enzo.

Stepping down from her nest, Ember walked across the clearing straight at me, her eyes never leaving mine. There was a moment I began to think everything I'd crafted in my mind, all the whispers, dreams, and conspiracies, could be wrong. Maybe I wasn't being targeted, and I could actually be chosen to become a Phoenix Soul. Ember halted before me, her feathers shimmering like flames over her body. I reached out with a hand only to be stopped by a piercing screech.

"Thief," Ember said and walked further down the line to stand before Korr, head bowed.

My heart lurched down into the pit of my stomach as my fears were confirmed without a doubt. It was hard watching Korr accept the gift of the Phoenix. To see him glow with power as he mounted Ember's back before they took off. It was hard to see something truly magical only to know you will never obtain it.

"KORR," Baras shouted in celebration. His voice deep and joyful. Not quite enough to break me from my depression, thinking how he took our pact literally.

Flint stepped forward next. His path mirrored Ember's as he walked up to me. This Phoenix stood tall above me. Wings flared out in a threatening show of force. I smiled at him meeting his gaze with stubborn pride.

"Light-fingered maggot," he called me before moving over to Fitz. The initial shock of my fate had passed and I could now truly be happy for my friend. It put a smile on my face to see Fitz chosen. He was going to make a magnificent Phoenix Soul.

Baras stepped forward once more, fist raised in celebration. "FITZROY," he shouted as Fitz mounted and departed in a blaze of glory.

Baras caught my eye and I could only smile at him. He returned smile in one of those rare moments, reminding me of when we were kids getting up to mischief.

I turned my attention back to the Phoenix and took a step back as Haze was barely a few cm from my face. There was a crimson flame burning in her eyes as she stared at me.

"We trusted you," the voice was soft, almost sad. I wished I was the person they knew cos then I would at least have known what I'd been accused of.

The Firebird turned with such sorrow it almost broke my heart. Haze had clearly been hurt deeply by what had been done. Moving a few metres away, Haze came to a halt before Baras. The look of relief in the man's eyes almost matched the depth of pain within this Phoenix. As no one made a noise, I took it upon myself to step up.

"Oh, oh... BARAS," I said, my fist mimicking Baras's movements moments before. I made sure to over emphasis a manly tone just to get a kick out of my friend. There was definitely a smile on his face as he mounted Haze. Looking back at me, it looked as though Baras mouthed the words *thank you* before he was gone from view.

The final Phoenix. The final insult. I took a deep breath as I watched Ash approach. "Would you like to add to what your kin have said or will you move along silently?"

"You will rot for what you did," Ash said. Turning, he took two steps to my right to come before Dustin, bowing his head.

Dustin didn't move. There was despair upon his brow and a dread in his heart. The Phoenix looked up once more.

"Choose Caeli," Dustin said, his voice barley a whisper, as tears formed in his eyes. "Choose... Caeli."

"No, you don't have to do this, Dustin," Caeli cried.

The bird chirped at Dustin, nudging him in the chest. It wasn't going to have a change of heart. It chirped once more then suddenly paused, sniffing at the air. Sniffing Dustin's side, Ash immediately reared back.

"Choose Caeli," Dustin said with a little more weight in his voice.

The bird turned away from Dustin and my heart froze. It was moving away from Caeli as well. Passing me once more, the Phoenix stood before Kymberlin. Head bowed. Nobody cheered this choice and my soul was slowly being crushed under the cries of Dustin.

"You were supposed to choose Caeli," he cried. "Caeli was supposed to be chosen." He fell to his knees slamming his fists into the ground. "Caeli," he said again, tears falling to the thin layer of snow. Caeli was immediately by his side, holding him close.

"Why, Dustin? We both agreed, no matter who was chosen we'd be happy and accept it." Her tears were just as strong and face smeared with fluid as she placed her head on his.

That's when I saw it. The crimson trail in the snow. Tracing it back to Dustin I could see his wrists were covered in blood and I realized just what the Phoenix could smell. "Caeli," I let out a shriek.

Looking at me, Caeli followed my line of sight and her eyes grew wide. "What have you done, brother? Oh my God! what have you done?"

His body was now laying in her arms, not having the strength to keep himself upright anymore. His arms shaking, Dustin raised a hand to Caeli's cheek.

"I just couldn't do it. I couldn't live a Phoenix Soul when my own was sentenced to death." His face was deathly pale as the words came out soft, barely audible.

"You stupid, stubborn man," Caeli said kissing him tenderly. Eyes closed and foreheads together, she spoke only to him. "I love you."

"I... love..." a final, deep, shuddering, breath left Dustin's body as he passed from this world. Caeli wailed loudly, clinging to him and I could do nothing in this moment to lessen the wound of her heart. I stood by watching, my tears flowing freely.

"Well, I ain't staying around to watch this melancholy scene progress. Coming Kiarrl?" Pythia said from behind us. I found it rude but they hadn't formed any kind of connection with us so it was only natural for them not care.

"Nothing better to do," Kiarrl replied. "What a bust this was."

I didn't bother to even turn my head to watch them depart. There was no point trying to form an alliance with them either. They were never going to wait long enough to give Caeli the time she needed to grieve and, more than likely, bury the body.

A deep and horrifying scream came from the tunnel leading outside and my heart froze. It could only belong to Pythia. Moments later a second cry echoed around us as something took down Kiarrl. Yipping and barking reached my ears and I was certain there were Terror Hounds just outside. The growing noise indicating they were coming in.

I placed a hand on Caeli's shoulder. By the look on her face nothing else in the world mattered or even reached her.

"Come on, Caeli. We have to go," I said but got no reaction from the girl. The sounds of the hounds closer still and I kept eyeing the entryway expecting them to break through at any moment. I was forced to drag Caeli to her feet and push her along in front of me as I headed for the concealed opening Enzo had used to enter the dome. I couldn't be certain it would open again but I had to try.

As we reached the spot, the first of the Terror Hounds entered the Phoenix nest and slowed. More and more filtered in behind them and they fanned out around the sides of the area surveying the space as if they had done this before. And they probably had. Or at least their ancestors had brought them up on stories of the Souls left behind and trapped for them to feast upon.

To my great relief the trees moved aside allowing us passage from the area and I stepped forward but paused and looked back to find Caeli unmoving. The hounds, seeing what we were doing had sent a force after us while the rest made for Dustin's body. Caeli's breathing grew heavy and her shoulders began to shake. She lifted her head, and our eyes met for only a moment. Red rimmed, Caeli's stare was fierce as if a terrible anger was burning just below the surface. She pushed me back and before I could gain my footing the trees had already begun to close.

"Caeli, no!" I screamed but my way was already blocked and I could only watch from the small gaps in the tree line.

"Don't you dare touch my BROTHER!" Caeli screamed and charged towards Dustin. The first Terror Hound to reach her had been partially decapitated by a swift and powerful swing of Caeli's short sword. The blade left clinging to the flesh in the hound's neck. Vaulting over the next, A bow and arrow seemed to appear in her hand and with practiced accuracy took down the lead hound of the second group.

With a clear run Caeli reached her brother moments before the hounds, skidding to a halt with two daggers in hand. My heart was pounding in my chest as I watched what could only be the last moments of Caeli's life.

Four hounds fell to her blades as they slashed left and right opening throats and carving through limbs. For a moment, my hopes began to grow watching even with their vast numbers the hounds just couldn't break through until a misguided attack saw one of the daggers left lodged in the brain of a hound.

Taking out the sixth, one of the hounds behind her pounced and latched onto Caeli's arm. With a guttural cry, Caeli jammed an arrow through the hound's eye socket and up into the beast's brain. Knowing this was all she could do; Caeli accepted her fate. Spinning on her heel she fell beside Dustin to gaze upon her brother's face one final time. The last image I saw seemed to freeze in my mind as I turned away. A hound in midair, jaws mere inches from Caeli's neck. Pink leaves fell around the area and Caeli laying over her love, made for an almost beautiful

117

picture. Only, the gargling scream of my friend drowned out any poetic notions my mind could create.

"Caeli, no," I whimpered again, my legs giving way below me. I wasn't brave enough to look back upon the scene. Tears came unbidden to an already damp face as I mourned the loss of all my friends. I had no doubts now I would never see any of them again.

I don't know how long I sat in that dark and narrow passage, depression seeping deep into every fibre of my being, when a familiar tingling began in the soles of my feet. Dark and full of hate, I scratched at the skin trying to desensitize them before shifting into my spirit form. A dark blue energy line ran along the centre of the pathway, growing thicker as it headed for the West. The Lich was close, and a deadly confrontation was beginning to feel inevitably fated.

Wiping back my dribbling nose, I stood on wobbly feet. I knew the path I needed to walk but hesitated, not sure I had the courage to meet my fate. As if hearing my inner turmoil, the trees themselves began to encroach on my space, forcing me forward step by uneasy step.

The dark tunnel twisted and turned as the trees led me across grass, stone, and hills to come into a clearing beneath the breath-taking night sky. The river of stars flowing directly overhead, a witness to my existence. Elara had been here. The crescent moon, my only source of light, giving shape to the lands before me. And yet even with this sparse light, I strained hard to see through the darkness ahead. A large mass stood in the darkness, that I was sure, but to what it could be was another matter.

As if on some unspoken order, all around the area fireflies took flight in a magical display. It was as if the stars in the sky had come down to dance for me. A smile itched upon my lips, the recent worries almost vanishing into the bewitching show but with a physical pulse of dark power, I was brought back to the present. Within the darkness ahead, a blue flame came alight and with a sudden realization, I recognized the structure to be a large crystalline casing of ice. Long splinters shot out in every direction and from within, two powerful, swirling, purple eyes considered me.

"So, you've finally come to finish that which you began three hundred years hence, Elara of Three Pines." The voice was raspy, almost whimsical as it addressed me.

Three hundred years? This could only have been an ancestor of mine especially when Three Pines had been wiped from the map, or so I was told.

I still couldn't make out the figure within the towering ice structure.

Only the eyes seemed to float in a mesmerizing display back and forwards, purple tracer lines following the path. As a firefly got close, I saw echoes of soft blues and whites shimmering around it.

"I've been a maid all my life. I know not the wrong you believe I have committed or the woman you mistake me for... I," I said.

Scorching, blue flames filled the space within the crystal and from out of the curling wisps of heat, a deep blue Firebird emerged. Another Phoenix of blues, whites and purples. Stronger than the others with a deep hatred for me. I'd been wrong about the Lich. It was a Phoenix all along sharing in the energy the five held, seemingly holding onto life as long as it could.

"Don't you dare weave you're cursed lies with me again. Do you not think I can feel my power crackling within your skin? Do you not believe I have felt you stealing my life essence to craft your horrid ice magic? You think I don't see the makings of the immortal scar snaking its way into your clothes?"

I touched the frostbite at my neck, concern beginning to creep into my every thought.

"I bet you believed I'd be gone from this earth never to be reborn. When you first entered my life, I was but spark of the red flame, inexperienced in human lies and naïve. Because of your honeyed words and poisoned tongue, I have had to struggle to cling to this world for centuries. But now, you are the naïve one, too drunk on the power of the Phoenix to understand it was a mistake to come back here. To challenge me once more and try to take that which will secure you power eternally."

A deep resonating boom reverberated around the clearing as the ice prison shattered apart sending shards of ice in every direction. I lifted my arms in front of my face to protect me from them, gaining small slices upon my skin. I peeked out from within my cocoon to find those swirling purple eyes still locked on me, free to approach at their will. I could feel the blood run from my face as my whole body screamed at me to flee. Looking around I couldn't see the tunnel I had entered by. All around were layers of trees blocking the path and I looked back to the Phoenix in fear.

It drank in the fear and confusion upon my face, giving a loud twittering symphony of tweets I could only conclude was laughter. The flaming monster circled me, considering me as it relished in my pain.

"What? Little human upset I destroyed her *impenetrable* cage. You were so proud of yourself that day, crafting a fortress no other of the Fibonacci tribe could accomplish. To me it was a gift more than a prison.

For the last hundred years, I have been syphoning its power and weakening its bond to you. I have been able to take so much energy from it. Your little ice tricks will not work against me again. This is but a taste, human. I am going to enjoy scorching the very flesh from your bones inch by inch, feasting on your juicy meat. And from the marrow of your bones, I will forcibly take back that which you stole, leaving you to fade into the abyss where you belong."

The intensity of the flames grew all around it, eating up the fireflies and setting fire to the boundary of the clearing. Swooping down to skim inches from the ground, the Phoenix raged at me with the intensity of the sun and panic set in.

"What did I steal?" My voice came out in squeals as I threw my hands up and looked away.

With a swift diversion of its trajectory, the Phoenix reared up before me, wings outstretched, curling over me at the tips. It levitated a moment as if time had stood still before floating gently to the earth below. I had to crane my neck to look up at the giant creature, almost twice the size of any other Phoenix I had seen.

Those purple swirling pupils pierced my very soul as it stood, head slightly tilted, considering me.

"This will not do at all, you worthless human. You have abused my power, stretching your mind thin beyond measure. What is my name?"

"I haven't met you before," I screamed back at him.

"What is my name?" the Phoenix said again, its voice sharpening to match my tone. It latched onto my arm with its beak, threatening to snap it clean off.

I pushed against its fiery head, the skin of my fingers singed and crackling. "I don't know you," I cried and his beak's grip clenched tighter, the edges beginning to draw blood. "Shard, I don't know you. I've never met you... Shard!" I couldn't fathom how such a word had sprung to my lips in this moment, but the Firebird backed up. My arm tender but still attached.

"You tricked me, human. You stole the very essence that allows a Phoenix to be reborn and have used that power relentlessly. So much so, it has affected the memories of your previous lives."

"Then take it back and leave me be." It all sounded so surreal. Being reborn as the Phoenix are. Living multiple lives. Enzo... He missed me. Recognized me by my scar. Made love to me like we had done so a thousand times before. My face flared crimson.

"You would give this to me without a fight? You have not come to correct this adverse reaction to your overuse?"

"What is the point of having such an ability if I don't even realize I have it. To live each life like it is the only one I have while you are in pain, suffering from my actions. This can be my first and last life."

Shard's eyes narrowed on me. There was a touch of disappointment in his features, and I could understand it. Three hundred years, plotting and training for revenge to have it too stolen from him.

"Then give prayer to whatever Gods you find comfort in. You dine with them tonight."

There was a calm that washed over me. For a week I had been running scared from everything that could kill me. Now that I was face to face with certain death, I felt ready. I tilted my head in submission.

"I had hoped this would have a deeper impact on you but see what years of stealing your energies have opened within me."

The purple in shards eyes shimmered with a cold blue and from the ground ice began to form around me clinging to the skin and freezing me inch by inch.

I gave a soft smile to this creature I had brought so much pain upon and felt the ice engulf me, my body shutting down into the frozen nothingness. As my eyes grew weary and darkness sat at the borders of my vision, Enzo landed on the ground as if jumping in from a height. He rolled with the momentum coming to his feet to stand before Shard as Talon circled the area and landed a ways back.

"You need her," Enzo's voice filtered through. It was all I got as my heart finally gave out to the freezing cold. Darkness and an eternal sleep took my lifeless body.

Chapter 7

"I'll make it so she can never steal my powers again," Shard said leaning over the still form of Elara, her body dead but preserved in a crystal chamber these last 5 weeks. "This'll be your last life with her, Enzo TalonSoul."

"It's a blessing, Shard. Thank you for this gift," Enzo replied, bowing his head.

"It wasn't for you. I can't fight without a soul backing me and the humans won't send anyone for a Phoenix they don't believe exists. The others are fighting hard but they'll soon falter. All I could think of through my rebirth was getting back to them. I need her. Her icy heart and fiery soul are a perfect match to mine," Shard said. A reserved fury, sat, locked behind his eyes.

"If only for this reason it is enough," Enzo replied.

Shard leaned in close to Elara, the ice melting from the blue flames dancing across his feathers. A breath of golden energy flowed forth from Shard's beak to lay like shining droplets of water, beading across Elara's skin. Slowly, the energy sank below the surface, her body taking on a brilliant, golden glow beaming from her with growing intensity until Enzo needed to shield his eyes.

My eyes fluttered open, the haze of darkness still upon my sight as pins and needles attacked every inch of my body. I could remember the sensation after sleeping on an arm or sitting on my legs for periods of time but never had I experienced it with such intensity. Clenching my eyes once more, I tried as hard as I could to allow the sensation to pass through me with as little pain as possible.

"Elara, you need to open your eyes. There are minutes left at most."

The distress in this, somehow, familiar voice caught my attention and I forced my eyes open. Nothing could prepare me for the face looking back. Two swirling, purple eyes sat upon an overly large beak. The edges, opening and closing rapidly with a threatening click.

I screamed, my lungs burning as the air escaped. A hand slapped me roughly and I collapsed into a coughing fit, seeking the source of my pain. To the right stood a man with curly dark hair. His arms were tattooed in some sort of archaic design. Above all, the eyes drew me in. Flecks of gold and brown danced upon a dark amber base. It was alluring and breathtaking, I could get lost in those eyes for hours but the large bird before me, looking at me like I was dinner, got the majority of my attention.

"What the fuck is that thing?" I cried, pointing at Shard.

Enzo's brow furrowed, seeing for the first time, my memory was horribly fractured. "You need to listen to me, Elara. You died in this very forest. Your soul's been drifting in the void, barely tethered to your body."

"How can that be? I'm here speaking to you."

"No. This Phoenix has granted you a moment of life. He's given you the chance to either say your goodbyes or have another shot at life. You have minutes at most to decide before the magical energy inside you is used up and you return to death once more. Once it is gone, there is no reawakening."

"I have no one to say goodbye to," I said and the man looked physically hurt. This alone got me curious about the life I'd lived. Why couldn't I remember. "What must I do to remain alive."

The Phoenix screeched a god-awful noise at me and I drew back.

"She has not the ability to hear your voice anymore. Let me, Shard." The man turned back to me. "The Phoenix would bond with you. Share its energy and strength."

"And what do I give in return?"

"Even with your memory gone, you're extremely sharp. A Phoenix has no soul. They are a mass of energy with a body of fire formed around them. Without a soul they can't be reborn. They disperse into the air like they were nothing. Even should you die, the link with the soul you share remains until their rebirth. You share your soul with them; they share their power with you. You will also get to live a fuller life."

"Why me?" I asked. This all sounded terribly confusing.

"Because you are here and I am already linked to another," Enzo said, his voice beginning to strain. Kneeling down, he took my small hand in his. The fingers curling over to embrace me. They were so warm and my cheeks began to blush.

"Please, Elara. Please stay with me." His eyes seemed so sad as he gazed into mine. I couldn't hurt him further.

"Tell me what to do."

"Just accept in your heart and Shard will lower his head to yours, connecting the two of you."

Looking across at the Phoenix, I closed my eyes gathering courage and strength to proceed. I could feel parts of my body beginning to grow weak and my instincts pushed me forward.

"I... I am ready, Shard," I said and with a chirp, the Firebird approached.

My heart pounded harder as blue flames grew across his feathers down

123

to his majestic, almost peacock-like, tail that seemed to burn with the intensity of the sun. Though, surprisingly, I felt no heat from it as he placed his head against mine. All at once, power flowed through me like a dam had burst. The waves of energy filling every part of my body. Muscle, tissue and sinew all pulsed with heat and light as they repaired themselves. The organs around my body flared to life as if born anew, my lungs, almost painfully, flaring more than anywhere else. Even to the topmost layers of skin, all blemishes, cuts and scars seemed to magically vanish. All but the dark and intricate pattern running from neck to thigh like a tattoo.

Flowing through the bloodstream, the energy swirled up into my brain, and everything seemed to stall for me as it spread through the nerves. Comprehension of the world around me, the soft voice of my subconscious, even my senses, all stopped in that moment. By the conversation with Enzo, my brain needed the most work. And then just like that, everything rebooted and I was back in control once more. My memories returned to me from the youngest, most recent memories to the oldest and most educational.

...But one, single memory stood out above all others.

With a snap of my neck, I lowered a deadly glare upon Enzo. It was never me. I had never... fully, betrayed the Phoenix. Yes, I locked Shard away in a crystal prison, his body helpless and dying but when it came down to the moment of extracting the Soul attached to his body from a previously deceased Phoenix Soul, I couldn't do it. I couldn't bring about the final death of such a beautiful creature as Shard.

It was Enzo who harvested the Phoenix Soul. Enzo, who force fed it to me. Enzo, who brought me back from the brink of death so that he could live a hundred more lives with me by his side. Enzo, who sentenced Shard to death and, conveniently, bundled me up with all the blame.

It was always Enzo. He had already done something similar with Talon to the point that when Talon is reborn, so too is he. He was the one who gave me the idea in the first place, fanning the makings of a plan, using my love for him to persuade me. It was even Enzo who killed Shards last Phoenix Soul to allow for easier execution of the plan.

Oh, how my feelings had turned to hatred. I had searched for Enzo over countless lives, his Phoenix always seemingly stationed across continents from where I was. That and when a human is reborn, they fill the forming foetus of a new child. Because of this, I never knew what Enzo looked like. Finally, when I did find him, I couldn't remember what he had done and, therefore, fucked him in the forest feeling terribly infatuated with him. Echoes of my distant infatuation. He should feel lucky for that final ride.

"Come, Shard, let's take to the sky," I said, my eyes never once leaving Enzo's as I vaulted to Shard's back. It was only when we took flight, did I finally focus on what was ahead.

A sharp, crisp wind coursed across my skin as Shard pierced the sky like an arrow in flight. Winter was definitely close, with flecks of snow falling sporadically from the sky and a white sheet of powder lying across the terrain.

Trails of blue flame flowed from the Phoenix wings. It was a brilliant display of this majestic creature as it twisted and turned through the sky. If Shard managed to dislodge me, at least he would be free of that which he deemed a nuisance and possibly an enemy while still having the ability to be reborn once more. I was too confident in my seat, however, to let that happen, my legs tucked in just behind Shard's wings without impeding their ability to move.

So confident was I that I released my gentle grip on Shards shimmering feathers to stretch out my arms. Ice began to form around my hands to trail behind us a few metres shattering into a deadly hailstorm of crystalline fragments. The light of Shard's fire gave the ice an ephemeral glow creating a magical and mythical trail in our wake. It felt like my soul awoke in this moment as Shard began a series of corkscrews. I laughed, unable to hold back my euphoria.

Levelling out, I breathed in deep allowing my lungs to shiver with excitement rather than clench up and strangle me.

"It is wonderful to finally breath again. To breath wholly without fear. Too long has my body been denied the exhilaration of the cold due to its weaknesses. Thank you, Shard. That alone was worth the bonding," I said, sheer glee beaming from every part of me.

"Spoken like a true, Fibonacci," Shard replied. There was still resistance evident in his voice but that was to be expected. It was seldom I heard my ancestral name brought up. Not many now a days even knew of the clan's small sprint in history. Three Pines held the final resting place of my clan along with my true mother and father. Wiped from existence by BrongTa fire users because my clan had abilities in ice.

I laughed at the irony. On the day the BrongTa sacked my village and wiped out my clan, it was a young BrongTa that had saved me and allowed the line of Fibonacci to continue. What did he call me? His *Forbidden Fruit*. Enzo had a lot to pay for from both our clans but the pull of fire and ice was erotic and taboo. I could understand his reasoning.

I shook my head.

"How do we do this?" I asked.

"Do what?" Shard chirped back

"Link our minds. Share memories. Speak without words. I have something I need to show you."

There came a whistle and a shudder that ran through his feathers which I took to mean Shard was amused.

"I believe you're thinking of Dragons. Us Phoenix are a little more private."

My brow furrowed thinking just how much effort it was going to take clearing my name. I was about to speak when Shard flew up to the perch on Shatterstone Mountain where the Souls met Enzo for the first time. My mind came to a jarring halt, and I vaulted from Shard to look out over the kingdom that had been my home for most of this life. Fires burned freely despite the snow and smoke hung low over the area making it hard to find certain landmarks across the realm. My eyes sought any semblance of the land I once knew but it was almost impossible in the haze.

"How long have I been gone," I asked. The devastation made me think years.

"My rebirth and our bond were completed in only 5 weeks. Time was saved using your previous form preserved in the ice," Shard replied.

"Only 5 weeks. Who could have done so much damage?" I was incredulous. I hadn't heard of a single kingdom across any of my lifetimes that had the strength to come up against Telveria and decimate them so quickly to such an extent.

"Chimera," Shard said softly.

I tracked through my memories looking for any reference. Everything was so disorganised from my time without them and it was hard finding exactly what I was after. Finally, I came across a reference to a form of creature I read in a tome.

"The monsters made from grafting different creatures together? That is exceptionally dark magic."

"The worst kind," Shard said. "They have been slowly moving into Telveria even when you were climbing this mountain. It was they who killed the last Phoenix Souls."

"Why wasn't anyone warned?" I asked thinking of Enzo playing with the new souls while the continent burned.

"They were. Enzo informed the General and an assembly was called to begin naming Souls early. A Phoenix would usually go a year without a new Phoenix Soul. We tend to like the peace and quiet away from you

126

humans." Shard chortled and I knew for sure he was having a crack at me this time.

I just scoffed as I knelt on the edge of the cliff. Dipping my head, I shifted into spirit form. It wasn't a gift I received from my original birth but rather only two lifetimes ago. I was still getting used to some of the functionality but I knew more now than I had earlier this life. Especially, controlling both body and soul at once.

Holding my form on the clifftop, I sped faster than the speed of darkness to Telveria Keep and came to a grinding halt a kilometre above the walls. It was like the eye of a hurricane. A vast epicentre the smoke had yet to cover as if it were a soldier itself, the misty form travelling with the enemy armies. The clear grounds spanning four hundred metres around the high stone walls. Beyond in the haze came sounds of bestial creatures from every direction. It was a battle of the mind, playing on the fears of allied soldiers, with every man, woman and child set to die should our defences fail.

Drifting closer to the Keep, I could see the destruction and desolation already endured by the defenders. One in three warriors were free of any form of bandaging and everyone looked exhausted to the point of fainting. The only thing keeping them from falling asleep was the knowledge they would die if they did.

Along sections of the wall, the tops were crumbling and brittle. Large, dark scorch marks, stained multitudes of brickwork where the Chimera's army had attacked with fireballs and other such methods. On both sides there were piles of dead. Chimera laying in heaps at the foot of the walls where the soldiers threw them, and the Telverians, wrapped and placed in great pits to be burned. What got to me the most was the look of despair and loss in almost every soldier's eyes. I could see they all believed they were going to die. Now it was only a matter of how long.

Scanning the buildings, I spied the 4 Phoenix of my friends perched upon the taller building above the War room. Another flew in and I saw Enzo leap from Talon's back to make his way through the large iron doors. I followed.

"Finally," General Suniel said seeing Enzo enter. "I had long believed you'd fled these lands a traitor and a coward. Care to explain what you've been doing these last five weeks? We could have used you."

Enzo just shook his head and I glared at his back. He didn't need to wait for me to wake while everyone else was fighting. That was just selfish.

"It looks like you've been getting along fine," Enzo replied.

"Fine?" Baras roared and an aura of orange flames covered his body.

Clearly, his temper was still a part of his personality, but the flames were new. I began to wonder what I could truly do now I was a Phoenix Soul. "We have lost half the army to these bastards and most of the other half is too injured to last another night. Everyone's lost hope. We're planning how to salvage even a small scrap of it. How is that *FINE?*"

Enzo waved a hand at Baras dismissing him easily, his eyes still on Suniel.

The flames around Baras grew in intensity as a rage began to overflow him. "You bastard," he said in a low growl before leaping across the table.

Enzo stood by calmly as Baras surged forward and as the first punch was thrown, swayed ever so slightly down and to the left. Enough for the fist to graze harmlessly past his ear. Enzo's right fist twisted palm up and with a speed faster than most in the room could follow, landed an uppercut into Baras's jaw sending him catapulting back across the vast table to land unconscious in his chair.

I shook my head and drifted around to my friend. Placing a hand on Baras's shoulder I pulsed pure energy into him, healing his worn body, the two broken ribs, and kickstarting his brain once more. Filling him with calming energy, I watched Baras awaken and relax back into his chair.

"All I'm saying is, you ain't welcome here if you aren't gunna fight," Baras said. There was still a fire in his eye but his whole demeanour had clearly settled.

I moved on to Korr, then Fitz and finally floated behind Kymberlin. She reminded me of my younger self almost 300 years prior. Self-serving and feisty, I too would have taken the climbing equipment from someone I deemed weaker given the chance. Sure, I'd learned from my mistakes, but I wasn't about to hold it against her.

Pain flared in Kymberlin's face as I pushed through the healing energy. She held it tightly, straining in agony as the skin began to knit itself back together, the grizzly scar disappearing. Other parts of her body began to heal but that alone got people's attention.

Even Enzo paused in delivering some fanciful speech about finding a saviour to their *issues* beyond the walls. One brow furrowed as the other raised. Such an ugly man below the façade of beauty, I thought, watching him.

"I knew there was something about you," a familiar voice said and I turned, smiling to find Walan had shifted into his spirit form. He chose a form of pure light, but there was an aura surrounding him that could be no one else.

"Hi, Walan," I said, my soul gleaming in joy. There weren't any physical actions like hugging and embracing in this form but as the light of one's soul grows brighter it shows the joy and love between the two.

"You've changed a lot since last we spoke. Have you a physical form or just the lingerings of a passing soul."

I smiled. "I still live in the real world. I was able to wake up, learn about my long past. I'll be seeing you soon."

"Do not come if all you seek is a nostalgic death. Your essence is too pure for that."

"Trust me, I'm not as pure as you think. I'll be coming to help and maybe gain everyone a few extra hours of life they may not have had before. I will die with my friends," I said scanning those sitting at the table.

Walan followed my line of sight and smiled. "I see your journey was worthwhile after all."

"More than you know. Keep a watch. I hope to be here by sunset."

I left my friends as they spoke of war and other matters to float above the Keep. There wasn't enough in my reserves to heal all who still fought but, glancing at the line of blue energy now connecting me to Shard, I may be able to give those small scraps of hope, Baras sought.

Holding the energy line, I drew only what was required from Shard and rained down golden light on the soldiers and townsfolk. Touching the hearts of all those who lived, I brought up feelings of joy, old wonderous memories, Comradery, and just a spark that maybe there will be some hope, some cosmic fate, that could get them through this. It was all I could do and hoped it would be enough.

The energy line to Shard was clearly weakened. Enzo had been right in the spider cave saying I could kill the Phoenix. He was barley getting by as it was and then I come in and start stealing more of his life force. He will definitely need a sleep after tonight's decisive battle.

Flying over the walls once more, my breath caught as a lump formed in my throat. A voice had risen above the silence, their words a melody of life and love. Others took up the song and soon, all around the keep, everyone was singing. A smile kissed my cheeks.

"They're going to be all right," I thought and raced back towards the mountain range.

On my way, I finally saw the landscape clearly. Everything was destroyed. Crop fields decimated, forests flattened. Even the beautiful crisp rivers were now flowing with a dirty green ooze that looked like it would be sticky if touched. It would be years before the kingdom could begin to remake itself and that was if they were given the chance to by being left alone.

A scorch mark in the earth showed where the town of Hopstan once stood. There wasn't even enough of it left to know there had been a town. Further on and another town was in its death throes. There were two Chimera hunting the villagers and tearing them apart, their fiery breath burning all manmade structures in their wake. These two creatures seemed to be a mix of fox, bear, and some large scaley creature that could have been a snake, wyrm, or any other multitude of large reptiles. Along with the creatures were two men. I could only describe them as murderers and rapists for how they treated the woman and girls barely old enough to see their first bleed. I averted my eyes and continued on with no ability to help.

There was only one other village between here and the mountains, Valaos. I thought of the old shop keep, Fletcher, and prayed he was still untouched. My prayers were answered as I spied the town, still standing within the smoke haze.

A glint of sunlight on metal caught my eye and I turned to see another two Chimera and two murders approaching the village through the brush. My eyes widened but a determination steeled my heart. They weren't about to do to Valaos what was done to the other cities of this kingdom.

Fleeing to my body at breakneck speed, I slammed into it, physically throwing myself back onto the rock shelf as I merged.

"Come, Shard. There is a battle to be had," I called to the Phoenix before racing to the cliffs edge and diving over into a free fall.

A sharp whistle pierced my ears and halfway down I felt the gust of Shard's wings as he manoeuvred below me. It was a risk, I know, and with how Shard still felt towards me, I had half expected him to let me meet my end with the Earth's embrace.

The soft feathers cushioned my fall and the moment we touched, I felt myself become weightless, as if I was floating within the slip stream of Shard's flight. It was such a magical feeling.

"Small village that way." I pointed with an arm outstretched. "I owe them a debt and shall show them the same help they showed me when I was helpless."

"How many?" Shard asked.

"Two human, two Chimera," I replied and immediately felt Shard slow. "Take me or I head there without your backup."

"Even one Chimera will be a struggle."

"You have yet to see me fight after multiple lives of practice. Tell me what abilities I gain from you."

130

There was a moment of silence as Shard contemplated my words. I could see he was really struggling with the decision but finally, our speed picked up again. "You can wield fire in any form you like. The strength at which you wield changes from person to person."

"And how do I bring it forth?"

"Same way you do the cold. Focus on what you wish and think warmer thoughts."

"Thank you, Shard," I said softly as we came upon the village. The enemy had reached the outskirts with villagers now fleeing any which way they could. Thankfully, no one had been touched and I vaulted from Shard's back into a tumblers dive, rolling on landing to come up to my feet in a fluid movement.

The enemy charge faltered only a moment before one of the humans grinned a wicked smile as he and the two Chimera continued forward. The other murderer held back circling slowly as his pale eyes studied me, the only human feature I could find of his face below the helmet. I kept him in my peripheral as I levelled my eyes on the opponents ahead.

"Kill the Soul," came a devilish hiss and I realised it was the Chimera that spoke and not the human. Immediately, the man ran in, sword raised. He tried a clumsy overhanded swing which I batted away with ease before sinking my short sword under his chin, up into the brain. The man fell silently and I focused on the Chimera.

They began circling me in opposite directions. Their eyes displaying the pupils of the dominant animal within. As they assessed me, so too did I assess them. There was little in the way of flaws. Obviously, their cunning came from the fox. Their sheer mass and strength from the bear. The scaley skin worn like armour coming from a reptilian creature. Whoever crafted these things had put a bit of thought into their ingredients.

I breathed out slowly allowing my body to relax and react on its own. Shard was right to question me going up against these creatures as one was going to be trouble. Two was going to take a lot of luck.

The first charged in leaping at me. Its long arms were outstretched with sharp talons protruding like daggers. I dropped to one knee and watched the creature skim overhead, my sword skittering over the underside of its protected belly. I could see that not a mark was made and, as it cleared me, the rear knee knocked the side of my head sending me tumbling to the dirt. I had no time to react as the second Chimera charged in.

As I watched this beast helplessly, time slowing within the last metre, Shard flew in digging his claws deep in the creature's neck. A green

131

blood flowed from the wounds bringing with it a pungent stench to stick in my nostrils.

Faltering in its charge, the Chimera thrashed about trying to dislodge Shard. Shard, however, pulsed a continuous burst of blue flame, engulfing the beast and setting its flesh alight.

A horrific howl came from the Chimera as it contorted in pain. It was all I got to witness of the battle as the second Chimera attacked my flank. This time it used a breath of ice that froze the ground and strands of grass along the path to me. I did not try to block or dodge the attack. The cold would never be a threat to a Fibonacci.

Raising a hand, I let the freezing breath dance around my fingers and play along my arm. Water vapour in the air freezing into little icicles like sparkles to give the moment a magical feel. I smiled feeling the gentle chill run along my shoulders to brush past me.

"That almost reminded me of my younger days when I hadn't yet grown into my powers," I said.

"Impossible. A human, even a BrongTa Phoenix Soul, should not be able to withstand that attack," the creature hissed. It's breath crinkling my nose causing more discomfort than the ice.

"As you are protected from my flame with your scales, so too does your ice not affect me. But maybe..." Focusing my powers I tried for the first time to wield the fire within me. It came rather easy, having prior knowledge of elemental magic. Flames of blues and whites came to life over my skin. Pulling back in an intricate wave of my arms, I flung bursts of fire forward into the air. Channelling, I propelled the flames towards the beast in a large fireball. As a show of power, the creature stood without moving, imitating my stance with the ice. Just how I'd hoped it would.

The ball of fire hit the creature in the face, flames curling back around its skull and down its neck to dissipate across its body. The heat of the blue flames searing small scorch marks across its skin and the force within the fireball had knocked his head back. Its jaw spasmed a moment while its head twitched and, suddenly, the beast fell to the earth, dead.

I walked over and placed my foot on the shard of ice lodged in its eye socket. "Sure, my flames may have little effect on you, but my own ice magic is formidable," I said as I pushed the shard deeper into its skull. The blue flames were a perfect concealment for the ice. The trickiest part being the fluctuation of the internal air temperatures to keep the ice solid.

"Shit," I swore aloud then swung my head this way and that, looking

132

for the second murderer. I found him standing by a far building. There was a tilt of his head, acknowledging me before he disappeared into a misty haze right before my eyes.

"Did you see that?" I asked as Shard came up beside me.

"He has fled," Shard replied and I turned to look at him, blanching in disgust. Green blood was smeared all over his beak and the surrounding feathers. A small scrap of flesh was hanging from his beak and I almost threw up from both sight and smell.

"I think he fled from you, Shard. You need to clean yourself. That's disgusting." I raised a hand to my nose trying to block the stench.

"It's a delicacy," Shard said. He didn't understand the concern. "I haven't gotten to feast on Chimera in centuries. Not since you rendered me immobile in my crystal cage."

"Why did you save me after I leapt from the cliff face? You could have let me fall to my death. Have some semblance of revenge."

Shard considered me a moment. "I feel a change within you as if time to reinvent yourself has given you a deeper perspective on life. That and I can't be certain I will reincarnate just yet. The bond is there but it's fragile. If you were to pass so soon after our union I couldn't guess if the bond would remain true or not. I would be vulnerable and never again be able to bond. Meaning my death..."

"Would be final. I'm sorry," I said, my words barely above a whisper. I became quiet a moment, contemplating my next words. "Shard, I need to tell you something. You will not like what your about to hear but I will allow you to come to terms with it in your own time."

"You have already performed the worst deed a human can to a Phoenix. What could you say now that would upset me?"

"I did not take your ability to reincarnate."

"Liar!" Shard squawked. "If not you than who?"

"I will not name names right now. I only wish for you to know that when it came down to it, I turned away from the deed. I couldn't harm you. I trust in you, Shard. When you can tell me you believe me, I will know you trust in me too."

"That moment will never come."

"Then let us be off to the keep and better company."

"A moment," I heard a voice behind me and, smiling I turned to find Fletcher standing at the front of the villagers. Running over, a gave the man a hug.

"It's good to see you again, Fletcher. I'm glad I could make it in time," I said.

"It is good to see you too, Elara. I see I made the right choice in putting my faith in you. The whole village thanks you. Would you like supplies or food?"

"I can't stop. There are more battles across the kingdom. You aren't safe here."

"Where can we go? Our homes are here," Fletcher said.

"All I see is wood and dirt. Your home is the people standing at your back. The children looking up to you. The neighbours who lend you things in times of need. The families who would give their lives for you. Look at them."

Fletcher turned to meet the eyes of his friends and family. People he had known for years.

"They are your home. Your home is wherever they are. Not the wood and dirt of this land. Head for the pass and get to the villages in the West over the mountains. Tell them 'Elara Three Pine sent you'. You will not be mistreated."

Fletcher seemed stunned. "There is far more to you than I ever conceived. Do not fear for us. We will take your advice and disappear into the north." He bowed his head, two fingers on his heart. "Be safe, daughter of the earth and stars."

A lump formed in my throat seeing the gesture and hearing the words of my village from someone disconnected from my home. Though Three Pine was lost to time, the history and legends are still around today.

I mimicked the gesture. "Be well, father of the moon and sea."

Walking from them, I vaulted to Shard's back and the Phoenix took to the skies in a burst of blue flame.

A new battle had already begun by the time I arrived. A steady flow of humans clad in dark armour broke against the walls of the Keep. The defenders firing volleys of arrows, throwing spears, and heaving chunks of broken wall over the ramparts and onto the attackers.

Ladders were carried across the killing grounds to be raised against the walls. The fastest of the climbers racing to get to the top with the defender's attention thinned along the vast walls. When they made it to the top of the walls, the enemy worked at making more room for their allies to gain footholds and small pockets of fighting along the walls broke out.

I smiled as I saw my friends swoop in on their Phoenix to leap onto the battlements and close the gap. Baras took the one nearest to me, flames sweeping out like whips to thin the enemy lines. Further along Korr was... grinning, even smiling, as he carved through the ranks of the enemies. It was terrifying and I was so happy he was on my side of the war.

Even with the backup of the five Phoenix Souls and their Phoenix, anyone could see the soldiers in the Keep were at breaking point. A few more decisive battles, a number of deaths and there wouldn't be enough fighters to man the walls. The enemy could easily storm the Keep at this point and the kingdom would be lost.

The smoke wall didn't help with morale either. There was a constant flow of people appearing from out of the haze. They were endless and there was no way to gauge how many more may be in there. Not to mention the Chimera I could sense nearby. They seemed to be waiting for something, happy to let the humans do all the dirty work.

A horn blew from within the depths of the Keep and the heavy, thick, steel portcullis began to slowly lift. A terrible grinding noise accompanying the movement. At its base, a number of the enemy were rigging support beams under it in case it dropped again and from the smoke a deluge of warriors came running ready to breach the Keep's walls through the main entrance.

"There," I pointed to Shard and he swooped into action skimming along the ground at a deadly speed. Fierce, blue flames manifested themselves around Shard and he used them to set alight the earth in a large arc causing the warriors to divert their charge to the far corner close to the wall or wait for the flames to die away.

As Shard came around in a slow, smooth turn, I dismounted and rolled to my feet on landed. I was now standing between the gate and the warriors who wished for access. Gaining a moment from Shards flames to centre myself, I rushed the warriors rigging up the gates, taking out two. The other three turned to fight. None were ready and before any could even unsheathe a sword, my blade sang to the sounds of their blood. Only one lived through the first fatal thrust, his screams of agony a perfect backdrop for what was to come.

I destroyed the props ready to catch the gate should my allies take out the enemy who was currently opening it and turned to wait. The enemy warriors had just started to filter in through the small gap left by Shard. It was going to be easier fighting the smaller numbers as opposed to the vast horde and each of them I killed was one less the Keep soldiers had to deal with.

Charging in, I side stepped the first thrust, my sword coming up to open the warrior's throat. Spinning on my heel I loped off a second man's arm before thrusting the tip of my sword between another warrior's ribs to quiet his beating heart. Pulling my sword free in a spray of crimson I saw more of the enemy grouping before me.

"Ready to dance?" I asked, a wicked glint in my eyes.

Slashing horizontally, an arc of blue flame rushed forth to smash into the armour of the front most warriors. The metal melted instantly from the scorching heat to eat into skin, muscle, tissue and bone. The warriors screamed in horrific agony until the metal cooled enough to harden. Their bodies stiffening with the cooling metal until all they could do was rock in pain.

They became obstacles for the next lot of warriors to try their luck. As they clambered over their friends my sword danced to their dying screams, its hunger for blood insatiable as the body count soared.

From the wall came a battle cry and I glanced up to find Korr leaping from the battlements, that terrifying grin still etched into his features. He landed heavily on two of the enemy to break his fall and rose with a crimson, two-handed longsword cleanly severing the nearest man's head. The way he fought was like a scene from some of my darkest nightmares. He stood upon the necks of those he toppled, not giving an inch as they thrashed and fought for air. His feet came alight in bright orange flames to scorch and peel the skin while he took down one enemy after another with that massive sword. Two fresh cuts could be seen on his right shoulder, but they didn't disturb him at all.

"Look to fire. Korr take care of puppies," Korr said over his shoulder and I smiled. He was so sure of himself. There was so much confidence in his ability and yet it seemed right. Even in boasting or exaggerating, Korr knew who he was and spoke truth.

Turning, I was shocked to find a Chimera standing at the edge of the smoke. There was definitely characteristics of frogs and giraffes but the third... A salamander. The legendary creatures said to live in the depths of volcanoes. The flames did nothing to deter the creature and as it stood within the burning inferno, its chest and neck began to convulse as if it was going to throw up. Too late I realised its plan as a deluge of smoke began to spew out of its mouth to suffocate Shard's flames.

Firing off two ice shards, I took the creature in the head and throat, watching it drop silently but, alas, the damage had been done. A breach in the flames allowed for more warriors to spill in and as the portcullis was now fully up with the gates slowly opening, I placed myself between them ready to fight on two fronts. To my surprise it was Fitz and Kymberlin who emerged from the Keep and reinforced me.

I threw Fitz a friendly smile and nodded to Kymberlin, her face glowing after being healed. Hesitantly, she nodded back before we turned to face the enemy. They were moving slowly now, cautiously assessing us, waiting for a trigger when all hell would break loose once more. This came in the form of the Phoenix as Ash and Flint manifest fireballs and catapulted them into the ranks of enemy soldiers.

The three of us began cutting and slashing our way through the tide of soldiers, battling to get back to the breach in the flames. Steadily, inch by inch, metre by metre, we forced open a path and after 15 minutes were standing by the protective flames.

With a desperate use of force, I flung both my palms to the dirt and focused on ice. Great spires burst from the ground in every direction outside the fire. Many impaled the bodies of enemy soldiers as I crafted a 20-foot-high wall of ice stronger than any steel. The enemy would take a long time getting back to the gates after that. My knees gave out as Kymberlin killed the last of the warriors inside the safe zone with a deadly over hand swing, parting the flesh between neck and shoulder right down to their stomach.

Catching my head as it was about to hit the ground, Fitz gently positioned me so he could pick me up in his arms and carry me back to the Keep. Resting my head against his chest, I listened as horns sounded for the enemy's retreat. With a smile, I fell into a deep sleep.

My eyes fluttered open as light and sound started to filter in. There were no dreams to gauge the passing of time, but I felt rejuvenated and ready to fight again. I became aware of bodies moving around the room with a dark, fuzzy figure leaning over me.

"I can't believe she's still alive." That was definitely Kymberlin and I smiled.

"If you want something done right," I said to her and she scoffed.

"You're not worth the effort," Kymberlin replied.

"And, alas, this has been a common feeling so here I am." My sight adjusted and seeing her, I blanched. "Who would have thought a scar could help a person's looks."

Kymberlin's eyes narrowed and I could see a hint of humour playing across her cheeks. "Fuck off," she said, a small smile touching her lips.

Looking around, I noticed Enzo standing in the corner. I definitely wasn't ready to rip that band aid off yet. Then I focused on the man standing above me. Fitz had tears in his eyes, the emotions he showed for my life was touching.

"Enzo said that you made it out, but it's been so long. I began to doubt his words," Fitz said pulling me into a tight embrace. There was no pain in my muscles, either. I must have been asleep for a time.

"I had to die to be here before you. To be whole once more. To be more than the person you knew," I said and I could tell he didn't comprehend the significance in the words. I had no doubt he'd be thinking metaphorically.

"I saw Shard circling the keep. A blue flame Phoenix is rare indeed. Noone has witnessed one in thousands of years, Elara. But whatever the case may be, I'm just glad you survived. Were there... Others?"

I pursed my lips and looked away. This was answer enough for Fitz as I heard him take a shuddering breath.

"Caeli and Dustin died in each other's arms. They wanted nothing more."

Fitz nodded and hugged me again. "I'm happy for them."

"Where is she!" Came a familiar, heightened voice from the hallway. Baras paused at the door then raised a fist in triumph. "Elara!" he shouted as if he was standing back in the nesting grounds and I'd been chosen.

"Yes, yes. I made Phoenix Soul," I said blushing slightly. It wasn't often people would make such a big deal about me.

"I was watching from the walls. You were amazing, Elara. The way you held off the assault and your fighting ability. You've changed so much in the last 5 weeks you'd think you were a different person."

"There is some truth to that but let's say, rather, that I found myself out there in the woods."

"Well, I'm glad you did. The abilities you gained arrived just in time. There wasn't much fight left in this old Keep and now morale is soaring. Everyone is talking about how you single handedly held off the enemy outside the gates. This new you is incredible."

"It's nothing new. She has always been incredible," Enzo said from the corner and I turned on him, eyes deadly.

"I think Enzo and I need to have words," I said through gritted teeth.

"Anything we need to be aware of?" Fitz asked concerned. He placed himself on the edge of the path between me and Enzo.

"I'll catch you up later. For now, I'd like to speak to him in private," I said.

Fitz pursed his lips as he considered me. "Ok, Elara. We won't be far off."

As Kymberlin walked by, I caught her arm. "Leave me your gauntlet."

"Fuck off. Find your own gauntlets."

A shard of ice manifested right before her eye. With my grip holding her in place, the spike began to slowly move towards the soft, juicy eyeball, moments from popping it.

"What the fuck are you doing?" she squirmed trying to pull away. As she twisted her head from side to side the icicle followed. "Stop Elara...

138

Elara!"

"You have seconds at most. Your eye or the gauntlet. I will be taking one."

"The gauntlet. Take the fucking thing!" Kymberlin screamed as she wrenched the gauntlet from her hand and threw it at me before fleeing towards the door. The icicle dropped harmlessly to the floor already beginning to melt.

"Thanks, Kymberlin. I'll get it back to you shortly." Sliding out of bed, I slipped the gauntlet onto my right hand, flexing my fingers. It was such a nice fit.

"I see your powers have gotten more substantial, now. You never used to be able to levitate the..." Enzo said and I punched him with a hard right cleanly to the jaw. His head snapped sideways with the force and he seemed to freeze on the spot. What he said did have merit, but I learned to levitate my ice when I gained the ability to shift into spirit form. It was a mix of the two skills that had nothing to do with becoming a Phoenix Soul.

"I guess I deserved that," Enzo said as he spat blood and rubbed his jaw turning to look at me. Immediately, he was met with a second, straight right that took him between the eyes. A sickening crack sounded as his nose broke from the force, his head flinging back.

"Fuck, Elara. You're just as hard as you've always been." Bracing both sides of his nose with his hands, Enzo felt out the brake. It was along the same fault line he'd broken two times prior and with an awkward twist he forced the nose back into place. "If it weren't for me, you'd be dead by now. You'd be dead lifetimes ago."

"And I should thank you for that. I have died. Many times, and each time I have felt every agonizing moment. I have been ripped apart by wolves, had a mountain fall on me; that one lasting days of shallow, torturous breathing, drowned as I was dragged down in a ship, and tortured to death by those I held close. You forced this life on me. I said no and you forced it on me anyway, because, what? I had nice tits and a sweet arse?"

"I love you, Elara," Enzo said, his expression strained.

"Love? You covet me as if you own me. You treat me like an object as if I couldn't choose what was best for my life."

"You were dying, Elara. I couldn't stand there and let that happen."

"I chose in that moment to pass from this world. I know I was dying but I didn't want my last act to be taking the life of a Phoenix and stealing something so pure. For if I did that it wouldn't be me coming out the other side."

"Shard still lives. You've committed no crime of conscious. And you are alive, Elara. Can't you see? Everything worked out."

"I loved you, Enzo. I lived a long and happy life with you after you saved me from the cold. I was going to die happy, your face being the last thing I knew. But that's gone now. The girl you slept with in the forest was an echo of who I once was. Young and naïve with no knowledge of what I know now. You killed that girl. All there is is me."

"I know deep down you love me still," Enzo said.

I attacked again feinting with my right knowing he was going to be ready for it. As he blocked the swing, I rammed my left under his chin in a thunderous uppercut that almost lifted him from the floor. Enzo stumbled back, tripping on a stray bedpan and falling over. Rubbing his chin, he looked me in the eye.

"I will unfreeze that heart of yours and free your love for me once more, Elara. I don't care how long it takes. We are destined to be together."

I frowned shaking my head. Without saying anything more, I walked out. There was no point killing him at this time. His skills were needed for the fighting to come and he was an ally. Not to mention, he would just be reborn somewhere else. Maybe once everything settled down and the kingdom was safe again, I pondered. I admit the thought did fill me with warmth.

Outside, Fitz was leaning against the wall beside the doorframe. As I stormed past, he glanced inside and shrugged when he saw Enzo was at least breathing, if a little roughed up.

"Kymberlin?" I asked.

Fitz pointed down the hall and motioned out to the left. "You scared the poor girl pretty bad, you know."

I paused a moment raising an eyebrow.

"Most Souls do regrettable things on the trek to the nesting grounds. She may not regret taking your gear, but she has had a hard life and is actually a decent person. She has proven herself time and again on the field. Saved my life more than once," Fitz said and I laughed.

'I hold no ill will towards her. She is safe from me. I just wasn't in the mood to waste time arguing when I needed to thump Enzo."

"Yeah, I noticed that. What happened out there, Elara?" You may have scared me before as a maid. Now, I feel terrified under your gaze. There is a fierce storm raging within the depths of your soul. I cannot tell how it will manifest into the world."

"It would never manifest against friends," I replied.

Fitz's brow furrowed. "But you don't know Kymberlin."

"I've seen how much she loves this kingdom and the lengths she will go to to protect it. I wouldn't have healed her face if I held any ill will towards her."

Stumbling in his step, Fitz caught my shoulder. "Wait. That. That was you? How? Noone could explain it."

"I understand my spirit flights better. I can use my own energy to heal others. You all got a boost that day and the soldiers morale was influenced for the better."

Fitz was lost for words. I saw his jaw start moving but nothing came out. Rounding the corner, I saw Kymberlin sitting with her back against a wall, Baras comforting her. Seeing my approach, she made to flee, and I stopped, arms raised to show I meant no harm.

"I am sorry for my actions back there. I had been impatient and would have done the same to Baras or Fitz if they said no."

"But they wouldn't have said no. Why did you single me out?" There was fear in Kymberlin's eyes. "Was it because Ash chose me over Caeli or you?"

Closing my eyes I shook my head. "Everything that has been done is behind us. I hold no grudge."

"Then why?"

"I needed a gauntlet closer to my size. Using the others would have hurt me more than protected."

"That's it? That's the only reason?"

"As I said, I'm sorry." I knelt beside her and offered the gauntlet. "Sorry for the blood, also."

She was halfway reaching for the metal glove when she paused, her eyes landing on the blood smear.

"Is he?"

I shot her a disappointed smile. "He still lives but he does have a lot to answer for. It's the type of grudge that could transcend even death. You don't need to fear me, Kymberlin."

"It's hard not to right now."

"You once spoke of a conspiracy with the Phoenix. Is it to do with that?" Fitz asked cautiously. He didn't quite know if he wanted to open that unknown box. I could see in his eyes he wanted me to make the choice for him. Bring him into the circle only if it wouldn't destroy him.

I looked from Baras to Kymberlin to Fitz and smiled. "It has everything to do with the Phoenix, Enzo, and myself but nothing that will make you regret your choice to become a Phoenix Soul." Fitz's features physically relaxed. "It was just as he said, Enzo knew me and the Phoenix hated me for something they believed I did."

"How's that possible? I've known you since we were young." Baras said.

"Let's wait for Korr. We can use Baras's hut."

Baras shook his head. "There's a new captain. He has the hut now."

"That's rough. So where is safe to talk?"

"That's simple. We go to the tavern. Patrons are there to revel in life and are rather loud about it. They aren't looking to eavesdrop."

I considered such a simple option when a loud horn sounded from outside. I looked up.

"Shit. Here we go again. You can sit this one out if you need to, Elara. Two hours isn't much of a rest," Fitz said as the others stood.

"Only two hours...? No, I'm fine. We'll meet at the tavern later to speak of my return."

Everyone nodded and I turned for the courtyard entrance.

"Hey new girl. You may be psychotic but your rather dense. Your Phoenix is on the roof," Kymberlin said.

I smiled at her remark. It was a start. Kymberlin made the first move to close the gap and get past today's events. I raised a hand to rub the back of my neck.

"I forgot about Shard, actually." Following the others, I made my way to the rooftop where Shard waited with his kin. None acknowledged me as I vaulted onto Shard.

"Weak little human got some rest?" Shard asked with a whistle.

"Don't forget I can feel your energy lines too. You weren't far off tumbling to the earth yourself."

"That'll never happen," Shard squeaked then took to the sky.

I laughed and scratched Shard at the base of the neck under his feathers. A shiver ran over Shard's body.

"Stop that. We are heading into battle." Shard chided.

"When we win then," I said with a giggle.

Shard ignored me.

The smoke around the Keep didn't seem as thick now and I wondered if it was the Chimera I took out that was controlling it. There would need to be a number of them to keep up the haze. It was something I stored in the back of my mind to bring up in war council.

Scanning the battlements, I saw a number of the Phoenix already diving in to seal gaps in the defences when I spotted a lone fighter. Two ladders had been set against the walls of the Keep in the south, enemy soldiers spilling over it like water over a cliff. There was only one warrior stationed at that point and he was beginning to be overwhelmed. Wielding a lance, he danced and swayed through the enemy ranks dispatching them with sweeping blows or straight thrusts. And though he was soon to be encircled, allowing the enemy to break past and his certain death, there was no give in him. He continued to battle them as if it was a game. Unlike Korr's maniacal laughter, his was humorous, almost playful.

"There. We need to reinforce the wall there before that child welcomes the enemy into the Keep without a warning to his allies," I said to Shard, pointing at the warrior.

Shard chirp acknowledgement and banked towards the wall and flow of enemy.

"Do watch your landing this time. A little more rotation in the last and you would have snapped your ankle," Shard called.

I scoffed at the comment as Shard swooped over the battlement. There was a moment I was waiting for when all the inertia of the turn spun back in on itself and there was a split second of weightlessness. When it arrived, I vaulted from Shard's back to land within a metre of the lancer. I had to hand it to Shard. He took everything into account from the angle and time it would take for me to jump. All this time, technically bed ridden, hadn't dulled his skills.

As Shard swooped over the plains before the walls raining blue flame over the massing soldiers, I shot the warrior a dirty look to which he just tilted his head coyly. I keep him locked in a singular glare for his ineptitude, only breaking it to divide the first enemy to attack in halves with my sword. The moment behind me, I was impressed with the Lancer's skill. He followed my advance with a flurry of spins and sweeps of his lance. His movements were so fluid and in sync with his weapon, I began to doubt I was even needed on the wall and whether he was just playing with the enemy all this time.

Our weapons danced in unison, complimenting one another as the enemy fell around us. The space in which we stood continued to grow as we made our way back to the ladders and the breach in the wall. The skill this man wielded was incredible. Even just keeping up with me was impressive. At least, when not using magic. There were still depths he would never reach when facing me.

I paused in my forward momentum and laughed. He had me in such awe of his skills, I'd just imagined a fight between us.

With one final push, we were able to force the enemy back of the walls, restraining them to the ladders. With an arcing sweep of my arm, an ice wall was erected atop the existing wall. There wouldn't be any more of the enemy breaching this section of the Keep. I immediately turned on him ready to give him a mouthful.

He removed his helmet and my eyes widened, a soft pink hue touching my cheeks. Those grey, steely eyes held me entranced. The cool and easy expression on his face giving rise to a roguish charm screaming at me that he was trouble. There were locks of wavy hair just hiding his ears as his chin and cheeks held a two-day stubble that only helped his looks. He was lithe and agile but there was definitely sculpting to his muscles beneath the leather armour.

He leaned across with a finger outstretched and gently wiped the edge of my parted lips. I could feel the dampness there and immediately swung around, my face going bright red. I couldn't. I wouldn't. How could I embarrass myself so much in front of this man by drooling. He was maybe, what? 20 something? And I...

"Are you okay?" the man asked.

"I'm 317 years old," I yelled at him and ran off to hide under a rock.

"Okay, I'll hold the fort then," the man called after me.

Chapter 8

"Here ya go. A nice pint of ale to harden ya the fuck up," Kymberlin said placing the huge mug in front of me. A moth had gotten caught in the froth on the way to the table and a shooed it off to fight for what little life it had left.

"I can't believe I did that. Who just stands there gawking at a man and then runs away screaming when he shows you attention," I said, face in my palms.

"I don't know what's wrong with ya. When I see a guy I wanna rut with, he ain't gettin' away. By end of the night, I got him singing high praises. Drink. You'll feel better," Kymberlin said nudging the mug closer.

"Poor guys," I said. Lifting the mug to my lips, I took a swig and blanched, almost spitting it out onto the table. I felt the fluid burn down my neck as I swallowed. "That's not ale."

"Good girl. Most will spit it out first try. Least I know you can keep it down." Kymberlin was grinning like it was some sort of game.

"The fuck's in it?"

"Well of course there's ale. Ain't getting no froth without it. Bit of whiskey for the burn, and some of that clear stuff the pansies like with their fruit juice. The stuff made from potatoes."

"You mean vodka. No wonder it's got a kick." I took another swig, ready for the turmoil of alcohols on my system. "This is terrible."

"But it's got ya stoppin' ya whining over not getting laid."

"Who's not getting laid?" Fitz asked, taking my mug and sitting next to me. He took a swig and his eyes bulged as he sprayed the drink over the table. "Dammit, Kymberlin. I told you to warn me when you set your concoctions down on the table."

"This'ns hers." She said nodding to me then turned in her chair. "Barmaid, vodka with a widdle juice for our widdle man over her."

Fitz just glared as I laughed.

"Our girl here left some prime meat up on the battlements," Kymberlin continued.

Fitz swung on me with a curious grin, the topic not even worrying me anymore.

"Does this *meat* have a name?" Fitz asked.

"Nah she ran off screaming at a touch." Kymberlin laughed and I turned red once more. Maybe it was a little worrying.

"I see. Must have really had it in for that one. Enzo seemed…"

And I killed his line of comment with a deadly glare.

"Now, there's a man you need to tame. If only I could get my hooks into that one." Kymberlin said unaware of the building tension.

There was an anger swirling inside me. A deep ingrained scar that pulsed with pain and anguish. At the far back of my mind, I knew it wasn't Kymberlin's fault in any way. She was just there and poking at my sores.

"What happened to '*When I see a guy I wanna rut with, he ain't getting away.*' I said, sarcasm dripping from my words.

Kymberlin must have felt the well of anger behind the words and stood. "You think just because you rut with him once, he's yours. I have the nerve to go take him from you with that attitude."

"I would love to see you try," I said. Then took a number of great gulps from the mug of alcohol.

Fitz could see the argument building and noticing Korr and Baras walk in, motioned them over quickly. I slammed the mug on the table and without another care, made to attack Kymberlin. Baras caught me just in time, locking an arm under my elbow as I was mid swing. Korr jumped in front of Kymberlin who was now to riled up to let it go.

"Enough!" Fitz yelled at the two of us and we relaxed just enough to listen. "We came here to listen to a backstory of Elara's that involves Enzo. I can't say it holds any weight on the situation we are in now but I would bet all the whores I've yet to pay that bringing up that man's name is triggering you, Elara."

I pursed my lips knowing he was right but threw in enough stubborn not to admit it.

"Sit down. Tell your story. And you..." He turned on Kymberlin. "You're just triggered by aggression. There isn't a night we don't see you beating some guy senseless. Get your arse on that chair and listen to what's said. If each of you still want to work out some frustrations afterwards, take it outside and give the barkeep a break for once."

Belar, the barkeep, paused polishing his mug with dirty rag he carried long enough to give Fitz a thankful nod.

We each sat down tenderly watching the other to make sure they were doing the same. Baras and Korr relaxed a little, sitting beside their current ward.

"Okay, Elara. What has you so touchy?"

"It be that hunk of man meat she didn't gobble down on the wall."

"Kymberlin!" Fitz growled and I couldn't help myself. The laughter that exploded from me was liberating. Kymberlin didn't change one bit from moment to moment. After a second, she joined in the hysterics, our voices over powering the crowd.

146

The men just stared at us as if we'd lost our minds. In the time it took us to calm down, Baras and Korr were onto their second drink while Fitz was still nursing his first. He seemed worried somehow and I reached across to rest my hand on his as I wiped away a tear.

"Is something bothering you?" I asked.

He looked at me and his brow furrowed. "I just don't like things that are unknown in war. You were supposed to be dead. You disappeared for 5 weeks and then all of a sudden, you're back, more powerful than ever. You interact with others, argue and carry on, like it's nothing. You're a completely different person than you were when we left."

I tilted my head in question.

"Not that it's a terribly bad thing, mind you, but if there was a secret fountain of strength we missed or something that might turn the tides even more than you have, I'm all for it. That said, if there was some deep, dark secret surrounding the Phoenix that might come back and bite us in the arse later on, I'd like to know about that as well. I just want to know what happened." Fitz said. The whole time he was staring into his drink as if afraid to make eye contact.

"It's nothing like that Fitz. I'm just not quite the person you remember. Well, I am, but I've always been something more as well. I just didn't realise it."

"How can that be?" Baras said. "I've known you far longer than anyone at this table, all the way back to when we were kids. Unless there is some hidden training in the snowy ice caps of some faraway range with a race of bald, robe wearing, warriors, I don't buy it."

"There weren't any bald, robe wearing, warriors in my past..." I said raising an eyebrow at his imagination. "...But long before you and I met, I had been trained in a number of weapons and fighting techniques. One of my masters from your village, Korr. A Master Gamlin who trained students in an eccentric yet highly effective form of martial arts."

Korr scoffed, possibly for the first time ever. "Master Gamlin live 300 year ago."

"I know but I was 28 at the time so that made it only 289 years ago. His hair was snow blessed with age but no one was stupid enough to test themselves against him."

A hush came over the group. Everyone was waiting for the butt of the joke not quite seeing the relevance.

I smiled. I would have doubted such fantasies too had I not lived them. "Phoenix are marvellous creatures. No one knows just where they came from but, once, they lived in abundance until the humans of old began hunting them. They used to ground bone of a Phoenix to dust just to

147

start fires. The feathers of a Phoenix were used to heat their huts and caves through the long winters. In this age, the death of a Phoenix was eternal. It wasn't until they'd been hunted to a definite extinction, the six remaining Phoenix being all males, did they find a path to rebirth after death. They used part of the life essence of a human to be reborn, but not just any human. The Phoenix and the human needed to share a special bond."

"Our souls are to be consumed when we die? I didn't sign up for that." Baras said, suddenly sober.

"It's only a small amount. Enough to kick-start a beating heart after their bodies burn away and a new egg is formed from the ash. In time those they created bonds with were granted abilities and extended an invitation to soar through the skies with the Phoenix. Such was the closeness of the Phoenix and Souls.

"Over thousands of lives, the Phoenix experienced life in both male and female forms but found that at this point they had become infertile and could never procreate again. It was a sad realisation for the Phoenix and still a sore point today. Through all of human's written history there has been six Phoenix, and then five in the most recent years. As the humans learned different, faster and safer methods to craft fire, cook and be warm with, they began to worship the Phoenix almost like Gods. Constant, magical and mythical."

"Blah, blah, blah. Oh my god, the Phoenix are so amazing. Get to the good stuff," Kymberlin said making no move to stifle her yawn.

"Then shall I talk about myself?"

"No, that's even worse," Kymberlin droned.

"Well, drink up cos that's the only way you're getting through the next section." I looked around at the others and was greeted with focus and attention. "I was born to the Fibonacci clan of Three Pine Village. I am the last of their line and was there the day the village was raided and burned. I escaped and fled into the forest. Being too young to assimilate ice and snow..."

"You did what to the snow?" Baras asked trying to get his head around the bigger words.

"My family blood line can manipulate ice. You have seen me use it at times. That doesn't come from the Phoenix. Though Shard can manipulate ice, he got that from me and the innate ability now locked in my soul. I'd been too young to use ice magic to stop myself from freezing back then. It was only by luck that a child about my age had been wandering through the woods. Said he was in training to be a Phoenix Soul. He wore only shorts as the cold didn't touch him."

"He BrongTa?" Korr asked suddenly, his whole body shifting as if waking up. Made me question just how much everyone was really listening.

"He was BrongTa. He was also Enzo," I said. Korr seemed shocked beyond words as he tried to process the information.

"You said this was happening 300 hundred years ago. How can Enzo be there?" Fitz asked.

"He did say he knew me as a child. And I did get a memory of a child helping me after my parents died. This was Enzo and the memory was from another age."

"So, what are you then? Some kind of Goddess amongst humans? I ain't worshipping you, that's for sure," Kymberlin said.

"Maybe after a few more drinks you'll be on your knees," I smirked.

"For Baras maybe. Ain't getting your sloppy pocket anywhere near my lips," Kymberlin retorted and I laughed.

Baras just cleared his throat. "Ladies, if you please," he said. I could see Kymberlin's comment had clearly gone to his head.

"I am human, much like yourselves. I spent a lifetime beside Enzo, training and fucking. It was a beautiful and fulfilling life and I was a fool. In time Enzo became a Phoenix Soul once more."

"Will I regret asking about the 'once more' comment?" Fitz asked.

"I was unaware that Enzo had been a Phoenix Soul in two previous lives. He found a Phoenix willing to accept a deal and craft a different style of pact. One where both Phoenix and Soul are resurrected."

"Could we all make such a pact?" Baras asked.

"If the Phoenix accepted than yes, but let me warn you. The Soul used to kick start two hearts is that of the Phoenix Soul. Slowly, their soul is worn away until there is only enough left to resurrect the Phoenix. After a long, long life, you will cease to exist even on the spiritual plane."

"Maybe that's not the pact for me then," Baras said, hiding behind his ale.

Enzo had already formed an alliance with Talon and when he met me, he slowly twisted my mind to believe it was what I wanted as well. I could spend an eternity with my love and even death couldn't keep us apart. It was Shard that we tried with back when he was of the orange flame. It was Shard that said no. For one: He still had a Soul bonded to him and for two: he didn't want to be stuck with the same Soul across every lifetime. Where was the wonder in that? Where was the growth? He told us what Talon did was a mistake and no other Phoenix would extend the same offer. Enzo raged for days after that. He spoke with Talon at length but Talon wouldn't help him. And then suddenly without warning, Shard's Soul died."

"You mean?" Baras left the question hanging.

"It was a long time before I found out what Enzo had done. How he helped pave the way to my resurrection. He continued pushing me, manipulating me, twisting my mind and bending my will to hate the Phoenix and formulated a plan to steal the resurrection ability form Shard so that we could live for eternity together. And me being so completely in love and blinded to his games, I went along with it.

"When the fateful day arrived, Enzo spurred me on to enter the nesting grounds. The large dome like area where we were chosen is only open to Souls at a special time of the Phoenix choosing. This time was definitely not it and I was not a Soul. On this day, Shard was alone in the nesting grounds. He was furious when he saw me. Anyone else would have been dead but he gave me a chance. Tried to have me leave, Enzo was arguing my case as I couldn't understand Shard but when that failed, I locked Shard in a cell of solid ice. It subdued him and as I was about to steal the very essence of his former Phoenix Soul, the droplet of a soul that would give me new life, I looked into Shard's eyes. I had never truly looked at the eyes of something so pure, something so majestic and bewildering, that I immediately regretted my actions. I told Enzo 'No' for the first time in my life and his face grew hard. Shard had, by now, passed out and did not see that it was Enzo who stole his only link to a new life. At this point Shard was mortal and dying. Enzo had force fed me the Soul essence and from that time on when I died, I was resurrected into a new womb."

"It explains why they were so angry?" Fitz said.

"Not quite. Enzo spun the story that it was I who stole the Soul Essence from Shard. They hunted me as I hunted Enzo across my lives. I was lucky enough to be born into a Drifter bloodline gaining the skills to transition into my spirit form. It was only this life when my soul was beginning to wear thin that the effects of so many lives began to show. I couldn't remember my previous lives anymore and thus would get echoes from time to time of all the past lives. I had believed they were dreams or events from my childhood but it was true that I lived them all."

"How did it come to pass, then, that you are a Phoenix Soul with full memory of your lives?" Baras asked. He finally hit a fairly intelligent question.

"When Enzo saw me that night outside our camp, it was like I was young and naïve once more, getting swept up by a hot and rugged guy."

"Yeah, he is," Kymberlin said.

"Enzo believed I had forgiven him not realising the mind degradation that had occurred. I escaped the nesting grounds and found my way to Shard who had been kept alive by the energy of all the other Phoenix."

"The Lich?" Fitz said.

"Yes. It was Shard all along and he wasn't stealing the energy. He was being fed by the others. They were trying to get me back to Shard to return that which *I* stole. I gave it willingly. I had nothing more to live for after seeing my friends leave me or die in the woods. And it was not in this life's nature to keep something of someone else's from them. Shard used it to resurrect himself but not before Enzo talked him into allowing me one more life. The war and need of a fast Soul was what convinced Shard and they put my body on ice. When I woke, I was worse than before with minutes to live, minutes to make a choice of Phoenix Soul or death. I chose to become a Phoenix Soul and Shard healed me, opening the pathways in my mind, allowing me to remember the revenge I had been living so long to take. Shard had also closed off the pathways to future resurrections which I am grateful for."

"So, what are we bloody well waiting for? Let's go kill Enzo." Kymberlin had already slammed her mug down and was rising from her seat. I waved her back.

"Sit, Kymmie," I said.

"Excuse me? What the fuck ya call me?" Kymberlin turned on me, a fire igniting in her heart.

"Just getting your attention. To kill Enzo now would just see him resurrect again somewhere else. It'll be years before you can track him again. The Phoenix don't know either and I want it to stay that way. There will come a time when I take my final revenge but now isn't that time."

An arm fell gently upon my shoulders and I looked across to see the warrior from earlier holding me. With a tingle like lightning running through me, my heart fluttered uncontrollably. The slanderous words I was about to use on whoever felt the need to touch me, catching in my throat.

"What are we all talking about?" The man asked shifting around the table to face me.

Kymberlin looked from the man to me and back again, her eyes glistening with mischief. She mouthed the words 'man meat' to me and I shook my head in terror mouthing back 'don't'. Kymberlin turned on the man.

"Man meat!" she shouted excitedly.

"Man meat?" he said, taken aback. "I prefer Riven." His attention shifted back to Elara. "I saw you across the bar and just wanted to thank you for your help earlier. You took off before I had the chance."

I looked downwards unable to make eye contact. "Yaww... You're welcome." My voice was so soft and mouse like, it was embarrassing though I had no control over the soundings. It was like my whole brain wanted to shut down. After a moment of silence waiting for a reply, I looked up to see if he was still there. I rocked back finding him leaning across the table, face right in front of me.

"Sorry I didn't quite catch that. Little louder if you could," Riven said, tilting his head and tapping his ear a couple of times.

"She said, she wants to get naked and rut on the wall where you met to celebrate such a momentous victory," Kymberlin said in an easy tone as if rattling off a grocery list.

"All that from a little squeak. Your friend must either have very good hearing or you two have cracked the language of mice," Riven said to me, ignoring Kymberlin completely. His arm grazed past me as he reached for something on the top of my chair.

A shiver spread out across my shoulder and down my side leaving goosebumps in its wake. After a moment he pulled back a large metallic object that had been balancing behind me and as he brought it to his head, I realised it was his helm.

With a grin, Riven placed the helmet atop his head, covering his face. Only his grey, steel eyes broke through, their allure powerful. "Is this better? The last time I took it off you started screaming about being 317 years old. A rather specific number."

I blushed.

"You told him before us," Baras said surprised.

"No." I swung, shaking my head.

"You said it was about 300 years. We didn't even get an exact number. His information seems to be more accurate," Fitz said with a cheeky grin.

"I didn't tell him... Did I?"

"Should I come back?" Riven asked.

"No. Sit. Drink. Have merry," Korr told him, gesturing to a nearby chair and placing one of Kymberlin's specials in front of him.

As Riven sat he made to remove his helmet but Fitz caught his arm. "Best keep that on a little longer unless you want our princess here to become completely mute."

"Hey," I whined and everyone started laughing. Even Korr grinned. It was only Riven who remained calm, his eyes focused on mine ensnaring me. I finally had enough wits about me to realise it couldn't get more embarrassing and I found my courage to speak at least.

"Why were you fighting alone on the wall?" I asked.

"I was positioned there. Hadn't been in the Keep long and was untested by the hierarchy. I guess they thought the position wouldn't see much fighting."

I scoffed. "You were all that there was holding back the tide that flowed over the wall. That was a terrible blunder. Can't they see everywhere is a threat in war."

"There was another lad. Boy of about 14. He took off when the first ladder touched stone. You never looked over the side of the wall, did you?" Riven asked and I just looked stunned.

"Why would I? Two ladders came up over the edge. There is a significant risk."

"If you had of looked, you would have found a large gaping hole where the latrines that had been dug decades ago hit a natural pocket of emptiness. When the lands started to fall in, they were worried they would lose the wall all together. It was only luck that sees them still standing."

"Were you based on Dagger's Wall," Baras asked considering the kid. "By the sounds of things, you have enough skill to keep from being positioned there, though I'm glad you had been. We haven't had anyone even try to cross that crevice. So that means you're not from around here. From where do you hail?"

"Geopti down in the Sou-West. It was mostly left alone until about 3 weeks ago. Since then, I've been slowly navigating the smoke on my way to the Keep. The sudden lull in the veil of smoke allowed me to find the Keep. It was like the smoke vanished from one sector and all that stood before me was the Keep shining like a beacon of hope."

"Geopti...? I wouldn't exactly list it as a Telverian town but some of the outlying houses have a little cross over. Some of the best beef though. Probably why Telveria likes to claim you. Personally, it was the view from Mount Brueshair that did it for me. Very few people have stopped to watch the shimmer of a golden sunrise on an ocean, thousands of miles away. It was breathtaking." I realised I was staring off into that distant memory and refocused my eyes on Riven. He had his head cocked as if assessing me.

"What?" I asked blushing under his gaze once more.

"You're rather well travelled for a maid," he said. "And talented. Even some of our best climbers have trouble on those cliffs and that's without climbing before sunrise. But I know the beauty of which you speak."

My eyes narrowed on him. "You're well informed for an outsider. Been

153

researching me?"

"As I said, I wanted to thank you. Was it wrong of me to ask around?" He gave a shrug.

I smiled. "Not so much," I said and lent over, the tips of my fingers pulling at the edge of his helmet. A hand came up and caught me.

"A warning. Many a fair maiden has uncovered the horrors of what's waiting below, their tongues turning to stone even as they shrieked in disgust."

"Oh shush, I was just unprepared for such horror the last times. I'm over it now," I said and pulled the helmet up. Nope. Nope. Nope. Nope. Nope. I immediately slammed it down again not quite as ready as I thought. After taking in great gulps of air, I slowly pulled it up once more. "There, see? Completely immune."

Riven just lowered me a glare as he rubbed his head. "Glad to hear," he grumbled.

"I know right, now we can talk. Where did you get that mark on your head? Looks nasty."

"Just some whimsy girl who thinks too much of herself. Had trouble holding up some equipment." He laughed to himself.

I glowered at him. "Would you like another one?"

"I think ones enough though I get the feeling if I hang around you there'll be plenty more."

"Plenty more," I said with a smile. I found my eyes focusing on his lips as I spoke, my mind running to places they shouldn't be going. The more I tried to keep images of this man... naked... his head between my legs while I sat upon the battlement of Dagger's Wall... out of my mind, the more intense they became. Head between my legs... hand between my legs, mouth upon my breasts... cock between my legs, my arms supporting my body on the wall as it hung over the chasm below.

"Elara?... Elara!" Riven's voice rose.

"Yes. Me. I'm Elara," I said without thinking. Looking around my face paled as I found my friends had left me alone at the table with Riven. I couldn't even say when it was they left.

"You're rather odd, aren't you?" Riven said then with a chuckle. Care to take a walk with me? I have a craving for some fresh air." Standing, he offered me a hand.

Hesitantly, I took it but it wasn't a deep warmth I was met with. The hands were cool to touch. Not a clammy, irksome cold that riled the skin and turned back one's attention. It was crisp and refreshing like a winter morning. The sun glistening through the frost covered leaves, your every breath turning to little puffs of smoke. It was vibrant and alive and spoke

154

to my very soul. As a Fibonacci, the cool sensation flowed into me, relaxing me. I finally felt like I was seeing straight.

"Your hands," I said standing beside him. He made to pull away but I held tighter.

His eyes narrowed. "Most would say too cold, but you don't seem to retract."

"They're a perfect temperature. I wish to relish in this feeling a little longer."

"Relish away," he said as his hand relaxed in mine.

Leading me out into the dark streets, I got a sense of where I'd felt a cold such as his. As winter was beginning, the nights held a chill. It was such a wonderful feeling as the freezing breath of life washed over me.

"Such a beautiful night." I shifted closer, my fingers intertwining into his. There was a tingling in my chest as if a million fireflies were skittering around setting my soul alight. I don't know just what it was that called out to me, that made me feel so weak at the knees, but this hand, this person, was so comfortable to behold.

"It's a pity the stars are being smothered by the smoke. With the Keep this dark, they would have been amazing," Riven said. He hadn't reacted to the more intimate touch but rather flowed into it. His thumb slowly grazing up and down the spot between my thumb and forefinger.

"It makes the small glimpses into space we do get all the more special. Their vulnerable and fragile existence enhancing even the smallest shimmer of light. Their life fading into moments with the turning of the world."

"You like to speak of philosophy. There are so many facets to you, Elara. In just this small moment I've shared with you, I have come to see the many ways you shine. How many more am I going to get to see before you and I fade?"

My heart fluttered like the brilliant fireflies within me and I bit my lip as I gazed into his steely, grey eyes. Warmth, passion, lust. The feelings swirled around me and I couldn't hold back in that moment. Pulling him close, I leaned in to steal a kiss and closed my eyes. The cool, crisp shiver as our lips met was invigorating and in the same moment the heat of it was overwhelming. As the moment ended, I was left giddy and coy, feeling both embarrassed and scandalous all at once. Many times, across many lives, I'd laid with men, felt their strength and my passion soaring but this was the first time I'd been so moved. And by so little. It just felt right. Even Enzo never made me feel such feelings. I opened my eyes to spy the man who held my heart and soul so delicately.

Riven had been smiling as if waiting for me to come back to the world.

155

Taking a step back and dropping my hand, he overemphasised a shy and embarrassed persona.

"I'm 478 years old," Riven said with a squeal before he shot off down the road.

Too shocked to move at first, my eyes finally caught up with him halfway down the street.

That bastard, I thought recognising the moment he was referring to. A small flame burning inside me for his light teasing. "Hey, old man," I called after him and he swung back with a cheeky grin. "I was gunna take you to the walls where we first met and have my way with you. Guess you miss out now."

"With the way you fight, there will be plenty more time for stolen kisses and heated tussles but when I give you myself for the first time, I want you out in a field with the light of all the stars in the heavens as witness to the merging of our souls."

A breath caught in my throat for this man actually trying his hand at romance. "You're not like any guy I have ever known."

"I am man enough to know I need to cool off right about now."

I bit the edge of my lower lip, my eyes taking on an air of seduction. "There is this wall I know."

"Tch," he chided me. "I will see you on the morrow. I look forward to initiating the kiss this time."

"You better," I called after him as he continued off into an alley.

Leaning against a wall, my heart was pounding as if it was about to burst from my chest. My knees quivered and I slide to the hard cobblestone street. Distractions in a time of war? I heard my mind question. The implications and risks involved made me terribly vulnerable.

War in a time of distractions, I heard my heart counter and knew in that moment I would never be free of Riven again. I would never want to.

The youngest persona that was Elara never dreamed in her wildest imaginations she'd be stepping through the large iron doors of the Keep's war room. There was never a circumstance that could arise to give need for it.

In actual fact, I had stepped through these doors on three occasions across my numerous lives. Twice to provide intelligence in exchange for the location of Enzo TalonSoul. Once under the cover of night to steal intelligence of a peaceful cult travelling across Telverian lands. A simple act to help the sun worshippers who saved me when I'd been poisoned.

Stepping into the room, it was no surprise it hadn't changed. There were some extra chairs placed around the table to accommodate the Phoenix Souls and there was a new face to fill the Commanders roll Jermaine left vacant. She had a look of steel and was perfectly formed. She filled the full armour as well as any man could. Her eyes rolled over me, assessing me with brow furrowed before moving on. There were no lingering looks to portray her judgement. She got what she needed and that was that.

I smiled, warming to the woman instantly for her dismissal of me. Sure, most of this life, I was weak and humbled with asthma but it wasn't strength I needed to be formidable. This body was almost perfect in how flexible and agile it could be. That was all I needed to make nations crumble.

Scanning the room, I found Walan standing beside his chair at the back edge of the room. He was shaking his head as our eyes met.

"And to think you could barely parry a dagger when I named you, Elara. Look how far you've come."

"It's great to see you again, Walan," I said and embraced the man. "Thank you, for believing in me."

"There was a spark of the unknown hiding within the depths of your soul. Truth be told you were a wild card and your soft nature and shy manner worried me. I hoped more than believed." He motioned to a chair beside him and I sat.

"Whatever it was, you had done more than kill me that day. You gave motion to my rebirth. And in doing so I was able to make right something that had long weighed on my soul. Thank you, Walan."

"You should do more than simply thank the man. He single-handedly convinced the council to allow such an inappropriate and downright insulting candidate to be allowed the trials," General Suniel said from his seat at the head of the table. "I for one didn't want to throw the life of a perfectly good maid away on a whim. But to see you come back a Phoenix Soul riding the mythical 6th Phoenix. I couldn't believe it. And blue flames at that. You are without a doubt the most powerful Phoenix Soul to grace these halls in millennia."

I looked at Enzo for the first time this morning. He was leaning against the wall by the door seemingly not paying attention. As my eyes fell on him, he grunted, looking anywhere but at me and I smiled. That comment got to him.

"Hadn't you heard, the blue flamed Phoenix are for Mage candidates," I said turning back to Suniel. The General's eyes bulged. Maybe now they might give a little thought to the potential of Mage candidates.

"Either way, Shard and I have centuries of history we needed to sort out."

Suniel raised a questioning eyebrow at my comment but it was the new Commander who spoke.

"Pipe down girl. Phoenix Soul or not, I will not allow you to make a mockery of our council. Hold your tongue."

I smiled, eyes locked to hers. "Yes, Commander. Council can proceed without my mockery now."

She glowered at me, eyes full of disdain before slowly turning back to the council. A woman that sought to keep only the powerful and the mighty around her. Intelligence was for the weak and the dead.

Walan leaned in as General Suniel began to debrief the war efforts since the last meeting. "Mockery?" he asked. There was an intrigue within his words. Definitely a sharp one.

I shook my head. "A spark of the unknown," I replied simply and he grinned reading the depths to my answer.

"...Riven of Geopti to speak," General Suniel said and my eyes shot up to the door.

With a creak, a burst of natural light entered through the large iron doors and there he stood. My heart by now was a mess, stuttering as that goofy grin and steely grey eyes landed on me. The grin deepened before he circled the room to the head of the table, my eyes never once leaving him.

"General, Commanders, Phoenix Souls." Riven greeted then looked at me. "300-year-old maids playing at war."

My eyes narrowed and I mouthed the words *'Fuck off'* much to his delight. Glancing at the female commander, it looked as though she was about to have a meltdown. Her face was deep crimson and set in a stern look as discipline made her bite her tongue.

"There is little I could report that may be worthwhile. Geopti as a whole was largely untouched when the enemy came through. They seek the end of Telveria for reasons unknown and the border towns had only been raided for goods without resorting to death. Taxes for the new and rising power they called it. In my heart I was Telverian and day by day watching the land I love become engulfed in flame and smoke. Well, it broke my heart, it did. Taking up my lance, I decided that if Telveria was to die then all of it would die as one. That was when I made the trek across country to the Keep."

I rolled my eyes as he upsold himself. Riven still had a few of the more ridiculous qualities men seemed to share.

"There were pockets of the enemy all over but the smoke helped to hide my scent as it did to hinder them from view. If you remained quiet and listened for the footfalls of groups of soldiers you could bypass them rather easily. One thing I noticed however after piecing some stories together was the whole trek, not once was there a break in the smoke screen. Not once until the Phoenix Maid took down one of the smoke spewing Chimera."

Everyone turned to look at me but I kept my eyes on Riven. The look he got told him to expect trouble later and he was looking like he revelled in my reactions. Enzo couldn't help but notice the interactions between us and a cold, dark jealousy grew within him.

"I'm sure even Commander Lianha can see the smoke screen has been crafted by the Chimera," Riven continued and the female commander nodded. She was too dense to realise he was having a quip at her, singling her out like that and I smiled. "If we could locate and kill the Chimera creating it our view of the world will grow substantially. We could safely navigate the fields, even at night under the stars."

I caught his double meaning and my cheeks burned furiously much to his amusement. He continued with a quirky grin.

"I would guess the enemy can't just recreate them easily either or we would be overrun with horrid creatures by now."

"Agreed," Baras said sitting close to the front. "Did you get any indication of the enemy's human numbers?"

"Without seeing more than 50 metres at most I couldn't say," Riven spread his arms. "Though I will say one thing. There isn't as many out in the field as they would have you believe."

"Why do you say that?" It was Commander Scrause who commented. This man looked almost as old as the Keep itself with grey hair and beard. His experience was invaluable in many war efforts, and he was a prominent figure in the Keep for speeches and the like. Though he looked as old as the wind, he still kept himself fit and strong. Many soldiers manning the walls would have trouble keeping up with him.

"Just a feeling. If there was an army out there, I should have had more difficulty reaching the Keep. At times it felt like groups came out of nowhere to land within throwing distance. I just don't believe they are out there."

"We can't plan off of what ifs and maybes, Riven," Suniel said. "They attack with such numbers and consistency that it proves they are out there."

"Sir, I just don't think..." Riven said.

"Good," Suniel cut in. "Leave the thinking to the Commanders. You're a fighter. Your place is on the wall."

"General," Riven saluted but I could tell he was holding back, what? Contempt? Quiet rebellion? I couldn't blame him. The disdain he got from the General was thick in the air. I shook my head. Given another 15 years of peace and another up and coming would have taken Suniel's place and the whole Keep would have been turned upside down with how things were done. Unless it was Lianha. She would have been a perfect match to Suniel.

"So how do we tackle this new problem?" I asked and Suniel's eyes narrowed on me. "Let's say the fields are full of the enemy. Their lungs struggling to sift through the smoke for the oxygen, their eyes stinging and watery. We need to see. I believe the Chimera are our best bet."

"Your position does not afford you a voice in this council, *Phoenix Soul*," Suniel replied, his voice filled with as much disdain as he had for Riven. It was already clear they didn't believe I held any worth in this room. I was a maid after all and to them, I never once considered war tactics. The other commanders all had a similar look on their faces and a hand came to rest on mine at my side. I turned to look at Walan expecting a similar look. He, though, just rolled his eyes and nodded. He couldn't say it out loud but I knew the man had my back.

My friends as well. Baras was fuming in his seat, knuckles white. It was his strong discipline holding him back. Fitz was in quiet contemplation, lips pursed, his eyes on me. Korr was slowly rolling a ball of flame back and forward across the table top, the first time he'd brought flames out at the meeting. I liked to think he was considering who to throw it at first. And then I turned on Kymberlin. She was smiling openly at me taking pleasure in my reprimand. I smiled back knowing that was her friendship language. She had trouble showing it any other way. I glanced at Enzo but he wasn't showing any emotion either way. He knew my history and my strengths. He understood I was a big girl and could take care of myself.

I turned back to Suniel and cocked my head. "What is my purpose in this council, *General?*" I asked giving as much disdain back as was provided and smiled as the General's face went beet red.

"You are an asset to the defence of the kingdom. You go where we tell you to go. Fight who we tell you to fight. Your position grants you a sit in on the council so that you are better equipped for the front lines."

"And what if a Phoenix Soul chooses the kingdom over the General and his assets?"

"This is treason," Lianha growled.

"No, you dung brained sow, this is questioning my position so that I may better serve the Kingdom. I was only asking that if Telveria is in its

160

death throws and a new power was about to control the Kingdom, who do I defend?"

A chair was thrown back across the room as Lianha rose to her feet slamming a fist on the table. "How dare you speak to me that way."

"How do you want me to speak to you? In your natural tongue? Der derpity derpity der. Is that better? Did you get the dung brained sow part this time?"

The rage was palpable as I could visible see Lianha shaking. Her face had drained of all colour now and I knew she was about to make a mistake. At least it was about to become a little quieter.

As Lianha stalked around the table I looked to Kymberlin and tilted my head in a plea.

"Ha," Kymberlin laughed and tossed her gauntlet across. "You need to get your own."

Slipping the gauntlet on, I looked up in time to see the silver trail of a knife thrusting towards the underside of my chin. I scoffed and with all the time in the world, side stepped, delivering a thunderous right to Lianha's Jaw. The eyes rolled back in her head and she dropped silently to the floor.

"Sorry, *General,* I tripped into your commander. She definitely didn't make the mistake of attacking a Phoenix Soul or anything stupid like that."

Suniel just glared at me and I turned back to Walan.

"That was Jermaine's move. Does everyone in that position like that move?"

"Apparently," He replied. He seemed in shock watching me easily take down a commander and acting so calm about it.

"So, back to my question, Suniel. Does a Phoenix Soul fight for the Kingdom or the people currently residing in it?" I asked innocently.

He glared at me and when he spoke his words were low with a hard edge to them. "The people are the Kingdom. Even should the lowest beggar still live then so too does the Kingdom. That is who you fight for. Who we all fight for."

"Good response. I'll take my leave now. Come, Riven," I said gesturing for the man standing by, awkward and forgotten. Happily, he made to move but Suniel stopped him.

"We aren't finished with him, yet. Or you for that matter. You will remain until the council has finished," He commanded like I was some maid girl to fall in line.

"You forget yourself, *General.* A Phoenix Soul may take anything they wish at any moment. That is their right. None have the right to

161

command me. I am taking my leave and I am taking the old man." My eyes remained locked to Suniel's threatening him to argue. The General returned the look long enough to save a small amount of pride before turning away to address the rest of the council.

Flicking my head, I motioned for Riven to follow. There was a bounce in his step as we made for the door. Pausing in my stride I turned back to Kymberlin and slipped the gauntlet off.

"Sorry about the blood," I said tossing it back to her.

She scoffed. "I really don't believe you are."

"No, not really," I shrugged and continued out the door, Riven close behind.

"That's one," Riven said holding up his forefinger.

"Hmm?" I asked.

"A new way to see you shine," he said with a cheeky grin.

I returned the smile. "I thought you were showing me how high you could count. It was a very good try by the way. So smart."

Riven laughed long and loud.

"Elara!" Enzo's voice cut through the fun. "What are you doing? If you piss of the hierarchy they will make it harder for you."

He walked up to me, completely cutting off Riven in the process. So, it was jealousy then.

"Let 'em be pissed. You of all people understand the way this world works. You know there is no worth in drowning in politics. Or are you happy throwing away the lives you have to be a lap dog?"

"I'm no one's lap dog!" he yelled spitting at the last. The reaction was a little over the top, even for Enzo, but he was trying to act tougher than the real man behind him that he tried to eclipse.

"No? Just addicted to that which the Phoenix has allowed you and too scared to lose it so blindly follow."

"What is your problem, Elara? The world isn't against you. I am not against you."

"You forced me into a life I never wanted. I thought I loved you. I was ready to die with that love being the only love I knew. But your addiction for life and your fucking greed almost killed Shard."

Enzo leaped forward covering my mouth with his hand. "Shh. We don't want our friends on the roof to hear this conversation." He suddenly stopped and glanced downwards at the sharp edge of steel. "You will remove the blade from my throat or I will kill you, grunt."

I hadn't even seen Riven's lance in the war council yet her it was, held to Enzo's neck. Or half of it, I thought, looking closer. In his right was the bladed end and in his left was the other half as if it could be pulled down into two.

"You're welcome to try," Riven said and my eyes grew wide as I shook my head 'no' trying to warn him off.

I felt Enzo's hand drop away to his side. "Don't do this, Enzo," I said, then to Riven. "Get out of here. He is far more dangerous than he seems."

"The firebug needs to learn some manners. It isn't right to treat a woman that way." Instantly, Riven bounced backwards as a blade slashed through the air where he stood moments before.

Enzo fell into a flurry of stabs and slashes I knew all too well. He was going to kill the one person I was beginning to fall for and I taught him the combination of moves. It was almost unbeatable, especially for someone with only years of experience and not centuries.

I couldn't turn away or hide my eyes. It was bittersweet but every stroke of Enzo's large curved dagger could be Riven's last moment. The last I would see him breathing, moving, living. I couldn't give it up, yet with every stroke, Riven swayed, and dodged, and blocked Enzo's attack, living life a hair's breadth from death. My mind tried to persuade my heart but hope began to grow. To grow knowing how futile it was.

There was one moment in the assault when Riven could turn the tables. One weakness I wove into the tapestry of the combo. A weak opponent would never make it so far but a strong opponent... he would either take the moment or die in the onslaught that was about to proceed. If he took it though he would die sooner. When the strong opponent took the moment thinking they could turn the tides, I would turn it straight back and kill them instantly. Enzo knew this too.

I almost counted down the strokes until the moment arrived. Watching intently, I traced every movement of Enzo as speed slowed to milliseconds lasting minutes. The quick slash to the left and a curving cut back up and right. Enzo's guard opened completely with his sword arm twisted awkwardly.

The moment had arrived and I was frozen to the spot as Riven reacted instantly swinging his spear like a sword intent not to kill but to knock him out.

"No," I squeaked as Enzo's wicked smile filled my vision.

Dropping his blade, he flicked his wrist to catch the handle in a reverse grip and swung to knock Riven's spear away. This in turn would send Riven off balance with the tip of the blade in prime position to thrust straight through Riven's neck.

A part of me clicked and I found I could move once more. Leaping forward I knew it was too late. The weapons connected and my brow furrowed as the distance was still too far. There must have been a discrepancy in the angle or my eyes didn't focus right but as the sound of weapons clashing should have resounded around the space, there was only silence. Enzo's blade phased through the shaft of the lance as it continued to smash into the now off balanced Enzo. Enzo's head snapped back and I saw his eyes roll into the back of his head as he fell to the floor. Skidding to a halt, my body was in shock over the outcome.

"What...? What just happened?" I stammered trying to make sense of the scene.

Riven shrugged. "There was a fight. Men were being macho, fighting over a girl. One ended up unconscious."

I shook my head, my eyes closed. Slowly, I turned back to Riven. "His weapon. He was about to block you but the curved dagger just slipped through your lance."

"Oh," Riven laughed. "It was a fluke really. I noticed too late the predicament I was in and I hesitated a fraction of a moment. I think it saved me as the lance shaft struck right at the point it could slide around the curve of Enzo's blade."

Replaying the memory over and over in my mind, it shifted and remade itself until I saw the whole scene perfectly. "That actually makes more sense than I'd believed."

"Oh?" Riven asked.

"Nothing. It's more embarrassing to speak of it now. Let's go see what we can do about dispersing that smoke. Come with me to the roof."

"Lead the way," Riven said, stepping over the unconscious Enzo.

I could feel his eyes on my arse as it swayed up the stairs.

Chapter 9

The other Phoenix were all hissing and cussing at me as I spoke to Shard, but I ignored it. Their words meant nothing when I knew the truth of my past. I held no ill will towards them for Enzo's manipulation.

"I will not carry him," Shard said with a squawk.

"It's only a small distance and you're strong. I don't doubt you could carry five times... No, ten times the weight of Riven and I combined," I replied playing on his ego if one did exist.

"By the time we finish arguing he would have made it beyond the wall on foot." Shard ignored my comments. He seemed rather adamant he wouldn't give Riven a lift beyond the walls, a steel will pulsing from his eyes. Stubbornness I say.

"Yet he hasn't left yet and now we are still in the same position as when I arrived. Why do you need to be so stubborn?"

I found it amusing watching Riven standing awkwardly hearing a one-sided conversation. I could see he was trying to decide if I was all there upstairs.

"If I may?" Riven stepped forward and Shard let out an ear-piercing whistle.

"Tell the boy if he doesn't step back, I'll be feasting on his eyes," Shard said, a menacing glare levelled on Riven.

I waved Riven back. "Best not be getting too close. I don't think he likes you."

"The eyes," Shard reiterated and I smiled.

"Step back little boy, or Shard, here, will be feasting upon your eyes," I said, the smile still on my face.

Riven's eyes widened a moment, and he bowed his head to Shard as he took a step back.

"Happy?" I asked.

"The harmony a Phoenix and their Soul produce in flight cannot be recreated with another. It is like we are connected intimately, more than any mere rider could produce. I know you've felt it, floating as if on a cloud in the slipstream. Only you could feel that way. Only you could be so light upon me. I may discard him before we ever reach the walls. I am not built to carry humans." He paused taking in a deep, relenting breath and sighed. A sound so oddly wrong coming from a bird. "I will carry him in my Talons. He will be dumped outside the walls. It will not be gently."

Jumping to embrace the large, blue Firebird, I began scratching up Shard's neck. His flames pulsed brilliantly and a shiver ran through his feathers before he shook me off.

"Don't do that," he said, his tone almost sounding embarrassed as he glanced at the other Phoenix.

"Aww, Shard," I said in a soft, enticing voice running my fingers up and down the front of his neck. I could see he was fighting the urge to let me continue, my fingers scratching all the places he couldn't reach easily on his own. I knew he was enjoying it but finally Shard butted my hand away with his head.

"We are not a mated couple nor are we the same species. Refrain from such intimate approaches again," Shard said, clearly ruffled by the touch.

"But Shard, just a moment ago you were saying how we connect so intimately when I ride you," I said with a cheeky grin.

Riven raised a concerned eyebrow listening to the one-sided conversation. "Anything I should know about?"

Turning on him, my whole being dripped a lascivious and impure essence. "That I've ridden my Phoenix? All the time in fact. More than I can say for you."

His eyes narrowed and I could see the corner of his mouth teasing at a smile. "Best we rectify that soon."

"Soon may not come quick enough and you find I take you down and satisfy my own needs." Biting my lower lip at one edge, I let it slowly fold back to place as I winked at him.

"Are you about done?" Shard asked.

I turned and patted his cheek. "Just teasing, Shardy."

"Shard!" he whistled sharply.

"Ok my big, strong Phoenix," I said absently scratching softly at the base of his skull. This time he only tilted his head away as if in protest.

"So, what's the verdict?" Riven asked.

"Shard's going to carry you in his talons to the wall and toss you over. Best compromise I could find."

"Riiight." Riven didn't look convinced.

"Take it or leave it," Shard chirped, his amusement back, though, he had yet to stop my scratching.

"Come on. We're wasting flight time and I have a need to see the stars once more," I said vaulting to Shard's back.

My words brought forth a warm, rich smile from Riven that set my heart alight and made my body tremble. There was no mistaking how hot that man made me feel.

"Where do you want me?" Riven asked taking a few steps towards the centre of the roof.

'Everywhere," I replied, my voice husky.

"Can you not do that while on top of me. Tell the puppy to remain where he is," Shard said.

I smiled. "Stay puppy. We'll pick you up. Arms." I jabbed mine out to the side a couple times as Shard took off with a burst of air. I watched with amusement as he stuck his arms out wide.

"Arms?" Shard asked.

"Girls gotta have some control over her man."

There came a chirping noise from Shard I could only take to mean he was laughing as he flew in a large, arcing curve to line up with Riven. It delighted me to see Riven had his eyes shut as Shard swooped in swiftly as if predator on prey. As his talons curled around the man's shoulders, I felt Shard's whole-body tense while lifting him into the air. He seemed to do so with ease but there was a terrible discomfort in Shard. I hadn't realised it would affect him so badly.

Gaining height quickly, Shard pulled his wings in, diving swiftly towards the nearest section of wall. The distance was eaten up in moments. As the wall passed below us, I felt Shard drop below the lip of the wall then pull up, instantly flinging Riven into the air out over the field.

"Riven, No!" I shouted, watching Riven twisting and curling through the air at a height that would seriously maim, if not kill on impact with solid ground. Focusing on and drawing in the cold from all around me. The tempered ice floating on the breeze, the drifting cool clinging to the underside of the clouds, the chilly morning dew still solid in the shadows. I drew it all in and extended my arm to force it to my will. I had never formed such solid ice across this distance before but if I didn't, Riven... I needed to focus.

With great effort, I formed a sloping ice sculpture in my mind to catch him and cool his momentum down to a soft slide across the grass. Pushing the image forward, my anxiety heightened as Riven fell close to the ground before the ice slide even begun to form. I couldn't say that it came out just as I imagined but it was coming together none the less.

The breath, held in my lungs, gave way as Riven met with the slide smoothly. His body followed the path of the slide and I released a soft whimper seeing him get to his feet.

"Why, Shard? Why would you do that?" I screamed at Shard from the middle of his back, the extreme moment settling. "I know we joked about it but I didn't believe you truly would."

The muscles and tissue all across Shard, relaxed as if an incredible burden had been released and he began to glide.

167

"I could not hold him any longer. I am sorry, Elara, Child of Fibonacci," Shard said, a real sorrow in his voice.

I couldn't help but feel for the Firebird in that moment. It was I that forced the matter to begin with regardless of Shard's feelings.

"Riven has survived. Let's not try something so terrible again. Take me to the horn blower on the wall," I said.

As Shard turned sharply, I glanced back at Riven standing close to the smoke screen, lance in hand. Within the smoke green flashes could be seen lasting ten seconds or more at a time. It was eerie but with the smoke so dense, I couldn't get a good look.

Turning away, I focused on the task at hand. As Shard hovered above the wall near the lookout tower, I called out to the guard on duty.

"There are going to be some enemies filling the fields soon. I don't want you sounding the alarm unless that man in the field falls," I said pointing to Riven. "Or the enemy begins climbing the walls. The men are ready so will not lose anything in waiting. It is vital to my mission. Understood?"

"Yes, Phoenix Soul," the guard said with a salute. "And as you say, here they come."

I turned to find small groups of warriors entering the field as if they shimmered into existence on the spot. "We need to begin," I told Shard and he darted across the field. Watching the way Riven fought, I wasn't worried for his life. The way he wielded that lance, sometimes sweeping in one long piece, other times blocking two people at once with the shaft split in half. He was formidable and almost unconquerable as he danced across the field. He was always in motion and always in balance. He was a natural at war, far beyond his years. Riven knew how to bring death.

More green lights flashed in the smoke haze and I pointed. "Get me above that area, Shard."

Shard swung instantly, and brought me to where I desired.

"Rain fire," I cried.

Great balls of fire manifested in thin air to fall from the sky randomly through the smoke. As they passed within, the smoke began to eat away at the intensity and ferocity of the blue flame but it was too strong to be fully engulfed. Hitting the ground the fireballs exploded clearing small pockets of air for me to scan.

"Come on. Come on," I whispered. My eyes travelled from spy hole to spy hole until I found what I was looking for. "Gotcha, you bastard." I growled, sending a shower of ice shards down upon the exposed Chimera.

A howl echoed into the morning air as the beast went down and soon the smoke thinned. It didn't clear in large patches like I'd hoped but that just meant there were more in the area. More Chimera to slaughter.

"Come, Shard. Let us hunt."

Shard let out a whistle of approval and we kept moving. Three more firestorms found two more Chimera and a large patch of the horizon came into view. Almost a third of the landscape had been revealed from 15 minutes work.

I glanced at Riven to relish in his dance a moment. With the horn remaining silent I knew he was safe. There was a fresh cut upon his cheek but the bodies piling around him was a testament to his ability.

A flash, like sun on metal caught my eye and drew my attention. I scanned the fields when another flicker of light brought my attention to a signal tower on a large hill skimming the edge of the cleared smoke.

"Survivors," a said to Shard motioning to the signal tower. Another shimmer of light on metal. "There, see?"

"They were smart not to light the signal fire. It only would have brought in the enemy," Shard said back to me.

"We need to help them. Circle close to Riven then we can head over to the tower."

In a trail of blue sparks, Shard circled around and slowed above Riven. He was currently engaging four warriors who looked to have a little skill and tact in taking on Riven. They had him hemmed in. Riven's movements hampered with stepping over countless bodies as they circled him.

"Riven," I called and saw his head tilt my way while his eyes remained on the warriors. "Take care of your friends and head over to the signal tower in the East. We have survivors."

He waved and dove to his left rolling between two of the warriors. Pouncing to his feet, Riven strolled to clear ground and waited. His eyes narrowed, when he noticed two of the warriors were pointing to the East after Shard and I. A few yards and they could be lost in the smoke to hunt me and the survivors, gathering any enemy they found along the way.

Without hesitation, Riven sprung forward. It was getting hard to keep my head at this angle but it was amazing to see him dance. Feinting to the left he spun back to the right, the lance blade twisting like the harsh winds of a tornado to slice the neck of the first. The second went down as Riven split his lance in two, blocking the sword thrust aimed at his stomach and ramming the bladed end through the man's heart.

At a run he sped after the two retreating enemy. Without missing a step and in perfect balance, Riven threw the lance like a spear to pierce the nearest warrior's skull at the base, toppling him forward. He recovered the lance in his strides and raced after the last man. Riven was faster with only leather armour to hold him back where the other was dressed in full bronze armour. As the last was about to enter the smoke haven, Riven spun the lance around himself before sweeping it down to slice the tendons in the enemy's knee where the two plates of armour met.

I saw the man go down, crying out in pain with Riven slowly stalking him but that was as much as I could witness. Shard had picked up the pace feeling I had seen everything I needed too and shot towards the outpost.

The tower was badly in need of maintenance, the kingdom overlooking proper repairs to the crumbling brickwork. A number of external wooden beams were holding the structure upright, the integrity of the foundations remaining intact without the added stress of the tower leaning over. Long, creeping vines had crawled up the outside of the tower like a spider's web adding a contrasting green to the dark surface. At the top was a fire pit with a stack of wood set out to catch fire easily and quickly. The drum of oil nearby and the stock of chopped wood and whole logs ensured the flames would burn long and bright to be seen for miles around. Further South, I spied a similar structure like a small imitation model, high on a distant mountain. There was no doubt to be more along the trails to our allies. A message for help could cover vast distances in only a few hours.

There was only a single pathway leading to the ledge where the tower sat and I noted this was barricaded with wooden structures and what looked to be bricks that had dislodged themselves from the tower. There had definitely been someone here, hiding away from the war that plagued the land. Of all who may have been here, I couldn't tell if they all survived but at least someone got a signal out. Scanning the grounds, I spied the man I was after hidden in some bushes near the ledge waving a small piece of metal. That he hadn't seen my arrival was surprising but I realised he may have been at it for hours just hoping to get someone's attention from the Keep and was more than likely half asleep.

"Put me down near the man over there." I indicated to Shard and he circled round to land on a clear patch of grass a small distance away. That the man didn't react to the Phoenix's approach was also disconcerting.

Vaulting from Shard's back, I approached the man cautiously, sword in hand. The bushes were covering him completely except for the hand that was still holding the small piece of metal. It was laying just outside

170

the bush twitching back and forwards.

Creeping forward, I peered into the bushes and found the man looked half dead. His eyes were closed, and lips were dry from lack of water and exposure to the winter air. Quickly, I sheathed my sword and pulled a small leather skinned pouch with some water in it from my belt.

"Hey, wake up," I said shaking the man gently.

His eyes came open suddenly as his awareness booted up and he stumbled backwards, wide eyed and afraid.

"Easy, friend," I said holding the water skin in front of me. "I saw your signal. I'm here to help."

The man was looking from side to side expecting to see enemy soldiers all around the area. When no threat was evident, he began to settle down again looking at me as if for the first time. Cautiously, he leaned forward taking the water skin. With a final sniff at the contents, he drank deeply until the skin was deflated and only a few drops were left.

"My name is Elara. I am a Phoenix Soul from Telveria Keep. I saw your signal. Is it just you up here?"

"Oh, sweet heavens, thank you. No, there are others in the tower. We were beginning to think no one was going to find us. The smoke was just too thick."

"It's ok now. Go inside. Get everyone ready. There is a soldier on his way here. When he arrives, we will leave for the safety of the Keep."

"A soldier?" the man asked. There was concern etched into every weathered wrinkle on the man's face.

I offered an easy smile. "He fights like no one you've ever seen. He and Shard will get us through."

"Shard?"

"My Phoenix," I said pointing to where Shard still sat. His blue flames glowed deeply and I could feel the warmth emanating from him. I was touched by his gesture to warm the air around the area. The man's eyes widened as he spotted Shard.

"Now that is a beautiful sight to behold," he said.

"Isn't he just," I replied with a smile. These were the moments I found all this fighting and warring was worth it. It went without saying, moments like these wouldn't be necessary at all without the warring and fighting. "Go tell the others. Wait inside until we are ready."

His knees shuddered under his weight as the man pulled himself to his feet. It was obvious how weak he was but I was sure the sight of Shard and promise of safety pushed him to work through it. As the man passed Shard, he bowed low, offering his thanks. I was glad to see Shard return the gesture.

"It warms my heart to see such happiness," I said, walking over to stand beside the magnificent Firebird.

"Are you ill, Fibonacci?" Shard asked.

I glanced at him raising an eyebrow. Shard held a steady expression, and I got the feeling he was joking with me.

"It is not often your kind would speak over the joy of warmth," he continued.

Smiling, I shook my head. "You need to work on your humour." I laughed. "And it's just an expression."

"I've not had the opportunity these last 300 years."

A twinge in my heart crippled my happy mood. "I'm sorry, Shard." I said and sat beside him leaning into his burning feathers. He was soft and cool to the touch and actually, really comfortable. "Just say so and I will travel anywhere with you. Experience anything you have missed these last few centuries."

Shard remained quiet and I couldn't be sure if it was distrust in my offer of just stunned by my words that held his tongue. And so, I let him have his solitude of mind. He deserved that much.

Gazing out into the dispersing smoke fields, I saw movement and a sudden jolt like lightning brought me to life. I felt my heartbeat quicken and my breath catch as my eyes swam over Riven's form. He was jogging through the thinner sections of smoke, shimmers of light dancing over the sweat highlighting his muscular form. A hand came to my face as I turned a deep crimson. I couldn't deny the feelings building in me nor did I want to, anymore.

"Would you leave that boy if I said the word? Would you give up on your lust filled feelings to show me the world?" Shard suddenly asked, his voice held a sharp edge.

I looked up with concern in my eyes and a fear in my heart. "You seek to hurt me?"

"I seek to gauge the integrity of your words. It seems I got what I needed."

Looking away, I shook my head. My soul deflated under the weight of this decision. It knew the thoughts and feelings of my heart and my head and neither could allow Shard to feel trapped anymore. "You seek to take from me the first good thing that has come along in these last 300 years so of course I hesitate. Still, who am I to deny you that right when, through actions I took part in, you lost anything good, bad or otherwise you may have experienced in that same time period. I would leave Riven behind so that you may see the world once more."

From within the smoke a Chimera stepped into Riven's path. I could see it wasn't one of the salamander cross Chimera spewing out smoke but that only made it more dangerous. This one was built for fighting. With an upper body and elongated arms that were covered in fur I could almost mistake it for a gorilla. The only give away to the contrary was the massive lions head with matching dark mane and powerful, stallion legs. This creature approached on its hind legs wielding a two-handed battle axe in one long arm.

My heart leapt into my throat and I stood, taking a few steps towards Riven. "Riven, No!" I shouted still too far away to help. Yet he seemed as calm as ever. Lowering his head, Riven began a slow jog towards the creature, eating up the distance. Separating his lance, he threw the blunted end, aiming for a point directly in front of the creature and started sprinting towards it while the lance half was still in mid-air.

I watched with bated breath as the massive axe came up for a devastating blow. When the creature tensed his muscles for the attack, Riven timed a jump to step upon the blunted end of his lance like a stilt as it landed upon the ground. Riven then used it to launch himself high above the Chimera as the axe blades whistled less than an inch below him.

Positioning the sharp point of the lance below his feet, point down, Riven descended onto the creature. The massive lions head turned to look up too slowly and Riven embedded the lance half, tip and shaft, into the Chimera through the eye socket to lodge somewhere in its lungs. The creature dropped silently as Riven bounced to the grass with little effort.

I could only stand in stunned silence as he recovered the lost half of his lance by connecting the two pieces and dragging the shaft out of the body. There was a spray of blood that covered Riven's leather breastplate as he waved my way.

"Be weary of that one," Shard said, walking over to stand beside me. His head was level with mine as he spoke.

"Weary why? Riven is skilled but he would never hurt me," I said watching as Riven continued towards us. He was close but still out of earshot. This conversation, whatever it was, needed to be sorted quickly.

"I cannot vouch for the boy's integrity or honour. When I carried him, I tapped into a power hidden deep within. Pain erupted all over me as I tried to prod it, exploring its potency and possible origin. It was why I threw him from the wall. I couldn't hold him any longer."

"A power?" It was true, Riven was highly skilled for someone so young but I'd never sensed anything unsavoury from the man. Nothing that suggested he was more than he claimed.

"Whether he is aware or not, something quite strong hides within him.

173

Be on your guard." Shard made to launch skyward but paused, wings spread wide with little wisps of blue flame dancing around them. "If you had chosen him, I would not have offered you this warning," Shard said before taking flight as Riven ran up the rise to the tower.

Stopping before me he tilted his head in question as he looked at me. I was probably acting quite strange in that moment, as Shard's words resounded in my mind. I had not the capacity to be happy or cheer on Riven, up the hill. I could only stand with a concerned look as if I'd been given bad news. A possibility yet to be seen.

Shaking my head, I forced a smile. "Sorry, my mind was elsewhere. I'm glad you bested the Chimera."

Riven just waved a hand. "That was nothing. On the trail to the Keep, it wasn't uncommon to fight more than one at a time. I've had plenty of practice."

"I'm glad for it. Your skill is amazing. Way beyond your years. It's a pity the Chimera wasn't a smoke type Chimera. We've made such a dent in their smoke screen."

"My father was a lancer before me. I used to train with him even before I could walk. Or so my mum would tell me. I guess I got a valuable head start. Did you find the person who was signalling? We should get back before more Smoke Chimera fill in the gaps around the Keep and we need to walk blind."

"Yeah. He said there were a few more hiding in the tower," I replied. "I told him to go get them ready."

Nodding, Riven looked to the tower. "Shall we get them moving then?"

Walking passed me, Riven knocked on the door. The tower was short and there could only be room for the spiralling staircase inside but when the people started exiting, I couldn't believe my eyes. 24 people were hiding in the cramped space. They would have been hard pressed against one another and by the look of them, had been there for days at least. Fear could push people to amazing lengths for survival.

From the group, I counted only one woman and one child swaddled and held in a sling. The child's head, a little more than a baby, was resting on the woman's shoulder. Otherwise, the group consisted entirely of men. They all held beards or the rough growth of about a week and each looked like they'd seen their fair share of fighting in their time. I was glad the woman seemed comfortable in their presence and she didn't look ill-treated. The young child most likely scared them into line.

Riven already looked as though he'd made friends with the signal man as I walked up. He was highly charismatic and the man laughed at some

174

off handed comment.

"If you want to take point, I'll protect the rear. Shard will protect the flanks with a rain of fire where necessary," I said, interrupting their comradery.

"I have an idea on the terrain. I'll get us home safely," Riven said with confidence. His smile would put anyone at ease but it filled me with such warmth. I needed him to take me, make me moan to the four winds and the endless sky. I'm sure there would be plenty of stars out tonight and if Shard actually wanted to leave, I needed to make him mine sooner rather than later.

I found that I'd stalled a moment and the group was already filing out down the hill. Shaking my head, I fell in beside the woman and child bringing up the rear.

"It's such a long distance and there are so many of us. Are you sure we'll be safe?" The woman's voice was low and timid and she didn't raise her eyes as she spoke.

"I won't lie to you. A swift ambush or sudden arrow could see any one of us downed. In war there is always danger just like in life. A missed or crumbling brick in the foundations of the tower could have seen it fall with everyone inside. Stick close to me and I'll protect you. I know we don't look like much but Shard, Riven and I are worth 100 of the enemy... Minimum," I added thinking it sounded even better. Thinking about it, the woman probably didn't care about my ramblings. She just needed to know she was safe. Focusing my growing list of abilities, I crafted a small ice rose that could fit within my palm. Inside the rose burned a flame of vibrant blues that sparkled and danced upon the ice surface. I was getting better at mixing the elements, I thought, as I offered it to the woman.

Her eyes grew wide as they fell upon the ice flower. She reached out a hand tentatively but pulled back. "It's beautiful," she whispered. There was a hint of sadness in her voice.

"It's yours. You can take it if you'd like," I said, bouncing it a few times as I offered the flower again.

Slowly, the woman reached for the flower, her eyes longing to hold it but she pulled away once more. "I can't," the woman apologised. "The flames... scare me."

An understanding dawned on me and I smiled removing that element of the design before offering it once more.

This time the woman took it happily. "Thank you. I've had troubles with flames before," she said showing me large patches of scar tissue from past burns. She peered into the ice marvelling at how it kept its

175

shape in her warm hands. "You are a Phoenix Soul?" She asked.

"I am. My name is Elara ShardSoul. Shard is the Phoenix circling above."

She seemed confused, her face becoming serious as she peered into the ice rose.

"Anything wrong?" I asked.

"Sorry," she shook her head. "It was my understanding that Phoenix Souls worked with pyromancy. I hadn't realised they could take on other elements. But I haven't seen a blue Phoenix either. Does that have something to do with it."

It made sense why she'd be confused. I smiled softly. "Ice manipulation was an inherent ability I was born with. Long ago, there were more like me but they have been hunted and killed. I believe I am the last of my clan to still exist. Shard's colour on the other hand is due to the intensity of his flames. Blue burns stronger than orange or yellow flames."

"I'm sorry. I didn't know," she said in her soft voice.

"Not many do," I replied.

There was a long silence before the woman spoke again. "I'm Bella."

"It's a pleasure to meet you. It's nice to have another woman to talk to. It can start to get a little masculine at times with the company I keep. Even the women act more like the men but that's to be expected in their line of work. Am I right?"

Bella just nodded keeping her eyes low.

I pursed my lips, considering her. "Were you ill-treated in the tower? Is there someone you would like dealt with?"

Her eyes came up to meet mine, wide with worry. "No, nothing like that. I kept to myself and so did they."

"Are you travelling with anyone? Your baby's father, maybe?"

There was a sadness that washed though her like a dam that suddenly burst. I knew then it was the wrong question to ask. "He never made it out of town. It was only because of him that I could get away. When I found the signal tower, I bunkered down with the occupants. More seemed to turn up over time until we grew to the group you see now."

A refugee then. She wouldn't have a home to return to now if the number of raids I witnessed in my spirit flight was anything to go off. "Well, I'm glad you and little...?" I said indicating the child in a silent question.

Bella glanced at me and then over her shoulder. "Oh, umm."

Blue flames rained from the sky all around as Shard spotted the enemy creeping in through the smoke screen. Bella screamed as the flames rose, boxing us into a narrow corridor. I could see Riven was dealing with the few soldiers that weren't incinerated and I reached out to take Bella's hand. "It's ok. Shard won't do anything to hurt us. Right now, he is doing everything in his power to protect us. Watch." Reaching out I trailed my fingers along one of the flaming walls as Bella backed away a few steps. "See? Shard chooses who will feel the heat of his flames. They won't harm you."

Shaking her head, Bella began to back away further. She looked like she was about to break and run, the fear seeping into every inch of her soul.

Appearing around the edge of the flames, a soldier locked eyes with Bella, a wicked grin etched into his face. Raising his sword, he waited for the hysterical woman to walk back the last metre but before his blade could fall my hand shot out, a dagger appearing in the soldier's eye socket.

"This way, Bella. It's too dangerous back there," I said, holding out a hand but she was too far gone. Instincts had taken over and she turned to run. Having not even realised the altercation with the soldier occurred, Bella tripped over the body.

Falling face first into the dirt, she skittered around, fumbling with her hands as if searching for something. To me it looked as though she was searching for a way to stand, to retreat from the area, when she caught the soldiers arm. Eyes, already wildly seeking freedom, saw the dead body under her and grew more terrified. Her body began to tremble as a scream was born within her chest. It swirled and grew at such a horrific pace that soon she couldn't hold it any longer. The shrill cry encompassing everyone and everything nearby as Bella scrabbled away.

Reaching her, I pulled her close but the frantic movements almost forced her way loose. Finally, I felt no other choice than to slap her and with a bit of force I did just that. I felt bad in doing so but I needed to get her under control and out of the hostile area.

A spark of clarity focused in Bella's eyes and she started shaking her head. "I can't go back in there," she said, and I felt for the girl but couldn't accept her answer.

"Close your eyes. I'll guide you through. You won't even know you're in the walkway. Trust me," I said and offered my hand.

Hesitating, Bella just stared at my hand.

"Just close your eyes and everything will be all right."

Before I could convince her, Shard lowered the fire walls with the nearby enemy eliminated, Helping Bella too her feet, I froze in shock with a deep, shuddering, almost painful breath. I couldn't move, couldn't utter a word as Bella began the trek once more.

Noticing the change in my posture, Riven signalled to Shard to circle the area and ran back to me. His forehead showed deep worry lines as he rested his hands on my shoulders and looked in my eyes.

"What's wrong, Elara? Are you injured?"

"Dead," I could barely mutter. The word coming out in a hushed whisper.

"What's that?" Riven asked.

"The... child. It's dead."

Riven glanced back at the child in the sling. As if for the first time he was seeing it for what it was. Many would have only seen a small child resting peacefully on their mother's shoulder but look a little closer and you start to see the signs. Pale skin, the way limbs and the head moved about weightless, the small hole in the back of the material where an arrow must have pierced. There was dried blood blended into the red material of the sling and someone had snapped the end of the arrow, the final piece hidden within. It was evident though that the child had passed a day or two ago.

Closing his eyes and mouth tight, Riven slowly tilted his head to the side as if there was a great pain growing inside. I saw him clench and unclench his fists a number of times before it looked as though he regained control.

"Don't bring it up with her. She is currently in denial. It happens in war. She either doesn't notice the child is there or might even believe it is still alive. We cannot know what she might do if we shatter the illusions right now. Best to get her behind the walls in the safety of the Keep, first. There are doctors there that can help." He continued to watch me, gauging my response but I could barely produce one. It was an event I wasn't ready to witness. I was not a soldier bred for war, tempered to the harsh and cruel nature of the creature that was human. Just a wandering warrior hoping to put my past to rest.

"Elara, snap out of it. Mourn in the Keep. Right now, these people are your responsibility. You need to protect them. Don't allow anymore death."

The words filtered in slowly but they made sense. I needed to build that wall around my heart. I needed to temper my being as war does with all those who would survive. I was these people's guardian. I needed to be strong for them.

Closing my eyes a moment, I gathered myself. Then with one foot in front of the other continued bringing up the rear. Riven shook his head and returned to his position at the front but it mattered not. No one would be getting through again.

There were no more ambushes as we came into sight of the Keep. We did happen to stumble upon a Smoke Chimera which Riven dispatched easily. And as the smoke cleared, a horn burst sounded from within the Keep. Moments later, a second identical burst sounded signifying allies returning.

"Look, Sisha, it's our new home," I heard Bella say as she stroked one side of her daughter's cheeks. My heart tore in two and tears came unbidden. It was too much and I fell to my knees, crying unashamedly. The world was so fucked up.

A hand squeezed my shoulder as I felt someone fall to their knees in front of me. Through bleary eyes I was able to make out the features of Baras in front of me and a second even stronger wave of pain washed over me. His arms pulled me deep into a protective embrace and I cried relentlessly.

"The child's dead," I spluttered through tears and a nose running nonstop. "She doesn't even know."

I felt Baras tense around me then he stood quickly.

"Suniel," he called. "The woman."

"What, No!" I squealed. "Why? What are you doing?"

General Suniel was walking the field towards us flanked by a group of allied soldiers. As Baras's voice caught his ear, Suniel side stepped as a figure loomed to his right and just in time. Where he once stood a blade cut through the air with disciplined accuracy.

I couldn't believe what I was witnessing. Bella had pulled a short sword from within her clothing as a terrifying expression contorted her face and was attacking the General. I tried to race forward, tried to put a stop to this. Bella was a grieving mother twisted by the brutality of war but Baras held me tight not letting me escape. Slowly he brought me back around into an embrace, holding my head to his chest.

"Don't look, Ellie. This is not your world. You are too pure for what is to come. I never wanted this for you," Baras said.

As much as I wanted to see, Baras wouldn't let me turn back. The sound of steel on steel met my ears as if a battle of a large group had broken out and the only thing keeping me calm was that Baras didn't feel it was threatening enough to let me go. It was over quickly as silence fell.

"Let her go, Baras," Suniel's voice broke through the silence.

It was a long moment before Baras complied, allowing me to turn back. He stayed by my side in that moment of undisguised shock. All around the main gate, the group of men I rescued were laying where

179

they'd been slayed. And at the forefront was, Bella, a large sweeping gash carved across her chest. Her child still resting its head on her shoulder.

The scene became too much for me and my stomach churned causing me to empty its contents to the earth.

Suniel shook his head, his eyes glowing with rage. "Look at them. Look at the mess you have caused, Elara ShardSoul. You brought the enemy to our gates offering them a free pass to rape and kill. All of the pain they could have caused would be on you. Your ego and selfish attitude put everyone in danger. If Baras hadn't of made the woman, the Keep would be down a commander, its soldiers and the townspeople you swore to protect. Your actions were traitorous."

The words cut straight to my soul, biting into it with jagged teeth. Baras tensed as if he wanted to step in but he didn't and that hurt more, made the statements all the more sharper. He actually believed the words enough to allow them to pass.

"I didn't know," I said weakly.

The words only causing Suniel's rage to rise. "No, because you're not a soldier. You're a maid playing in a game you know nothing about. You gained a little power beyond your means and all of a sudden you felt invincible. Invincible and incredibly stupid and that makes you one of the most dangerous people to our allies. In war, no one moves on their own. If you find survivors, we plan on how to retrieve them. If you spot the enemy, you pass the information on so that we are aware. You do not go out into the field alone, crippling any plans that may involve you. You don't run off to rescue groups of people. Even if they are allies you put them in grave danger from attack trying to get them home. AND YOU DON'T HAND OUT COMMANDS THAT UNDERMINE OUR DEFENSES!" Suniel's voice rose extensively. "WE WERE ATTACKED WHILE YOU WERE OUT. THE ALARM DIDN'T GO OFF UNTIL THE ENEMY WAS ALREADY BREACHING THE WALL. OUR ENTIRE OPERATION WAS ALMOST LOST BECAUSE YOU FELT YOU WERE BETTER THAN US. TWENTY GOOD MEN DIED TRYING TO PUSH THE ENEMY BACK."

Even I couldn't argue with his words now. I was being selfish. I did think I was better than the soldier hierarchy. I believed that lifetimes of experience and knowledge far outweighed the experience gained from living through war. And now that I was twice as powerful with the abilities of the Phoenix backing me. I really did feel invincible. And because of that more innocents died.

My head lowered and voice became shaky. When I spoke, it barely held a spark of its former tone. "I'm Sorry."

"Sorry? Oh no, a soldier doesn't get to be sorry. A soldier that makes a mistake, lives with the consequences of their actions as a reminder. They will never earn forgiveness. You will not be forgiven for acting as you did. But if you want to remain a soldier, to help rather than hinder, you will become a part of this team," Suniel said, a hand motioning in a large sweep to encompass the Keep. "Only you can decide your fate."

My mind fizzled away. I couldn't bring words forth to string even a sentence together. No forgiveness. All these deaths that scattered the field on my head. The weakening of the only place keeping hundreds of innocent lives safe. It was all on me and started to become too much. Pulling away from Baras, I fled over the bodies of the fallen and in behind the high walls. I could hear Baras calling for me but there was nothing he could do right now. Though I grew up in this Keep as a maid, I became lost in moments, finding a dark, isolated corner to fall into pieces.

A rat, plump and wobbling on its little legs, skittered by me. The fur rubbing over my ankle as it passed by, checking within the cracks and crevices for discarded food scraps. The fear and disgust I held for these creatures barely two months prior would've had me leaping and dancing around trying to get away no matter my state of mind. Remembering the time I had to feed on them raw when I was trapped in a cave-in, though sickening, really put things into perspective. Anything, even something so small as a rat could both insight fear or open the path to survival in times of need.

I felt so insignificant. I was lost in a world I had no right to be in. And what had I done. Incited fear. Made those I wanted to protect become weary of me. In this time of need, I didn't help at all, as this lowly rat did me.

The chill in the air embraced me gently, soothing my sorrows. I couldn't tell now how long I'd been sitting here in this damp corner, nor how long there was left of such a sad night. A gentle haze of cloud kissed the moon in passing and the stars danced, grateful to be free once more. Seeing them woke a spark of wonder but nothing that could save my tortured soul.

Maybe he could make me forget. Maybe if I gave myself to him, I could get those dead, staring eyes of Bella out of my mind for just a moment. I stumbled to my feet and dragged myself along the wall, leaning heavily to hold myself up. Not a single drop of alcohol had passed my lips today but it felt like I'd been on a bender for months.

Swaying down the street, I first needed to find where I was in town before I could track my way to where Riven waited. I finally found a landmark I could be sure of, a sordid little inn in the far Western outskirts that had a church open across the street. The priest felt his best work needed to be accomplished in the hole where sin could be found. I always feared for the kindly, old man, but it was unnecessary. His charisma and joy for life won a place in this world of sin, won the acceptance of his presence. The amount of sin never did fall but an extra act of kindness here and there came out of it. That in itself was worth the effort.

From here, the barracks were only a 5-minute walk along a sub street. The Keep began solely as a central hub to maintain the armies between the Capital in the North and Telveria's Southern expanse. The centre of the town included barracks, mess halls, living quarters for the elite, meetings rooms and training grounds. It was designed exceptionally well to allow for smooth operation.

In time, the town began to grow around it but unlike some places that allow the peasant population to build however they would, the original commander took control. He commanded the soldiers to build the homes and shops, roads and alleyways to follow a set plan. Everything was thought of from wide roads for ease of access to waters wells placed throughout. Even the sewerage systems were built to be so vast, anyone trying to enter through them would be crawling for hours with multiple grates. In times of siege a number of structures were designed to be toppled to create internal walls against the enemy.

It was a work of love, tactics and a lot of ingenuity. The only thing they could have done better was work out a brighter lighting system for the darker end of night. It really came down to the lazy ass soldier who couldn't be bothered to maintain them.

"What's a pretty lady like you doing out at this time of night."

I glanced across and rolled my eyes. Here they are now.

Ignoring the two armoured men walking my way, I continued towards the barracks.

"Hey, I was talking to you," a heavily bearded man grunted.

I waved over my shoulder and honestly, I knew it would, but this made the soldier angry.

"Don't ignore us. We're talking..." His voice droned off and I glanced back. He was looking past me now, unsure of himself.

I focused forward again and saw another figure standing in the shadows, gentle flames swirling in the air around him. I felt my whole-body tense in recognition of Enzo and blue flames manifested in response.

"Shit, it's the Phoenix Maid. Let's get out of here before she kills us too," the second, smaller soldier said.

His words ripped through me, cutting right to my heartache and self-loathing. My flames vanished instantly to the footsteps of the men.

"What are you doing here, Enzo? I'm not in the mood," I said softly, any essence of motivation gone.

"I could ask you the same thing, but it seems rather obvious." Enzo glanced back at the barracks. "Off to see your little boy toy?"

Fuck he makes me angry. Or maybe I needed someone to hit but something about him just sets a fire in my soul full of rage and darkness. It was a rather easy balance to my current mood, though. I stuck my chin out in defiance. "So what if I am?"

"He's dangerous, Elara."

"Why? Because he knocked you out? Is your pride hurt widdle boy? Do you need a cuddle and be tucked in to bed?"

"What he did with his lance was not natural." A glint in his eye showed his annoyance and I smiled for the first time in a long time.

"The lance comes apart. You're just annoyed a little trick knocked you flat."

"No, Elara, the lance didn't come apart. It swayed and moved around my blade as if it was alive." Enzo stepped closer to me backing me up against a wall.

"I think you got hit a bit harder than you realise," I said, hard eyes locked to his.

Slamming a fist against the wall, he growled. "Listen to me. That man has power. He is dangerous. I visited Geopti today. I spoke to the elders there. Nobody remembers him by description or name. You can't trust him, Elara. Stay away from him." Enzo leaned in dangerously close.

'Be weary of that one,' Shard's words echoed in my mind, and I lowered my head. Doubt began to flood my heart but before it could sink its teeth in, I felt lips upon my neck. Enzo had taken my moment of submission as an opening for his own desires, and my body was already reacting to his touch in a way my mind wouldn't normally allow.

A shiver ran through my body like electricity, and I let out a soft moan. I almost lost myself in that one moment, my body using my low self-esteem and depression to latch onto any joy and good feelings it found. I almost lost myself but for the single flash of Enzo force feeding me Shard's soul essence. That one, still image broke through the desire and kick started my brain.

Eyes blazing with blue flame I pushed Enzo back to the street. "You will not touch me again, Enzo TalonSoul." I said, my voice edged in ice, but I couldn't muster the rage I normally felt towards him.

Eyes narrowing a moment, Enzo just laughed. "I see the truth you bury away. You will be mine again, Elara *ShardSoul*." The last held a ripple of sarcasm.

And didn't that make my self-worth plummet. I muster strength, courage and pride to tell this man I once loved to leave me alone and he disregards it like a used and torn rag. He held no respect for me, so why should I keep any myself? I walked off, less of the person had been.

Glancing at the barracks, there was no desire anymore, no want to mask the pain I felt. Riven was deceptive and would only make me feel worse if that was possible.

My feet moved on their own at that point. They knew these grounds intimately and soon I found myself outside the door to my old room. I tried the latch, but it was locked. It had probably been reassigned when I left the Keep as a Soul.

Resting my head against the cold wood of the door, I knew I couldn't be alone anymore. I needed help, friends, family. Anyone that could pull me out of this pit I found myself in because I couldn't do it myself. I feared myself in that moment and the darkness I could dream up.

Baras and Kymberlin were out on patrol, their Phoenix seen circling as I wandered. To wake Korr and Flint was selfish at this time of the night. My mind was already resisting the need to find help without me realising. It believed I could make it alone and made excuse after excuse to leave my friends out of it. They didn't need my pain heaped upon them.

Swaying down the hallway, I reached the stairs. Instincts pushing me left and down, I chose against the grain, taking right and up towards the flat, open roof. Nobody would miss me. My family died off 300 years prior and I'd already lived beyond my care. It should have ended in the Phoenix nest.

Reaching the top steps colours and light began to play on the walls in a ripple much akin to water. "Shard," I whispered under my breath realising the source. How could I forget him? I reeled at how far I had fallen tonight, what such depression was capable of bringing out in me. I never believed I could have such dark thoughts. And then I hesitated.

Would he even want me to crash his evening? Would he even care for my troubles at all? I was the one who locked him away for three hundred years.

"I can feel you there, just out of sight, my Soul. Come sit with me." I heard Shard say and immediately I burst into tears. Racing up onto the rooftop, I threw myself into his feathers, burying my face as the emotions spilled forth.

"Thief."

"Light fingered maggot."

The Phoenix's taunts were broken by an ear-piercing screech as Shard filled the roof top with waves of blue flame asserting his Strength.

"No more will you speak ill of my Soul. To do so is to speak ill of me," Shard commanded. The other Phoenix quietened but they never took they're judging eyes from me.

It didn't make any difference though as I didn't look their way. I didn't see more then the wisps of flame twirling from the feathers of Shard. His words helped to sooth my aching heart. He had every right to hate me like the others but he stood up for me, defended me. He was majestic and noble.

"You seem upset, Fibonacci."

"You caught that, did ya, Shard?" I said but his probing eyes saw straight passed the humour, sending my lip into a quiver. "How do you do it?" I wept crying into the feathers.

"You need wings to fly," Shard replied evenly. I paused a moment as my mind tried to comprehend the answer.

"Did you just make a joke?" I asked in a whimper. "You cut mine down and to give back your own?"

"I have spent enough time with humans to pick up some humour," Shard said looking rather proud of himself.

"It was terrible," I said with a soft chuckle, sniffing my nose and rubbing it up an arm. So unladylike.

"Yet she still laughs. What do I do that you cannot?" Shard extended a wing out to encompass me in a tight circle. The stares of the other Phoenix annoying him more than myself.

I frowned trying to find the words. "How do you live for so long? How do you watch everyone you know die? How do you die and then come back to find the world completely changed from what you knew?" I looked like I was about to burst into tears once more and Shard went to speak but I pushed through.

"I can't keep it up. I never wanted to live so long. It was all En... It was all him and his stupid selfishness. Latifa, Jason, Tim, Eli, Idris, Daniel, Gaia, Gemma. I have lists and lists of all the people I have met, befriended, loved, and lost. They live in my waking moments and visit me in my dreams. How can I get past this hole in my heart? How can I be happy that I'm still here when they are not? Even now, it affects me. I have new friends. Friends that love me and care for me but I'm running from them. I haven't talked to them properly in days, weeks even. Ever since I got my memories back. I was happier as a maid. I couldn't remember anymore. I couldn't feel the pain anymore. I could act like a friend and a human. I was scared and each moment felt finite. Everything was beautiful. But now... It's like I'm living in a grey and empty wilderness. I'm drowning in nothingness."

"And would you wish to be a maid once more? To forget all the lives you've lived and fall back in line with your human friends?"

"With everything I have come to know and learn of the world, yes, very much so. But as I was? Drowning in a sea of work, tied to this Keep where even the cold I love so much could have killed me, no.

It all came around full circle. I can't live forever and I can't live a normal life. What I want is to have passed from the world when I should have. Knowing one love in my life and having it be enough.

"I am sorry, Shard. I'm so sorry. I'm sorry. I'm sorry. I'm sorry. I'm..." flames running over the surface of Shard became warm as I spoke. Then hot. The heat grew to such an intensity, it forced me to leap back, refocus.

Instantly, the heat of the flames settled and I was left devoid of all my words as Shard locked eyes with me. What more could I say now that I didn't before. This was a creature of legend. A god of death and rebirth of his own design. I only got a taste of their life and it almost destroyed me.

"I've gone through periods like you, little human, where the world and this long life were more than I could bare. We all have." Shard said encompassing the other Phoenix on the roof including Talon who had landed only moments before and was trying to piece together my mess. "The only difference is we have each other. We can back each other up and pull each other back from the brink. You've been going it alone all these years and everyone who could have helped was gone in the blink of an eye. The first few hundred years for us were the hardest. All of the family and friends we ever knew were gone. Ground to dust by you humans. Only six survived. Those years were dark. In those years I would have given anything, like you, to turn back the clock."

"How did you get through it?" I asked. "When all of you were going through the same thing?"

"It was Haze. He was already alone in the world. Born an orphan and had known his share of pain. He brought us back one by one. 1000 years passed in a blur before we began to build ourselves up again. We are still not whole, even now. We do not make friends outside of our circle and Souls. The Souls we carry with us through our lives, the circle we bounce off when we need but we are not whole."

186

"Then why continue? Why do you keep pushing through?" It seemed like such a sad life and if the taste sat so bitter in my mouth, how did theirs...? "Do you have a tongue?"

Shard's head twisted to an unnatural degree.

"Umm, ignore that." Crimson graced my cheeks. "It was relevant but unnecessary."

"Humans." Shard just shook his head. "When we started it was for longevity of our species. To remain alive in a world that would use us for warmth. In time, it became more about the routine of living than actually living itself. We will not be here forever. We are in our death throes. We just can't accept it yet. We live stubbornly for the sake of those small moments we can smile at. If we can smile even once over a thousand years, that moment is a magical memory."

"And if I feel I couldn't smile again?"

"Because you tried to do good and learned a harsh lesson."

"That the enemy could be anywhere?"

A quick, shrill, chirp cut through my words. "That even alone in the dark, dying in a horrid world, you have family you can rely on. We are all dust eventually. Allow yourself to love fiercely and depend desperately. You're are not alone, Elara ShardSoul."

My mouth pursed in a joyous pout as a saddened crease cut across my forehead. His words had been terribly touching and it was everything I needed. Tears slid down my face once more and I hugged Shard.

"And she cries again."

Laughing through the tears I reached up and scratched Shard's neck through his feathers, feeling the shiver run through his body.

"Don't do that, little human," he said but didn't pull away.

I smiled. A magical memory.

Chapter 10

Standing before the large iron doors of the war room, I hesitated. I knew I was on the outer for the way I acted. It was going to be a long road gaining everyone's trust again. I was going to get a lot of flak for what I did. It was a stressful and terrifying moment to reach for the door handle but I needed to if I was to find anymore happiness in my life. I couldn't run from this and let it hang over my head.

With a deep, steadying breath, I grasped the handle and turned to a satisfying click.

"Well, it's about bloody time. I thought we were going to be standing out here all morning," Fitz said from behind me.

I shot around, eyes wide and face beet red as I looked up at my friend. I'd been so focused on taking that step that I hadn't even heard him... or Kymberlin, come up behind me.

"Ain't that the truth," Kymberlin said grinning from ear to ear. "Come on. Pay up. I at least gave you a little me credit. Half an hour, I guessed. Closer than the 5 he said."

Fitz reached into his cloak and produced two silver coins from a hidden pocket he'd hand stitched. Tossing them to Kymberlin, he gave me a quirky look that suggested he wasn't gunna apologise. When did they even have time to make that bet. They couldn't have known I'd be just standing here unless they were standing...

"Were you making that bet while standing behind me?" I couldn't believe I'd missed their conversation.

"And arguing with a guard who'd fetched the wrong item from my room," Kymberlin said.

"You're pulling my leg," I replied. A hushed conversation I could accept, but with the way Kymberlin argues? Half the garrison would have thought we were under attack. The other half had most likely been on the receiving end and were trembling in a corner somewhere.

"Look, here he is now," she said pointing at the guard coming down the hallway. I looked at Fitz and he just tilted his head with a smirk.

"I'm sorry, both boxes looked the same. Is this the item you were after, Phoenix Soul?" the guard said handing her a box the size of my forearm. As he apologized my jaw dropped. He just confirmed what Kymberlin said as true. I couldn't believe I was so far out of it.

Then my mouth shut tight and my brow furrowed as I watched Kymberlin lean over and kiss the guard on the cheek with a cheeky grin.

"How many of the guardsman here have you slept with?" I asked.

Kymberlin wasn't offended by the question but rather looked up to the left as if she was trying to recall. "Only the guardsman?"

"Soldiers, townsfolk. The people within these walls regardless of rank." I said.

"Only the ones I argue with," Kymberlin replied shooting a playful wink at the guard. No wonder they're in a corner trembling somewhere, I thought, laughing inwardly.

"You flirt. Wait. You've argued with Baras..." I shot a questioning look at Fitz who only held his hands up in defence, shaking his head. "You've argued with me. Where was my invite?" I laughed.

"You know where my room is. I ain't chasing you down. You're often aloof anyway." She offered me the wooden box the guard got for her.

"What's this?" I asked curious to be receiving anything from Kymberlin.

"Just take it." Kymberlin pushed the box into my chest forcing me to take it from her to relieve the pressure. Slowly, I opened the lid to peer inside and my heart fluttered in my chest. Within sat two polished gauntlets of about my size. Down the sides had been etched a Phoenix with wings spread wide. A blue and black hue had been added to the metal around the Firebird, an artform the blacksmiths do with flame and some powder mixture. It was almost a perfect replica of Shard. These were amazing and looked to be made by a master blacksmith.

"I... I have no words, Kimmie," I stammered with a tear forming. "Thank you."

Her eyebrows dipped dangerously at the use of her nickname. "Stop, fuckin', stealing mine," she said and pushed passed me to enter the war room.

I smiled after her before looking back at the beautiful gift.

"I believe that means you're welcome," Fitz said coming up beside me and peering into the box. "She really does like you. She doesn't get along with many women. Most end up beaten and bruised."

"I remember," I replied. "The 'maid' Elara would never have been able to handle her but I've known a Kymberlin or two in my time. She's fun."

Fitz just scoffed. Then his voice got quiet. "How are you fairing, Elara?"

I couldn't look at him straight away and when I finally turned, he saw the sadness in my eyes, instantly.

"Raw. In the course of 24 hours, I've been smashed down into thousands of little pieces. All the pain, and suffering, and hurt, and depression, and dejection, and just utter regret. All these negative emotions I had caged up within me these last 300 years, every barricade had been smashed down and I was engulfed, forced to confront the darkest, most hideous recesses of my soul."

"So, another Monday then?" Fitz said adding his humour into the mix.

"Almost," I replied with a soft laugh.

"Do you need to talk? We can..." He nodded back down the hallway.

I shook my head. "I don't believe you have experience and understanding enough to help. I broke down over three hundred years of shit. Yesterday just triggered it all. I'm doing better."

"But do you have anyone? You said Enzo...?"

"No," I cut in holding up a finger. "He's one of the main reasons I'm hurting so badly. I found myself breaking into Shard's feathers. I don't even remember how I found him but he related to my pain. His words brought me back. Gave me purpose."

"Purpose?" Fitz raised an eyebrow.

"To find a reason to smile. To enjoy the subtle things in life we miss because we're rushing from moment to moment. We try to fill our lives with everything at once only to miss the beauty and wonder before our eyes."

"That..." Fitz just stood thinking a moment staring off into oblivion. When he refocused, his eyes had softened and a natural smile touched his lips. "You're going to be just fine, Elara. Come on. Let's get into the meeting."

Fitz understood life with an odd view of the world. He was able to understand the world intimately and, out of everyone, may have had the greatest chance of healing me over time. But to see his reaction to my life goals, I knew he was one of the good ones in this world.

Every eye in the room fell on me as I entered. I could almost hear their thoughts as they judged me with those eyes. Well, except Baras who stood as a sign of respect, and Korr who, hand on heart, bowed his head to me. My friends, I could not do this without you, I said silently.

"Before you take another step, Elara ShardSoul, speak your intentions," Suniel said from the head of the table.

Standing to attention, or what I thought was close enough, I replied. "This Keep is a family. Everyone plays their part to keep our family working, keep our family whole. For a long time, I felt like I was on the outer. That I didn't belong for one reason or another. This caused me to act in my own interests and in ways I thought may impress or allow me to be accepted. I have been wrong for so long. I am a part of this family and intend to do what is required of me to help and protect. I owe it to the soldiers whose lives I didn't keep safe."

With pursed lips, Suniel nodded. "Take a seat with the rest of your family."

That was it. That was all he was going to say. I glanced at Fitz, confusion evident as he simply motioned to take a seat with a smile. I sat next to Walan as seemed right.

"Is that all he will speak on the matter?" I whispered to Walan.

The man just nodded. "You aren't the first solider to make a mistake causing death. The General needs to accept such things as a part of war and plan accordingly. He spoke everything he needed to yesterday. If you came in this morning unchanged you would have been dismissed. You are a valuable asset, excusing the term, and if Suniel can use you to your potential and his grand plan, he will. You seem to understand now there is more to war than just killing and protecting. Generals and commanders have their uses. Trust in them."

"I'm beginning to." I turned my attention back to the front and this time listened with my mind and not my ego.

"From the 5 scouts sent out, only 1 returned and missing an arm at that. He spoke of green holes in the air before the enemy was upon him and Verin," Lianha reported.

Baras just shook his head, a look of dismay etched into his features. He would have known every soldier stationed here personally and each loss was going to hurt.

"I noticed them yesterday. Green flashes in the smoke before the enemy appeared. Shard believes it may be some sort of portal." I said.

"I've seen similar instances," Fitz replied.

Lianha glanced my way and nodded. Or possibly a nervous twitch. It was barely a movement of her head in my general direction. "Before he fell unconscious, Liam mentioned a larger force gathering in the denser sections of smoke. They are about a day's march to the Keep and if they begin, we'll have a hard fight ahead of us."

"We need numbers / a count," both Baras and Kymberlin said splitting the difference at the end. Baras seemed to blush as he looked back at Kymberlin who winked.

Catching Fitz's eye, I mouthed 'What was that?' to which he made his hands look like two... I tilted my head. Ducks? And then proceeded to smoosh them together a few times where their lips would be.

"No!" I said loudly, eyes wide before realising where I was. I looked around at the other commanders, hands up and face bright red. "Sorry, my mind became overwhelmed by the army descending upon us."

"This is why we don't bring *maids* to war," Commander Dren commented shooting a look at Walan. "As I was saying, we'll send all the Phoenix Souls to gather intel. We cannot risk more scouts and if the enemy has numbers, one or two Phoenix may not be enough."

191

Walan had taken an interest in my back and forwards with Fitz and leant across. "It was two weeks after your friends returned as Phoenix Souls," he said quietly.

"What's that?" I asked confused.

"It was rather natural how they got together. When they finally saw each other for what they were, everything just fell into place." I realised he was looking at Baras and Kymberlin.

"I really didn't know. Not with all the other guys. Is Baras really ok with that?"

"There is no one else. She may be speaking big around you but every night she is with him."

"How can you be sure?"

"I keep tabs on the Souls with my limited abilities. It's my role in the council," he said tapping his nose.

I thought a moment and then remembered he had something of the Drifter's abilities himself. Then it hit me. "You're a pervert." To which Walan almost choked.

"I don't go that far, Elara. I see them meet. It reminds me of... Well, that doesn't matter." Walan seemed distant in his hushed tones.

"So why does she need to act tough around me then?"

"You're Baras's childhood friend. Someone he holds dear. Wouldn't you want to get in good with Riven's friends?"

Narrowing my eyes, I shot the man a dangerous look. "Stay out of my affairs."

He smiled and turned back to the meeting.

Opening the lid to the gauntlets once more, I looked them over. I noted the craftsmanship and detail that went into them first glance but knowing what I do now, it was a big gesture. Kymberlin must have really gone out of her way to not only track down a master blacksmith but the amount she would have paid. Unless she just used her Soul privileges to force the matter. Then the gift would be meaningless. A thought for another time.

It was surprising that Baras chose to be with her after how Kymmie treated me the first time we met. He would have been harbouring a deep grudge against her with how protective he gets. And it's only how poorly she treated me that I can accept it now. She must have really been something special to him, got deep under his skin for him to forgive and even fall for. I smiled at the thought. I had never known him to be in love. Guess as his best friend it's required I tease him a bit.

Sliding my hand into the internals of the gauntlet, I was surprised to find just how comfortable and snug they felt. Compliments to the

192

blacksmith because he got my size perfectly. I flexed my fingers a number of times before making a fist. Everything moved and flowed along with my movements as if they were a part of me. This was a princely gift and would be cherished.

"Any more questions or clarification on the mission? Phoenix Souls gather information, assess the enemy strength, get back here with haste," Suniel asked. "Anyone looking to go it alone?" His eyes were trained on me and I smiled.

"Walking the line, sir... Umm, General," I said with a clumsy salute. Perplexed was the only word I could find for his expression. It was as if he was trying to figure out how I had survived so long. I then turned my attention to my friends.

"Kymmie, they are a perfect fit," I called across the room and a set of deadly eyes found mine. Crossing to Kymberlin I drew her into a hug before she had a chance to retort. "Never got to hug you earlier. Thank you, Kymberlin, but can I ask you one thing?"

Strong hands slowly withdrew me from the hug and she stood with raised eyebrow. "What?"

"How did you acquire these?" My expression serious.

"I didn't steal them if that's what you're asking. And I know you think our right as a Phoenix Soul is an equivalent of stealing. Alagos, will not honour a Soul's request either. He is one of the only people with an exemption to that rule."

Hearing her name, the kingdom's greatest blacksmith, settled my worries. Alagos once went on strike for having to reshoe a horse for a Phoenix Soul free of charge. She soon gained that exemption.

"Then I accept you as sister, Kymberlin." I leaned in close with hand to the edge of my lips. "Just try to keep it down when he bends you over the edge of the bed. Especially if I'm around to hear it. Not an image I want making a home in my mind."

The squeal was worth it as Kymberlin brought her hands to her burning face. Sparks and small swishes of flame began to manifest in the air around her as her emotions spiked. "How? How did you find out?"

"It was starting to become a little too obvious, even for me."

She pursed her lips looking worried.

"Don't worry." I shot her a reassuring grin. "It seems right but let me break it to him that I know, ok?"

"Ok," Kymberlin replied sheepishly.

"Thank you." Baras was just finishing up a conversation with Suniel and I bounced across to him.

There was relief in his eyes as he saw me smiling again. "With the way you left yesterday, I haven't been at ease until I saw you again this morning. I was really worried, Elara," Baras said pulling me into an embrace. It was a rare occurrence and it felt more brotherly this time. Unlike when I was a maid and held a spark for the man.

"Thank you, Baras. You've always been there for me and I think it's time to call it what it is."

He seemed confused but didn't break the hug so I pushed on.

"We've been dancing around the edges of it for a long time but I want us to stop dancing."

"Elara, are you ok? What's this about?"

"Us, Baras. I want us to be together. To spend all our time hand in hand. To kiss and make love and destroy a bed or two. Baras, I want us to finally make a go of it."

Pushing me back, Baras looked wild as he glanced from me to Kymberlin. I think I almost broke him in that moment and to my absolute bliss, Kymberlin was nodding in confirmation. I knew she thought I'd just admitted to knowing their secret which made this all the more fun.

"You don't seem happy. Are you?" I brought my hands to my mouth. "Are you cheating on me?"

With a ghostly complexion, Baras was at a loss for words. He could only shake his head rapidly as he dodged around me and retreated to Kymberlin. There was a moment of utter confusion as Baras and Kymberlin conversed, then I saw her eyes go wide and she turned to lock onto me.

"Fucking bitch!" she said. As she pushed passed Baras, I bounced over the tables laughing gleefully, making my way to the exit. At the doorway I turned to find Kymberlin had given up pursuit having messed up climbing onto the table. She was now halfway upside down.

"Sorry, Baras. I had to. You too have fun, you here." Baras was in mute confusion and Kymberlin just sent a rude gesture my way as she retreated back to claim her man. There was a small smile gathering on her face knowing that Baras would choose her.

Heading out the door, a hand caught me and pulled me back into the corner. The hand was cool upon my arm and I knew instantly who it was. Looking up into those steely grey eyes, my internals twisted and churned. The fluttering of my heart, a call to innocence and love, was in turmoil with the caution of my mind. He was still a mystery and a possible threat. In the end it was my mind that won out and I turned away

His hand came up under my chin. With soft encouragement, Riven was able to bring my attention back to him.

"Have I done something wrong?" he asked.

I wanted to lie and tell him he hadn't done anything. I wanted to but I couldn't. It wasn't a lie. There was nothing Riven had done that had turned me off him. Just rumour and conjecture from a reliable source and a bias source. That they both said the same thing didn't help but Riven hadn't actually done anything.

I shook my head, with sorrow in my eyes.

"I'm sorry for yesterday. I tried to find you. Searched most of the night, before some comrades dragged me back to the barracks. They would all suffer if I was found truanting but I still couldn't sleep. As the sun broke free, I started my search once more until I decided on something drastic. Your Phoenix doesn't like me much, does he?"

My eyes went wide hearing that Riven would go so far for me. "Shard has a particular taste." I replied.

"Well after he tried taking an arm with that beak of his, he finally told me I could find you here. Well, gestured really."

"You would have just barely missed me." I drew into myself a moment trying to decide how much I could truly open up to this man. I wanted to cut through the walls and lay myself bare for him. To let him experience everything that was Elara but if there was some deep, dark secret surrounding him, would I just be setting myself up for more pain?

Shifting to my spirit form, I looked over Riven's soul. Vibrant blue swam in his veins, rich and strong. It lit him up like a massive pyre for a King, flowing back around to merge into a large pool of power within his stomach. This wasn't anything unusual as everyone looked similar. Just the strength of his soul was impressive.

But then I saw it. Small, glittering flecks of orange caught in the ebb and flow that was Riven. They trailed through the body latching onto muscle and tissue with a large congregation within the brain. Tilting my head to get a better view, I was shocked to find a large, orange tentacle like strand of energy attached to the back of Riven's skull. It was clearly a foreign energy with the orange line trailing away through a wall.

Reaching out to detach it, the strand pulsed an orange flare that sent me reeling back and toppling into my body. Physically it looked as though I almost feinted and it was only Riven's close proximity that allowed him to catch me. Whatever that thing is, it's strong.

"Are you ok?" Riven asked, worried.

It was definitely confirmed what Shard had said. There is a power around Riven that tended to fight when threatened. To what end this power held was still yet to be determined but I needed to be weary.

195

"I didn't sleep too well last night and allowed my body too much leeway when choosing to stay upright or not. I am fine really. And thank you for your thoughts last night. It was more about my past than what happened in the field but Shard helped me. He can be very protective over me. Even told the other Firebirds not to harass me."

He peered into my eyes a moment longer as if looking past my walls and deep into my soul. It felt wrong to hold so much of myself back but I didn't know what to trust and right now I didn't have the time. Still, as long as I could, I held to those eyes. They made my mind fuzzy and my loins warm. Or was it the other way around.

Without thinking, I leaned forward and stole a kiss. I hadn't even been prepared for the move and we both found ourselves retreating a fraction assessing the others reaction. Without a word or motion passed between us there was a pure understanding and we both engaged in the kiss.

Immediately, I was reprimanding myself because I was about to head out on mission, yet I couldn't stop. Couldn't disengage these perfect, soft, cool lips.

"Ahem..." Baras cleared his throat behind us.

"I'm sorry, Elara, but we just wouldn't work. Someone else fills all the spaces in my heart. Roof in five."

I shot him a cheeky grin and nodded. "I know. Just saying my goodbyes. Not that he knows yet."

Baras simply bowed his head a moment and turned to walk away. Pausing, he shot over his shoulder, "Look after her."

"I will," Riven replied then he turned back to me. "Goodbye? And what was the other stuff about?"

"I wasn't hiding it. Our conversation just hadn't provided the right opening yet. Also, I asked Baras to run away with me and make lots of babies."

Riven choked on his next breath, not expecting the answer. "How many's lots?"

"5 or 15. Somewhere in that vicinity." I flailed my hand about to contextualise the statement.

"Ha. I always thought he had a thing for the feisty one," Riven said then.

"You've been here all of 5 minutes and you could already see it. I'm terribly off my game when it comes to matchmaking."

"That you are. There is a match in the making right in front of you and you're talking to others about making babies."

"Well, come back here and finalise the match." I said wrapping my arms around his neck and moving in for another kiss. Before I could a finger came up to rest on my lips.

"Aren't you forgetting the goodbye?" He asked.

"That comes after the kissing... and maybe before as well."

"Then it seems, all the criteria have been met. Just for today?" he asked.

"Why? You gunna miss me?"

"I missed you last night when you weren't in my arms."

And I swear I almost melted in that moment. "We are on mission to assess the enemy's strength. I'll be..."

Riven's expression became wild and his hand gripped my arm tightly, almost painfully. "You can't!" he almost shouted in my face. And then, as quickly as it came on, Riven's whole demeanour relaxed. "I'll see you when you return," Riven said calmly before walking off without another word.

I was too stunned to speak or even react at that point. I couldn't help but think that maybe I'd done something wrong. It was a head spin and not something I had time to deal with now.

"Your boy's got some rather big issues," Enzo said coming up beside me.

I looked at him a moment, shook my head and left the same way Riven did.

A blaze of fire lit up the morning sky as the Phoenix streaked through the air. A wondrous and awe-inspiring display of fiery reds and yellows, cut and polished with the deep veins of blue. Floating in the slipstream of Shard's wake, I allowed my body to curve, dip and rise with every movement. Our bodies attuned, weightless and in sync, was one of the greatest and most intimate feelings I've ever felt across all my lives. To say I was lost for words every time I went up with Shard was underplaying it as I couldn't keep the smile from my face.

I have flown before. I have left my body and watched the world fall away. I've drifted far outside the realms of this world to watch the birth of galaxies and define the essence of eternity in the loneliest corners of the universe, but nothing compared to actually feeling the experience. In spirit there was movement without a sense of touch. Awareness without feeling. In flight, there was pure life.

And now there were 5 others flying alongside, tracing reds, oranges and yellows through the sky. I always worried about the embers floating through the air, falling to the grass and catching into a massive bushfire. Shard tried to ease my worries stating Phoenix will choose the heat within their sparks but I was still nervous. If any of these Firebirds got bored with their immortal and exceptionally normal lives, this was a great way to spice things up.

I felt guilty putting everyone out in the field for what was deemed such a dangerous mission. My abilities should have been enough but I didn't want my first day back in the war room to seem like I was taking over and going it alone again. I realise now that all choices made were to lessen the chance of death and pain for all.

I should have spoken up about my Drifting and not held back. Or have Walan throw me under the carriage. He knew my abilities and could have opted in. It may have just meant he knew better than to speak for me but I needed to try now. It could mean we didn't need to scout further and my friends could return home. I couldn't rest easy if anything happened to them.

"Fly straight for me a moment," I said to Shard.

"Do not throw up on me, little human, or I will toss you to the wind," Shard replied instantly.

I scoffed. "I'm just going to scout ahead. Stay steady until I'm back on board."

Shard chirped and I took it to mean he understood. Slipping from my body, I drifted apart from Shard a moment who, suspiciously, looked straight at me. I should have realised they can see me after the number of times the Phoenix tried to attack me in this form. The sight was amazing from this angle watching my form floating on a legendary bird. I'd dreamed of this in my first life but never believed it was going to come about.

Letting the image fall away, I raced ahead to assess the danger. It was amazing how far we had come in such a short time and I recognised a few markers through the smoke.

Our destination should be close and I just followed the smoke as it grew thicker. Soon, I found myself staring at a swirling dome of smoke that blocked any chance of seeing through.

Maybe Walan just knew there was a dome hiding the enemy from spiritual spies. No, his skills were limited.

I trailed around the outskirts and found it could hold a huge area inside. A huge army. Floating down to push inside, my eyes caught a glimpse of light. A shimmer that sent chills through my soul, and not the good kind. It was faint at this height but as I got closer, a lump formed in my throat. The orange light stretched out like long strings of rope across the land. And it wasn't just one. Hundreds could be counted around the dome. The strings reminded me of the blue energy lines that ran across the Northern expanse feeding Shard.

What really crushed my soul was the lines I was looking out were the same colour as the line of energy attached to the back of Riven's head. Everything was beginning to come crashing down much along the lines of how life was running lately. It was a surprise that life would choose to dangle Riven in front of me and bob him just out of reach but I had a lot to be accountable for with karma.

I couldn't think further than whatever was in there had a hold on Riven and I needed to get in and find out the truth. Rushing forward I made to enter the dome but the moment I touched it a pulse that felt nothing short of lighting shot through me, repelling me, and sending me back into my body with a painful thud.

The world spun as I tried to regain my bearings. A rush of blood to the head started to shut down my mind as darkness crept in from the edges of my vision. The last thought as I passed out was realising the spinning world wasn't in my mind at all but my falling, twisting body as it plummeted away from Shard.

There was no way to tell just how long I was out but when I came to, Shard watched over me. His flames gaining in strength as I opened my eyes. Leaning down, Shard rested his forehead gently against mine. I was still trying to piece things together, but the gesture was touching. Lights filtered in and I realised everyone was standing around me watching. Even Enzo was standing at the back, facing away, but he was still there.

"Having trouble keeping your seat, Ellie?" Fitz commented. I knew it wasn't a question but a jab.

"I ride that bird better than Korr does," I smiled at him as he nodded sarcastically.

"I can see." Fitz returned the smile.

"Korr is goat," Korr said suddenly and the three of us laughed as the others looked on confused. Kymberlin, Baras and Enzo were never privy to the mountain climb and I was suddenly reminded of Caeli and Dustin. I knew them only for a short time compared to the years I'd lived but the pain for their loss was still sharp. It would've been a much nicer sit down with them around. Even without making Phoenix Soul, their company would have lifted my heart.

But everyone disappears from my lives, one way or another.

"So, what did you find out?" Fitz asked. He was always quick to understanding things.

"Very little. There is a shield protecting the enemy from view. When I tried to enter, I was filled with pain as if struck by lightning. I see it affected me physically too." I thought it better to keep Riven's possible spy status quiet for now. Especially as Enzo would have loved to hear. I didn't know anything for sure and there wasn't any need to worry everyone just yet. Speaking of which. I shifted my sight to spirit vision and checked the others for any signs of the orange energy. Nothing... Except for Enzo, who was all orange and no tail. I could at least trust everyone here, if not like them.

"Do you think you can ride?" Baras asked.

"Let the princess sleep. She's already delayed us enough," Kymberlin remarked.

"Ain't no delaying you from getting home when you bring your snuggle pumpkin on mission," I laughed.

Kymberlin scoffed. "She can ride," Kymberlin growled at Baras.

"So can she, it seems," I also said to Baras, eliciting a squeal from Kymberlin.

"Let's just go," Kymberlin said turning to face her Phoenix and Baras followed after, knowing better than to say anything.

An arm reached down before me and a cheeky grin filed my view. Rather surprising to see Korr getting involved in the relationships of the group or even seeing him show much emotion at all but it was becoming a tight nit group. A family. I took the offered hand and Korr lifted me to my feet with little to no effort. There was so much strength in that man and I was glad he was on our side.

"Captain Snuggle Pumpkin," Korr said, and I could have sworn there was a small chuckle from the man, but I was too stunned to think straight.

"Was... Was that a joke? Are you amused Korr?"

Korr just turned and began to walk away but a deep, rumbling laughter burst from the man as he climbed upon his Phoenix.

"Captain Snuggle Pumpkin," he repeated with a laugh as Ember took off into the air.

"Well, that's a first," Fitz said.

"Something resonated. Think it's gunna stick," I replied. We were both standing astonished by the normally placid man's show of emotion.

"For Korr's sake, most definitely." Fitz grinned mischievously. Then he turned serious. "You're ok?"

"I'm ok. There is something strong out there. I lost the spirit battle, is all. My physical body is still strong."

He looked into my eyes as if reading something deeper, looking for any sign of weakness. Satisfied he nodded and indicated to the Phoenix.

"We best get after Captain Snuggle Pumpkin before he gets too far ahead."

I laughed. "Oh yeah. That name's stickin'."

Vaulting to Shard's back, I settled against the soft, blue feathers. His powerful wings beat only once to get us airborne and two more times to reach full speed. A chill of excitement ran through me, rejuvenating body and soul as the world sped by. This was right. This was how life should be. One big adventure with friends. Even Enzo, bringing up the rear, couldn't get me down right now.

"It's taken too long to realise," I said to Shard as his wings spread to glide along the air currents. We reached the others almost instantly and Shard had to slow down to match pace.

"What's that?" Shard asked. He twisted his head to look back at me with his misty, purple eyes. The swirling, shimmering purple was mesmerising to view and hypnotising to keep eye contact with.

"I wasted that which was stolen from you. I used the gift of resurrection to walk the paths of revenge, always out of reach. It's only now that I could return that gift to you that I appreciate each moment I'm alive. It's more precious than before."

There was a nod from Shard, but he made no comment. He wasn't in the position to give up his resurrection ability. It may have even made him sad knowing the life I was speaking so highly of, he could never touch. Over thousands of years, he would have forgotten the feeling of living a short singular life. I dropped the subject making a mental note to not bring it up with him again.

Up ahead, the swirling dome of smoke came into view. Even at this distance it was massive, seemingly bigger than when I was in spirit. No light pierced the surface and we were going to need to punch through if we wanted to see what was happening inside.

"That's the dome you came up against?" Shard asked and I confirmed.

"It didn't feel quite as big in my spirit body."

"They are building an army inside. It reminds me of a battle I was part of 4500 years ago. If the thing inside is what I think it is we are all in danger," Shard said before screeching loudly at the other Phoenix. Everyone began circling the dome cautiously as they moved inwards.

"What do you think is in there, Shard? I asked but was abruptly shushed.

"Quiet, I'm speaking to the others."

"Speaking?" there was no noise coming from Shard or any of the other Phoenix and it dawned on me they were communicating via telepathy. "I thought you couldn't use telepathy."

"I said I was more private than a dragon. Not that I couldn't. Now hush and let us talk."

To think I would be hushed by a Phoenix. Sure, a number of Fibonacci have experienced it in the family history, and it wasn't so unlikely but usually that would have resulted in a deadly battle straight after. This was considerably different, and I would guess a number of my ancestors wouldn't approve either. Fire and ice should never mix.

Drifting silently in the slipstream, I waited on Shard's private council to conclude. I wondered if the ability was only shared between the Firebirds or if I could join the party. The way he spoke made it seem like linking our minds was possible, but I'll be patient. I couldn't say Shard, honestly, trusted me, both after what I had done and being a Fibonacci. I'll allow him his time.

"We're going in," Shard said suddenly. "We need to know if it's him. Hold on tight."

"Wait. Who's in there? What's going on?" I asked but was ignored. Shard turned sharply and I needed to hold tight to his feathers to keep myself steady. There was a sound much like a grunt to show it had hurt Shard but he ignored it and flew straight at the smoky dome with the other Phoenix.

Flames reminiscent of a meteor encased us as we scorched across the sky, faster with each moment and as Shard was about to hit the barricade his muscles bunched as if he was expecting a collision but the smoke parted easily and we burst into the inner sanctum.

Turmoil and darkness met us as we crossed the threshold. The sun couldn't pierce the wall of smoke and the little light there was was coming from each of the Phoenix as they broke through. The winds were horrific inside and twice I was almost ripped from Shard's back before I anchored myself to him with arms and legs. The muscles just above the wings, a perfect handhold for me.

A crack of static thunder burst in the air as tendrils of lightning lit the area a few brief moments and my heart jolted haltingly. The field was full of warriors all looking towards us with malign hatred etched into their features. Woven in and around the human army were creatures of terror, fuel for any child's nightmare. Large wyrms, kin to dragons without wings or limbs, coiled around the field. Chimera of all species and mixtures were scattered, throughout. Some even looked to be shouting commands with the humans obeying but the strong winds killed any noise that confirmed this. And drifting through the sky were three Phoenix, their flames dark as the night's shadow. These seemed to cause the most distress for our Firebird friends and with good reason as there should be no other Phoenix alive.

My eyes shifted to their spiritual form to read the energies of the room and I was met with hundreds upon thousands of orange lines like web intertwining and rolling back to a central position. The area glowed in such strong hues of orange and black that I couldn't see anything physical within. Shifting my focus back to my physical side, I tried to peer through the darkness to see the creature that might be behind all of this evil, but the darkness was too dense as if it lived to protect the creature's identity.

Lightning pierced the sky and shadows fled in fear. For a terrifying moment that seemed to hang between space and time, I spied the enemy and my heart shattered. Turning ghostly pale, I locked eyes with a figure pulled straight from my own nightmares. A sunken face with glowing orange eyes, dense and menacing, had a crown of boney thorns sitting above it like a demonic halo. The body was wrapped it a dark and shredded cloak, its torn ends dangling around thin, bare feet. A Lich King without fable or legend to keep it within the realms of myth.

Dread static buzzed down my spine causing me to shake in fear of this creature as a look of recognition passed its features. A skeletal, white hand, rose pointing at me from its dais and a shrill scream pierced my soul as it directed its minions towards me. Legions of soulless eyes turned to face my direction and instantly weapons came up and snarls erupted through the staging area. Arrows loosed at me got caught up in the winds creating a deadly flurry of sharp projectiles to navigate through.

Shard screeched as the dark flames of the enemy Phoenix dive bombed us. I was forced back to my senses as Shard dodged left and right, fleeing this brutal bird's assault. At one point, Shard inverted himself to lock talons with the creature in a test of strength while I was left dangling and spinning in the fighting freefall, we found ourselves in.

"We have to flee the area," I called to Shard over the cracking thunder.

A burst of flames knocked the dread Phoenix back and Shard was able to manoeuvre away. "The others have tried but the winds of the dome are two strong. It's as if there is something else holding us in."

"We can't take on the whole..." I pause as Shard corkscrewed through a flurry of arrows. "We can't take on the whole army of the damned."

"Use your spirit to feel out the barrier. Find a weakness. If you can't then we will bloody well have to fight."

I doubted I could even keep my seat with the way Shard was flying but he was too agitated and focused to argue with now. If I didn't try, we were as good as dead. "Keep me alive," I shouted.

"You overestimate my ability," Shard replied.

A disconcerting comment but I needed to keep it from my mind.

Shifting into my spirit form, whips like orange fire attacked and an onslaught of pain rattled my form. It was like I was being stabbed with thousands of sharp knives and I transitioned back, fleeing it.

Barely hanging to consciousness now, I forced my mind to focus. There was dizziness and a darkening around the edges of my eyes, but I held myself in check by force of will alone.

"What have you found, Elara?" Shard's voice penetrated my mind. It was flowery and soft as it echoed within my head. I barely recognised the telepathy but had not the thought to make any more of it.

"Only pain. I will go back in in a moment," I said wearily.

"Pain or death, Elara. They are coming," Shard said, the urgency in his voice pulling me back.

Green portals beyond count opened through the air and flocks of harpies began filling the space. They were an odd creature with dirty brown wings in place of arms on bare breasted, humanoid women. There legs were much like a rooster, leathery and thin, coming down to three dark talons dripping with poison. A new sound of screeching and screaming filled the dome and it attacked the mind peeling back all conscious thought.

These were creatures I only knew of from legends as they were extinct long before the Phoenix were immortal. The Lich wasn't just manipulating those who were alive but was using necromantic powers to bring the dead back to life. It made me wonder if everyone under the control of the Lich was long dead or there were some exceptions.

"Riven," I whimpered in the depths of my mind.

"If you want to find out what the boy is find us a way out. Every second counts," Shard screeched.

That he heard my thoughts was unnerving, but he was right. I had moments before the Harpies reached us. Steeling my will and preparing for the pain, I shifted to my spirit form. Instantly, a feeling much like burning red needles piercing the eyes sockets, sparked in my brain. A pain I have felt and will know intimately through all my lives.

But the torture of one life can prepare you for another and I held my head long enough to get a snapshot of the world and the energies around me. In a fraction of a second, I could trace the energy lines holding the dome together and found it was being strengthened by three Chimera around the grounds.

Seeing the battle getting tense, I rushed back to the sanctuary of my body. The changeover was easier this time and adrenaline pushed me into action.

"Go," I yelled, and realised Shard was glowing bright blue.

With a shudder of tense power, the glow became too bright to look at and in a moment an explosion of blue and white flame burst from Shards body to engulf any harpy that got within 20 metres, disintegrating them instantly. Cracks in the flying demons defence opened up and with no hesitation Shard was at full speed, weaving through the mass of wings and fangs.

"Did you get our key?" Shard echoed in my mind. He had no ability to speak at this speed.

"Three Chimera need to be destroyed. How can I get their locations to you?"

"Picture the image in your mind. I'll get them."

I pictured two of the three creatures in my mind, showing where they were in the scope of the field and from left and right, the other Phoenix Souls peeled off, one after another. I was thrilled to see they were all, on the most part, whole.

My focus caught the tail end of Enzo and Talon and echoes began to fill my mind unbidden. Thoughts of the moment we stole Shard's immortality. Of fighting back and being forced into the life I only thought I desired.

"Focus, Elara. The third Chimera is more important than our quarrels," Shard beamed, breaking through my thoughts.

He was right. I forced the past from my mind and concentrated on the beast we needed to slay. Shard picked the location from my mind and swooped in a long curving arc to come down upon the beast. His talons scrapped and clawed at the creature but I could see they made little difference. I knew what I had to do.

Pulling my short sword from its sheath, I leaped the few feet from Shard's back to the ashen earth below. I almost lost my footing as I landed thinking the earth was more solid than it turned out but on closer inspection it was exactly like ash. Soft and grey, clinging to my ankles where it touched. If I was to rub my finger across it, I had no doubt it would have smudged.

The Chimera rolled from Shard's attacks and circled around glaring at me. It was a more traditional beast with a lion's head, body of a shaggy goat and the tail of a snake. Within the eyes, the dark pupils were the hourglass look of a goats that always irked me for some reason. The fangs, however, were definitively the lion's and it snarled aggressively as it bared those sharp rows of teeth.

Closing my mind to the outside world, I let my body relax, ready to react to whatever attacks came my way. In that moment, I wished I was a Berserker as Fitz discerned. I had known a number of them in my lives

205

and they were always a ferocious foe to battle. Usually, the enemy would die to the berserker even had the berserker received mortal wounds. Alas, the 'maid Elara' was fighting with only muscle memory even when she had no actual memory of it. It took only a few fights for the body to fall back into old habits.

The Chimera leapt and I rolled to my left, clearing the talons by inches. As I came to my feet, I batted the snake's tail strike awake with my new gauntlets. A blindness took me as the snake spat venom in my eyes but instead of clearing, them, I jumped back feeling the wind of the snake's seconds strike roll over my neck.

Blinking rapidly and rubbing excess venom from my face, I looked around for the Chimera, already feeling I'd tempted fate long enough, and found Shard had caught the snake in his talons, pulling it away. The Chimera was getting enraged as it tried swiping this way and that behind itself but Shard danced just beyond reach.

Taking the opportunity, I brought thumb and two fingers to my lips as if I was holding a glass blowers' tube. With a deep breath, I blew a deluge of blue flames to cover the Chimera. My breath release was slow and consistent to allow the greatest and deadliest flow of flame I could.

Two of the zombified warriors had stumbled to where I stood and without the ability to turn my head had to fight them off with short sword and peripheral. I was happy to gain only a small cut on my arm, my concentration returning back to the Chimera as the flames died away.

A quick movement and the Chimera had leapt for me, pinning me below. The shaggy coat of the goat had burnt away and the skin and muscle tissue had begun to melt. Shard was circling back towards me screeching in despair for my safety as it held the shredded snake's tail in its talon's.

With my arms pinned and my neck bare, I reacted instinctually as the beast attacked. The razor teeth of the great maw circled my throat, scrapping the skin as it tried to rip into me but couldn't sink any further. Behind the rows of teeth, I had crafted two thick rods of ice that took the force of the jaws, holding them open and buying me moments. Even now as the harsh, rotten breath assaulted my nostrils, I could see thin cracks beginning to form in the ice. As the creature struggled to break through the wedges, I twisted and turned, inching my arm out from under the beast's body. With a wicked twist that almost dislocated my shoulder, I pulled my arm and short sword free before turning it in on the best and jamming it into the back of its throat to sever the spinal cord.

Immediately, the Chimera slumped onto me as dead weight, the last of its life fading into tremors. I couldn't move it. The weight was too much for one arm alone and even Shard could barely make the thing rock in any way.

I could see more of the resurrected warriors closing the distance. It was such an awkward position and I knew it was only a matter of time but I wrenched the short sword from the Chimera's throat to a spray of green blood. I now wished I hadn't as the putrid smell filled my nostrils, threatening to be the final thing I'd smell in life.

Swinging the sword, I managed to down two of the enemy with ankle cuts and dispatched them with jabs to throat or temple. The latter saw my sword get stuck, leaving me weapon less before an approaching hoard.

Weight shifted off my chest. Swinging my head, I found Enzo and Korr rolling the Chimera's corpse from me. Korr leapt into the attack as more warriors reached us. His bastard sword drinking in the blood of his foes. Enzo yanked me to my feet and pointed to Shard, who had now landed next to Ember and Talon.

"Get on Shard and get out of here, Elara. The others have already retreated outside the dome," Enzo commanded with a shove. "They are a league to the North."

I nodded to Enzo and fled with him close behind. Glancing back, Korr was in a fighting retreat with that wicked laugh filling the void. I was sure now that war and battles, maybe even danger in general, were a type of fun for Korr and I turned to vault onto Shard.

As I jumped up a sharp, piercing pain punched through my shoulder and with a burst of blood, an arrow head exited my chest. A second shaft hit my arms sideways, bouncing clear before a third punctured my side and I tumbled straight over Shard to the soft, grey ash behind.

"Elara, No!" Enzo yelled but Shard had already scooped me up in his talons and was fleeing the area. I could hear the eerie cry of the Lich as we made our escape. I held to consciousness knowing that, could we reach Fitz, I'd have a chance. He could remove the arrows and patch me up. Sensing my need and the dimming life-force within me, Shard picked up speed. He could see more than I, the amount of blood I was losing to the sky and the precarious placement and angle of the second arrow. There was little he could do but fly and distract.

"It was 100 years give or take," Shard's voice echoed in my mind.

"What?" I tried to mumble but he stopped me.

"Don't waste energy trying to talk. Think to me and I will hear you. I now accept you as a true Phoenix Soul."

"As opposed to?" I was a little sceptical about how this all worked but

was happy by his comment.

"A thief who I was forced to link with in a time of need. A Fibonacci girl, mistrusted and despised for your past discretions by the ranks of Phoenix alive today."

"You've held such strong and sad feelings towards me all this time?" I asked.

He paused a moment and I could hear the echoes of his internal thoughts. They were too fast to catch and discern and the little I got was confusing. "Honestly, no. There was a short time after I broke free of the ice cage that I wanted nothing more than to eat your eyes and suck out the tantalising brains inside your head. I wanted you dead and it was a fragile line that kept me from doing so."

"Why... you... why didn't you?" I could feel my mind starting to slip but felt this was important. I couldn't die without hearing Shard's thoughts of me.

"It was selfishness and fear. I needed a Soul after so long without and feared for myself every second I tempted fate to find someone worthy."

I scoffed. "I was never worthy of this title."

"The moment I watched you jump from that mountain with the intent of saving that village, not knowing whether I would follow but believing in me, I knew you were worthy. That you had always been worthy and I was just blinded by tradition and our interactions in every life we shared. You have shown me every moment after that you were the only choice I could have made."

I was too touched for words; my mind filled with emotion. Tears dampened my cheeks as a 300-year regret began to break.

"It was 100 years before I could fully appreciate what a gift mortality was. One morning, I woke to find the sun shimmering through the ice sending rainbows to dance around the earth. Warmth of the rays filtered over my feathers and bathed the skin, relaxing muscle and tissue. It was the first moment since I was trapped that I found no more hatred and anger bubbling below the surface. I was able to just sit and take in my surroundings. Be happy with the world I found myself in. That cage had forced me to slow down and face the demon's I held to all the years of my long life. The last of it fading when you made your leap from the cliff. I had thought to myself in that moment that here was a girl to follow. Here was a woman I could live for and share my world with. Here was a true Phoenix Soul. Here was Elara ShardSoul."

"EHEhkklsmmmmmmm..."

Chapter 11

"Elara? Elara, hold on," Shard said aloud, spotting the Phoenix camp in the distance. As Elara drifted in and out of consciousness, he dove sharply. A trail of blue fire blazed behind him for nearly fifty metres as he landed abruptly in camp and pushed Elara forward towards Fitz.

"Pull the arrows," Shard ordered. "I don't have the finesse for this. Be quick and precise, but if you can't... rip them out."

Fitz hesitated, staring at the wounds. "I can't just..."

"She's dying," Shard snapped. "I can only reach her mind for a moment longer. She can heal herself, but not until the arrows are gone. Don't be the reason she dies."

Fitz faltered, still unsure. She would bleed out if he pulled them wrong. With an exasperated sigh, Kymberlin shoved past him. "Oh, for gods' sake, I'll do it."

She knelt by Elara, grabbed the first arrow, and snapped the shaft cleanly before pulling it through. The second was worse; its head was still buried deep inside. Trusting Shard's words, she braced herself and yanked it free.

Blood seeped lightly from the wound, but the sudden pain jolted Elara's body. Her grey eyes flew open and locked on Kymberlin.

"Elara!" Shard's voice roared through every corner of her mind. *"Use your spirit. Heal yourself. Heal yourself!"*

The camp held its breath. Heartbeats dragged like hours, tension twisting into panic. Enzo landed hard nearby and sprinted toward them, just in time to hear Elara's last gurgling breath as her body went limp.

"What happened?" Enzo demanded, his voice a snarl. His gaze darted to Fitz. "Who pulled the arrows?"

Fitz shook his head, but Enzo's eyes caught the bloody shafts in Kymberlin's hands.

"You! What the fuck have you done?" he roared, lunging.

Enzo charged at her, fury radiating from every muscle. Baras intercepted, tackling him to the ground, and Korr, having just arrived, leapt in to hold him down. Even then, Enzo's rage threatened to break free, his eyes blazing like a demon's, fixed on Kymberlin. She went pale as chalk, collapsing to her knees in terror.

Only Fitz's rushed words cut through the chaos. "Wait! The wounds. They're closing."

Enzo broke free and shoved him aside, eyes assessing Elara's body. It was true, the twin wounds in her shoulder, front and back, had already sealed. The deeper one at her side was slowly knitting shut, inch by inch.

Elara was healing herself. Drained and unconscious, but alive.
Elara was alive.

My eyes flitted open enough to take in the soft pink highlighting the small tufts of clouds as the sun set into the west. The darkening twilight still felt harsh on my eyes, causing me to blink and squeeze them tight as I tried to wake them up. I had little energy to waste and laid still trying to piece together how I came to be at this point in the world with night approaching. The last thing I could remember was the eerie cry of the Lich as we made our escape from its territory.

I panned gently, looking to the right and saw Shard seemingly asleep with Talon beside him. To where the others were, I couldn't say and hoped beyond all else that they made it out safely. I also hoped that Enzo maybe didn't and that Shard was comforting Talon for his recent lose. Panning my head the other way I saw it wasn't the case as Enzo was sitting next to a small campfire. His head was bowed as if asleep and it looked as though he was keeping himself supported upright with his sword. The tip was in the ground, and his shoulder was resting against the blade just below the hilt.

Seeing him like this reminded me of the old days when he wasn't such a self-centred and scared little boy. Maybe he always was but my naivety helped craft him into something more. After all this time hunting him and hating him, I couldn't do it anymore. I'd calmed my own regrets and grief I wasn't strong enough to face. I thought the answers to my own troubles lay in destroying this man, but I was running away, myself. I needed to face my demons and give all I could to making it right with Shard.

Three hundred years I marched to catch him in an unshielded moment and now that I look upon the sleeping figure of a man, I felt only pity. He would hate to hear that but what could have been between us faded into the abyss and I am so far removed from him, I couldn't say I knew the man.

But he hasn't changed at all. He's stuck in the same perpetual spiral of death and rebirth the Phoenix are. Never any need to grow and learn and live for others when you had a multitude of lifetimes ahead to do so tomorrow. A lifetime of tomorrows you would never have to face.

I had no intention of waking the man. Of giving him reason to interact with me and feel in charge of the moment. My mind was only on saddling Shard and escaping awkwardness. As I twisted trying to gain perch on an elbow, I drew in a breath sharply as pain flared in my side, a grunt escaping my lips.

Enzo came awake with a start, BrongTa dagger in hand before him, then settled back as he saw me. I could have sworn there was genuine relief on his face.

Slowly, I turned back to lay on the soft earth. I needed a little longer to recover and get used to being awake. The stars were beginning to appears in the heavens and I admired the display.

"I think." Enzo drew a deep wavering breath. "I think I was angry with you, Elara," Enzo said. Flaring with the words, I tried to sit once more but again the attempt failed. The pain was only half as much now and becoming manageable but still pushed at some tender points. What reason had he to be angry with me.

Enzo only held out a hand to calm me.

"Sit. Let me talk a moment. We get very little time to just be alone these days."

With little choice, I nodded, my gaze tracing back to the heavens.

"In the early days, I couldn't understand why you stayed away. Why you didn't seek to keep what we had alight. I understood there was some adjusting to be done. There was wasted time while you were a child and getting used to a new body. I thought you could have been reborn a male as the Phoenix do and were embarrassed by this. I began to think maybe the transition failed and you weren't reborn at all but seeing Shard each rebirth cycle confirmed you were out there somewhere. Living. Without me. I couldn't understand what I may have done to hurt you so after giving you such a wondrous gift."

"Then I saw you on that mountain top. You stood there ignoring me, giving me nothing until it was made obvious who you were. The way you so casually said my name... I couldn't take it. The rage I kept at bay broke free and I threw you from that cliff top to teach you a lesson. What was one more life time? The Firebirds would live hundreds of lives after even we have passed from this world so what was another 100 years or so to get you back to where they wanted you to be. Even then I had faith in your skill to survive. To take that split second to notice the rope and pull yourself to safety. In that time, I had calmed and you filled my mind once more. I couldn't keep away from you and found you still desired me, after all this time and how you remained distant, you still wanted me. Memories or not, you were drawn to me as I have always been to you. I vow to you here and now, Elara."

Here we go, I thought to myself.

"I vow to find a way to restore your immortality. There will come a point in time where Shard won't be able to resist any more. I can see you working on his tender side, becoming close to him, making yourself

211

irreplaceable. I will work the other angles. Angles that may get my hands dirty. I will do it for you, Elara. When I saw the arrows hit you, I was beside myself. I couldn't lose you again and I won't."

My eyes bulged and a burning dread coursed through my veins at the thought of more pain being bestowed upon Shard or worse, another lifetime in this world full of regret. It was well past time for me to pass from this world... And Enzo too. I looked across at the man, a serious, almost maniacal look contorting his features.

Pushing through the pain, I rose to my feet much to his worry. He too began to rise, a hand raised as if to calm me.

"Rest, Elara, there is nothing more we can do right now. The others have warned the Keep of the dangers and until the dome comes down, we have time. Rest."

"You pompous, self-centred, selfish cretin. Who gives you the right to play God over others? What makes you so much better than anyone else including the Phoenix."

His brow furrowed at my outburst. "Elara, you're going to hurt yourself. I'm doing this for you."

"For me?" I laughed loudly. "You have never listened to what I want. You are doing this for yourself alone, anyone else be damned. I won't have it. You fuck with my life again and I will rip the Phoenix essence from your soul. You will never be reborn again and I will make sure the rest of your pathetic life is short and terrifying. I will not have you harm Shard or any other Phoenix again."

Enzo visibly calmed and a smile crossed his face. "You could never harm me, Elara. I know you are a soft and loving soul and cannot do what is needed. It's why I'm stepping up. Why I will do what must be done for us. I will protect your honour as much as I will protect your lifespan."

I was incredulous. I couldn't believe what I was hearing and knew there was no arguing with him. A number of retorts filled my mind but I bit my tongue. What was the point of this argument. I would never reach Enzo when all he can hear is himself and his greed. He made his choice and now I know my path. I will end Enzo.

Shaking my head softly, I turned and walked to where Shard was resting. There was a slither of light between his eyelids and I knew he was awake. Watching, listening, ensuring I was safe. This was protection and I scratched the back of his neck. He was smart enough to piece together the implications of our conversation and yet he gave me my space. Shard allowed me to deal with the issues myself.

"Time to go, Shard," I said, climbing up into position on his back.

212

Leaning in close, I whispered. "Do not trust that one."

"*I never have,*" Shards words filtered into my mind and I realised we were still linked. It wasn't just a delusion after my body shut down.

As the earth fell away and a weightlessness washed away the pressures and burdens of this world, I thought of the ease of communication I was open to now. I could show Shard just what happened in my first life to lock him away.

"No need," Shard called back using his real voice.

"Pardon?" I asked. Surely, I wasn't speaking out loud.

"You already flooded my mind with a deluge of images about it before you passed out. I know enough to know what happened."

"I..." I looked away, emotions bubbling inside. "I didn't mean to show you that until you wanted to see."

Shard curved along the peaks of a mountain range. The crisp evening air sending tingles over my skin and cleansing my body with every breath. An underground spring flowed out the side of the cliff face to dissipate into the air in a shimmer of colour and sparkles set off by light of the dying sun as it caressed the mountain tops. Catching my fascination, Shard skimmed the cliff face sideways, allowing us to pass under the misty waters.

"I have known many souls in my time. At the time we have made our pact and our minds link, the first thought of a human is always their darkest secrets. The dirty abyss they never want the world to find out. It's as if, knowing I can read their minds, they seek that which they don't want me to know to confirm that it is still locked away in the depths of their souls. Tainting their hearts. That the deepest secrets and regrets of yours were over another's deeds and your part in it was finding your conscious and fighting back. I am amazed you remained so pure with hundreds of years behind you."

"It makes sense. Those are the thoughts we would be persecuted for but you haven't seen my whole existence. I can be a dirty girl too."

Shard screeched suddenly and I needed to hold my ears a moment as the high-pitched tone passed.

"Not those types of thoughts," he said. "I don't need to see humans that way. And no. chasing off your dad's sheep because he reprimanded you for climbing the tree overgrowing the cliff side doesn't count either."

I chuckled at his discomfort. "How much have you seen?"

"Almost everything," Shard replied. "Your mind is very active when unconscious or asleep."

"Will I ever get to witness your lives?"

Shard went quiet a moment and we just glided over a distant forest.

213

When he finally spoke, there was a pit of regret and pain in his voice.

"We do not share memories from before our Soul's birth."

"What happened?"

There was more hesitation, and it felt like even answering this was pushing the limits.

"There had been Seven Phoenix who could pact with humans. Because of the information shared with a human, six remain. Smokey was the last of us who could bare chicklings.

The regret I felt at even reopening that wound was terrible and I made certain I wouldn't ask again. "I'm sorry for your loss. Humans have all but destroyed your existence."

Shard didn't reply and I could sense he was ready to drop the subject all together. A speck on the horizon announced the approaching Telverian Keep and I realised I remembered very little of the scouting trip. Only patches of darkness, horrific enemies and the Lich.

"Can you show me from when we entered the dome to when I passed out, Shard? My mind is in a haze and I'm going to need the information for the battles ahead."

Almost instantly, the memories played before my eyes showing me the scene from Shard's perspective. I got a better grasp of the enemy and what happened to me. Subconsciously, I reached up to feel the arrow wounds but found they already healed over. A feat only I could have achieved unless another skilled Drifter had been wandering close to the smoke dome.

Then the gentle and emotional words from Shard echoed in my mind. The words he used to keep me aware, keep me functional. I could hear the underlying tones showing how genuine the words and feelings behind them were. Honestly, I was flawed as much now as I had been being carried in Shard's talons.

The mist of the memories pulled back from my sight and I found we had already landed upon the rooftop at the Keep. Tears had dampened my cheeks and I sat unmoving, just looking at Shard as he waited patiently for me to dismount. With a rush of emotion, I flung my arms around his neck and hugged him tightly.

"She is strangling him," Flint screeched.

"Free Shard," Ash cried.

The other Phoenix bobbed and swayed as they darted this way and that around Shard looking for a clear opening. The way these intelligent beings acted reminded me so much of the common wren or squawking parrot that I couldn't hold back. What began as a lofty and rolling rumble in the back of my throat churned and swirled until I was laughing in a ridiculously loud manner. My eyes were tearing over and I was having trouble breathing but I couldn't stop. These creatures were so innocently hilarious I lost all control.

"She mocks us," Flint spoke again.

"We must get Shard out of her grasp," Ember chitted.

"It is a hug," Shard almost growled. He was beginning to become annoyed with both the other Phoenix and my affection.

"Shard lives," They chirped and danced as if they had a hand in his wellbeing.

Finally finding some moments of calm minutes later I apologised to Shard and scratched the back of his neck sending his feathers into a tizzy.

"Stop that," He squawked. "Haven't you somewhere to be."

I smiled and jumped from his back. There was little pain in my limbs anymore and I felt almost fully healed. Only minor aches reminded me I had almost lost my life. A thought occurred to me.

"How long have I been out, Shard?"

"A good part of three days. You used up too much energy healing yourself. That alone almost killed you but you were dead without it. Your heartbeat even stopped a moment. Ember says the others are at the bar. Go, be with them. Talon has contacted us and war is now marching on the Keep to arrive this time tomorrow."

A sigh escaped my lips as the thought of tomorrow grew heavy on my shoulders. I'd already lived and died enough that once more didn't worry me. I was here now and that's all that mattered.

"Your enigma is at the bar also..."

My head slowly turned to lock eyes with Shard, a wicked little grin curling my lips. You didn't need to be linked to know where that open sentence was heading. "I thought you didn't like to think of human's that way."

He chirped at me and cocked his head away. "If it helps you relax for tomorrow, I am not against it."

"He may be the enemy," I said softly.

"Then stick him with your sword instead of letting him stick you. Go. Have fun," Shard said.

Some rather dirty thoughts entered my mind. They had been on a completely different tangent to how Shard meant but a devilish grin began to grow.

"That won't count either," Shard called after me as I skipped down the stairwell.

My friends seemed down and out sitting around the bar table. There were drinks in various mugs but no one was touching them. Each was lost in their own little world. Their faces etched with lines of worry and contemplation as they pondered the likelihood of tomorrow. By now the Phoenix should have passed on the information that the enemy was marching. It was strange to me they wouldn't just teleport into the Keep and kill everyone inside but I guess it made us all suspenseful. There wouldn't be many that slept well tonight and that alone would help the army of the dead.

Of course, the Lich would have its own strategy and tactics. We still couldn't know for sure what that creature could be after or why it chose now to attack. Maybe he might... Looking around the room, I couldn't see Riven anywhere and my heart sank. That, most of all, I couldn't understand. There was every possibility he was the enemy. A plant to weaken us in some way. Maybe open the gates at an opportune time or kill the General, tactfully cutting the head off the snake. It was hard to know just what his game was but to why I still wanted that man naked, hot, against me. That was something I couldn't understand. There was only pain down that path.

Not surprisingly, it was Fitz that saw me first. He was always the more perceptive of the group and having the only chair that faced straight at the door helped. Immediately, his face lit up. His features almost coming alive in colour and radiance as he sat bolt upright. Such a beautiful smile touched his face and I could only return one with similar feeling behind it if not such natural beauty.

The others began to catch on one by one as Fitz raced over to embrace me in a strong and gentle hug. Everyone was on their feet as Fitz finally let go, their faces mirroring the enthusiasm of Fitz's earlier.

"Hey, everyone," I said giving a quick wave and feeling suddenly bashful with all the attention.

"Welcome home, Elara," Baras said. There was a shimmer in his eye that looked almost like he was tearing up.

"Was it wrong to leave you with Enzo? He didn't give us much choice," Fitz said quietly leaning in as if even bringing up the name could somehow harm me.

I shook my head and placed a reassuring hand on his shoulder. I remained just as quiet. "It put a few things into perspective. I'll be killing him soon enough. I just need to work out the right way."

"Oh, I bet Elara was on him the moment she woke," Kymberlin said smirking and I blanched. "There was plenty of unfinished sexual tension after the journey to the Phoenix nest."

216

"Fuck off, Kymmie," I replied, flipping the Firebird. A flurry of flames and sparks danced around my middle finger.

"We can all see the bounce in your step. It's like sunshine's beaming out your arse and you want everyone to know. If only man meat was here to witness it. Maybe he'd try to smother it with his own light."

"Well, of course you'd recognise the signs but you couldn't be further from the truth." I turned to Fitz. "Riven?"

"Still around, just hasn't been out much. Take no heed of her words. She's been the most worried." Fitz said.

"Bullllshit," Kymberlin growled. "And what did you mean by of course I'd recognise it? I'm not a slut."

"Sorry, I just assumed Baras had been filling you with something to get you walking crooked. You seem more lopsided now than the last time we drank."

Her mouth hung open a moment before jamming shut. Kymberlin looked away as if contemplating something, her face growing increasingly red. Finally, her eyes returned to us. "Come for a walk Baras," she said grabbing his shirt and dragging him to his feet.

As they stumbled from the bar, Baras shot me a look saying 'what have you done?'. I burst out laughing.

"I'm glad things haven't changed very much since my absence. You all looked lost."

"War come. Phoenix Soul die. Many die. Much to get right with self before battle," Korr said. There was a large possibility that we won't be breathing tomorrow. It took a lot to come to terms with that fact.

"And I interrupted your soul searching. I'm sorry."

"We were beginning to get too depressing anyways. The other soldiers could feel something inevitable was coming and it wasn't going to be good for morale. You brought light back to our world and this dark little bar. That arse of yours really does shine," Fitz said before smacking my butt.

A squeak escaped my lips and a number of patrons listening in began to laugh.

"Here's to the Phoenix Maid's arse and having it home where it belongs," Fitz called raising his glass to the room.

"Here, here!" Came the roar of everyone within. There were cheers and laughter as my face began to burn like the heart of a Phoenix, rich in crimson.

"It's been a dreary place without that arse wandering our halls," one person called.

"She's got an arse like a brewer's prize cask, round, firm, and begging

217

to be tapped," another cheered.

Fitz's brows rose at the last comment and glancing at me, he just shrugged enticing a giggle. I hadn't realised just how legendary my arse could be.

"Let's go raise the troops morale," Fitz grinned.

"Fine, but just know you started this. I draw the line at tapping this aged beauty, though."

I let out a squeal as Korr picked me up effortlessly and sat me up on the counter, much to the amusement of those around us.

With spirits high, I seized the moment, and one of the soldier's mugs. Standing up on the bar, I downed the gritty ale and threw the mug across the room.

"Who wants a song and a dance?" I cried. If I didn't have the crowd's attention before, the cries and cheers now would have woken the commander in the Keep's stronghold. "We need a song then," I smiled walking the bar top. Many songs had been shouted in that moment. Songs of bravery and heroes. Songs of buxom beauties and memorable nights. All I had learned across my lives and all I could put on a show for.

"The dragon's lament," Korr said near my side and those around him grew quiet. They became thoughtful as if reflecting on their own worth. And as the mentioned name circled the bar, not a soul was so rowdy or so cheerful as the moments before.

It was a sad and inspirational song talking of the balance between life and death and how our deeds echo through time in legends and fable. Though we are all to die it is how we choose to take that quest that makes the difference. I had seen the stone dragon once, sleeping in the distant mountains of the West. A village was built around it to tend the beast and protect it. I never got to hear the full legend but the dragon had once lived and breathed, a menace for many, but when an even greater danger threatened the way of life for the people in the area, the dragon gave its life to protect them. It was cursed with a petrifying spell and now rested in the town square.

The room was quiet as eyes began to fall on me, expectant. It wasn't the song I had believed would be requested but I felt it was right. Standing upon the bar, I closed my eyes and began. I couldn't boast the most melodic voice but the emotion I could fill the words with had many shed a tear. Slow and rolling, I let the words free:

"In the heart of the square where the old stories dwell,
A dragon of stone in the cold, ceaseless rain,

Children in whispers recall what befell,
The echo of thunder, the shimmer of pain.

They gather for warmth as the night settles in,
Longing for magic to stir from within.
Once, elders would speak of a time it had soared,
Alive in the hearts of the meek and the worn.

They swore on the wind that it opened its eyes,
Guarded their sorrows as tears matched the skies.
Now, moss on its claws and the silence grows deep,
Carrying legends no one dares to keep.

But still, in the rain, hope stirs through the gloom, ·
For courage is found in the cracks of a tomb.
Though stone may not rouse and lost dreams decay,
The memories burn all the shadows away.

A roar in the silence.
A promise remains,
Strength can be born from the heaviest of chains."

The song faded into the tavern. Opening my eyes, I found the soldiers around the room were entranced. All eyes were on me as the tune echoed in their minds. And as if a spell had broken, they all began to move, one by one. Each held hand to heart and bowed their heads towards me.

"Phoenix Soul." The words were repeated around the room filling in the silence.

"We would follow you into the depths of the abyss itself," one man said, and a general murmur of agreeance rose up.

"And I would lay down my life for each and every one of you," I replied, moved by their display of affection. With the use of Fitz's offered hand, I stepped down from the bar top and made my way through the crowd. Stopping here and there to shake a hand or give some words to a warrior who looked especially down. By the time I had made the door to the bar, I'd learned of a number of warriors names and a lot of their hopes and back stories. I had no intention of adding more people to the long list of names I'd outlived but the caring and uplifting nature I nurtured wouldn't let me pass quietly.

"It doesn't look as though you've had it rough lately."

Stepping from the bar, my head swivelled towards the voice I'd longed to hear again. Leaning against a wall was Riven, a smile etched into his features. Without the ability to keep myself at bay, I took the few steps between us and leapt into his arms. His cooling embrace washed over me setting my heart alight. I melted into the embrace, loving the feel of the man's strong chest as a cushion. I couldn't say whether it was the highly emotional mood I was in or the small amount of alcohol that was impairing my system, providing a nice euphoria, but it didn't even cross my mind that Riven could be an enemy.

For a time at least. When my senses began to sharpen and I was able to gather some wits about me, it was all I could think of.

"What are you?" I asked without letting go. My voice soft, almost too soft, and for a time I couldn't be sure he heard me.

"I am what you see. A warrior following the orders of his lord," Riven replied.

"Me and Korr are going to head, Elara. We would hate to shadow your reunion," Fitz said and I tensed. I'd already forgotten they were with me, and I was about to say some things that would cause issues for Riven. "Try to get some sleep."

Lifting my head from Riven's chest I nodded to them. "I'll save any sleepless nights until after the battle," I promised much to the dissatisfied look of Riven.

Fitz smiled and Korr... Well, Korr's expression didn't change at all when they left.

"No sleepless nights even with the stars shining above?" Riven asked.

"We don't yet have a field with the enemy about," I countered taking a moment to get my thoughts straight and tyring to fend off the awkward moment that was about to occur as long as possible.

"Then I guess we better clear the fields."

"Will you?"

Riven just stared a moment waiting for the end of the question. "Will I?"

"Will you clear the fields of the enemy?"

To have such a question of loyalty asked of him didn't seem to affect Riven in the slightest. He just continued to gaze at me with those steel grey eyes, a crooked smile the only change in his demeanour.

"Of course I'll clear the field of enemies."

"And what enemy will that be?"

His eyes narrowed. "You had best ask the question you are skirting around."

"Are you an agent of the Lich."

"In the broadest of terms, yes," Riven said simply.

"Just know my eyes can see more than just... What?" I asked softly, my mind taking a moment to process the words.

"I am alive because of the Lich."

"You are an enemy," I whispered taking a retreating step backwards.

"I am not your enemy, Elara."

I was shaking my head in disbelief as I took another step back.

"The Lich has control over you. You can be triggered at any moment to cause great upheaval for the Telverians. Give me one reason I shouldn't sound the alarm right now?"

Riven looked away, sadness creeping into his eyes. His chin furrowed.

"You can't, can you? You don't even trust yourself," I said, a sorrow entering my voice.

"I'm fighting him," Riven said in a sudden outburst, the stress and worry of everything etched into every line in his face. His arm flailing for dramatics. "I'm not just some worthless hunk of meat to be manoeuvred and manipulated at a moment's notice. I can feel his link to me. I can feel him pushing back. Sometimes he catches me off guard like when I tried to warn you about your latest mission but I will not let him take me."

By the end, Riven had tears in his eyes. I could see how much this was affecting him, but I couldn't be sure I could trust him. What if this was all a ruse and the Lich is manipulating me, working on my humanity to keep his spy in our ranks. This was all too much and I needed help.

Taking another step back I froze in sudden realisation. To take my eyes from Riven, even for a moment, may be the last time I see him. The Lich would know he is compromised. It may even speed up his role in all this. I needed to keep him distracted until we destroyed the Lich.

Steeling myself, I took the first step towards Riven. "So, you've lied to me this whole time. Played me with your pretty words. Flirted and kept me at arm's length," I stated. "Can a Lich even love another being?"

A dark look crossed his features as if I struck a sore spot. Without a word, Riven turned and began walking away.

"Do you believe I will let you leave? To run back to your master?" I said and he paused mid stride. He didn't turn back but I could see he loosened up as if he was expecting a fight.

"I have no master."

"Then prove it," I said softly. I hadn't realised until I said the words how much I needed it to be true. More than anything, I needed Riven to be an ally. To mean everything he said to me.

Head turned to the side as if speaking over his shoulder, Riven replied.

"And how do I do that? Tell you all the secrets my mind could hold? No. That could come from the Lich. Then what? Kill myself? Show you I'm not a threat by not existing at all? I will not do that!" He swung his arm out as he spun around to face me.

I could never wish his death even if it proved anything. With a rush of emotions, I dove into Riven's arms, wrapping my own around his body. He drew back surprised but didn't push me away.

"Stay with me," I whimpered. I couldn't say why this affected me so much. Why I felt so strongly for this man when he could quite easily harm me. I couldn't even say I knew anything about him. "Just... Stay with me. Be by my side and watch the sun rise over the fields. Fight at my side tomorrow and protect my back. If you turn on me and I die it will be right. I won't want to live without you by my side. Just stay with me and show me you're true."

Leaning back, Riven brought his hand up to rest upon my cheek. "Until you command me, I will be nowhere else."

Our eyes met in a perfect moment, and I couldn't want anything more. I wanted him. Leaning in, I closed my eyes as our lips met. Lightning surged through every part of me. Our bodies, minds, souls, entangling into one another. Every atom shared between us came alive to dance and sing. A choir of love, a sonnet of life, a saga of eternity shared between us in that one moment.

I shuddered as we came apart. I hadn't missed anything so quickly and so wholly in all my life. And this was only heighted by the sharp intake of breath from Riven. I could see, he too, was taken. Lost in the ocean that was Elara.

"Let's go back to my bed," I said, my voice husky with desire. And a strangled, almost heartbreaking look crossed Riven's face.

"Do you fear bedding me that you may lose control of yourself?" I asked hoping that was all it may be, but he shook his head and the beginnings of a lump formed in my throat.

"I don't want to have to tell you no, Elara. I meant every word I said to you," Riven replied. "I want our first time to be in the open fields under the stars. I want to shout your name to the earth and the sky and let the rocks tremble and the waves crash in frustration knowing you are mine and I am yours."

It was a relief he still wanted me but there was such a need for relief right now. I know I'll have gone crazy by the end of the night.

"You meant every word?" I asked.

"I have always tried to be honest."

"478 years old ring a bell? How honest could that have been?"

Riven just remained quiet, a smirk on his face. He stood waiting for the penny to drop while I felt so overconfident that I had caught him in a lie. The silence grew dense and I began to question his words; find some hidden meaning I was missing.

"You can't be 478," I said before the thought of the Lich and his ability to manipulate life crossed my mind. My eyes grew wide. "You're 478!"

"It's why I'm able to fight the Lich's mind control. I've had centuries of becoming accustomed to it. The harsh power fades in time yet the creature doesn't seem to care so much when it has vast hordes of bodies to manipulate."

My mouth was hanging open as I just stared up at him. "You're four hundred and seventy-eight years old." He was older than me. The thought sent tingles running through my body. It was how I liked them. And I believed it was impossible this day and age. It was funny as I will have soon slept with two out of two men who fit the build this last year alone. Lust and longing filled my eyes as they settled on Riven. "You will follow me to my bed," I said, a hand on his chest.

"But I," Riven stammered before I placed a finger to his lips silencing him. My hand then trailed slowly down his chest to where a part of him began to grow. Curling my fingers around Riven's manhood, I bit my lip as I felt his girth. A thick cock, I began to gently caress up and down its length.

"He is safe," I motioned to my new friend. "But I will have you hold my tonight and long into the morning before we are required on the field. Just know, either yours or my hands will be busy because I cannot wait so long without release."

Turning I began to walk off after shooting a wink over my shoulder. A sound echoed behind me, halting at first. I smiled as I heard his footsteps coming after me.

Chapter 12

By midday, we emerged from my room energized and ready to take on the world. Riven treated me with gentle embraces and soft caresses. I'd been wrapped up in his arms all night and never felt so safe and at peace in my lives.

It was going to be a terribly hard moment if I ever had to sink my sword into his chest. And with that, I knew I needed help.

Walking from the main gates to the open plains beyond the Keep, I scanned the horizon. The smoke haze was still out there circling the Keep but the enemy was now pulled back to a more comfortable range. I didn't know strategy as well as I thought I did but it looked like they enemy wanted us to meet them in the field. They allowed just enough room between them and the walls for our armies and a killing ground.

I saw the General, along with the other commanders and Phoenix Souls already out on the field. It was a mid-morning strategy meeting and it looked as though it was already underway. I glanced at Riven.

"Wait by the gate and remain in view. I don't want to have to chase you down but you know I will."

Riven grinned sheepishly. "I walk where you do," he said before jogging back the few metres to stand by the opening. The gates had only been opened enough to allow the General and the meeting group to pass but didn't risk any more, allowing for a quick lockdown.

As I got close to the group, I was able to get the attention of Fitz. Tilting my head he got the message for a private moment and walked from the meeting to stand 20 metres away.

Standing uneasily, I tried to work out what to say. Even making eye contact was hard knowing what I was about to disclose.

"That bad, huh?" Fitz said breaking the silence.

I just nodded.

"Something to do with your boy back there?" Fitz indicated to Riven.

I pursed my lips. Fitz was too good at seeing to the root of things. "If I asked something of you that danced along the lines of treason, what would your next move be?"

Fitz studied me with narrow eyes. "Is now the time for this with the General right there?"

"There can be no other time. It is either you or Baras I will ask?"

His hand rose subconsciously to his mouth as he considered my question. "I honestly cannot say without knowing more. I can dance the lines of treason like any soldier but for some that line is closer or further away. With Baras you will find the line is closer to honour. Only your history may sway his decision. You can only trust me to do what is right. Right for you or right for Telveria is the question though."

"If I asked you to kill a man for me, would you do it?"

"Enzo?" Fitz asked.

"Enzo's mine," I replied with a smile. "Riven is the target."

The absolute shock on Fitz's face was amusing as it was the last name he would have guessed I'd say.

"You need to tell me more," Fitz sputtered.

"You know I can transcend my body?"

"Will you two be joining us any time soon?" Suniel called.

"One more moment, sir. Just acquiring some information I requested. Vital but not relevant."

Suniel nodded and turned back to the others. He put a lot of trust in Fitz's word.

"I know of your ability. Give me everything and be quick. We have little time."

"I transitioned into spirit to investigate something Shard mentioned of Riven. There is an energy line from Riven back to the Lich."

"A spy?!" Fitz's eyes grew dark.

"Not completely. Riven is fighting the connection. He has been fighting it for centuries, gaining better control every year. He is as in control as he can be now and it takes brute force to hijack Riven's mind for even a short time. I would ask you to kill him should he step out of line."

"I would prefer to kill him now," Fitz said, hand resting on the hilt of his sword.

"And I thank you for the effort you have put into staying your hand. That alone means more than anything. I have asked Riven not to leave my side throughout the battle. I would like to make my final decision then and I need your input."

"He knows you know?"

"He does."

Fitz growled as he paced back and forth. "You're too close to him, Elara."

"It's why I brought you in. I will trust your decision even against my own heart."

Fitz hesitated only a moment longer. "Fine. One foot wrong and he dies."

"Thank you, Fitz," I said.

He stuck up a warning finger. "Not for this, Ellie. If anything goes wrong, it's both our heads."

"You knew nothing about it. In fact, I'm sure you'll try to stop it. I'm not thanking you for what you're doing. I'm thanking you for your friendship. It means so much to me. We see the world differently, you and I. Your life is fragile, fleeting like falling glass. Everything has more urgency, more weight. It is this I need as I have been tempered across many lives. I see passed things that are important, neglecting the fleeting and the fragile details."

With pursed lips, Fitz angled past me. "Let's just get back to the meeting. Thank you for keeping him distant."

I followed closely. There was no doubt I put Fitz in an impossible position and he was feeling hard pressed about it. Most likely thinking back to the moment we started our journey to become Phoenix Souls and contemplating the myriad outcomes that could have occurred if he had just left the young maid be. He at least wouldn't be in this predicament.

General Suniel took one look at Fitz and his brow furrowed. "Anything we need to know?"

And the impossible position just got worse. This was the moment Fitz was to decide if he was to back Telveria or myself.

"Seems we have a possible traitor in the Keep," Fitz said and my heart sank. I did say I would back his decision no matter the outcome. It was still sad. Suniel's expression however turned grave.

"How deep?"

"New recruit. No access to anything important. Only the ability to get close to those in power."

"You have leave to take care of the matter. If it suits, take Riven. Lad's been rather useful to us lately and his skill is beyond his age."

"I might just do that," Fitz said and my eyes bulged. Suniel then turned on me.

"Elara ShardSoul, we do not bring our entertainment to meetings. It's not on."

The soft embers of embarrassment crept across my face as a raging turmoil of worry and doubt churned in my belly. I watched as Fitz had a few words with Riven before those steely greys looked to me. I nodded and Riven took off after Fitz into the Keep. I prayed they both returned.

"Phoenix Maiden no more," Kymberlin joked but I let it roll on passed me. I wasn't in the mood to argue back.

"If we are quite done," Commander Dren said, his impatience palpable.

"Commander, General," Kymberlin bowed her head and stood casually, attention back to front.

"We will make an assault on the field. A swan song, so to say. Our troops will stand together as one right her."

"Would not the Keep provide a greater defensible position? We've been holding off the enemy so far with an acceptable death rate," Baras asked.

Too hear any rate of death was acceptable disturbed me greatly but times of war demanded sacrifice. That at least is the majority belief and words such as Baras said could be forgiven by the survivors with a favourable outcome.

"The problem is that Wyrm. The enemy need only harry us with the Harpies, keeping our attention distracted while the Wyrm gets in behind the walls. Once that happens, the close quarters will make it impossible to overwhelm it, while the beast just slithers through the streets as if it was in its den. The defences will be our end. We fight in the field where we have a slim chance. The Phoenix can rain terror through enemy ranks without fear of hitting the Keep and we can focus on the rest."

"What's the likely hood of our victory?" I asked. Even my untrained eye could see the possibility we'd be here tomorrow as low. I just wanted a straight answer from the General. Know what I'm fighting to thwart.

"Do not let your fear show on the field, Phoenix Soul. I know that you are a maid and of humble background. That you have lived this long is thanks to the strength of the Phoenix who bonded you. If you allow thoughts of victory and defeat to sway your battle sense on the field the army's morale will fold and crumble," Suniel said dismissing me.

To say Baras looked galled by Suniel's words was an understatement, but it was not his words that filled the silence.

"Speak no ill of Elara, General," Enzo said stepping forward. There was a terrible look in his eyes that promised pain and death. "You have much to thank her for in this moment."

Eyes narrowed as he met Enzo's, he waved a dismissive hand. "That she has done her part in the war is to be expected. I have seen her fight and seen her stand. It was just friendly advice for one who has spent her life in serfdom."

"She is more skilled than..." Enzo began but I stepped up and resolved myself to place a hand on his shoulder. The gesture irksome in itself.

"It is not your honour you banter for. Still your tongue for my sake. We will have fighting enough come this afternoon. The General only sought to help me understand my place."

"He speaks out of turn," Enzo said quietly.

"He has the only right. Stand down," I growled.

Oh, he did not like that. To be put in his place, Enzo's temper was silently bubbling below the surface. I smiled at him then. A smile that spoke of his empty soul and the depths of his selfish pride but he misread the gesture. There was something in his eyes that tended to lust and he took a step back.

Whatever works. I turned back to the general. "As you were."

A grunt escaped the General and he turned back to the group.

"If we are agreed then let's move to the more intricate details," Suniel said.

He started pointing at different parts of the field. A debate beginning over the types of troops to be placed and where. There were merits and negatives among the arguments and Baras seemed to be in his element.

I never realised just how much planning went in to not only saving the lives of the realm, but in doing so with as little loss as possible. I was truly impressed with the role of the Commanders and General. I will never again think of them as some blood thirsty hoard seeking to profit and fill their bloodlust through war. At times, especially in defence, it was needed. Little would survive a true bloodthirsty hoard.

As the day wore on and the hours grew thin, I grew bored with war tactics. So much so that I felt more like what I had originally perceived the General and his men to be than what they were. One venture may lose five lives where another could lose ten. I was currently at a point I didn't care enough to squabble over one or two extra lives. It felt a little over done when a simple stone in the field could trip a single soldier avalanching into a series of catastrophes and death. Luck was the only true balance on the field.

After the first hour, Fitz had returned giving a nod to the General. I let out a sigh of relief seeing Riven back by the gate though his face was now weary. Whatever transpired between Riven and Fitz seemed arduous but that they both returned showed Fitz at least trusted him enough. That is all I hoped for.

There was a short break and a meagre meal of black bread and cheese. Enough to refuel the body and chase away the ache in the empty stomach but not enough to make one sick during battle. A battle that was fast approaching if the advancing smoke screen said anything.

Tremors of a horn blast echoed over the field and through the Keep. The enemy had been sighted on the high walls. The commanders filed back to the gate as men began to enter the field and form rank.

Liahna took control of the right flank and Dren the left. Each led their soldiers to designated positions out in the field. I was glad to see old Scrause hang back to command the archers with Walan above the battlements commanding small siege engines and sending information of the war movements in real time. A handful of other Commanders,

Captains and the like, were scattered amongst the field leading smaller strike forces, ready to step up if the chain of command became broken.

It was amazing and inspiring to see the full force of thousands of soldiers in the field. For those townsfolk hiding under beds or in pantry cabinets, it would lift their hearts just that little bit to see such a disciplined force protecting them.

Myself, I was just happy to have Riven back at my side. The Phoenix Souls each stood at equal distance apart along the front lines. I was second from centre with the leading position going to Enzo. He was the most well-known being a Soul for many years longer. Lifetimes if you want to get technical but the soldiers wouldn't recognise that. They just needed a known face to follow.

"Will the Phoenix not be in the battle?" Riven asked.

I looked back at the Firebirds sitting on the battlements. They'd been spaced as equally as their Souls, sitting behind their bonded.

"Gathering intelligence for your Master," I quipped nudging Riven with my elbow. He didn't seem impressed.

"Was it necessary you sent the ranger over to hound me? I almost preferred death after listening to him droning on for over an hour."

"It's no surprise I am biased when it comes to you. I cannot trust myself to thrust a sword into your heart should that circumstance come to pass. Fitz is my insurance. I needed someone I could trust more than myself to do what was right. It was Suniel that suggested taking you on a mission. He's been impressed with you of late. It was just happenstance you and Fitz were thrust together after he found out your truths."

"Anyone else know?" Riven asked. "Should I expect any more lectures?"

"Only those I felt the need to tell. And Shard but he suspected something of you when he carried you the other day."

"I noticed he wasn't too happy with me."

"You still hadn't thanked me for saving you with the ice slide by the way."

Riven raised an eyebrow. "I hadn't realised it was you that saved me. Thought the lady of luck was on my side with a freak end of season ice formation."

I was beside myself. "The only ice wielder in this kingdom at your back and you send your thanks to the elements."

"It was your bird that tried to kill me," Riven pointed out. "Couldn't say whether you both shared objectives."

I punched him in the arm and relished at just how padded my hand was with Kymberlin's gauntlets. "Watch yourself old man. And don't worry. The Phoenix will reign terror down on your kin when the battle begins. That was always a given."

Riven laughed breaking an underlying tension that was niggling at my mind. I'd been worried I'd gone too far bringing Fitz into the circle of trust and Riven was wary of me. His infectious laughter told me not to worry so. That we could be from opposing armies and still be this comfortable with one another was remarkable.

At 400 paces the smoke screen finally halted its advance. It was massive and if the size was anything to go off, then so too was going to be the army inside. I already knew it was big. I'd seen it first hand with the Lich still bringing in troops.

The General rode out a few paces and turned to face his men. Here, in his shining battle armour he voiced an inspiring and riveting speech. He spoke of honour and bravery. There was the calling to defend the families of all Telveria. To put aside the fears we harboured and be the heroes we were all born to be. It was this hour we would fight and die. It was this hour we would crush the enemy into the dirt. Each and every deed performed on the battlefield would echo through history. Now was the time to become immortal.

At least that's what I hoped he was yelling about. It was quite hard to hear him with thousands of people fidgeting and buffeting around in steel armour. Even when I stood fairly close, most pf the words I needed to fill in myself.

The speech ended with Suniel thrusting his sword into the sky and giving a tumultuous battle cry. I like to think he was trying to stab some imaginary god who suddenly broke his focus but this cry alone was unifying for the soldiers. Like a ripple, it was picked up all the way down the lines of warriors. Even to the point I found myself echoing the gesture. In that moment, I felt there was no need for long winded speeches. He just needed to ride out, attack a god and yell. Everyone would be as one after that.

But any hope of keeping that energy in the charge was lost when the smoke dissipated. I looked over the forces and even I felt the cold hand of Death resting on my shoulder. At least ten times the number of soldiers stood across the killing grounds. Harpies as thick as clouds hovered above the masses with dark feathered Phoenix gliding above. Chimera of all shapes and sizes could be seen standing alongside the humanoid dead. I swear I even caught a glimpse of a unicorn. At the far back coiled in a large weave of scales sat the Wyrm. The fierce and giant creature alone was going to be enough to instil fear into the men.

I looked over the paling, faltering faces of our soldiers. If something wasn't done and quick we were going to have mass desertion.

Suniel was no better. Though he had been warned of what was out there, nothing could prepare a man to witness certainty of death. I feared those wide, terrified eyes were going to be counted amongst the soldiers fleeing the field but when he suddenly tempered himself, I was impressed. I could only guess that years of training and fighting had let him find that inner sanctuary he could store his fear.

"Heroes of Telveria, onwards to the glorious feast in the halls of hell," he cried and charged the field.

I felt so sorry for him in that moment. No more than twenty paces and he turned to find no one was at his back. Sure, there was a Commander or two in a similar position but the soldiers remained in rank, frozen to the spot. Some had made to step out, to follow their leader into the fray but with the majority held in a state of fear, the braver stepped back.

Now the ranks of warriors were sitting on the edge of a knife. Fear itself was like a plague. Everyone infected by it battled within themselves to keep it in check. It would take only one person to fail, to break and run, for the fear to grow and take the hearts of all around them.

Scanning the eyes of the men I knew it would be only moments before the weakest in the chain snapped. We were about to lose the battle without even swinging a sword or loosing an arrow.

"Are you with me, Shard?" I pulsed back at him through our mind link.

"Even unto a true death," came the response and I was filled with a calm I didn't think possible. Where fear was a curse, so too could bravery be the antidote.

The enemy began a slow and steady approach. The silence of it almost worse than hearing a horde shouting a battle cry as they bounded down on you.

And then the first man broke... and a second... and five more, before soldiers were fighting each other to flee.

"In the heart of the square where the old stories dwell," I thanked lady luck my voice was strong and true. I stepped out towards the approaching army giving a moment for my voice to reach the soldiers ears.

"A dragon of stone in the cold, ceaseless rain,
Children in whispers recall what befell,
The echo of thunder, the shimmer of pain.
They gather for warmth as the night settles in,

Longing for magic to stir from within."

My heart leapt as another voice echoed my own. Riven had taken up the tune giving body to my voice. Then another warrior and Kymberlin and Fitz. The song grew in strength as I began to jog. I had no need to look back upon my allies. With their support or not my only path was forward.

Once, elders would speak of a time it had soared,
Alive in the hearts of the meek and the worn.
They swore on the wind that it opened its eyes,
Guarded their sorrows as tears matched the skies.
Now moss on its claws and the silence grows deep,
Carrying legends no one dares to keep.

By now it was all that could be heard. Soldiers all over the field had offered their voices to the words and joined in the cry. I picked up the pace as I heard hundreds upon thousands of boots beating over the hard earth to follow me.

But still, in the rain, hope stirs through the gloom,
For courage is found in the cracks of a tomb.
Though stone may not rouse and lost dreams decay,
The memories burn all the shadows away.
A roar in the silence. A promise remains:
Strength can be born from the heaviest of chains."

The piercing cry of the Phoenix roundest off the verse as fires of oranges and blues created a canopy in the sky above, taming the flying beasts.

We picked up the song once more from the start, the verse flowing like an enchantment, fuelling courage and steeling the hearts of men.

With the chant high, I clashed into the enemy ranks alongside comrades. I was blessed to die beside these men today.

As the ranks folded in on one another, it became more a contest of push and pull. The area too crowded to swing a sword properly and many men went down when the enemy found an angle to thrust a sword first.

Even I almost fell to a skinny, half dead corpse when I got my sword arm stuck. Diverting a blow that would have taken my head with a gauntlet, I pulled a knife and rammed it into the enemy's throat before getting it wedged into the eye socket of the woman pinning my arm.

This bought me a little space to move and with a sword aimed at my stomach blocked by Riven, I began to cut and slash my way through the enemy ranks.

"Use your ice. Use your flames." Riven yelled. "It's why they separate you from your Phoenix, to double the magic users."

I was astounded I had forgotten something so ingrained into my being that I would fight with sword alone. This was how big the moment I had had with my allies was.

I began to laugh. Not as crazy as Korr sounded half a field away, but many would think me mad after this. Yet, still the men rallied to me.

The first Chimera I saw didn't get a chance to attack as I put it down with an ice shard through the eye and up into the brain. The tail of a snake was still biting and I crushed it under my boot as I passed. Columns of flames burst from the ground setting enemies alight and toppling many to the earth. If anyone was in danger of my flames spreading to the allies, I would quench them immediately and ram my sword home ending the enemy's fleeting life.

With a chain mace of searing blue flame, manifested in each hand I began to dance through the enemy ranks. Each chain ignited what it touched and as it was made from flame passed through the enemy warriors without disturbing my dance. The spiked ball at the end had sharp fangs of ice hidden in the flames. As one would lodge into a soft piece of flesh, I would form another to replace it and continue my spinning and twirling.

Even the Chimera, normally impervious to flame, fell to the intense heat of Shard's blue flame essence and my ice crystals. None stood a chance and my comrades did all they could so that I wouldn't be out flanked. I saw one soldier even dive in front of an arrow for me. The arrow lodged in his shoulder and I paused my dance to ensure he was evacuated to the healer's quarters just inside the walls.

I kept an eye on Riven and he was in perfect form. It was hard to tell his kill count amongst the bodies piling up around him but his lance was ever hungry and he never seemed to tire. He glanced across at me while dispatching a warrior and winked. I pointed to both my eyes with a stern look and then back to the field, telling him to stay focused and encouraging a joyous laugh from the man as he went back to twirling his lance.

He better be good with a stick, I thought as I watched his beautiful and well-balanced performance. The temperature on the field was pushing towards uncomfortably warm levels, though anything above a soft, alluring chill was uncomfortable for me. This was different.

A shrill, heart trembling roar pierced the grounds as the Wyrm reared up, towering over the field. It was late to enter the battle and was used perfectly to dampen the growing morale of the men. I could see within the minds and hearts of the soldiers around me that there was a strong and terrible fear building within but no one was at risk of faltering. No one looked as though they were about to flee the field. Everyone stood strong behind me, following my lead. This alone quelled my fears, pushing me to be more than I felt I was.

With speed, the Wyrm attacked. Like a javelin, it barrelled through the ranks of Telverians sending bodies of those unfortunate enough to be stuck in its path hundreds of feet into the air. And the damage the Wyrm brought upon its enemies it also did to its allies. There was no care of sides to this creature. Just the destruction of all who fell in its path.

"Stand true, heroes of Telveria. Keep this rabble from reaching our homes and our families while I deal with that little thing," I called above the fighting.

"You seek to flee leaving us alone to die," A voice reached me and I let it slide. The frailties of the heart in the midst of a battle could be forgiven.

Shard, I need a lift," I relayed to my Phoenix before addressing the masses. "The last guy I rutted with was bigger than that thing, so I have nothing to fear. I'll slap that Wyrm down and be back by your side in no time. Just watch Shard. If he flees, so can you."

"If you want a real challenge, find me after the battle. Ain't no woman has tamed my beast yet," A soldier called to the laughter of his friends. I recognised him from the tavern the night before. A lively, black bearded fellow who loved to dance on tables.

"I see you, Ojin, and will look forward to my shot but Riven will be the one I'm taming after the battle."

Ojin looked terribly embarrassed as I called him out by name but it was Riven that made me smile. It was possibly the first time ever I had seen him falter in his movements. The moment ended quickly and he was back to fighting without a word.

Raising a hand above my head, Shard collected me from the field and flung me to his back. "We need to attack the Wyrm," I shouted.

"Easier said than done. It was born of flame with scales that would deflect even the sharpest and hardest of metals," Shard replied as he swung toward the beast. Though many of the archaic Wyrms had wings, it was an encouraging sight to see this one had none. There were two large bumps on its back where the wings could have reduced to down the

234

lines of Wyrm but there would be no great aerial battles today.

"Even if we cannot harm it, we need to distract it and get it away from our soldiers."

"I already expected as much," Shard said.

With a twist and a dive, Shard began to plummet towards the Wyrm at an alarming speed. Stretching my arms wide I manifested hundreds upon thousands of ice daggers around us. Just as Shard arced out of the dive, I flung my entire arsenal at the creature's face and body. The eyes were going to be a good target but everywhere was going to be peppered. If there was a weak spot, I'll see it on my next approach.

Banking hard, Shard brought us around and my face paled dramatically. There hurtling through the air with pinpoint accuracy was a great maw sporting hundreds of razor-sharp fangs. The Wyrm had coiled back and sprung after us moments after our assault and now with the hard manoeuvring we had no way to escape. I now stared down my final death.

A streak of yellow and orange tore through the sky crashing into Shard moments before the Wyrm could tear through us, sending Shard spiralling out of control. I was flung from his back and as we hit the dirt hard and I tumbled through the mud to be facing the sky.

The Wyrm was descending to the earth, a large flaming wing still sticking from its jaws.

"No!" I screamed. "Who...?"

And a deep cry burst from nearby. The kneeling form of Korr could be seen watching the events unfold, a single hand outstretched reaching for his Phoenix. It was heartbreaking to witness.

Ember's essence would already be travelling back to the nesting grounds to await Korr's energy for rebirth. They will be together once more but never again in the way they have been. I couldn't say how devastated I'd be if I lost Shard.

Slamming his fist into the ground, a grim determination masked his emotion. With eyes on the Wyrm, Korr slowly unsheathed the large broadsword on his back. It was surprising he hadn't used it until now having been fighting with only two short swords.

"Shit, Shard, he's going after the Wyrm," I pulsed, my head swivelling the find where he landed. There was a pile of rubble across the field and I could see him rolling back to his feet. *"Get the others, we need to provide Korr a distraction."*

"He cannot take on the creature. Especially without his Phoenix Soul abilities," Shard replied.

Oh no. I'd forgotten about the flames. They meant so much to Korr as a BrongTa and now they too would be dimmed.

Watching the big man charge into battle, his sword began cleaving through their ranks as he opened a path to the Wyrm. At moments, I could see him trying to produce flames to push through the enemy, but only smalls wisps of fire came forth. Echoes only of his BrongTa ability.

Coming to terms with this fact only seemed to enrage Korr further. Cracking his fist into the face of one enemy, Korr completely decapitated the head of a lion bred Chimera that burst into his path.

No more was there a crazed laughter spilling over the field. Only growls of pain and anguish every time Korr swung his sword.

"Then protect me," I yelled, my pain evident in that moment.

Rising to my feet, and racing to the enemy closing around Korr, I shoulder barged a younger looking warrior to reach his side. There was a moment as our eyes met as if Korr was staring into my soul, reading my own growing pain. He nodded and we fought back-to-back, holding the enemy at bay, inching ever towards the rampant Wyrm.

Cool flames, engulfed us, harrying the enemy. Looking skyward, Flint and Ash hovered above us encompassing us in a deluge of fire. They protected us from the worst of the attacks.

"Go forward veering to the left. It's cutting across field. You need to get in front of it," Shard sent to my mind.

"Quick, Korr, this way. The Wyrm is on the move," I called and without looking, took off at a run following Shard's direction. Keeping a flame barrier up, the enemy stepped out of the way creating a path for us to follow.

"Right there. It's coming right for you," Shard said, and my eyes widened. I hadn't actually wanted to be in its path. As the flames died away the creature was barely two hundred paces off and closing quick. Korr readied himself but I stood frozen, my mind blank.

"Use your damned ice," Shard's voice screeched through my mind and a wicked grin crossed my lips.

With a curving, ascension of my arms, I raised a massive ice wall. It had a bend like a wave as it began to curl over onto the sandy shore. Quickly, I reinforced the back of it with great ice spikes, preparing for the impact.

There was no time to test or harden the structure any further. When the Wyrm struck, a great shudder rippled through the land. Many warriors, allied and enemy alike, stumbled to the earth and looked our way. Even Korr, usually in perfect balance tripped over but had his wits enough about him to catch me on my way down, keeping me stable.

A large crack splintered the ice structure, shattering the topmost section and sending a rain of ice over us. In the swing of a hand, I transformed the ice into water to land harmlessly upon the dirt. Though the barrier was now gone, it completed its job.

Towering over us, were four dark eyes with blood red pupils. The snarling jaw, was full of the fangs that almost took my life moments earlier and I shivered remembering the wing of Ember sticking from its mouth. A large red feather was still lodged within its great maul but as I looked upon it, the flickering red fell apart to an ashen mist.

"Ember!" Korr screamed, reminiscent of a battle cry as he ran in.

Flames sprung to life along the twin edges of the blade, ignited by his BrongTa abilities and he swung a deadly over arcing slash to crash against the shimmering, forest green and brown scales of the Wyrm.

There was no effect on the scaled beast and with a cry of frustration, Korr began a flurry of swings and strikes against the creature.

"Korr," I cried trying to get through to him. "Korr, we need a better tactic." My voice was lost on his ears.

After two more strikes, the metal blade couldn't handle the barrage anymore. The two-handed longsword broke close to the hilt rendering the weapon useless. All flames expelled upon the churned earth.

And still the Wyrm stood over us. The way it swayed its head back and forth was almost mocking our efforts in laying it low. With a flick of its rough tail, both Korr and I were sent flying, barrelling over a number of fighting men as we landed.

I was feeling for Korr in that moment. Such pain for the loss of a bonded friend. Feeling little self-worth not only in losing Ember right next to me but disappointment in failing to avenge her, either. And now the Wyrm was slithering slowly towards us, stalking us with a hungry, slavering tongue.

A spark of light caught my eyes and I looked skyward to see Enzo riding Talon. A fireball was even now racing towards Korr with growing speed and intensity. My eyes widened in shock that Enzo would attack an ally and could only imagine he was sending the soul essence required for Ember's regeneration back to the nesting grounds. Korr had yet to see its approach and there was now no time to warn him.

Raising my arm in a dying attempt to protect myself, the fireball struck the ground with a burst of air and a roar of flames. The closing enemy fell in searing pain as the flames ate their flesh to the bone, but no ally was harmed. I hadn't felt anything that could have been heat and even Korr seemed in one piece.

Looking to the impact zone before Korr, I spied a glint of metal wedged into the ground. It looked familiar and my mind seemed to shut

237

down in providing the answer when I needed it most. It wasn't until I saw Korr's devilish grin that I realised it was Enzo's BrongTa knife. He was sending Korr a weapon. Not trying to kill him.

Wrapping his fingers around the hilt of the knife, Korr channelled his BrongTa flame through the meteorite steel. A flash of fire enveloped his body. His high emotions fuelling his power. Setting off at a dash, Korr charges the Wyrm so big he could have almost fit between the gap of the creatures front most teeth.

Calling on my draining reserves of power, I began flinging ice shards at the creature's face. I had no real hope of piercing the creatures thick armour but I needed to do something to distract it. For Korr's sake.

Tendrils of fire poured in from the sky as Phoenix began circling the Wyrm. They too had the same idea as me knowing an orange and even blue flame could barely annoy the beast. My heart lodged in my throat watching them circle in the sky. Even Shard was there, knowing the creature's agility and speed.

"Get out of there," I tried to call, sending pulse after pulse through thought when speech failed but the Phoenix ignored me.

Korr had reached the base of the Wyrm and I smiled as he began to scale the scales. Somehow, he managed to wedge his fingers between the gaps making hand and foot holds where there shouldn't be.

The Wyrm, feeling the human's ascent, rolled in the dirt and writhed this way and that trying to dislodge him much like a horse would but Korr was too skilled. He swung and jumped from point to point, using the Wyrm's movements for his own benefit. At one point, almost like he was in slow motion, I marvelled at how Korr confidently launched himself over the Wyrm as it rolled, catching the creature on the other side as if he had not even moved.

In my distraction, something sharp pierced my shoulder and I let out a gruelling cry as a large mass barged me over to sprawl through the dirt.

"Oh, you better be ready to die," I said picking myself up and shaking off the dirt.

I shot a deadly look at my attacker to find myself staring at a Unicorn. Strong and muscular, the flanks of the horned horse were covered in the blood of battle. A disturbingly twisted and serrated barb had my blood splattered upon it running to the Unicorn's white and black patterned fur on its forehead.

Snorting at me, the unicorn pawed at the earth, ready to charge. Keeping my eyes on it, I raised a hand to my shoulder, my thumb running along the open, jagged wound smearing the blood. Using my soul power, I was able to close the wound but not fully heal it. The scar would remain until I had the power to close it. Still, it may make a fun story to tell at the bar at night about a unicorn giving me the scar.

"Come on then, you horny, wretch. Come at me," I taunted and used two fingers to motion it forward.

With head lowered and barb out front, the unicorn charged. I realised it couldn't see in this position and easily sidestepped it. As the unicorn rounded for another try, I stepped three paces to the left. After an adjustment the unicorn charged again but this time its hoof fell into a hole I put between us.

With a sickening snap the leg bone shattered and the unicorn went down screaming in pain. The noise was jarring but I wanted this to be harsh. I wanted the enemy to know I wouldn't be playing anymore.

Placing a metal boot onto the creature's face, I wrench the barbed bone from side to side trying to drag it free. When that didn't work, I grabbed the tip of the horn and slammed my fist into the base of it a number of times before it broke free.

With barbed horn in hand, I put the tip to the erratic eyeball and began to slowly push it in. It writhed and bucked under my weight but would never get free.

"Not so nice, is it? Die."

Feeling the barbed horn bottom out, I twisted it savagely and the Unicorn went limp. Ripping the horn clear in a spray of blood, I rammed it into an approaching axeman's throat. Simple humans seemed too easy now.

My mind then shot to Korr and I looked up the Wyrm trying to find the small figure of the hulking Korr still attached. The Phoenix were still swarming and the creature was thrashing about as if Korr was still climbing it like a flea on a dog. This at least gave me hope.

Then I saw him. He was rounding the last bend of the neck to reach the flat of the Wyrm's head. There were more hand holds in this area with horns and ridged spikes all around. Not that Korr used them.

Confidently strolling to the centre of the creature's head Korr raised the BrongTa knife above his own.

"KORR... IS... GOOOOAAAAT!" He screamed and a brilliant white flame surrounded the dagger as he plunged it through the Wyrm's scales and into its brain. The soft organ boiling and bubbling instantly under the heat of the white flame.

The massive frame of the Wyrm began to shake and shudder as its eyes rolled into the back of its skull. Soon, they too melted away as white flames burst from the eye socket. The great creature slumped to the ground, crushing a number of warriors and Korr leapt from it, rolling to his feet and returning to the fray once more.

All around the fighting grounds, people were chanting his name with renewed vigour. It was the turning point of the battle as Telverian soldiers started to gain ground in the field pushing the enemy back.

A quick glance through Shard's eyes showed me the Wyrm had done far more damage to the enemy than it had us and we were only at a disadvantage of about 3 to 1 now.

Just three more kills each and we can go home, I thought before scanning the field for Riven. I'd forgotten all about him in the battle with the Wyrm giving him the chance to get up to all kinds of trouble.

After a moment, I found him stalking the field with intent. A few metres ahead was General Suniel and I could see Riven was making ready to attack. I noted Fitz was battling like crazy to get to him but was never going to make it in time.

"I'm sorry Fitz," I whispered as Riven thrust his lance.

The General had turned to find Riven attacking and raised his sword to defend. The lance scratched the edge of Suniel's face to take a leaping warrior in the chest, holding the enemy suspended in the air.

My eyes went wide and Suniel seemed to pale considerably as he turned sharply to find a dagger inches from his temple. He turned back to Riven, clapping him on the shoulder and finding another enemy to hunt.

I couldn't tell what was worse. Riven actual killing the General or saving the man's life and paving a path to get closer to him. If the Lich had a man at the right hand of the General, we could never win.

I made a mental note to ask Riven to leave with me for somewhere far distant and out of the way of war. In that, we may be able to live happy lives together. No more mistrust.

Fighting my way back across the field, I was happy with the clean up the Phoenix accomplished in the sky. There was barely a harpy left and the few that were still airborne were being chased and killed by our Phoenix. I couldn't say where the black flame Phoenix went.

"It was one of the first to die. We couldn't let our kin be controlled like that," Shard echoed in my mind.

"Thanks, Shard. Feels like we only have a tidy up of the field to do. See if you can thin the enemy numbers some more. Really tip the scales in our favour."

I saw Shard and Flint peel off from the others to begin burning through the ranks of the enemy soldiers. And as our men pushed forward it wasn't long before we outnumbered the enemy and could over power them. Unlike other armies that might buckle and break, the

240

armies of the enemy fought on. It was annoying to risk our lives for the last few but when you don't have feelings of your own there is nothing lost in continuing to fight.

As the last of the enemy near me fell to my sword, I let out a sigh of relief. I gained a few small cuts that had already congealed over but in all I was exhausted. My magic reserves had long depleted, and I was loath to steal from Shard while he battled the larger masses.

"My essence is yours to use as you will, Ellie," Shard said in my mind. It was going to take a long time to get used to him listening in on my inner most thoughts. The use of my nickname was nice though.

"I have no care for the thoughts of humans. I can see your heart... Ellie."

"Quite it, Shard. I was capable without the magic and as a last resort would have dipped into your pool of power."

"We know your stubbornness wouldn't have allowed you."

"Humph," I sounded, a smile touching my lips.

Turning, I found Riven standing at my side. Apart from the time with the Wyrm, he never left me once, contributing to the victory of the Telverian forces. We didn't fight against the Lich and there'd be many battles to come but I was satisfied with the man's heart.

Leaning into him, I listened to his heartbeat and it was soothing against the adrenaline still flowing through my veins. I felt I could fall asleep in that moment.

"Get your rest, Beauty. The greater battle begins tonight," Riven whispered in my ear.

Leaning back, a look of confusion crossed my face and he just winked at me. The wink and the gaze sent butterflies rioting in my stomach and my face caught alight. I snuggled back into his chest picturing what mischief we might be getting up to tonight. I wasn't tired enough to miss that.

"Elara," a voice called and I puffed out my cheeks, pouting. Turning back, I saw Suniel walking towards me, a smile brightening his features.

"General. You have need of me?" I asked hoping I could get some free time with Riven.

He shook his head and I breathed a sigh of relief.

"I wanted to commend you on your achievements today."

"We all won this battle, Suniel," I said sheepishly. "I know how unlikely it is for someone like me to make it as far as I have since being named Soul but all the soldiers out here done their part."

"This victory is yours, Elara. Without you, no regular soldier would have remained on the field. Everyone, faltered when I charged. I knew in that moment the ranks were about to break and run. It was you. Your voice. Your ability to win the hearts of your men and have them follow you into darkness and defeat that won out. I will never doubt what you will bring to the field again."

Thank you, Suniel. It means a lot," I replied, my gaze barely meeting his.

"Now where is Korr? He deserves some praise also."

My eyes shot up and I shook my head. Reaching out, I placed a hand on Suniel's wrist for emphasis.

"What? He single-handedly killed the Wyrm."

"We lost Ember," I said quietly. "Korr is mourning her."

The General became speechless, mouth flopping around like a fish out of water yet no sound came out. It took a moment for him to find his wits. Scanning the horizon and the descending sun, Suniel finally nodded. "I hadn't seen her fall. I will call a meeting of the commanders to discuss the implications. The sun's getting low so I'll let you get to the peak."

With that Suniel turned and walked from the field. He called a young soldier to him and shouted orders. The kid took off at a run looking to have them fulfilled before Suniel entered the Keep.

"What's the matter?" Riven asked. I hadn't realised my brow had furrowed as I contemplated the meaning of getting to the peak.

We will be meeting atop Mount Shatterstone. Ember's journey is to begin again in the dying sun, Shard's voice sounded in my mind. A strong burst of wind at my back signalled he landed swiftly behind me. "And leave the boy at home, Elara."

I looked between Shard and Riven, torn over what to do. In the end it was my heart that won out over my lust.

"I will meet you under the stars on the hill, there," I said pointing to a hill a little distant from the Keep. "I must farewell a friend first."

"I could join you," he offered and I smiled.

"This is for the Phoenix Souls and their Phoenix. Nothing will keep me from our battle." I winked.

Riven returned my smile and bowed lowed. Then until that moment, you may have your leave."

"The boy finally agreed to rutting you. He is finally becoming a man," Shard commented.

"Shard!" I squealed, hands to my mouth, face churning a deeper red.

Arriving on the peak overlooking the lands to North and South, I saw Enzo standing with Korr. It looked as though Korr was having difficulty

242

returning Enzo's knife. The latter, holding up a hand.

"Keep it, Korribubugungalah. I, Enzo of the Phoenix Flame and Master of the Twilight Fires recognise you as BrongTa. You are a student of the White Ash Flame. This knife is proof of your standing," Enzo said. There was little in his words that made sense to me except that Korr was an accepted BrongTa. Holding the knife to his chest, Korr's emotions were on display for all. His cheeks were dampened by tears and he held himself with much pride.

Walking to the Southern peak, Korr let out a mighty roar over the land so that all may know his status.

"That was a kind thing you did for Korr. It makes..." I was about to tell Enzo that it made me remember the man I knew before ever meeting the Phoenix. The man I fell in love with but he cut me off.

"As BrongTa, I am forced to recognise one who has awakened to their true potential. That was a bloody good dagger I gave up." Enzo didn't even look at me as he spoke but rather watched the knife he gave to Korr.

I pursed my lips and could only stare at this self-centred man. His selfishness and greed left me speechless and I walked over to my friends. I couldn't believe how close I'd been to saying something nice.

Baras greeted me with a warm hug. At least this man's caring nature was true.

"How are you fairing?" Baras asked. "I haven't had the chance to catch up with you lately."

"I'm surviving as we all are. I'm no stranger to battles but the intricacies of war are what's getting to me. There's too much structure and discipline."

"Been my whole life," Baras smiled warmly.

"And I understand you much better now. I see the work and effort you've put into your job. You've done well Baras." I leaned in closer to his ear. "And I'm glad Kymberlin can reward you for your efforts every night."

His face cracked and a brilliant blush crossed his cheeks, going up over the bridge of his nose. I could see him stammering for words.

"She's good for you. Enjoy her and love her fiercely. I'm sure she'll do the same in return."

Placing a hand on his shoulder, I moved on. I could see Kymberlin eyeballing me from a distance. We'd shared enough pranks for her to be weary. Acknowledging her, I simply placed a hand on my heart and bowed, quelling her fears.

At the far edge looking North, Fitz stood alone. Walking to his side, I raised my palm as if splitting a line straight up the middle of the North. The land was now covered in a blanket of snow. If I ventured out there as a maid with my weak lungs, I barely would have made the forest.

"I say we cut straight up the middle, cut back at the last quarter," I said with a smile, my hand carving a path in front of us. He looked so deep in thought as if something was rolling over and over in his mind. Worry lines broke his brow and I just wanted to give him a little light.

He looked at me as if only partially aware I was there and I repeated myself.

"Only if you want to run afoul of trolls and drakes," Fitz said easily. There was a sad smile upon his lips, and I knew it was from stirring memories of Dustin and Caeli. "Sorry, I was thinking of future battles. The Lich can command hundreds of thousands of warriors and nightmare creatures. Because he can raise the dead, we don't know what extinct and undiscovered terror it could conjure up against us."

"We also don't know how much energy it takes him to do so. It may have been thousands of years to raise the army he did, and we may have pushed his efforts back just as far again. Come on, that's a worry for another time. Let's go farewell Ember."

As he began to nod, I put my arm around him and walked together back to the others. I didn't notice last time I was here but the rock pillars around the summit made perfect perches for the Phoenix. I saw them all surrounding us, heads lowered in silent contemplation or prayer.

As the sun touched the horizon, Korr burst into a chanting song. The pitch and flow were so beautiful it brought a tear to my eye even when the words were in a language I didn't understand. It was also the most I ever heard Korr speak.

"Flint's providing Korr with the words for the tune. It will almost be that he is singing through Korr," Shard said quietly. He then became muted as he and the remaining Phoenix added their musical voices to the backing of Korr's words.

As the sun began its final descent into the earth, only half visible, there grew a large dusty substance in the sky above Korr. It reminded me of the white, ashen remains of a fire long deceased. Then Korr's shoulders began to glow a deep orange. Tendrils of a flame like essence seeped out of the large man and played on his shoulders reaching for the ashen dust. As they merged, they grew and when enough of it had been released, the flames sprouted wings to fly up and combine with the ash as the sun winked its last rays of light.

The mixture of flame and ash bubbled and swirled in a random and hypnotising fashion. I thought it was beginning to die away as the flames shrank down into a small, solid ball. It caught me by surprise as a burst of bright yellow and orange flames took the form of Ember and I realised in that moment the ash called forth was the remains of Ember and the flame essence held her soul.

With a squeal, Ember spread her wings wide and glided towards the nest in the North to await Korr's passing. A lump formed in my throat as I watched her fly away. There were two possibilities I considered and each was as sad as the next.

The first had me never seeing Ember again. I would never be able to settle our grievances face to face. Never be able to talk about the things that were believed to have occurred and, therefore, never mend that one small crack in the eternal friendship of Shard and Ember until I passed. It was like her best friend, Shard, dating a mortal enemy and expected to be all happy together.

The other possibility was that I *would* see Ember again and fix everything I'd brought up in the first instance. My only grievance being I would never see Korr again after that. And I was awfully fond of the big guy.

Then the fire faded and the night settled in. The stars were beautiful this evening without a cloud or whiff of smoke to mare the view. I stood tracing the constellations, remembering the moments I'd shared with Ember. It was back when I could still say I was young. Back when I would frolic in the fields with Enzo and marvel at the beauty that was Talon.

I could remember a day when Ember was between choosing Souls. Enzo was on mission with Talon and I was all alone. I found her in the fields basking in the sun. She seemed sad somehow but didn't open up about it. Said it wasn't done and I only just now realised it was about her past Soul. Seeing her emotions sitting raw upon her feathers, I decided to keep Ember company. We could have fun without speaking of our pains. Tentatively at first, I curled up into her feathers as I had Shard a few sleeps back. It was this night I realised how much the Phoenix love neck scratches. We slept the whole night together and Ember even wanted to make me a Phoenix Soul but it wasn't allowed. Warriors were already making the trek to the nesting grounds and, though I was accepted a friend, I was not a candidate for Phoenix Soul. I was happy when Ember had been upset over it but I was also saddened for the same reason.

I would always remember her that way.

Everyone stood upon the cliff in silence as the stars made their way through the sky. I couldn't say just how long had passed but I felt it time

245

to say my final farewells and go live a little. Hand on heart, I bowed and stepped away.

"Ready to go, Shard?" I pulsed and there was a feeling of agreement from the Firebird more than any form of words.

"There's one last thing that needs to be dealt with."

"What's that?"

"He's already approaching."

I glanced back to find Enzo walking towards me then narrowed my eyes on Shard. By Shard's words, I wondered if it was he or I that needed to deal with the thorn.

"Fly back to the Keep with me tonight," Enzo said. When Shard didn't reply, I accepted it as my responsibility. If only he was being literal.

"An invitation or a command?"

Enzo hesitated. "An invitation. I know you were close to Ember. I just thought I could provide company tonight."

"So, you're just horny then. I've already lined up some *company* for the night. No need to trouble yourself."

He was clearly taken aback by my statement and at calling him out. The initial shock soon turned dark as he understood who I referred to. "He isn't what he seems, Elara. You can't trust him."

"I don't need to trust him. I just need his cock," I said keeping myself neutral.

"Woo, yeah you do," Kymberlin called.

"Keep your dirty trap shut. I don't need some alleyways, gutter slut to get involved in serious matters between Elara and I."

My eyes went wide at the insult and Baras was literally burning with anger. He took a step forward before Kymberlin held out a hand. She seemed unperturbed by the insult but for a steely glint in her eyes.

"I love you for this, Baras. I truly do but I got it. Just have my back. Not my front," Kymberlin said before directing her words to Enzo. "Do you want to talk about serious matters between you and Ellie? How 'bout startin' with what you got up to 300 years past?"

Enzo turned sharply on me.

"All Phoenix Souls know the truth. Whether their Phoenix are aware, I cannot say but I doubt they won't be curious after this conversation. Shard though is fully aware having seen my memories."

I smiled as Enzo's eyes grew wide.

"Any words you want to get off your chest, Shard?" I asked.

"It's not the time," he pulsed at me before speaking. "Enzo. You of all people understand the nests need to be safeguarded while a Phoenix is awaiting rebirth. That is even more vital now that a Lich has been

246

confirmed. You will take on this role."

"Get gutter mouth over there to do it. I have better things to do."

She does not have your ability with both flame and weapon. Nor does she possess the many lifetimes of knowledge you have over the Phoenix. You will... accept... this role." Shard made it perfectly clear he would be bringing up past matters about Enzo should he not accept.

I spied his knuckles going ghostly white as he squeezed his hands into fists. He desperately wanted to fight this command but knew to do so would see him exiled.

"Fine," he said through gritted teeth.

"Well, glad that's settled. Shard, shall we?"

I said with a grin. My eyes met Enzo's and there was something desperate and dangerous there, like a wolf trapped with its back to a wall. May his watch be long and lonesome, I thought.

As Enzo took off into the north on Talon, I departed for the South and Riven.

A giddy feeling of playfulness and an undying youth sent shivers spiralling across my skin as Shard gently landed on the preordained hilltop. This turned to electricity as Riven stepped out to meet me. He must have been practicing this moment half the night as he caught the shadows perfectly, keeping his naked form from revealing the spicy parts. The missing lance only heightening my arousal.

"Thank you, Shard," I said softly, scratching his neck. "Now off with you. You don't need to witness what's about to happen."

"Which is why you chose one of the most open hilltops within miles of the Keep."

"Tch," I said and slid from Shard's back. The Firebird lifted off into the night and made for the Northern lands. I wasn't going to need him anytime soon.

Keeping my eyes on Riven's solid form, I began walking slowly towards him. My arse swaying salaciously with every step.

"We have the stars," I said, removing my cloak and belt. The weapons clattered upon the smooth stones as I let the belt go

"We do." Riven's voice was deeper than normal sending my heartbeat soaring.

Loosening the lace holding my pants, I let them fall free. Steeping cleanly past, I shivered with power at being so free. Only my tunic kept me hidden, and though I would love to rip it clear and stand naked and free before Riven, he too was teasing me.

"And we have an audience," I said, motioning to the lights of the Keep a short distance across the field.

"We have," Riven replied. His simple answer so sexy. I could see he was focused and it was all on me.

Two more steps and I raised a finger to trail down his chest. My own rolling with every steamy breath. His body was perfect and I couldn't keep my eyes from him.

"And will you help me find my voice so that I may scream my love for all to hear?"

"I will," Riven replied. His hands slid up under my dark tunic gently pulling it upwards. I raised my arms to allow the soft fabric to slip over my head and fall to the earth.

I let out a deep, trembling moan as he drew me against him. Nothing in this world was between us now and I could feel the heat rolling down my thighs in anticipation. Gazing into his eyes, Riven brought his hand up to cup my cheek tenderly. I'd never been treated with such gentleness and adoration in all my time upon the earth. It felt as though I was the most precious thing in the world to him and he would love me into eternity. A part of me was dying to be bent over a rock and pulverised but this was all new to me and I wanted to explore it.

With slow, easy movements, Riven sat back upon a blanket he brought to the hill and tugged me forward. He wouldn't let me sit upon him but rather he drew a leg up and rested my thigh beside his head. My foot crossed over to the other side of his back, the angle giving Riven such a view of my exposed lotus flower.

He was barely a few inches from it and gently blew a whisper of a breath across my dampness. The contrast of the heat from my vagina and the chill of Riven's breath almost sent me over the edge there and then. Ecstasy like lighting, running up and down my spine.

"Keep that up and it'll be the fastest I've cum from such little effort," I said through heavy breaths.

I couldn't see the expression he wore with his face so close but his eyes were still able to meet mine. His cheek grazed along my inner thigh as he kissed around the edges.

"Mmmm." I moaned.

He kissed the same point on the other side...

"O Ohh."

...before his tongue trailed up the length of my damp lips with inhuman patience that, by the time he grazed the tip of my clit, my whole body, all my muscles from head to toe, were contracting and spasming in one of the most powerful orgasms I'd ever felt. So much so I lost control of my ice, freezing the ground and crafting spires of ice in criss-crossing directions.

"MMMmmMmMmMMy God! what are you doing to me." I cried as I finally got my voice back. His head became wedged between my thighs just waiting for me to calm.

"That's just the beginning. A warmup, so to say. The more I can make you cum now, the longer I'll have you riding my cock later."

"Wear me down like that again and I may not make it to your cock."

"You'd be able to say no to five more of those?" Riven asked with a cheeky smile. He was leaning back to talk while supporting me by holding my butt cheeks.

"Yes... No," I then whimpered as my body craved more. "You could bend and break me so badly and I'd still be crawling back, pleading for more."

I couldn't believe the words coming from my mouth. That orgasm. That drop of heaven itself, all but destroyed me but I wasn't done. Far from it.

"No less than five," I demanded of him then.

With a wicked grin he went back to work. His tongue became more adventurous, breaking past my lips and lapping at the honey nectar now dripping from me. The sensation of his tongue entering me was amazing. The thick, wet, muscle gliding through me, twisting this way and that as it reached areas I'd only hit with a finger. To say another orgasm wasn't far off was inaccurate as it already hit like a tidal wave against the shores. This one even stronger than the last.

And his tongue hadn't finished. Riven focused intently on my engorged clit, twirling his tongue around it before sucking upon it in a long continuous draw. Blood was pulled into it making it hypersensitive and, as a finger penetrated me to begin slowly pumping, one last lick sent me straight off one orgasm into the next. My vaginal walls clamping around a finger that was still moving within me. The pleasure still flying ever higher until I couldn't take it anymore. Pushing him back, I fell to the earth in a writhing mass of passionate ecstasy drawing in great gulps of air.

He sat there smiling at me as I began to finally come to. I locked eyes on him and a fierce determination took over. Rising to my wobbly legs, I grabbed his shoulders, straddling him.

"You're fucking mine now," I said and, guiding his curved cock to its new home, I thrust down hard. My eyes rolled into the back of my head as I felt we became one, smiling as Riven moaned my name. Biting my lip to keep myself in check, I started moving to a steady rhythm.

It wasn't about speed or power or domination. This was about the melding of two souls into one. This was where I belonged. This was my heart and my home and I could live like this for always.

Feeling his cock begin to twitch and stir more than before I slowed my pace to pull all the way up Riven's shaft. Every nerve ending between my legs going off like fireworks until I reach the very tip. Pushing back down, I found he felt even bigger now as my inner walls clenched tightly. This was insane. I could feel an orgasm desperately calling for release but at this speed I kept it at bay just as I did Riven's. It was torturously erotic in nature.

Shaking his head, Riven held firmly to my back and sped up the pace with those strong arms. Pushing me up and down, I felt him breaking through the wall holding my ecstasy in check. Still, he got faster, and as his eyes clenched tightly, I could see he was on the verge of exploding, himself.

Like a geyser, Riven flooded me with a throbbing flow of warmth that brought on yet another climactic finish of my own. We both shuddered holding each other tightly as we hit a heightened euphoric state.

It was some moments before we could possibly even breath again, let alone talk and I knew I wouldn't be walking straight in the morning. My eyes began to focus once more as I sat upon this amazing and breathtaking man, his cock still within me though smaller now. I felt a mixture of our love seeping free and smiled.

"What amuses you so, Beautiful?" Riven asked.

"I would have screamed your name to the world tonight but you were so good you stole my voice all together," I said and Riven chuckled.

'You still have one more orgasm left. Let's see if we can't find that voice of yours once more."

"Let's save that one," I said, still trying to catch my breath. "We have all night to play. Just hold me now and let's watch the stars drift across the sky."

I leaned into him turning to look up but a shining glint caught my eye from left and right. Looking around I found the whole area had been frozen solid right down to the smallest blade of grass. I could only guess that I did this in my heightened state of pleasure.

"When two Fibonacci make love, the world freezes over in their wake." Came a voice from behind the frozen brush. Riven had rolled to his feet as the screen was shattered into smaller, ice encrusted pieces. Beyond were a group of soldiers numbering at least 15 at a quick count.

I stood defiantly, unashamed at my state of dress, ready to take them on when the words ran through my head once more.

"Why do you say 'two Fibonacci'," I asked looking from the group to

Riven. He stood with a stern look on his face and I began to guess the answer. It would explain why his body was always in such a perfect state of cold.

"Would you like to answer that, Riven Fibonacci?" The leader said with a disgustingly smug look on his face.

"We'll talk about this later, Ellie," Riven said before extending his arm out to the side, palm open. Swirls of blues and whites danced around his hand forming his rather unique lance. More answers were supplied knowing the reason the lance was detachable and apparently moveable was that, to a Fibonacci, their soul weapon would become alive. It could be manipulated and wielded as the owner saw fit.

This wasn't just something to shrug off and sweep under the rug, either. For all my lives, I had believed the BrongTa had destroyed the Fibonacci line. Now I find one alive and breathing right before my eyes. I wasn't about to wait. With a swish of my arm, blue flames erupted in an arcing curve to block the mercenary group's advance for a small time. I was low on energy as it was and holding the flame wall active would eat the last of my recovered strength.

"No, we talk about this now. You understood I was Fibonacci?" It was still very distracting as he turned without any clothes on. The moonlight turning the skin to a milky white.

"I did know," Riven admitted calmly.

"And you felt a need to hide this from me? Why?"

"It would have changed how your feelings grew. I didn't want to risk telling you and having the information sway you for good or bad. I didn't want it to be the only thing that defined me. Of course I would have told you. I never felt my heritage was a big thing. I just didn't know if you did and wanted to get to know you, and you me, first."

"Well, it's a shock, of course. I didn't believe there were any others of my... our clan, left." I corrected. His answer wasn't a bad one. A lot of people like to open up slowly over time. It won't make them any less who they are. "You could have shared your worries, but I understand. I won't be that woman that demands everything of you immediately. I guess we really can talk about this later."

He nodded. "And just for the record, this little bit of information rounds off the 'everything I am'. You have it all now."

A tender smile graced my lips making me feel giddy all over. I looked to the enemy and couldn't feel confident in the fight to come. *Shard we're going to need you,"* I pulsed but couldn't be sure how it worked over distances or whether he was even connected right now knowing what Riven and I were up to.

"*I don't give rides and I don't join in human activities.*" Came the return almost instantly and I puffed out my cheeks.

We were definitely still linked but Shard was doing his best to ignore me.

"*The enemy are here.*"

"*On my way.*"

At least I was confident that we could hold off a few warriors the couple of minutes needed to be evacuated. In the same fashion as Riven, I brought forward a weapon crafted through my gifts as a Fibonacci. It was a curved sabre like I used to use when younger. Though I try to keep practiced in all forms of weaponry, this style of sword was definitely my favourite.

Inspecting my weapon, I saw small patterns upon the blade and realised it was the blue flames of Shard dancing over the surface. My soul had truly evolved this last life.

As I was about to lower the flame wall a thought hit me.

"When Shard threw you from the battlements, was it you or I that crafted the ramp for your landing?"

Riven just shot me a wink and a smirk.

"Bastard. I thought my distance magic was getting better."

I let the flames drop and stood ready to meet the enemy. There was no hesitation from them and they charged at us like a surging river braking through a dam wall. Riven reacted first swinging his lance and slicing clean through the first at the waist before two more took his place. More swept around him to come after me and I let my sabre dance and play. The first lost his head before I thrust my blade through a second man's heart. Turning to face another warrior, I panicked when the two men who should have been dead kept coming.

Hands grabbed my arms locking me down and I cried out for help. This was no use when I saw Riven was in a similar predicament. The half a body of the first warrior he took on was now grappling with Riven's legs while other limbless and dismembered bodies encumbered Riven to the point he went tumbling over. Still the man fought on and it took the hilt of a sword to the head to knock him out and still Riven's struggles.

I could see the light of three Phoenix speeding towards us. The blue flames of Shard, screaming ahead of the others at full speed, but it was covered by a man with a sword as he stepped in front of me. There was no way I could escape what was to come as the Phoenix were too far off.

"*I'm sorry, Shard. May your next Soul be everything you could want.*"

"*Don't you dare die. Ellie!*" Shard cried.

The man standing above me looked over his shoulder at the approaching Phoenix before smiling with a gap tooth grin. The maniacal stare was disturbing. Green light appeared giving the area an eerie glow. I had sense enough to realise it was a portal transporting them back to somewhere distant without hope of rescue. The man grabbed me by my dark hair and thrust me into the portal before collapsing, as if he had always been dead. The light began to fade and I was left alone in the dark.

"I'll find you." Were the last words to filter through before the green light blinked from existence. Now my mind was void of any words. It was like our mind link had been severed and all was darkness. Pressure built upon my mind, draining energy reserves, and sending my body into shutdown.

Chapter 13

I awoke with a start, my breath racing. Trying to find my bearings, I looked around but there was nothing in the darkness. The void so absolute, I found no essence of light to catch and adjust my eyes to. I felt around the eye sockets, pawing frantically at my eyes through closed lids. There was nothing that hurt or suggested I was blind. On the contrary, where I touched, I saw trace lines like white marks following my finger. I felt it meant something.

Fighting for calm, I sat down steadying myself. There was nothing I could do in the dark until I assessed my surroundings. If I was to freak out now and start running in a random direction, I'd probably knock myself out on what I ran in to. Settling my breathing and lowering my heart rate, I shifted into spirit form.

...

...

Except, I couldn't access that part of me. There was something holding me anchored in the physical. Something heavy preventing me from flying free to determine my location and let Shard know where I was. My breathing hastened once more threatening hyperventilation. I felt alone in the dark. Isolated. As naked as when they captured me.

I'll find you. The final words from Shard played through my head again. Calming. Reassuring. I wasn't as alone as my kidnappers wanted me to believe. The words feeding my strength and keeping me calm. I needed to hold out long enough for him to rescue me.

A horrid snarl sounded to my left and I froze, listening intently for anything that may even hint at an attack. Delicate, like the thin sheet of ice on a window pane, a sound found my ears. The padding of soft paws on stone. Paws too big to be one of those domestic dogs popular in Western societies. No. This was the paw of a wolf or lion. Something big with claws that rapped at the end of each step. With the way the sound echoed, it was either moving passed me or circling and I kept an ear focused in on the sound, waiting for a change.

Stretching out an arm, I focused on crafting a short sword. I couldn't be sure of the space I had and whether I'd be able to swing anything larger. When I closed my hand, nothing was there. No sword. No ice. Nothing but the emptiness of the void I found myself in.

The lack of abilities was jarring and I couldn't risk a flame in case I drew in the beast that may have been passing by. The very hairs over my body stood on end waiting to see if I would be safe or end up fighting the unknown beast in the dark. No doubt it was going to have greater senses than I did. And it was most likely raised here and would have adapted to the dark.

A terrible thought crossed my mind. If it was a chimera, it would have been bred with the dark in mind. I would've added some sort of nocturnal creature into the mix to remove any chance it wouldn't adapt to the dark.

The echo of foot pads slowly began to grow dim, and I let out a deep breath. I couldn't even say when I started to hold it. At least my survival skills were at full force.

Waiting until I couldn't hear the sounds of the beast anymore, I tested my flames. This at least produced some promise, if only a spark. But that spark made my eyes itch as they tried to adjust to the sudden onslaught of light. I tried again and again and each time couldn't get more than a spark or two to appear but that was enough. My eyes we readjusting to the miniscule light. The itch reduced now to a dull ache, and I was beginning to get a sense of the room I was in.

Most of the walls were solid stone enclosing a room about the size of the space I held at the Keep when working as a maid. It wasn't huge but it was manageable. Where there would've been natural flaws in the stone surface; holes carved out by the flow of water or something alien in the natural elements that wore away at a much faster rate, I could see the workings of human. Chunks of stone, glued together with a form of mortar I hadn't come across before. Grey and smooth yet incredibly strong. I gave up on the idea or tunnelling out using these crevices. I could see the dark makings of a door but dared not approach, keeping my scent as far back from it as possible.

There was never any worry of the beast stalking the outer halls attacking me. It passed a number of times over the countless minutes I'd been awake. It may have even been hours. Time was inconceivable without a reference. Possibly it was on a route to man the halls. If it kept to the same pace, time could be referenced in Chimeras.

My body began to protest the torment I'd been through of late. The great battles, both in the field and on the hill with Riven. Even the small sparks I produced, played their part in sapping my strength and my eyes began to close. I half rolled the distance to where one single worn sheet was placed and curled up into a ball as I began to doze. My mind solely on Riven and whether he lived beyond our last moments together. I hoped beyond all else we would see each other once more.

Darkness enveloped me.

Skittering around the edges of the room, a rat startled me awake as it brushed against my bare skin. With my arm reacting on its own, I caught it even as the rest of my body shied away, pressing against the wall. Tense muscles calmed as I realised what I had caught, and I smiled inwardly for being startled so while the rat began flailing against my grip. I caught it well enough that it couldn't bite me or escape.

"You probably know these halls better than most," I said to the flurrying creature. Its body was twisting and contorting on itself as I held it before me. "If only you could direct me out and away from here."

I produced small sparks as I talked. It helped to keep my eyes adjusting and in use while allowing me to see my new friend and food. It wasn't the first time in 300 years I'd been in a situation where I needed to force myself to eat anything I could to survive. It was disgusting and I was trying to put it off with our conversation, but I needed to regain energy. My body was already becoming heavy and my eyes just wanted to close again.

"I am sorry, friend. I know you didn't wake this morning expecting to be consumed but luck has not shone on you, and I am in need. Farewell."

A last spark fizzled as I brought the creature to my mouth and then paused, teeth on the verge of sinking below the fur. The taste and feeling were so horrid, I had to pull it away, physically forcing myself to hold back from vomiting.

Holding my mouth and swallowing down the bile, I looked over at what caught my eye, sparking the room again. Coughing, I closed my eyes tight as the bile ate at the back of my throat.

"Looks like you're lucky after all, my friend," I said letting the rat go. It skittered off quickly with a rather high-pitched squeal.

On the floor, a quarter of the way into the room, was a small plate with black bread and cheese. Next to it was what looked to be a silver chalice with red rubies adorning it. I guess there wasn't much need for pretty things when your army is loyal under your control.

Tentatively, I crept across the room. I hadn't ventured into this half yet and as I felt the tray against my hand, I sparked a wisp of flame. There were two things that bothered me in that moment. The first was the dark space I thought was a door was actually an open portal. The door had seemingly been ripped from its hinges and was laying in the walkway just outside. Second, and even more distressing, was a set of white shimmering eyes that were focused on me. Even when the darkness set back in, these remained floating faintly in the air and I remained frozen to the spot, unmoving in case it was watching for that.

Finally, I got the courage to set off a final spark and found an even more dreadful scene. As my friend crossed the threshold of the doorway, the chimera, with the head of a scarred and savage wolf, pounced instantly tearing the rat apart. It snarled a final threat before those eyes swayed away.

"Lady Luck is rather fickle at times, my friend. May you find happiness far greater in your next life."

Looking to the food below me, I allowed my fingers to be my eyes. The bread was crispy on the outside and from the dark colour I noted earlier, probably burnt. I pushed a finger deeper into the dough and found it could barely even be called semi cooked. All in all, it looked as though the dough had been thrown into a fire a few minutes before being recovered and placed on the plate.

I took a bite allowing the concoction to settle into my mouth. The dough slightly flattened trying to take on the curve of my tongue. It was deceptively chewy and the small pieces of charred crust gave a bitter taste and cringy texture to the whole ordeal. I began to wish I hadn't let the rat go. At least with that, I knew the terrible taste I was up for. This was just disgusting. I tried to wolf it down as quickly as I could but the mixture couldn't be rushed. Finally, it was behind me.

Picking up the cheese, it felt promising. It held a nice crumbly surface, dry to the touch with a few small pits much the same as an aged cheddar would have. With a little more enthusiasm, I took a large bite to flush away the foul aftertaste of the bread.

With the expectation of a solid consistency, my teeth plummeted into a soft and fluid core and, this time, I did throw up. The smell burned my eyes and I sparked again to find the whole inside of the cheese was a gooey, black mould.

My stomach twisted and hurled its contents all over the floor as I threw the cheese from the room. Reaching for the chalice, I misjudged the distance and knocked it, spilling some of the content. Recovering, I saved half the water inside and brought it to my lips. Closing my eyes, I paused as another lump forced its way up my throat but I held strong. I was able to force it right back down again with shear will.

Taking a swig of the water to rinse my mouth, I spat it out instantly. "It's fucking saltwater," I cried, hurling the chalice across the room.

With my head pounding, I went back to my bed and dreamt of the rat and the edible meal it would've made.

A long groan escaped my lips as I rolled over. The hard uneven floor wreaking havoc on my muscles. The muscle in the side of my stomach tensed in a sharp pain that made it hard to breath.

Sitting up, I rested against the far wall. It was a better position than laying on the stone but in my weakened state I didn't believe I could hold myself up indefinitely. I needed sustenance. I needed something or I was never going to see the light of day again.

The small sparks I could produce hadn't grown in strength, yet, didn't seem to drain me of energy like when I use the Phoenix flames. I knew it could only come from my link to Shard but for now it was enough. My eyes, still sore from the lack of constant light, were far better off, the more I sparked. It was all I could do to help myself. Food was another matter but if the right circumstances came about, at least I'd have my eyes functioning.

A dusty, green light began to register in my perception. It was an odd sight in the dungeon where no light lived and as my eyes began to focus on it, they started to see swirls and patterns while adjusting to something so bright.

I felt like I was beginning to lose my mind. That the lack of food and energy, was finally beginning to play with my head.

The hallucination seemed so real and I would have dismissed it but for a growing fear born in my chest. Hairs up and down my arm stood on end as goosebumps tingled across my skin. Some force, like static energy, was growing outside the room and the dusty green light became more dense and eerie in its tone.

My eyes were wide now as I stared at the opening, pleading to the emptiness that nothing would come into view. I felt like a child in their bed watching an open doorway expecting to see a demon, though this time I very well knew it was likely. My ears caught the sound of scraping getting closer. Not the harshness of metal or stone on stone but rather, something soft like flesh scraping across the floor. This only added to the dread feeling growing within me.

My breath was coming in shudders now as I slowly backed away towards the corner on hands and feet. As my back condensed into the far corner, the dark cloaked figure of the Lich drifted into view. A dense, green light spewing out from within its chest. I could see that it was floating, its bony feet inches above the ground and in its hand was a limp corpse. It was this that was dragging along the floor on approach. Now the Lich just floated within the room, staring at me, orange lines, tracing in the air with each movement of his eyes before fading away.

I was too terrified to look at the creature and huddled in a ball with head, covered by my arms, resting between my knees. It wasn't a question of fear or courage. I knew my limitations of both and how to overcome either when I had to. This was an innate dread born into me at the beginning of time when the first creatures breathed fresh air. It was a feeling from generations that now screamed at me to run and hide and not be anywhere near this darkness. The closer it came the more my instincts flared until I was this shivering mess in the corner.

"Why do you reject my hospitality, daughter of Fibonacci?" a voice broke through the emptiness. It was a hollow, strangled sound that grated upon my eardrums. Yet somehow, familiar. Forgetting my fears for but a moment, I peeked out from under my arm and to my absolute horror found Riven staring at me. He was being held at the back of the neck, suspended in mid-air. My mouth dropped and my eyes grew wide for it was not a sight I could even conjure up in my wildest nightmares.

The Lich seemed to grow impatient and repeated his question. The voice spoken through the husk of Riven. "Why do you reject my hospitality?"

"What hospitality?" My voice broke into a scream beyond my control. Somehow, against my better judgement, I rose to my feet. What it had done to Riven had set a small fire in my belly longing to break free.

The Lich seemed to glance at the remnants of the cheese and the discarded chalice and I understood its meaning a little better.

Flattening myself against the far wall, I spoke again, my voice still high but controlled. "Your hospitality would kill me. I'm not one of your fucking zombies. I need fresh food and water. Not the saltwater of the sea or rotting cheeses. I need real food."

There was a moment of silence as if the Lich was accessing some long-forgotten memory from a time in the ancient past where he may have known this knowledge. Then it was gone.

"How can I obtain a true rebirth?"

The question was left floating between us as my focus was stuck on Riven and the pain he must've endured to be before me right now.

"What have you done to him?" I asked quietly this time. With anger beginning to fuel my muscles, I slowly peeled myself from the wall.

Instantly, I flung myself back against the wall, head turned, trying to get as far from the Lich as possible as it took another step toward me.

"Tell me what I wish to know."

My heart was beating wildly with adrenaline pumping through my veins. If there was a cliff face behind me and this creature ahead, I believe I would have turned and leapt with all I had just to escape. But it wasn't fleeing that would save me now. I needed to speak, to give in to the Lich's desires so that I could escape.

"You will know once I do," I replied, admitting I didn't have the answer to true immortality like the Phoenix did. The Lich, however, took my

259

words as a defiant stance against it, asking once more about Riven. And it relented.

"I had to break him once more so that he would serve only me. Your influence on him stripped him of his loyalty. Now tell me the path to true rebirth."

It was a long moment before I realised what happened and another to understand the implications.

The Lich needed me. Needed information from me. Wanted me alive to provide an answer to his questions... The creature was mortal.

The feeling of dread remained but I felt just that little bit less timid. The creatures need beginning to fuel my courage.

"I need water... Fresh water before I can speak of it. My throat is dry."

There was a great anger that seemed to sweep over the Lich and it threw Riven hard against the rock wall of the cell. His body slumped to the floor and the Lich let out a blood curdling cry before stalking away.

The sound almost had me shivering in a ball once more but for Riven's body. I raced to him and swept Riven up in my arms, cradling him.

"Riven," I whimpered. "Riven, please don't be gone from me. I need you here and now."

There were tears trailing down my cheeks as I looked upon his still form. "Come back to me," I whispered.

Alone in the dark, I cried over the still form of Riven. There was no spark of life within him. No breath upon his lips or cool quip to brighten my day. He was as dead now as he had been for the last 400 years but it felt more final. I couldn't feel even a small trace of him within this husk of what he once was.

I wept, knowing I would never again experience our quick and overpowering love in this life. The tears fell freely until there was nothing left to give. It was almost enough to give up on life entirely. To be free of the darkness and pain in this world and be reunited with Riven In death... Almost, but there were friends I had who were still searching for me and I couldn't leave this world with the Lich still breathing.

... Or Enzo.

I couldn't say how many Chimeras had passed by since the Lich left but the green light had begun again in the halls signalling his return. I looked down at Riven's soft, calm face, my hand on his cheek, and knew in that moment just how Caeli had felt holding to Dustin.

"Hold on just a little longer, my love. I'll be with you soon," I said with a final tear coursing down my cheek.

With the chimera swaying back and forward in the doorway, eyes locked on me, the Lich entered. It was using some form of telekinesis to levitate in a bucket of water, placing it by a wall away from me. The moment with Riven had broken whatever fear and instinctual reactions I had towards the Lich leaving me indifferent to its aura. It was annoying to have to get up, and I glared at the creature, taking it in for the first time.

It wasn't exactly a walking skeleton wrapped in a cloak like I first believed. There was skin, and tissue, and muscle, and sinew, criss-crossing the bones. They were shrivelled and dried out over time and were so thin they could almost be considered another layer of the bone. It denoted the long and empty life of a creature that would never see the beauty in even a single moment.

Placing Riven gently on the floor, I crawled to the bucket. My lips a were parched and tongue was dry. If this was saltwater, I was in deep trouble. I scooped a small amount up with a hand and brought it to my lips. There was a feeling of tearing as the centre of my lower lip pulled apart and a taste of blood touched my tongue, but the water soothed this. A fresh, almost sweet taste, filled my mouth as the water was immediately absorbed before it hit my throat.

I took two big gulps before leaning back, coughing and spluttering with trouble swallowing. Half of the second mouthful was wasted splattering to the floor as I took a few more tender sips allowing the fluid to gently trickle down my throat.

"Tell me what I wish to know or I'll set the Chimera on you." The strangled comment was accompanied by a growl at the entry. The chimera was slowly pacing back and forth hoping for the opportunity.

My heart shattered as the blood drained from my face. I slowly turned to find a bony, withered hand holding Riven aloft. The tortured vocals sounding far worse than before and his lifeless eyes peered at me with tragic emptiness. I shouldn't have let him go. It was obvious Riven's body would be used to communicate but it just didn't cross my mind.

"How are you immune to death?" The words came out more abrupt. Harsher, as if his patience was wearing thin. My eyes grew dark as I stared past Riven into the creature's eyes.

"I am immune the same as you?" I said.

A dying cry gurgled from the throat of the Lich forgoing Riven's voice box. It was a cry of annoyance and desperation as it tried to make clear the consequences of my silence and the meaning of its words.

"You are nothing like me. My path to immortality has been a lifetime of research and experimenting. When you die you are reborn. For me my Phyl..." It went quiet a moment considering its next few words. I could see he almost slipped in telling me something I shouldn't know and

261

stored that last incomplete sentence in the back of my mind.

"Tell me now, Daughter of Fibonacci. Why do you keep it from me?" The Lich growled.

I scoffed. "I'll die soon enough anyway. Why not deliver it now?"

It was now the Lich's turn to laugh. It was robotic and monotonal and at the very essence of the action, wrong.

"You wish to be reborn somewhere far from here." The laughter continued. "You will not escape me so easily. Your energy will seep into the walls and floor to flow back into me. I will gain your powers, as weak as they are, and though it is quicker to extract information directly, I will gain access to your memories. Already I feast on your strength, keeping you weak. Your Accipitridae provides such rich and continuous energy."

"Excuse me, my what? What did you do to me while I slept?"

There was a jarring pause as the Lich was trying to work out the proper jaw movement for what he needed.

"Your birrrd," it said, the word slurring.

"Leave him alone." There was a dark edge to my voice as I thought of Shard. I couldn't risk hurting him and the Lich saw it.

"Give me the answers I need, and I will leave your Accipitridae in peace. It's the only one I offer this to," the Lich said, a grin forming on Riven's face.

With grim defeat my shoulders slumped. "What makes you think I even have the ability to come back?"

"7 moons past, I trapped a Soul of the Accipitridae, a BrongTa mutt. For his freedom, he offered up you."

I looked up sharply, eyes raging in destructive fire, physically manifesting at a greater intensity than my simple sparks.

With great delight, the Lich shivered, drinking in the rush of energy.

"What did Enzo tell you?" I demanded.

"The mutt showed me a memory of your rebirth and your 300 years of life. He offered this freely and I saw no alteration or deceit in the vision. It is why I seek you."

Pinching the bridge of my nose, I gave a soft chuckle. All the fighting, the death, despair, pain, suffering. It was all to track and capture me. The chuckle turned into a laugh which avalanched into hysterics.

Standing with a stern look on Riven's face, the lich waited patiently.

"You seek the one who has nothing to give on the words of one who has everything." I was still laughing as I talked. It was a culmination of all the hardship and struggles I'd gone through in recent times leading to this one moment. The dirty irony of it all... I just couldn't help myself.

"Explain your words, Daughter of Fibonacci," the Lich said.

My laughter evaporated as I realised, I'd said too much. I had no care to throw Enzo under a carriage. He deserved everything that was coming to him. I just knew the Lich would continue this war until Enzo was captured and the truth finally recovered from him. What was worse was if the Lich gained control over true immortality, everyone was in danger.

"I will not rise again in death. The Accipitridae have removed that which gave me mastery over death. You have come too late," I said.

"Explain to me the meaning behind the words *'of one who has everything',"* the Lich said then, refining to precisely what he desired.

"There is nothing for you, Demon of the abyss."

"Would it surprise you to know I am but a human and a scholar?"

"You became far less when you took on this form. What once may have been human died when you deigned to break the natural order of things."

"Then we are of similar make."

"I am nothing like you," I screamed, swinging my arm wildly. Deep down a voice began to question, is he really that wrong?

Without any more words, the Lich glided across the floor. Green mist swirled and danced upon his free hand and as he came within reach, he thrust the hand inside my chest. My eyes flew to the heavens as a gut-wrenching pain pulsed along every nerve in my body. I stood with mouth hung open in a silent scream. Shuddering in a mind-numbing fit, the Lich seemed to be searching within me for something.

The hand slowly withdrew from my body to the sound of snickering from the Lich. I drew in a hard breath, forcing it down my tense and throbbing windpipe, before collapsing to the floor.

"There is something there. Remnants of power, sweet to the taste. What is it?" The Lich asked. Its own, shrivelled tongue shifting in the air much like a snakes would.

"It is gone." I coughed with a dry throat before taking another swig of water.

"It is Accipitridae. It tastes like yours. The one that feeds you from afar."

"You will get nothing from them," I cry. Already, it knew too much.

"It is true, for they take from you the means for their own revival. This is a great disappointment. I have tried Accipitridae before, they are a loose end in themselves."

I remembered the black Phoenix on our scouting mission.

"No. It is your soul. I must find out this key because now I have confirmation it is possible."

263

Turning the Lich, left the room in haste. Tossing Riven's body aside, it hit the door frame before landing heavily, half outside the room. My heart shuddered as I saw the Chimera salivating over the body, stalling only to make room for the Lich's departure. Even as the beast pounced, I had been a moment quicker, dragging the upper half of Riven back into my cell and relative safety.

Gliding my hand through Riven's hair, I find it soothing as if he was somehow comforting me. I knew it a fancy of the mind but it was better than contemplating the regret for my words in the last conversation with the Lich. Slowly, I allowed myself to drift into sleep.

"*Elara.*" My name came across, soft like a whisper, but enough to stir me from my sleep.

"Mmm," I moaned not wanting to wake yet.

"*ELARA!*"

My eyes shot open and I looked around the room to be greeted by silence and darkness.

"Hello," I called to the emptiness I knew wouldn't reply. The voice had been Shard's and it brought a soft smile to my lips. He was trying to break through. With the Lich distracted in research or whatever drew it away, Shard had a chance. He was still looking for me.

Trying to shoot out a telepathic message, I wasn't surprised to find the jarring barrier set in place, strong against my mind. It must have only been in sleep and born from instincts that I made contact. I'd best not let Shard down now.

It almost became habit, clicking my fingers to bring on the sparks. I was sending out a constant stream now, my eyes taking in the surroundings and my brain beginning to piece everything together. Even obstacles like the bucket and Riven were etched into my mind and I felt at ease navigating around the room without incident.

Near the door sat another tray of food. I approached it cautiously not wishing to make the same mistakes as last time. Resting my hand on the small stack of red meat, I found they were still warm from recently being cooked. There was no way to tell the type of meat it was but right now I didn't care. Next to it was a firm pear. With a little pressure, I forced my pinky finger into the fruit all the way to the core. A stream of juice rushed past as I found it was fresh inside. Finally, there was a pile of peanuts on the side. I left these where they were having had a life where my body violently reacted to eating them. I knew it wasn't likely to be reincarnated into another body, but I couldn't now bring myself to risk them again.

The moment I began eating it was like my body reawakened an addiction. The meat was so moist and tender that it fell apart in my mouth. Juice dribbled down my chin and with the length of my arm, I wiped it away not caring about etiquette or manners or any other rule passed down from nobility. All there were was the sustenance I craved and how to cram it down my throat.

Reaching for the next slice, a pout formed as I found the pile had been depleted. Moving onto the pear, my teeth sunk deep into the flesh. Sweet nectar danced over my taste buds sending a shiver of delight down my spine. Of all the fruit I had tried or neglected over my lives, this one piece would live in my memories as perfection. Ambrosia to the Gods wherever they may be. Scraping my teeth along the core, I tried to savour every last sliver I could before setting myself to my impossible task.

In trying to keep my spirits high, I settled on improbable instead. I had no clothes, no weapons, no layout of the facility and yet I would attempt my escape either by an exit or through my death. I desperately wanted to see my friends again and would do anything I could to get out alive, but if it was death that greeted me... then I would at least haunt them.

I smiled thinking of all the wicked little tricks I could play on Kymberlin. With all her high and mighty talks, she seemed most likely to be spooked by ghosts. I giggled forgetting myself, lost in my illusions.

Shaking my head, I slapped my cheeks trying to drive a little focus in. The sting was a refreshing wake up, chasing back the head spins I was having. There was little time left until I'd be too weak to function properly. I decided, after my next sleep when the food had digested properly and my energy was at its highest, would be my best... and only chance.

Stumbling to the doorway, I stopped sparking so I could listen better. Each breath whistling from my mouth, the sound over exaggerated in the darkness.

"Where are you?" I whispered to myself as I cocked an ear this way and that, trying to hear the soft footfalls of the chimera.

And then it filtered in. That undeniable footfall that haunted my dark isolation. Stepping a foot from the cell, an immediate acceleration pounded down the hallway. There was no hesitation in the creature, no warnings for doing the wrong thing. If I hadn't pulled my leg back in that moment, the sound of the beast crashing into the floor where I touched gave no doubt it would have ripped the unruly limb from my hip and feasted on the flesh.

A guttural snarl filtered through before the beast padded off empty handed.

Thrice more, I tested my bounds. I counted the circuit the beast took to be 250 seconds and after verifying this a few times played with the numbers at 125 seconds the creature was on me in 30. 140 seconds and the time was even shorter. When I tested it at 110 seconds, I was surprised to find the amount of time I had went up to 40 seconds before the Chimera came barrelling through. I could only assume it hesitated coming up to half way in moving forward or heading back the way it had come. Maybe it wasn't even that smart and I gave it too much credit where it still ran forward at that distance. Whatever the reason, this was going to be useful.

By now the creature was frustrated, walking back and forward in front of the doorway, eyes directed at me.

"Your master bids you guard these halls, you slovenly mutt. Away with you?" I said creating a tch noise for emphasis. It looked to be about to move when it paused looking back up the hall.

A soft green light, beyond that of my sparks, made my heart sink as the Lich approached again. Taking a step back the Chimera bowed its head to its lord as he stood in the doorway. The Lich gave a slow sideways look at the empty food tray before walking up to me. I tried to move aside or lessen my imprint in the room but he was on me so quickly and my eyes widened as I saw that same swirling green around his hand.

One quick thrust, faster than I was able to grasp in my weary state and the hand entered my chest. Agony had me falling to my knees but for the strength of the Lich keeping my aloft. This only heightened the pain, and a few minutes of deafening screams was all my body could take. I welcomed the slow, cold kiss of that unconscious embrace.

Eyes fluttering open, I felt a form against me. Cold to the touch with head resting on my shoulder, I pulled him closer into him. For a moment only, I believed the kidnapping and torture from the Lich all a terrible nightmare. That I was still on the hillside with Riven and life wasn't so bad.

My eyes shot open to be met with absolute darkness. I created a stream of sparks and found my predicament hadn't changed but it was Riven who was curled up at my side. He would have needed to drag himself a few metres to reach me. It was too sad to sleep by his side as he was.

"Riven," I cried stroking his face. "Riven are you with me?"

Gentle lines creased the skin of his brow as he showed signs of life. My breath caught in my throat, watching, hoping beyond all hope that he might wake. And tears streamed from my eyes as his slowly opened. Drawing him into and embrace, I wept openly for several minutes.

"I see you missed me," The hoarse whispered words reached my ears. "Give me some room. Let me breath the air once more."

I pulled back. "Sorry," I said, creating sparks to see him better.

A hand reached up cupping my cheek. "You need never be sorry to me," Riven replied, with a warm smile.

"How are you here? How is this even possible? I thought you finally passed from this world."

"Abacus has full control over my body. He can..."

"Wait," I said, placing a hand on his bare chest. I couldn't say if it helped emphasise my words or I just needed the comfort of touching him. Probably both, if I was being honest. "Abacus is the Lich, right? That thing has a name?"

Riven nodded and began coughing into his hand. It was a terrible and grating cough that was born of his body's time in stasis. After a moment's pause, he talked again.

"He can control whether my body is animated or not. With me, he never got the process right. I still have my mind, as it is, but you can't remain attached. You can't let him use me to make you fold."

"I can't make that promise. I love you, Riven," I said, my voice barely a whisper.

His hands reached out and caught mine. "I can't tell you to forget me or act like I'm nothing, but I am Abacus's reanimation. If he hurts me, it is only a show. He cannot touch my soul."

"But," I say.

"He has yet to retrieve from you that which he desires most. He will do everything he can to make you talk. I was reanimated to break you. But that's all I am now. A reanimated torture device."

"We need to get you away from this place," I said, searching for something in the dark that could help.

"We can't. He'll just shut me down again."

"Then I'll stay here." The pain was beginning to overwhelm me. I couldn't think straight. All I knew was I wanted to be with this man and nothing in this world could pull us apart again.

A soft and sorrowful expression crossed Riven's features but he hid it quickly. "I love you, Elara. If only we could have met under better circumstances."

"Don't speak like this is the end. I'll save you."

"You already have." Pulling me down, Riven kissed me gently. There was great love passing from those lips.

As I opened my eyes to gaze upon my lover, the putrid green light was back. "He returns," I whispered without looking from Riven, who just closed his eyes and nodded.

Drifting across the floor on silent feet, Abacus made straight for Riven. There was no emotion in his eyes. No depth of soul to suggest pleasure or regret in what he was doing. Just another immortal husk, empty of the emotions and quirks that make us alive. There were no words this time when he picked Riven up. No trying to negotiate, threaten or trick the secrets out of me. There was only pain and screaming as he tortured Riven.

Riven's muscles contracted in a flood of agony and torment as his screams echoed throughout the small cell, building upon themselves until nothing more could be heard. It was heartbreaking and I ran in trying to tear Riven from Abacus's grasp. My weakened state conspired against me and I was unable to help.

With a back hand, Abacus sent me sprawling across the stone floor, coming to a rest on my side. I saw Riven drop something clear to clatter open the floor, before he looked up at me and mustered a smile.

"Reanimated pain," he said, his voice stressed to a grated whisper.

Those words made it clear just what he meant before. What he was trying to tell me. He knew this was coming. He was ready for it. Abacus used him only as a device for breaking me and Riven made sure it wouldn't happen.

Sure, it would stop if I broke. Abacus would win and Riven wouldn't be useful anymore. Or I could be defiant and indifferent. Maybe then, Riven might be seen to be useful that little bit longer.

Pulling myself to my feet with a mighty groan, I wandered back to Riven and Abacus. The torture had begun again and it was all I could do to ignore such pain.

Standing before Abacus, I bent down to pick up Riven's item and smiled. I stood tall, staring straight into the Lich's soulless eyes.

"I will never give up the secret of true immortality. Your death at my hand will be sweet indeed."

Realising the use of Riven was futile, Abacus flung him aside and came at me with a soul chilling scream. Its bony fingers reached for my neck as I stood strong, my eyes locked to his dimly glowing, green orbs. There was a cruel and triumphant look as those fingers curled around my throat to begin squeezing.

This was nothing. I needed him close; to believe he could win over me. It was my best time to attack. Riven, his power clearly still active, was able to provide me with a small and wickedly sharp, ice dagger. Even as he was being tortured, he was looking out for me and I'd be damned if I didn't make it count.

Letting the ice blade slide to my hand, I jammed the pointy end into Abacus's eye socket. There was little resistance entering or sinking in behind, so I couldn't say just how efficient the target was.

Almost immediately, he threw me back wailing in pain. I had to hold my ears to the sound as Abacus scrabbled at the hilt.

As he began to fall back, I winced at the sound but made to advance. Too late, a green portal enveloped him as he teleported from the room. Slamming my fist into a wall, I swore as darkness once again enveloped us.

There was a soft groan from Riven and, forgetting everything else, I rushed to his side. Relief washed over me seeing he was still functioning, his face contorting in pain. I stroked his hair.

"Abacus has fled. You're safe for the moment," I said softly.

"What happened?" He asked, recovering enough to speak. He still sounded battered and thin.

"I used your dagger. I was able to jam it into his head. It wouldn't be something a normal person could survive."

"Then I won't have long," Riven said with a deep sigh. "He'll have jumped back to his p... ph... He will have gone to regenerate. Minutes or hours, the moment Abacus can think properly, he will disconnect me and be back for you."

"What can't you say? Is it the secret to his power?"

Riven nodded. "There are things hardwired into my mind I just can't cross." He looked terribly concerned. "You need to get out of here, now."

I reached out a hand but he slapped it away.

"No! Get out of here. Leave me."

"I won't leave you," I said. I couldn't compel myself to be from his side. Not if it was to be his last moments.

"You must. If I'm with you, even if we flee miles from here in a random direction, he will use me to easily locate you in moments. He wants you to make that mistake."

"I need you. I need your abilities. I can't use my spirit form or my ice. The best I can do are these small sparks that help illuminate the cell."

With a gentle smile, Riven shook his head. "Your Fibonacci abilities cannot be blocked. Abacus has tried with me too many times to count."

"Then how?"

"You were never trained properly as a child, were you? All you need is moisture and your abilities will work. Abacus can pull all the water molecules from the air making you feel like he crafted a wall around your abilities. The elite can wield ice using the fluid in one's body like I did. Even if you can't, the bucket of water you were given will suffice in crafting weapons. It wouldn't work with saltwater, though."

Things began to make sense now as to why Abacus served me saltwater to begin with. Only risking the fresh water when my belief that my abilities were locked down had been solidified. And he had me fooled.

Sliding to the water bucket, I dipped a finger in. Small refracted crystals formed around my digit, fuelling my confidence and allowing me to believe there was a possibility of escape.

Looking to the door, there was only one, true, first step on the path to freedom. And it needed a sword. Reaching into the bucket, I visualised a lance like the one Riven would use, then gripped the shaft and slowly pulled the weapon of hardened ice crystal from the bucket. The water level dropped to a third the initial amount but it was necessary.

"I'm not strong enough to walk, let alone fight, Elara," I heard Riven say after he saw the weapon in the refracted light of my sparks.

"Who said anything about you fighting, old man. Let me clear the way for you," I said with a grin and headed for the door.

There was no sound of padding feet and I couldn't be sure where the Chimera was at the moment. At this point it could attack from either side and I didn't have the patience to wait any longer knowing Riven might pass from this world at any moment.

Stepping into the hall, I stood silently listening for any movement. In my head, I counted, giving me a rough deadline for where the creature may be. At about 28 seconds, I heard the pounding of feet at full run, coming up fast behind me. With jittery nerves, I waited until the very last moment. Flinging myself sideways into a roll, the wind and surly breath of the creature sat strong upon me as I slowed the battle, ducking into the cell.

Rolling to my feet, I skidded back into the hallway and with a spark or two, dropped to my knees. The crystal lance shimmered before me as I locked it into a loose cobble. With the mentality of the creatures this Chimera was crafted from, it lost its footing in the dark and slid along the stone trying to turn. When it corrected itself, the beast charged at me, leaping at the last moment. It was the only move I banked on, the only move that would save me. The only move I knew of predatorial creatures attacking from above, giving no chance for the prey to escape.

The weight of the beast fell full-force on the end of the crystal lance. The tip pierced just below the throat to skewer the chest and heart, exiting somewhere out the lower back. I was left fighting with the Chimera's death throes. The sparking nerves sending its talons flaring in odd and unpredictable ways. I was just happy the weight of the creature wasn't enough to have it slide all the way down the lance on top of me and I was able to shimmy out from under it.

"See, old man, nothing to it."

Pulling the lance for the Chimera, I recrafted it into a sabre. A favourite of mine and easier to wield in narrow hallways if we were attacked.

"I can't follow where you go, Elara. You can't take me with you."

Ignoring Riven's words, I walked to the bucket.

"Ready for a show?" I asked with a wink and snapped as many sparks around me as I could. I made sure they would last a few seconds before dying away and as Riven gazed at me, I lifted the bucket and poured the contents through my hair to store for future use. I was never going to carry the bucket and the sword with what I was about to do. The excess water trickling down over my naked body. In those last few dying seconds, I could see it set a blaze in Riven's eyes and most definitely, his loins.

The water felt crisp and cool as it flowed over me. Every touch was tender and intimate in a way that spoke to my icy soul, invigorating in both life and motivation. It was orgasmic to my very core like nothing in this world could be. It was pure and primitive and... I needed to tease Riven more.

Sparking an array of light around myself, I strode to Riven. The light took in every curve and enhanced me with soft shades. The light faded away as I reached him and with a tracer image I used for navigation in my mind, dropped to my knees and took his face in my hands. The soft moan that echoed in the silence was all I needed to know I got him. Leaning in, our lips found one another in a passionate embrace.

When we finally surfaced for air, I caught Riven by the arm and drew him up over my shoulders to carry him more easily. Even then, he was heavy for my frame, but I was determined now to save him and there was nothing in this world that could stop me.

"No, you can't do this. He'll find you through me. Let me protect you," Riven cried as he realised what was happening. He tried to wriggle out of the hold, but he was in a far worse state than I and had no chance.

"Don't even think about it. I'm not some defenceless little girl that needs rescuing. I am Elara Three Pine, Soul to the Blue Phoenix Shard, and daughter of the Fibonacci clan. You should tremble at my feet but for the love I hold for you, Riven," I said setting off into the hallway, one foot at a time. "And anyway, you still owe me an orgasm. Don't think you can get out of it so easily by dying."

"Ah, so now the truth comes forth," Riven laughed, his body too tired to fight me.

"And try to keep that thing under control. I can feel it having a go at my ear."

Riven just laughed again and winced from a sudden pain in his side. "When you bring it to life with your little water display, I will never be able to wrangle it under control this side of taking you."

I smiled wickedly. "Then I better get you out of here quickly and find those stars because I don't care if you can only lay there and experience me, I am going to tame that demon beast."

Out into the corridor, I looked left and right with a moment's hesitation. Making for the left, I felt Riven's hand tapping my chest.

"Other way," he said.

Slowing to manoeuvre easier, I turned around and headed back, taking the right path. It was a terrible balancing act to hold my sword and

Riven, while sparking to give myself a small chance of not running head-first into a wall but we began making progress.

"See, I still need you to make my escape," I said, and he grumbled some inconceivable words.

Around this corner there will be some stairs up and down. You need to head upwards. Just beware of the guards at the top of each flight."

"Makes sense. How far underground are we?"

Riven shook his head. "We are far above the earth. Maybe 15 levels. There are two levels above and a climb down the outside. For one who has scaled the cliffs of Mount Brueshair, you will be skilled enough to make it. Even in your current state."

"Why so dark?" I asked peering around a corner trying to perceive movement in the pitch black.

"Because those that reside her need no lights where captives and prisoners do. There is light outside."

A giddy, excitement begun in my chest sending goosebumps over my arms. There had been a high likely hood of never seeing the light of day, hanging over my head and now with the promise of light and fresh air only moments away, it was almost overwhelming. Quickening my pace, I turned into the stairwell.

"Stop," Riven hissed but it was too late.

On my next spark, a face came into view within arm's reach. A zombified human with threads of skin and body tissue hanging from all over its body as if it had been decaying for decades. Beady, sunken eyes came alive as it regarded me entering its domain. With the creature producing a loud scream, much like Abacus's true voice, I blanched as the breath of compounded death assaulted my nostrils. In the dying light, I saw it raise a broken sword above its head, short but still enough to take my life.

My sword arm moved before I had time to comprehend the attack, blocking the savage blow. Deflecting its momentum, I twisted to cut out the creature's legs. The undead fell past me down the steps before it let out another blood curdling cry. This was answered above and below with a series of similar replies. My heart sank.

"It was gunna happen regardless. Get moving," Riven grunted in my ear.

My legs began pumping as adrenaline fuelled my body. Around the top of the stairs and up the next flight, I could feel the sickly damp fingers of another undead on my back but with no clothes to get a grip on, it didn't hinder me.

Light started to filter in and I could make out the figures of humanoids upon the stairs. Some held weapons while others squared up to me with bare hands and jagged teeth. I could see at least five in my way and with a quick burst barged into them knocking the front few off balance. As they tumbled, they took others with them and I hacked and slashed my way over the top.

Leaping the last, I swore as a hand caught my ankle sending me sprawling to the floor with Riven tumbling ahead. Hacking off the hand, I was disgusted to find its grip held fast and I couldn't shake it from me nor give time to removing it with a pounding of feet echoing up the stairs.

Looking around for Riven, I realised the sky had opened up above us and I stood upon a bare, flat roof top in the centre of a deep valley. The sun hung low but in this moment was hard to tell if it was rising or setting. Mountains surrounded the area and across a deep gorge stood a vast forest filling in the gentle curve to the stone cliffs. Everything looked far more natural than I believed it was going to.

A low growl brought me back out of my reverie as I saw the undead that caught my leg, dragging itself towards me with its good hand. Taking Riven under the arms, I started dragging him towards the nearest corner as a horde of undead entered from the stairs, flaring out on the rooftop.

Taking a quick glance over the edge, I knew it was futile to try and carry Riven down with the horde dogging my heels. There was barely even a moment long enough to get myself over the edge. Turning I faced the enemy with sabre in hand. They were slow and unskilled, but this was balanced with my low energy. I just needed to get through them before I was spent. An unlikely outcome but at least I had my back to the ledge.

"Experience everything you can in my stead," Riven said, and my eyes shot down. He raised his head just enough to smile at me.

Before I had a chance to speak, spiked pillars erupted from the rooftop to a height above my head, locking me into a secluded section of roof. In the centre, Riven was lifted within, to be supported as if standing.

"You can't do this. I can fight." Tears had come unbidden to my eyes.

Shaking his head, Riven kept that smile trained on me. "I can feel his grip growing on me once more. I have minutes at most."

Decaying arms reached through the gaps in the ice pillars, grasping at the air as they tried to break through. The pillars remained strong and yet I was dying in a more torturous way. My love was dying before my eyes and I could do nothing now to save him.

"I need you to go while I can still hold this," Riven grunted.

Tears caressed my cheeks as I reached for Riven's. "I love you," I said and leaned in to kiss him deeply. I could feel him flinching below my lips as if there was pain coursing his body. I didn't want the moment to end keeping the kiss alive as long as I could but a cold spike caught me under my arm and dragged me back towards the ledge as Riven mouthed, *I love* you, too. His eyes clenched tightly.

In that moment, seeing his face in the small hole of the barricade, a terrible flash of memory started to merge over the scene. I was a small child once more in my original life. My mother's face peering through the hole in the wall of Three Pine's defences. "I love you, my darling girl. Be strong," she said to me before a sword pierced her chest and she coughed up blood.

"No, not again," I screamed at Riven. "I can't do this again. Let me fight with you!"

He smiled, the same as my mother had before a spear punched through his throat. I could only watch his torture as the icicle dragged me from the edge of the roof.

"Riven, Nooo!" A shrill cry escaped my lips as my world shifted and I was being dragged backwards towards the earth, the rooftop falling away fast. A sudden turn and my momentum was broken being flung back up and around a metre or so above hard dirt. I was being lowered more gently now but before I could disembark the ice shattered into a million tiny pieces along with my heart as I fell the small distance to land hard.

"Mother!" I cried, then, as the emotions threaten the swamp me, my voice softened. "Riven," I whimpered, slamming a fist against the stone wall of my prison. I knew in that moment, his life force was gone. I made a pact with any God who would listen that I wouldn't again let Abacus resurrect Riven. His form would not be disgraced for the Lich's pleasure.

"You hear me Aba...Shit." Glancing up, my eyes grew wide with fear.

The armies of the undead were flinging themselves from the rooftop and plummeting towards me. I knew intuitively they'd be getting up momentarily after landing to chase and harass me. I hadn't planned my next move beyond fleeing the area but when I realised I was heading towards the valley bridge, there was some small semblance of relief.

'*It's not the time. It's not the time,*' I repeated over and over in my mind as thoughts of both my mother and Riven merged and threatened to paralyse me. To let myself grieve would mean certain death. Either, I get out of here and find the time to grieve later or I part from this world and see my love and my kin once more. Regardless, I needed to keep moving and the mantra was all I had.

Telling myself never to look back, never to give myself the fear of doubt, should the enemy be approaching, I disregarded the warning. My eyes glanced over my shoulder...

"Fuck," I swore and pushed even harder to get to the bridge that was just ahead, around the corner. The undead were starting to find their feet and beginning to focus on me.

A gut-wrenching cry sounded from behind me and I heard a multitude of footsteps upon the hard earth.

"*It's not time.*'

As I round the stone corner my heart sank. The bridge was at least 10 metres above. The colour of the stone was significantly lighter than that of the stronghold and the rough and rocky underside looked natural. It was as if the whole top of the bridge had been carved in the natural stone and the stronghold built later from darker stones, acquired in distant quarries. There was a chance, but it needed to be quick. Should any of the undead round that corner before I could hide myself then I was dead.

My legs pumping hard, I thanked the Gods they didn't cramp at this vital moment. My eyes scanned the underside of the bridge looking desperately from shadow to shadow until I saw one that might suit.

Using the water held in my hair I crafted an ice platform below my feet. I forced it to grow quickly, catapulting me up to the crevice. Pain flared in my head as it glanced from a small jutting rock but I ignored it and scrambled into the tight space, wedging my body as deep as it could go and sent a prayer of thanks it was just enough to be hidden from the ground.

Transmuting the ice to water, it splashed upon the earth just as the first of the undead came upon the scene. My breath held as I watched it slow into its disjointed gallop, its head twisting this way and that, trying to find me.

'*It's not the time. It's not the time.*' I could feel my muscles wanting to shudder, to break down and tremble, but I didn't trust myself in this small hole. I couldn't give in just yet.

Confident in my sanctuary, I let my body fall away. The spirit taking flight into the dying sky. With the sun now kissing the horizon, I floated higher and higher. In this, I got to witness a reverse sunset. Or maybe I should call it the sun rising in the west. An odd sensation that once more began on its natural course as I reach an optimal height. Beyond the valley there was no life to be found. Open fields of grey ash that pushed on as far as the eye could see in every direction. North and east held active volcanoes. The Northern one spewing magma high into the air to fall back and run down the mountainside in orange, glowing rivers. I could only guess the valley was saved by the high, rocky cliffs.

Heading out aimlessly towards the west and the light, I soared over lands and oceans I had never seen in all the time I'd spent on the earth. All I needed was a single landmark. Something to give me direction, to give me hope. But every new hill or tree or river looked the same as the last one I passed and soon it was all I could do not to fall deeper into depression. Slowing in my drifting, I settled upon a high mountain and simply rested my head in my hands.

"*ArarrrahhAaaAAAaAaAAAAAHHHHHHHH!*" I screamed to the ephemeral winds. I just wanted to be home in my bed. I wanted warmth. Of all things for a Fibonacci to say and I couldn't deny that need of warmth... and clothes. Too many cuts and scrapes could have been saved by that thin piece of material covering my body.

"*Elara?*"

My head shot up, and I looked around. "*Shard? Oh my God, Shard! Is that you?*" I could have burst into tears then and there, but in my spirit form, I controlled it easily.

"*I'm here. Reach out. Feel my energy. Come to me,*" Shard said then.

It couldn't be that easy. Closing my eyes, I concentrated on the energy of Shard. The blue, warmth that filled me with such light and love. I reached out for it and found it all around me, holding to me, drawing me... further west. As quick as I could, I followed the line of vibrant, blue energy and soon found myself floating over familiar lands. If I had of just keep moving, I would have found my home even without the guiding vibrance of Shard. I just needed to keep going.

Like a blue meteor, Shard found me in the air, and I settled onto his back holding to the feathers. It was the most comfortable and welcoming place in all the world and I never wanted to leave.

"Elara, your energy is dim. Tell me where you are."

"Can't I just rest a moment, Shard? Your back is wonderful," I said. My eyes were getting heavy in the safe and loving embrace.

A loud piercing squawk brought me back into focus.

"You of all people know you could fade from existence using too much of your Qi. Tell me where you are and get back to your body. You need true sleep." Shard admonished me.

He was right. Using my spirit force was always dangerous and I needed to replenish it. Relaying the location to him, showing the path through shared memories, he nodded.

"No one has been there in millennia. I cannot enter that valley without great pain. Can you get to the cliff tops?"

"I can only try. Night is upon me. I'll try for tomorrow afternoon."

"I'm coming for you. Get some sleep. It is a day's flight for me at my best. The stars may be out when I arrive. Wait for me."

"I will, Shard. Thank you."

"You will survive. Get some sleep."

With a last hug, I blinked myself back into my body to wake at the edge of the small crag. The emotions filtered in once more along with thoughts of Riven and my mum. Footsteps on the ground below alerted me to the search by Abacus and the undead. My body was afire with pain and a stiffness that threatened to have the muscles cramping.

'It's not the time. It's not the time." My mantra played endlessly in my head as I hugged my knees. I rocked a little and tried to keep myself sane until the gentle hand of exhaustion swept in and pulled me back into a dark and silent slumber.

Chapter 14

'It's not the time.' My eyes fluttered open to find myself staring over the edge of the craggy opening. The sight didn't haunt me or send my sprawling into the confines of the shelf. I was already far past caring if I lived or died by some freak accident. Don't get me wrong, I would fight to the end, but if my end was falling into the abyss while I was asleep, I wasn't going to complain.

Watching the rain upon the pathway below, I relaxed into the sound of the water upon the stone bridge above. A sound that began to irritate me as it was too heavy and too out of sync with the light shower I was watching. Shifting to my spirit, I passed through the stone to get an idea what was happening. The enemy had given up on the paths below and were now searching the woodlands and free space between, down to the bridge. It must've been the night squad coming back in, refreshed by a new set of eyes. It was this changeover that woke me and sounded like a poor imitation of the rain.

Drifting back to my body, I settled in waiting for the sound to settle down. It was too open to try to cross over the bridge. Too easy for them to hunt me down once spotted. I scanned the drop below finding sheer cliffs to a dark abyss. That wasn't a viable option either. The only way now was underneath. From the quick scan coming up to the bridge it looked doable. Hard... but doable.

I smiled suddenly, thinking of Korr, inverted, bounding along on the underside of the bridge as if gravity itself had reversed just for him. And when the imagery ended and all the pain rushed back in to fill its place, I couldn't decide if the thought of Korr was worth it or not. Only the darkness felt stronger.

'It's not the time.' I shut myself off to my emotions, trying to concentrate on the task at hand. Contemplating the best way to go about getting out, I decided to go over the edge, feet first on my belly. It was an all or nothing shot and if I found no hand holds my strength couldn't keep me up indefinitely.

Taking a few deep and stabilising breaths, I jumped right in before my mind could tell me no. Sliding to my stomach, legs dangling over the edge, I planted my hands on the ledge in a more favoured position and kicked back. The weight of my body threatened to destroy my grip and drag me back but I held on, skin and nail.

I couldn't believe just how far my strength had fallen in captivity. The centuries of knowing my limitations had been shattered in that one moment and I played a sharp line of waiting too long to find I didn't have the strength to continue and pushing forward too quickly before I had processed the shock of that one manoeuvre.

My eyes ran one hold ahead as I began swinging myself under the bridge to the closest side, barely two metres away. I needed to take the dead weight from my arms and transfer it to my legs. They were stronger and would allow me time to rest along the way. Looking at it now, it wasn't a terribly hard climb and the bridge span was shorter than it seemed on the roof. I just knew now, I wasn't fit enough.

With a quick glance out passed the edge, I checked for any guards that may be scanning over the side and, more importantly, for the nearest handhold. With no one in sight, I made the awkward transition around the bend to grasp a small nook. Locking my fingers within, I brought my body around and, scrabbling with my left hand on a hold only big enough for the finger tips, my right gave way.

I felt the gut wrenching pull of gravity take over as I began to fall back, my hand scrapping over the harsh rocky surface. Instincts and a vast experience from an array of lives was all that halted my momentum. I'd formed an ice structure that snaked out into a number of nooks and crannies and wrapped it around my wrist, holding me aloft. The jarring pain of a shoulder at risk of slowly being ripped from its socket, tortured a grinding grunt from my lips but I bit hard on my other hand to ward it off. I could see a guard near the middle of the bridge, standing on the edge, taking a piss. The cool breeze pushing the yellow liquid back into the rock face and I cursed the man for it, even as I dangled. At least he wasn't directly above me, which was possibly the only reason he hadn't heard my initial cry.

I let myself hang limp as I prepared to boost myself back up with the tortured muscles. The pain had begun to subside as everything found a balance and settled into place. It would have been a sight to see. Soldiers running back and forward along the bridge while the prisoner they were seeking was dangling naked below. It was almost comical in its circumstances and a tender grin touched my lips. A grin that was chased away by pain and, because I was stubborn, was finally replaced with anger. Anger for the Lich and his unwillingness to let nature take its course, along with all the pain and suffering everyone else had to go through for him. Anger for Enzo, and his unwillingness to let nature take its course, at any cost.

Greed. Selfishness. I could see very little holding Enzo and Abacus apart when stripped down to their unrefined core. Each would put themselves in front of everyone else if it meant an extra day on this planet. They were both as bad as one another. Only, one, was less conspicuous about his actions.

The memories and the pain caused to me over recent and past years, built like a fire in my chest, fuelling the rage now coursing through my veins. With a low growl, I pushed for a handhold with my left, fighting through the new pain, allowing it to feed the anger and keep me moving. Soon, I had my feet below me, taking some of the weight as I shimmied along the bridge.

It was slow going, getting over the bridge. I moved until my limbs couldn't carry me anymore, rested and then began moving again in an endless cycle. It was the chill of the wind and the icy kiss of the rain that helped keep my senses alive. There was nothing more comforting to a Fibonacci, especially in times of great need and not knowing how long I was asleep for, I couldn't be sure when Shard would arrive to collect me. All I could do was keep moving and hope I didn't keep him waiting too long.

And with the sun beginning to get low in the sky, I was already going to need to waste an hour waiting for the dark. It was my best chance getting across the grassy clearing to the forest without being seen.

At the end of the bridge, the drop to the soft earth below came down to a few metres at worst. If I swung just right, I could even catch the gradient of the steep hill and slide down to what looked to be a goat's trail.

A small stream weaved its way down the hillside to fall from a ledge and into the darkness below. What caught my eye were some larger fish circling in the slower sections of water near the surface, keeping close to take any insects that may stray nearby. They were going to feed my empty belly. I never shared a taste for raw fish like some cultures but this afternoon's meal was sure to taste far beyond grand.

It wasn't long before I had the flesh of one of the fish dancing across my tongue. A little ice magic to freeze and send the fish my way was worth the small amount of energy used. It was always said you needed to spend a little to make a lot and I needed all the energy I could get.

Leaning against the slope of the hill just under the edge of the bridge, I kept a tentative lookout for any activity that might find me but when the enemy was mindless there wasn't too much danger where I was. None of them would think it through, just acting like ants covering as much ground as possible hunting their prey. Even ants, though, would eventually find what they were looking for.

Bringing one last fish to the banks, I relented in accepting my stomach wasn't quite as big as it once had been, after three bites. It was an unnecessary loss of life and I felt guilty I couldn't finish.

"I'm sorry, my friend. I will make sure the sustenance provided is put to good use," I said, placing the fish back into the stream and watching the body drift away over the falls and down into the darkness. I turned to look up the slope picturing the forest close by. "Time I got moving," I said to myself.

Upon my belly, I shimmied up the slope and peered over the top. One guard was on the bridge eyes forward and, after surveying him for 10 minutes, found he never looked to the sides. He was solely there to guard the bridge.

Rolling to my back, I wormed through the dirt making sure to cover every part of myself in mud. The days in darkness had toned my skin back to a whiter blend and to step out into the fields, especially at night, I'd shine like a beacon. Even ol' Sharp Eyes back there would notice me. Now, at least, I could blend in.

Making my way across the field without incident, I heard the sound I feared since fleeing my prison. The baying of terror hounds rang out into the night from little more than across the bridge behind me. Sure, they would need to find my scent but that would only save me 5 minutes at most as they fanned out across the field. I wasn't exactly far from the bridge and the mud wasn't going to do anything to hide the aroma I'd built since my capture.

Legs pounding, I raced into the forest. Low branches and harsh bark began to whip at me and graze the skin drawing a roadmap in blood. A spark of recognition that I was on the verge of panic sounded in my mind. As my mind screamed for calm, to take a moment and breath, the sound of the Terror Hounds kept me at the precipice.

A shadow moved to my right and I rolled on my shoulder as a blade whistled overhead, the slipstream of air rolling across my back. Sweeping out a leg, I caught the figure behind the knee and sent him crumbling to the ground. I pinned their sword arm and, finding a dagger at their side, slit their throat before they had a moment to recover. Taking the sword, I beheaded him for good measure. I spared only a moment to remove the man's belt and cloak, sweeping them around my naked, battered frame. There was no need for modesty or to hold back the cold. When it came down to having a thin layer of protection over your skin or none at all. Well, the choice was simple and I was going to need my hands free to climb so the sheathes on the belt were a must, also. If I had more time, I would have taken the hard worn armour but I could hear the hounds closing in.

There was a definite change in their barks, shifting to a more triumphant howl as they found my scent. Now, they would've all turned back to merge on the trail heading straight to me.

Climbing a nearby tree, I got as high as I could before leaping to the branch of a neighbouring tree. I was able to do this three more times before a lengthy gap forced me to make an ice bridge. I needed to get at least ten trees further along to give myself a fighting chance in making the cliffs.

Looking back, I smiled as the Terror Hounds found where I climbed and were, even now, circling that one tree. Some had sniffed around to confirm this was where I left the ground and returned to sit vigil. Their masters would be along soon enough but by then, I would hopefully be long gone and the hunt would continue. Every second counted.

The more I transitioned from tree to tree, the easier it became and soon I was at a comfortable distance away to begin running at ground level. That and the large clearing making my tree top advancement, all but impossible now. The cliff face was looming large above me and there would only be a short sprint through the woods to reach it. Even if the Terror Hounds took up the hunt again, I believed I could out run them.

Scurrying down the smooth, beige trunk, I skirted the edge of the clearing. Noting a small bush with purple flowers at the far end, I made for that so as to re-enter the woods at the correct position. I couldn't risk the open ground even with how close I was. Impatience could kill just as easily as the sword and I needed to be vigilant of both the enemy and myself. Forcing myself to move slowly, I focused on the small bush. It was unusual for any flowers to bloom in such a cold environment but the Lemna Raja flowers seemed to thrive in any environment.

"So, you will save me one last time? Thank you," I said to the bush remembering some of my more threatening bouts of asthma. I owed much in my life to this beautiful, dangerous creation of nature and as I reached the bush, tilted my head in respect.

Turning back, a shimmer of the moon played before my eyes and l bent back to my absolute limit. I could barely see the enemy and even the blade that would've severed my head from my neck had passed into shadow. But I had more pressing matters. Spinning on my heel and bending forward, I spun my arms in a circular motion trying to maintain my balance and not fall into the Lemna Raja flowers. I couldn't say how terrible the effect would be should my naked form fall into the bush, the cloak billowing wide from my efforts. With a last-ditch effort, I leapt forward into a roll landing hard on my back but clearing the flowers. A long groan escaped my lips as a throbbing pain spread throughout my body.

"She's here," my attacker yelled in a booming voice. Immediately, the baying of hounds began again. So, the hunt was heating up just like the anger in my heart. I was clear if not for this homunculus of Abacus and with an arcing swoosh of my arm, a crescent band of blue flame pierced the darkness. A terrible trail of destruction carved through the trees and melted the homunculus to mush and bone.

I stood in shock a moment. My flames were back. It'd been so long since I used them properly and had almost forgotten they dwelled deep in my soul. Turning to the sound of the hunt, a dark gleam filled my eyes. Palms upturned, fingers curling cruelly, I slowly raised them to the sky, summoning vast pillars of flame. The trees fell into ethereal blue tones making the woods a dark and twisted domain.

"Let's see those bastards get through that."

Fading into the woods as shadows danced across the bark, I found my way to the cliff face. The last ten yards was deceptively steep but it was now before me. My stairway to freedom and a life reclaimed.

"I'm coming, Shard," I said, the whisper more prayer than promise.

The hand and foot holds were strong and deep making for an easy climb and I was able to get all four limbs on the rock in moments. Confidence grew only to be strangled out of me as I was ripped from the wall by the throat and thrown to the earth. With a quick and awkward glance backwards, I paled to see a Terror Hound thrashing the cloak in powerful tugs, dragging me backwards through the mud.

Pulling out my blade, I hacked at the cloth material tethering me to the beast. With a swing that opened a flap of skin on my shoulder, I cut through the cloak and diminished the momentum by rolling to my stomach. Finding my feet, I stared down the hound as I held to the fresh wound noting only a small trail of blood.

The flesh of the hound was semi melted, muscles like jelly, threatening to slide off the bone at any moment. Shaking the cloak, it tossed the material aside and was now circling me. Assessing me. Seeking the perfect moment to strike.

"You've braved the fire only to find death awaiting you. Come dance with your fate, child of Abacus," I said and rushed in. The Terror Hound, met me head on, leaping with teeth barred in the same move that ended Caeli.

Brow furrowed and nose crumpled in deep hate, I side stepped, jamming the flat of my blade into its mouth as it tried to snap at me mid-air. Pushing it away and losing my sword, I produced a small throwing knife from ice and, pivoting, threw the blade to take the hound in the throat. It was a clean death and I couldn't tell just how long the agony would keep up but, recovering my weapon, I walked past the gurgling death throes to remount the wall without regret.

It was an easy climb on a cool night. The rain eased hours ago but flowing winds had kept the majority of the cliff face dry. Only some of the deeper holds had pooled water and this was easily avoidable. The clouds had moved on as well to open up the sky in a vibrant display of stars...

'It's not the time. It's not the time," I abolished myself mentally. The chase in the woods had almost made me forget the moments leading up to it. Almost... but never fully for the harsh reality lived just below the surface tormenting what could have been some of the greatest memories I could cherish. The stars would never be so bright again.

Against the dark backdrop of the sky, darker shadows had taken flight in a bobbing motion as they flapped their dirty brown wings. Fucking Harpies.

"Why can't you just leave me the fuck alone?" I screamed, my voice carrying across the stone. It was beginning to become laughable. Every time I found myself believing I could make the crest of the cliff top, now maybe 40 metres off, a new obstacle would dash any hope I could muster. There was little energy left as I put everything into climbing the cliff, leaving nothing for beyond. This battle was too much.

Closing my eyes, I held my breath to fight back the tears now threatening to spoil my cheeks. "Quick... sharp... breaths," I said breathing between each word. The change resetting my bodies emotional functions as it tried to adapt to me.

The first of the Harpies dove in, talons of the slender, human legs, positioned to dig deep into my flesh if they ever got a hold of me. It continued its dive straight into the cliff face and plummeted lifeless to the ground with an ice shard embedded in its eye.

More took up the attack and with waves of fire and ice from my precarious position, I fought back. Fought the Harpies assault. Fought the growing darkness in my eyes. Fought the vertigo threatening to drag me down. Everything attacked me, calling me to sleep my endless sleep, but that was not the promise I made myself. With even an ounce of energy left within me, I would fight to the end.

My arm shot out to produce a wave of flame but only wisps could be called. My ice, as well, had faltered and now my attacks came like sleet. Enough to annoy but not enough to destroy. I wobbled on my perch before my arm tensed and pulled me close to the wall. Talons raked at my back carving large scars across the skin and I swung the sword back and forth in a desperate attempt to keep them at bay.

One talon caught the belt at my waste and with strong wings, tried to pull me from the wall. Summoning the last of my pooled strength, I conjured ice around my left hand to hold me in place even as the Harpy pulled my legs almost horizontal. My fingers fumbled with the buckle, trying to remove the belt and when I finally got the latch, gravity pulled me back to slam hard into the rocky cliff.

Eyes bleary and seeing two Harpies where there should only be one. I thrust out with the sword somewhere in the middle and lodge the blade in its face.

With nothing left to give and the ice melting around my hand, I swayed. Back... forward... then back once more, over the edge to plummet down towards the earth and my final resting place.

I closed my eyes.

"I am here."

My eyes shot open to a rain of fire and flaming feathers, sizzling upon the enemy. The ocean blue flames edged within an arctic shimmer, filled my vision, engulfing me in a warm embrace, and silencing my fears.

Shard had come for me.

A bed of feathers caught me moments before the ground and I felt the sharp turn to ascend and escape the harsh prison of this valley. It'd taken everything from me. My love, my happiness, my physical possessions. My kindness and ability to trust splintering and threatening to break into a million pieces. The only essence of the girl I once was was dangling on a thin, silver line of hope. Even that was tender and I clung to Shards back as if he could disappear at any moment.

Breaking the crest of the mountain Shard set a course for home. The wind whistled past at speeds I hadn't experienced before. Far below, Lands accelerated underfoot and I was free.

... I was free.

...I'm free.

Tears began to form in my eyes and trail down my cheeks.

"No, it's not the time," I told myself.

'When will it be,' my subconscious shot back.

"You are free, Elara. You don't need to fight anymore," Shard added.

Whatever walls I had frozen around my heart, melted away and all the memories, all the pain and torment, the deep, scarring grief as I watched Riven killed, and the wakening emotions fuelled by my parent's death. Everything came flooding in to overflow my system. As Shard dipped towards a nearby clearing, my muscles began to shudder and shake uncontrollably. I tried wrapping my arms around myself to stem the tide but there was nothing I could do to hide from my tortured soul.

Hitting the ground, I leapt from Shard seeking solace, a sanctuary to save myself, but there were only empty fields around me. Empty and confronting. I broke down, dropping to my knees. Great sobs racked my body as the tears came steadily. I couldn't close my mind off anymore and I once again experienced my horrors in a waking nightmare.

Screams came unbidden, terrifying and heartbreaking. As one finished, I breathed through the suffocating emptiness of my deflated lungs straight into the next ear-piercing scream. I couldn't stop it or flee into my mind. I could only curl up into a ball upon the hard earth and suffer.

And Shard could only stand over me, wings in a dome of privacy and protection, to watch. His heart slowly breaking.

Chapter 15

There was no time for me anymore. Moments and events had all merged together in a jumbled mess until I found myself on my side in bed facing away from the door. The rest of the journey on Shard was a kaleidoscope of clouds, light, rain, a shimmering green aurora, and the patches of darkness that suggested I was asleep or lost in my mind. There was no recollection of who brought me down from the rooftop, tended to my wounds, or dressed me in a soft tunic. I only knew I was breathing and Riven was not.

Suniel was the first person my mind registered. He stood by the bed and I could almost picture him holding his helmet in one hand, his stance official and at attention. I didn't bother to roll over and find out, however. There was no point in wasting the energy. He spoke of the loss of Riven and how the man had the potential to be someone great. He talked of how quiet the war front had been since our decisive battle. The fields were empty now and the allied forces had a chance to recover some energy and reinforce the defences that were destroyed. The final message being *'to stay vigilant and should our surroundings look quiet, never roam the lands without informing a superior.'*

The last line reverberated in my head. It was almost as if... Suniel was reprimanding me! He was blaming me for mine and Riven's capture. He was blaming *me* for Riven's loss.

Swinging on him with fire in my eyes, I stared at his retreating back as he left the room. I was seething to think he would heap all this on my shoulders. I hadn't asked to be kidnapped and I sure as hell didn't want Riven dead.

But the feelings faded and with a heavy sigh, I rolled back into my foetal position, alone in the dark facing away from the doors harsh light. It was comfortable this way. Quiet. The walls still holding me as if in the cell I physically escaped.

Maybe this was all just a construct of Abacus, a nightmare to keep me pliable while he searched my mind for answers. It was a reasonable theory, but I finally shook my head dismissing it. Only reality could be this harsh.

More movement around the room. A tink of cutlery, the thud of a plate, my bed pan being checked and I could tell it was a maid. They were moving through the routine s taught to us by mentors. Place the food, clean what needs cleaning, remove old food on the way out. Without watching, I could see each and every movement the maid made right up to a point of hesitation. They were leaving the room but stalled in the doorway, their shadow etched into the wall above me.

"We all look up to you, you know. The maids and servants of the Keep. Even the townsfolk beyond. You are in all our hearts. We cannot tell you how much it means to us that even being of low birth you rose to the calling and protect us with your life. Thank you."

The maid moved away without another word.

"As long as you don't have to do anything. As long as you get to live, the number of bodies that have piled up below you don't matter." I mumbled to myself. I was sick of the timid and the scared and why good people must give up their lives with nothing in return. Why should only those of low birth get praise for putting their lives on the line? Even the knights with their castles and servants are worthy of praise if they risk it all for the protection of the many. Fuck this world.

I was in a dark place and I couldn't see my way out.

More fucking people, I thought as footsteps entered the room. A squealing, scrape of wood over wood sounded as my small chair at the table was being dragged across the room to sit beside me. Here we go. If they need to make themselves comfortable, I was in for an ear bashing.

A warm, calloused hand found my shoulder and I flinched at the touch. Settling moments later, a lump formed in my throat. Baras had never been good with words or kind gestures. Usually, his actions could be construed as threatening or mocking to the point of bullying when he was only trying to make someone smile. It was amusing at times and sad at others to watch him navigate interpersonal relationships. This though, he always got right.

A hand in the darkness to show he was always there by my side. At times when my asthma was fighting me or I was scared of a simple storm, this hand was all I needed.

Maybe there was some form of humanity still left in me fighting back against the tide, trying to keep its head above water. A single tear caressed my cheek to fall away and be absorbed by the sheets.

Reaching up, I rested my hand silently on his.

"She doesn't need you standing vigil over her, Baras. Take your weak ass gestures to the poorer sectors where they belong," Enzo said.

I felt Baras tense and my eyes flared with rage.

"Cunt," I growled, rolling to face the doorway.

Enzo was there. He was casually standing in my doorway with a smug expression on his smug face. Baras on the other hand was shocked at the language. He'd probably never heard me utter such a word. I never had reason before.

"Didn't quite hear you, Elara," Enzo said, his eyes locking to mine as hunter to prey.

"I know he can be a handful but..." Baras began.

"I called you a fucking cunt!" I screamed and hurtled an ice shard at Enzo's head.

It was close but with a swish of Enzo's hand, flames engulfed the dagger, melting the ice until only water was left to take him at the temple. A trick he had pulled off many a time when we used to train.

"Settle down," Enzo said, eyebrows furrowed on his stupid face.

I was going to cave it in. I needed to rip it off and feed it to the mountain lions.

"Settle...?" I was ropable, my body physically shaking trying to hold my rage in check. With a flick of the wrist, I sent a second dagger whistling his way, the aim just off as my muscles tensed. This time it was encased in blue flame.

It was almost too easy playing with Enzo's ego. No flame could touch a BrongTa and for a moment Enzo looked almost sorry for me, as if he was looking down at me like I was some unintelligible cripple in the market. There wasn't even an attempt at dodging, so confident in his invulnerability.

There was enough force to extract a grunt from him and as the blue flames dissipated, I could see the ice shard embedded a few inches in his shoulder. A trail of blood began over Enzo's leather breastplate as he slowly turned to view the wound. His eyes came just as slowly back to mine. There was a deep well of anger sitting just below the surface looking to break free.

"Are you serious right now?" His voice was low and dangerous as he dragged the ice dagger from his shoulder and tossed it aside.

"Deadly," I said imitating the tone. Hand stretched to the side; I formed a sabre. "You sold me out."

His eyes narrowed.

"Abacus. The fucking Lich. You sold me out. Everyone's deaths. All the warring, the destruction. This all started because you were chicken shit and sold me out."

"I think I'll let you both sort this out between you," Baras said hanging in the background with no clear path to exit.

"You would have done the same."

"I didn't do the same. I kept my mouth shut. All of his prodding and searching came up with nothing. The only thing he found was that I don't have the rebirth ability anymore..." I thought a moment and decided if he was so scared of Abacus, I should make it grow. "Abacus thinks you cheated him. He'll be looking for you now that he doesn't have me."

"You fucking bitch," Enzo said. His eyes flared. "You told him didn't you."

My right eyelid twitched at the accusation.

"Answer me!" He screamed.

There was a sense of clarity in that moment. He was never going to see passed himself. He was never going to bring light to this world. Only darkness. Taking a deep, refining breath, I looked at the twisted man before me.

He dies now.

Approaching, I opened with a lunging attack that rolled into a flurry of slashing, thrusting, moves I'd practiced and honed these last three hundred years. I hadn't expected to breech his defences straight away as he was just as skilled as I and knew a lot of my moves.

With a simple curved dagger, Enzo parried the lunge and used it to block the following attack. Booting me in the chest and sending me sprawling to the floor, Enzo stepped outside the room and drew a longsword from a custom sheath on his back. He needed the extra room in the wide halls to swing it and my quarters were too cramped.

Vaulting to my feet, I followed him out and ducked under Enzo's sword as he tried to take my head off. Sweeping his legs, Enzo fell to his back and instantly rolled, my sabre bouncing from the carpet floor. A crack appeared in my blade from the impact but I repaired it, remoulding the ice and hardening it further.

Enzo started into the same series of attacks he'd used on Riven and I smiled, finally understanding just how Riven managed to win. A gift from the Fibonacci. I allowed Enzo to proceed with the attack even going so far as to let the window I could use to turn it around, pass. We were fighting at superhuman speed compared to some of the soldiers in the Keep but to us, it was slow.

The moment came when I needed to block the attack. Bringing the sabre up, I ducked away as I manipulated the ice to allow Enzo's blade to pass through. Getting in close, I drew my sabre along his side, opening a deep cut.

With a grunt, Enzo jumped back with a scowl. This wasn't an attack he'd ever seen from me and I was planning to surprise him a few more times before I'd be able to sink my sabre into his gut.

Trading blows back and forth, we also began trading wounds. Small cuts had opened up on either side but nothing was fatal. I couldn't tell whether Enzo was fighting to kill in the beginning but there was no doubt in my mind he was after my head now. I recognised his certain quirks and movements that told me as much. Gaining the upper hand, I began pushing him to the stairwell at the end of the hall.

A gathering of soldiers and servants had started to crowd the halls. None dared get between us or cry out to stop. All were mesmerised by the raw skill and speed. It was motivating to be admired but, given an opening, I would gut Enzo before their eyes and be feared instead.

The fighting made its way to the stairwell and I continued my assault, pushing Enzo further up towards the roof. As the light of the sky began to enhance the stairs, a realisation struck me. Enzo was fleeing to the Phoenix. If he believed they were going to talk me out of killing him, he was about to be horribly surprised.

Any Phoenix that gets in my way will die at my hand too.

"Are you truly that upset?"

"Don't do this right now, Shard. He sold us out and set the Lich on us. It's the reason he's still alive in this form. It's the reason Talon survived when the other Phoenix died last rebirth."

A sword thrust came dangerously close to breaking my guard and ending it all.

"And we will deal with him properly," Shard replied.

"Get out of my head. I need to concentrate!" I yelled and Enzo grinned, seeing I was having issues with Shard.

He took a final step back out onto the roof. Fanning out to encompass the larger space. All the Phoenix sat around the perimeter enclosing the area. Shard was to my right but I couldn't see Talon anywhere.

Stepping fully to the rooftop, a movement at my back caught my attention. Spinning on my heel, I slashed upwards as Talon's beak snapped at my shoulder. The blade knocked the bird away, hitting him with a blunted edge after the sharpness melted. The proximity of Phoenix flame was too much for the Fibonacci ice.

As Talon recovered, slowly turning on me with its glowing, beady, little eyes, I could hear Enzo making a move behind me. Fighting Enzo alone was hard enough but a Phoenix as well was almost impossible. I couldn't even count on Shard to back me up in this battle.

Searing heat burnt my shoulder as a fireball knocked me from my feet towards Talon. I had to roll with the momentum as Talon, living up to his name, began a stomping walk where he tried ramming his razor-sharp talons through my chest. This only brought me within reach of

Enzo as he started a powerful sweeping blow. I felt my ace in the hole was my only option. I called it "The Hedgehog's Dilemma" for the swift spikey ball that formed which would impale anything within 5 metres. This was friend or foe as I had no control once I unleashed it. It was for this reason alone I used it as a final resort.

Closing my eyes, I focused for the fraction of a second I needed before I unleashed my attack. Spikes shot off in every direction before crashing into a secondary ice structure that encompassed me. A structure I didn't conjure. Enzo's attack had also bounced off this ice shield and my eyes went wide. I looked around through the blurry ice for the man I knew couldn't be there.

"Riven?" I whimpered.

"He's not coming," Shard replied in my mind.

"You did this?" I asked, looking at Shard. The shock even outweighed the anger I held dearly to. *"This is.... It's incredible to think a Phoenix could use ice magic so powerfully."*

"I will always step up for you when needed. Never doubt that. It just took longer than expected to set the ice in motion."

"That you did it at all was unbelievable."

I felt more than saw him smile. *"Your energy flows through my veins. I've watched and studied how you build and release the ice. We are a true match in Phoenix and Soul."*

A soft thudding broke through the sentimental moment and I remembered why I was here. Enzo had never forgotten, apparently, his sword still crashing down on the ice dome. The fact a Phoenix could use ice went right over the bastard's head caught up only in his selfish path.

"Drop the ice, Shard. I have every right to see out this battle with Talon after she attacked me. You cannot get involved. That is your law," Enzo growled, his face contorting into a snarl.

Shard let out a long high-pitched shriek that Enzo stood through unmoving. "I know our laws traitor. And I call for you to be exiled, always to fly alone should Talon leave with you."

Talon shrieked in defiance against the accusation and moved to stand between Enzo and Shard. He stood tall and strong and looked as though he would readily defend his Soul.

"She has turned you against us, Vashardiel." I didn't understand the term used by Talon.

"It is my hatching name. More an insult in this context," Shard

293

supplied and I made sure to put it to memory.

"How long before she turns him against the rest of us," Talon continued looking around the space at his kin.

"I have witnessed Elara's lives, walking in her footsteps, and learning her knowledge. Nothing was held back. She was not aware," Shard said.

Talon cut across Shard's path. "You accessed her subconscious without her permission. That goes against our most sacred laws you yourself helped make. And I would put forward your immediate exile."

My breath caught in my throat. I had not foreseen something like this could occur because of me. Shard seemed unmoved by the motion.

"Why would you do this?" Haze asked from the far edge.

"It doesn't matter the reason. He already admitted his guilt," Talon interjected.

My eyes narrowed. *"He already knows, Shard. Talon is trying to shut you down. Keep you quiet."*

"I'm aware," Shard replied.

"Then why give him the ammunition he needs?"

No reply came down the line.

"Shard is a special case, Talon," Ash replied. "There have always been exceptions to this law, and I would like him to answer Haze's question before we continue."

"Special? His Soul has already shown how volatile she can be towards both Phoenix and Soul. She is Fibonacci. She is the enemy, and Shard let her into our ranks. Now, he has been infected. We do not wield ice but look at the influence she has had," Talon said, his talons raking the surface of the ice protecting me. "Shard is tainted and will say anything to weasel further into our family."

My lips pursed and I nodded with clarity as a tame violence bubbled below the surface. Focusing, I pulsed out energy tempered in Fibonacci ice shattering the barrier around me. Capturing a few select pieces with wicked edges, I had them dancing around the throats of Enzo and Talon, manipulating the shards with my spirit energy.

"There was a moment in time, I was accepted by all of you," I said calmly, looking around the Phoenix. "Enzo brought me into the fold. Even rallied to have me become a Soul. And in this, Shard denied me."

Enzo could see where the line of conversation was leading. "Don't do this, Elara," He growled.

He actually growled at me like his big boy bark was going to scare me again. I tightened the ring of sharp ice around his throat, pressing them into the skin. Enzo stopped talking lest he slit his own throat and stared me down.

"The day I trapped Shard in the ice prison, I was madly in love and deeply enraged because I didn't get my own way. Shard wouldn't give to me the ability for rebirth like Talon gave to his Soul. I wouldn't get a chance to live out multiple lives with the one I loved. In this I acted out against Shard. I trapped him in a Fibonacci prison. I tried to take that which I didn't deserve."

"You didn't just try," Flint tweeted. "You cannot deny you have lived for over three hundred years in multiple forms to the point where even your memories faded to darkness."

I looked at Enzo who stood with a scowl on his face, slowly turning his head back and forth. The movement enough to slice the skin as a trickle of blood ran down his neck.

"There is no life in deceit," I told him before turning back to the Phoenix. "It would be foolish to deny that which is known to be true. I have lived many lives at Shard's and your own expense. You have fed Shard energy all these years weakening yourselves in the process. I am truly grateful you didn't let such a wondrous creature as Shard pass from this world at my expense. And he is a wondrous creature. Beautiful and majestic."

"You're laying it on a bit thick," Shard chided and I smiled.

"And it was this very quality that stayed my hand in the moments I would have committed such a grand sin. I did not proceed with taking the Soul Essence of Alistair." It was not common practice to speak of the Phoenix Souls who had passed. I felt in this moment it was necessary.

"Liar," Talon screeched, helpless and at my mercy.

"You don't need to cover for him, Talon. He is and always will be a selfish, misogynistic, bully. I don't know what he has over you or if you just feel like you need to see it through after choosing poorly in sharing your rebirths with Enzo. Either way, he would happily destroy all of your kin to keep this ability."

There was a stubbornness evident in his eyes. It would be more than words that would sway the Firebird.

"It was the first time I told someone no," I said, addressing my judges once more. I was surprised and moved that the Phoenix had been so patient with me, had given me time to say my piece. "Enzo had a temper tantrum of course, throwing fire around the nesting grounds like the wind to falling leaves. He made it out that I was hurting him. That it was somehow my fault for not hurting Shard. Enzo knew better than I, the ways of extracting the Soul energy and when I refused to embody it, Alistair had been force fed to me. I had no choice in the matter."

"Is this true, Aethalion? Speak your answer in our ancestral tongue," Haze said.

Talon could not hold the gaze of his kin and looked away without answer. I realised the name spoken was his.

"Vashardiel?" Haze then turned to Shard.

Shard replied with a series of chirps and whistles I could only guess was his native tongue, all the while translating to me.

"I have no memories of the moments after my capture. I have not witnessed it with my own eyes but I have travelled the mind of Elara ShardSoul in search of the truth and have witnessed these events as she says, through her eyes. It is true."

Ash hung her head as Flint looked at me with what I decided could only be remorse. They felt bad for the way they treated me.

"You did not seek to use her memories against her or bend her to your will?" Haze asked Shard.

"Until this moment, she did not know I had even dug so deep into her subconscious," Shard replied.

They are still judging him. The thought grinded in my mind in a terrible realisation. It hadn't mattered that Enzo was the bad guy. It was Shard that had broken one of their unspoken laws.

"None of that matters," I cried. "Shard has done nothing wrong. I don't recall my exact words but with remorse for my part in his capture, I told Shard that whatever I had, whatever I was, was his if it could make up for the lost 300 years."

Haze stood silently a moment, the others chirping softly. And then with a nod Haze addressed Shard once more. "You will not be exiled, Vashardiel. But your, Soul." He turned back to me. "You have attacked a fellow Soul and Phoenix. You have sought the deaths of our kin. You are human and therefore may speak once. Your answer will determine your fate."

My eyes bulged and I was about to argue when Shard's voice broke through my rage.

"Do not waste your voice on arguing. They will take this as your answer and you will be killed."

I froze and was forced to consider my words.

"When I had been kidnapped and held hostage by the Lich, Abacus. It was made clear to me that Enzo had recently suffered a similar fate when you all were in early rebirth. For his release, he offered up one who knew the secrets to stealing the rebirth ability from a Phoenix. He gave the Lich me. Because of this, the war, the deaths and my entrapment came about. I was compelled to rid your Kin of this cancer."

"What did you tell the Lich?" Flint screeched.

A part of me wanted to speak and ease their worries but I had said my piece. That was all I could say before my fate was decided. *"Right, Shard?"*

His eyes narrowed and I heard that birdish laughter in the halls of my mind. "Elara ShardSoul has spoken once. She will not risk death for speaking out of turn. A decision must be made."

"Yes, yes. She has nothing to worry about from us. Just tell me what you told the Lich," Flint said hastily.

I looked to the others and each Phoenix, feeling trapped in a corner, both by my unwillingness to respond and Flint's dismissal of my charges, nodded their consent and agreement.

"Unlike Enzo, I kept my secrets to myself and escaped from the valley without endangering the Phoenix further. I cannot say Abacus won't come after Enzo for lying to him."

They turn on Enzo.

"He cannot stay here," Flint said.

"Then let me kill him now and be done with it," I offered.

"It is not so easy to kill Abacus. We do not know accurate details of his creation. He was a child of..." Haze said.

"Not the Lich. I offer to kill Enzo."

Talon let out a strangled cry.

"You will harm neither, Elara ShardSoul. Talon's rebirth is not like our own. It is harder on him should Enzo die first. Painful even. They will be exiled for Talon's withholding of critical information and Enzo's role in placing our kin in harm's way."

"Our fight hasn't finished!" I said, ice sabre forming once more. There was a deadly look in my eyes daring anyone to deny me this battle. It came from an unexpected front.

"The battle is resolved and you have won," Shard said.

"Like hell she has," Enzo said defiantly.

My eyes blazed and I reached out with an open fist ready to close it and send the ice shards through Enzo's throat.

"He knows our laws better than you. If you kill him now, you will be killed on the spot, and he will only be reborn in a short span of time. We will need to kill Talon because as the pain he experiences sharing a soul is immense," Shared said quickly, keeping my attention. Then he spoke straight to me outside the realms of where he could be overheard. *"Pick your moment and make it worth it. I will not lose you for your own anger and revenge."*

I hesitated and, in that hesitation, I knew Shard had swayed me. The anger was still there bubbling below the surface. The want... The *need* to end this man's life was overbearing but every attempt I made at fulfilling this desire was defeated by a moment's hesitation. To kill Enzo now would satisfy a feeling in a moment but in the end, Enzo would live and I would die. The regret moving into the afterlife would be all encompassing.

I let the ice fall away.

"Fight me," Enzo said, his voice dangerously low.

"Fight him and he just begins again in a new body untouched by exile," Shard said.

My eyes narrowed on Enzo, fingers turning white as I gripped the sabre.

"Are you so afraid of his big boy bark?"

I smiled. "Look at you throwing my own words back at me," I said out loud. My whole body had now relaxed and I was able to let Enzo's words wash over me and pass by. Shard we right. To kill him now was to fall into the trap I understood not to do barely weeks prior. For Enzo to die, I would literally need to rip the soul... from... his body. I stood a moment contemplating the idea.

"I killed your parents," Enzo said with a harsh grin.

Yes, the heat of rage began to build in me once more but I was able to hold it at bay. "And you gave me plenty more parents to make up for it. Thank you, Enzo." Those words tasted like bile on my tongue but I didn't choke on them. I wouldn't choke on anything for Enzo again.

Letting the sabre fall, the blade dissipated into a fine mist. Enzo understood he wouldn't get to me and was forced to grit his teeth.

"Enzo, you are to leave this rooftop at once, collect your belongings, and then you and Talon are to leave Telveria until death takes you and rebirth renews you," Shard said.

With a scowl, Enzo stalked from the rooftop, his eyes burning into me as he left. When he reached the stairwell, he pushed through the crowd sending one soldier tumbling before the rest of the onlookers got out of the way. Haze, Flint, and Ash, all took off without so much as a goodbye. It couldn't have been an easy moment for them. They found out some terrible truths and had to exile one of their kin. That left Shard and Talon on.

"*Give me a moment, Shard.*"

"*My brother isn't trustworthy in this mood. The last time he was exiled he set a town on fire.*"

"*I'll be ok. There's something I need to say and I want the moment to at least feel private.*"

"*If you believe you can escape me.*"

"*I do not,*" I replied, my tone flat.

Shard laughed as he took off into the air.

"Talon?" I said gently, reaching out a hand to rest on his wing. As I was about to touch, he swung around and snapped at the air where my hand had been a split second before. The force in such a chomp would have taken my hand clean off.

Talon's enmity towards me was understandable. Not just for this afternoon's events. When he first met Enzo, things would have been exciting, wonderful, and new. I was the one who came between them and messed it all up. I made things extremely complicated for them. Enzo would have first shown his true colours about then.

"I'll make this quick, but it needs to be said. I know Enzo. His manipulations. His threats. His intimidation."

Talon screeched in my face but I found only an underlying sadness in his tone. As I looked into his angry, burning eyes, I could see past the surface into a well of pain and suffering.

"I see your truth, Aethalion. I see how hard you're trying to hold everything together, but you can't live such a harsh life. You needed to be broken down to find the chance of building yourself up once more. You know the darkness lurking in the depths of his soul. It is you that must stop him. He will never put you first and will not hesitate in harming your kin should he be threatened. You know this. But here's what I know. You are stronger than you think."

"What are you saying to my Phoenix?" Enzo said coming up the stairs. I saw the soft beginnings of a light in Talon's eyes immediately die out and he looked away.

"Just that if he felt so inclined to fight, I'm sure he would win next time," I said, the double meaning not lost on Talon.

"He never lost this time. We were just interrupted." Enzo vaulted easily to Talon's back. "And next time we fight, when I win, you will come back to my bed."

My eyes bulged. "After everything, why have you not given up?"

"Couples fight. Couples take time apart. They always come back together in the end. And there is not long to your end. You will be mine again."

I watched as Talon dove from the rooftop before spreading his brilliant, flaming wings and gaining altitude to speed off into the west.

"No, I won't," I said softly.

"You didn't go far," I said as Shard landed back on the rooftop beside me. Small wisps of blue flame danced around him to fade into nothingness.

"I don't think you'll reach my brother," Shard replied sadly.

I glanced at him and absently scratched at the space near the base of his neck, smiling as the Phoenix shuddered but didn't pull away.

"Don't write him off just yet. Enzo is choking him. Restricting Talon's freedom to the point Talon is forced to act out. Even to the detriment of his kin. I saw it there a moment. A deep sadness covered by a terrible fear. Enzo is selfish and abusive."

"It's a cycle. We exile him every hundred years and things settle down again," Shard said.

"Then this time we'll break it. Show him we're here for him. He needs support to break free. I believe Talon will put an end to this cycle of destruction."

"That is what I fear."

The emotion and sadness in those words were so strong, Shard couldn't voice them lest he break. My brow furrowed, confused by the reaction and I wanted to press further but I got the impression I'd be locked out. I decided to change the subject instead.

"The Lich is our first concern. It' true he'll be hunting Enzo for deceiving him, but he'll also be after me... And I hope he comes."

Shard just looked at me questioning.

"I've changed. I feel it deep down. The light of this world doesn't shine so brilliantly anymore. An anger churns within me, ready to lash out at anything and everything around me. I... I fear that dark room and yet I can't seem to escape it. How do I live in such a terrible and broken world?"

"You must find what it is you want to live for," Shard replied.

"I have a motivation driving me. If I fulfil this desire, there may be no returning to the world I once loved afterwards."

"What motivates you?"

My face turned dark as my hand came away from Shard's neck. "I will kill Abacus and Enzo. A true death at any cost."

I could see Shard's expression crumble further, his worry for me deep but that small voice that would normally show empathy towards him was quiet now. My conscience had stepped aside for darker deeds.

"Stop! This fight needs to cease now," Suniel said as he burst from the stairwell onto the rooftop.

Both Shard and I turned to look at him as he seemed to be scanning the roof in confusion. Baras came running up behind the General with Fitz and Kymberlin in tow. He must have gone to get them when things started to get serious.

"Where's Enzo? And the other Phoenix, where are they?" Suniel asked.

"A Phoenix does not watch the departure of one who is exiled." Shard spoke in my mind.

"Haze, Flint, and Ash, are all close by. Enzo and Talon are gone."

"You killed..." Suniel's eyes bulged but he calmed as his rational mind awoke. "No, a maid, even one blessed by the Phoenix, could never hope to match the prodigy that is Enzo."

A bubbling anger caught fire in my stomach. "I'm getting sick and tired of you categorising me as a maid. Judging my efforts and my strengths on that of the house staff."

"It's all you ever knew," Suniel said, his face set. I could see he was prepared for a fight.

"Fuck off, little boy. I knocked Enzo on his arse more times than I could count centuries before you were an itch in your father's ball sack."

"Had him on his back as well," Kymberlin supplied and I rounded on her with a dark glint in my eyes. She understood to back down.

"You will not speak to me that way," Suniel ordered.

"I will speak to you whatever the fucking way I want. You have no authority over a Soul. You're kidding yourself to even believe you did. The only reason the Phoenix have yet to put you to the torch is because you send them refreshments."

"How dare you!" Suniel was reaching for his sword but found it stuck fast in the sheath, my ice wedging the blade.

I felt a warm hand on my shoulder and didn't need to look to know it was Baras.

"Come on, Ellie. Let's leave." The voice was soft and caring.

But I ignored him shrugging the hand away. "How dare I. I dare with every right granted to me by your very own council in fact."

I walked over to him, Stood, just under his chin, squaring up to his dominant expression. An expression much like Enzo's. Stepping back, I slapped the General hard across the face.

"I challenge you, young cub. For all the insults you have thrown my way. For blaming me for Riven's death." The last came out at such a high pitch.

To say Suniel was stunned was an understatement. He held his cheek just staring at me blankly, like a white washed sheep surrounded by wolves.

"Don't do this, Ellie. Unless you're about to take the reins of command and lead the armies, we need him. I can't see you doing that in your current state. It isn't just Suniel's life that'll be lost," Fitz yelled.

"Speak for yourself, Soul," Suniel said recovering. His eyes returned to mine. "I have wanted to rid my halls of you since the moment you were named. You are a joke in the ranks of Phoenix Soul. Naive, selfish and undisciplined. I will not make it clean. I will make sure you suffer."

"Sir, stop this now," Baras tried to interject.

"None, will intervene," Suniel replied and I let him draw his sword as he began to circle me.

"As a deeper insult, I will not use my magic," I said falling into the rhythm of the bout.

"Suit yourself," Suniel replied before charging in with a strong overhanded slash.

I stood calmly, arm stretched out towards Baras as the general attacked. Promising no magic meant I couldn't use the Sabre I crafted and was now unarmed but I believed Baras would do the right thing under the circumstances.

With absolute faith, I stood stock still until right at the last moment when Baras grunted and tossed me his sword. The throw was good and I traced the path in my peripheral. He couldn't have timed it any better either. As I caught the handle in a reverse hold and with the momentum still going, brought the longsword across to divert the General's weapon harmlessly to the side.

Like a raging bull seeing red, Suniel attacked again and again. Each time I was able to deflect the attack with little to no effort. It was almost like I really was fighting a child. This was going to be too easy.

Growing bored of the varied yet simple attacks, I moved. Ducking under a cross slash aimed at my neck, I manoeuvred myself behind him on nimble feet before grabbing Suniel around the waist. In a practiced move against a number of opponents, I pulled Suniel backwards as I bent doubled over and slammed him head first into the roof top.

As the General scurried to his feet, blood rolling down his face, I swung two hard over hand attacks from each quarter pushing him back to lay upon the roof once more. I wasn't using strength like most pigheaded men would but rather attacked points of counterbalance, overwhelming an unenlightened opponent with physics.

Trying to catch me unawares, Suniel kicked out at my shin. Truth be told, he shouldn't have been able to make the move from the position he was in and it grazed past my calf muscle as I was slow to react. In response, I stomped his knee to the sound of a sickening crack and Suniel dropped his sword and held his knee grunting in pain.

"Mercy," he cried.

"It's not good enough," I said. The battle was over but I wanted to hear him scream. I hadn't been given the luxury of asylum in captivity. Why should he, who has done far worse than I, be granted mercy.

Taking the longsword, I positioned the point above a nice fleshy area just below the collarbone. Slowly and with great patience, I sunk the blade into muscle and tissue. The sharp edge severing nerves like butter as I slowly penetrated the man, a dreadful and wicked grin upon my face.

Screams and gargling cries echoed out over the Keep as Suniel couldn't hold back anymore.

"It's not enough," I yelled, my face close to his. "It. Is not. Enough."

Yanking the sword from his shoulder in a spray of blood, I chose another point. My eyes were wired and as I began to apply pressure, two strong, dark arms bailed me up and dragged me back. Arms I hadn't even seen reach the rooftop.

"No," I cried, thrashing against my captor. "Why does he get to get off so easily? Why does he get to be free."

Thrusting an elbow back, I took Korr clean in the face. A small part of me regretted hitting the big man, but even as a trail of blood flowed from his nose, Korr just smiled. There was kindness in his eyes and it broke my heart.

"Hit me. Hurt me. I don't deserve to be treated with love," I wailed still trying to break away.

"Korr feel Ellie heart. Korr touch Ellie Soul. Korr see true Ellie," Korr said.

"No, you don't. I don't want to be seen. I don't want to be heard. I'm alone, trapped in a darkness full of pain and suffering."

"Light shine still. Ellie fight darkness."

"Please don't, Korr," my body went limp in his arms as tears began to roll down my face. The sword dropped to the hard, stone roof and then in a whisper. "Don't show me love."

Korr just held me tenderly.

"I need to kill him."

"Suniel death not bring happiness. Not bring light."

303

"Abacus. I need to kill the Lich to be free. I lie awake at night fearing the darkness and block out the day undeserving of its light. I am trapped in a limbo I can't escape. I will never be able to escape until I know Abacus cannot take me again. Even with my death, he can awaken me."

"Then we will all take him down," Fitz said, coming up beside me.

"You need only let us in and we will help take your burdens and set fire to the darkness," Kymberlin said moving down the opposite side.

"Lead and we will follow," Baras added standing before me.

I looked at everyone and my shoulders slumped. "You can let me go now."

Korr slowly opened his arms allowing me to find my feet before fully letting go.

"All of you are idiots, you know."

"Steady on," Kymberlin said. "I will accept nothing less than alleyways gutter slut."

I shook my head and tried to smile but it was weak and unconvincing. "You're the worst of us all, Kymmie."

"That's better," Kymberlin replied with a genuine smile.

That everyone was ignoring the General's cries would have been amusing a few minutes ago but the moment was lost. There was only a depressive cloud dampening the scene.

"Do you have a thought on where to go next? Could we raid the prison?" Fitz asked.

"Abacus left through a portal. He could be anywhere in the world. We just don't have the history of the creature. We don't understand him well enough."

"Why not the capital's library then. I saw it once when I got lost, my first visit to Talivear. Hundreds of books. Maybe even thousands," Baras said. "If ever there was a place to seek information that would be it."

"No!" Came the shout of the General still writhing on the ground.

"Excuse me," I asked.

"I forbid it. I will not allow you near the King's city."

"You're long past forbidding anything," I said, my blood boiling once more.

Korr's arm rested gently around me.

"Do you want to go again?" I growled at Suniel, putting pressure against Korr's grip.

"Shhh. Ignore. Dog will bark. We still move."

I gave a moment's pause, letting the words sink in. Then, still high in anger, turned away. "To Talivear," I said and the others nodded. Korr, though, stood off to the side.

"Long journey. Quick flight."

It occurred to me with a heavy heart that Korr wouldn't be joining us in the capital. There was no way he could make the trip without burdening everyone else to a slow trek on foot.

"What will you do?" I asked.

"Korr see family. Korr see BrongTa. Korr White Ash." He banged his chest with a fist, proud of his achievement.

"I'm glad you found your spark, Korr."

"Ember help Korr. Friends help Ellie. Ellie now find spark."

There were no more words I could say. Nothing more was needed. He wasn't a man of fanciful words and didn't need to be flattered. He was wise beyond his years. Stepping in, I wrapped my arms around him, resting my head against his chest. He returned the hug, holding me as long as I needed.

"Thank you, Korr," I said and stepped away moving from the rooftop at speed. Another emotional cry was approaching, and I was sure I'd used up my quota on the rooftop.

In my room, I realised just how dark it was. I was using old sheets to block out the light making the room almost pitch black once the door was closed. The darkness somehow felt comforting but I could also see it was imitating the prison like environment.

Reaching for one of the sheets to pull it down, I hesitated. I knew I didn't need it. I knew I was free from my confines. So why couldn't I pull the sheet away? My hand began to tremble as I contemplated the dilemma. Why was I so afraid to leave the prison even after I had broken free? My words on the rooftop came filtering back, *I am alone trapped in a darkness full of pain, full of suffering*. I could not yet accept I was free and couldn't understand why.

A knock at the door pulled my attention. "We're heading to the roof. We'll meet you there," Fitz called without opening the door.

"I'll be out soon," I said, stealing my hand away from the makeshift curtain.

Moving to the footlocker next to the bed, I pulled out the ranger uniform with blue cloak and weaponry. I laid it on the bed neatly, placing each part separately. As I placed the blue cloak, my fingers traced the silver Phoenix broach. There was nothing about me that could make Fletcher's daughter proud now.

Rolling up the cloak and clothing, I hid it away within the footlocker once more. Instead, I donned the gauntlets from Kymberlin. Eyes roaming over the simple pattern, I began to craft a complimenting set of armour out of frosted ice. It started as a swirling shimmer of blues and whites upon my wrists forming the vembraces before moving quickly up my arm along the rerebraces to the cuirass. There hadn't been a need to craft anything around my elbows or shoulders as the ice was made in one piece. It was linked to my life essence and would move and shift as my body did, never leaving even a small crack to take advantage of. With a flare of elegance, I did accentuate spiked pauldrons over my shoulders. I hadn't liked the look of the bare minimal design. From the cuirass, I crafted the tassets to sit in the fashion of a kilt favoured by the high mountain men. Then I rounded it off with greaves and boots.

Looking in the mirror, I felt safe within the cocoon. Cold like the world. Cold like my soul. No more will an enemy easily touch my body. No more will my heart be left vulnerable. And never will I need to remove it.

I grimaced, realising a flaw in the armour. It was my barrier to hide away from the world in but it also hid away the cruelty this world was capable of. With only a thought, I shifted some of the frosted space to be clear ice, highlighting all the wounds I'd received in battle, the small black mark at the centre of my chest where abacus tortured me, and the immortal scar that ran down my body, forced upon me by Enzo. None of these deserved to be concealed.

All other belongings, I left behind. All other ties to the outside world. There was only me and the path ahead.

Making my way to the roof, I was greeted with woops and whistles as the others complimented me on my armour. There had been nothing like this crafted before and as the last of the Fibonacci line, no one would ever recreate it again. Even the Phoenix seemed to gaze in wonder at my creation. All except Shard. He stood unmoving and serious. He was the only one with access to the depths of my soul. Only he could see the torment that was there and the significance this armour held. It was a wall between us. It was a wall between myself and the world. But he remained quiet, allowing things to run their course.

"We fly for Talivear. On arrival, myself and Fitz will attend the library to find any references to Abacus or Liches in general. Kymberlin and Baras, you will entertain the King when he arrives," I said.

"Why would the prick even rise from his cushioned throne. I haven't seen him walking amongst the soldiers to bolster their spirits. He doesn't care for those below him," Kymberlin said and spat.

I turned to Fitz. "Wrong choice of representation?"

"I'll do all the talking," Baras supplied as Fitz just smiled.

"Not like the old geezer leaves his palace anyway. Too many fleas and cripples outside for his liking," Kymberlin said.

"She won't get a word in," Baras continued hurriedly.

"The King will greet us because he doesn't know if it is good news or tragedy we bring from the Telverian Keep. Especially if we all turn up unannounced. Also, even the King is below us. We win his wars for him. We fight his enemies. If he doesn't want to get his feet dirty in attending to us, he won't have Phoenix Souls to attend to."

Kymberlin stood thinking a moment before a wickedly curved smile crossed her face. "I hadn't thought of it like that. I'll make sure he attends to my every whim."

"On second thoughts, shall we reconsider the set up?" Baras asked.

Kymberlin leaned into him and started twirling a finger on his chest. "Aww, does my widdle Bary not want to spend time with me?" Kymberlin said, putting on a pout and drawling in an odd accent.

I choked on my breath, half way in, and struggled to recover before coughing. "I'm sorry, umm, what?"

Fitz had a calmer face, more than likely having heard this type of talk before.

"Widdle Bary doesn't want to spend time with me," Kymberlin repeated to me. I could see Baras turning a deep crimson and I laughed.

"Well, widdle Bary needs to suck it up and get the job done," I said imitating Kymberlin's tone. "Anything else?"

Baras remained quiet.

"Suniel was able to send messenger pigeons for the capital. He will no doubt be warning the King," Fitz said.

"Little concern. We'll be there at least half a day before any arrive. We'll have time. See any pigeons on the flight and burn them for good measure. If that is all. Let's go."

Turning, I walked to Shard and my heart sank. The moment of laughter, the touch of glee that broke through my defence had evaporated instantly as the weight of everything I was working towards filled my mind.

"She almost had you smiling freely," Shard sent telepathically.

I shook my head. "No amount of laughter will cure the ache in my chest," I said tapping the centre of my chest above the torture mark. "Even seeing my quest to fulfilment, I don't know if I could ever get back to where I was. I don't believe I will ever be free again."

"It is another scar you will learn to live with," Shard replied sadly.

"Live with but never recover from."

"I know too well." The last said softly, almost beyond what I could make out.

I mounted Shard and we took off for the capital in the far North West, tucked away where the mountains curved upwards towards the sea.

.

Chapter 16

The flight barely lasted an hour across the lush terrain. It was a beautiful land full forests and hills, hidden caves, and a vast network of snaking rivers and lakes. All of which passed under me without a glance. I wasn't here to marvel at the Earth's magnificence. Even the flight was not so wondrous as previous occasions. The weightlessness and cool breeze rushing over me didn't have the same appeal it once did. My mind was focused only on the task ahead.

"You riding me in that armour isn't the most comfortable either," Shard shot back.

This comment was also ignored. I could hear the hissing and see the bubbling of fire and ice mixing together as some sharp cornering brought us together. It may have been bearable for Shard having the Fibonacci energy running through his chakra system, but no other Phoenix would have accepted the discomfort.

"It is the only reason..." Shard began, then paused. *"There is a foul smoke upon the air."* Shard let out a sharp pipping sound to the others who then shifted closer together forming a dense formation.

And as if mentioning it was enough to awaken my senses, I caught a whiff of what he was talking about. It wasn't the smell of smoke from fires in the midst of winter but the acrid smoke of war. It had become so familiar around the Keep and even after clearing the Chimera away, there were pockets of the smell. The rest of the flight was clean and the war front didn't make it this far north.

"Keep on your guard," Fitz called from the flight formation. The smell must have already roused the suspicions of the others.

Skimming along the cliff face of the mountain ranges to the North, we cut around the edge to where the cliffs broke away and were stunned by the scene. A full-scale assault had begun on the capital. Undead warriors were scaling the walls to be fought back, again and again. They brought siege engines into play and all around were burning buildings and farmlands. Everything outside the walls of the capital was destroyed. I'd yet to see any Chimera or fantastical beasts that Abacus was capable of but I was sure they'd be along soon.

"It's Y'Borgiand," Baras called. "They must have seen the state of the kingdom and decided it was the right time to attack."

I looked again, confused by the remark. My eyes began to pick up things I didn't see a moment ago. Warriors being carried back to enemy medics when wounded. The use of banners rallying the warriors to their countrymen when Abacus had no need. Just the simple lack of the ephemeral realm.

A moment ago, I believed they were monsters for the destruction they were causing. Now, I could see they were just human. How far we had fallen from hunter gatherers to suggest this was 'just in our nature' and justify it with rule of want.

"Selfish bastards," I uttered under my breath.

"Survival of the fittest is the natural order of things across many species," Shard sent.

"Weeding out the weak. Taking your share and more to ensure survival. To have multitudes of concubines to reproduce with and spread your advantageous genes. Those with power are corrupted and egotistical. It is the lowly serfs that have real strength. They work enough to give most of their possessions to the rich who have plenty and still get by on the meagre scraps."

"Panda Pile," Fitz called referring to the formation of a continual fire storm raining down on the enemy from one Phoenix after another.

My eyes flared. "Are you attacking? We're not attacking. Stick to the plan," I screamed.

"It will come down as orders from the King the moment we land," Kymberlin replied.

"We're here to work out how to destroy Abacus. He is priority."

I couldn't believe they were all looking to waste time on this little side quest when the answer could be right there. No one listened as they tilted into formation.

A rage began to build within me with thoughts of all the nasty things I could do to them to bring them into line. Ice barbs to the less used fleshy parts. Barging their Phoenix with my own. Leaping upon the other Phoenix back and belting them.

"Enough!" Shard said. An ear-piercing screech sounded for a few moments, enough to force me to raise my hands to my ears, cutting off the line of thought I had. "They attack and alleviate some of the pressure from the walls then more of your common folk, more of the people with true strength, live. This isn't for the King or the lords and ladies. This is for the townsfolk who serve them. There was a time you knew that."

The pain and anger were there. I wanted to scream at Shard for taking their side. I wanted to destroy the world in that moment, but he wasn't wrong either. The conflicting emotions ran around in my mind fighting and waring with one another like the little figures in the fields ahead. It all became too much and I let out a gut-wrenching scream, making Kymberlin jump and the others look my way.

"Attack if you must. Meet me in the city when you can."

Without another word I turned off in a straight line for the capital and the richer quarters where the library would be found.

In a jolt and a movement, I was thrown to the left as Shard banked and righted quickly. I was about to give him a piece of my mind when a sharp gust of air rolled over my shoulder in the wake of a dark blur. Glancing back, a large barbed, harpoon was sailing away from us. There was no shock or fear of the ballista and the impact it could have had had it landed. There was only a sickening temper that needed to vent.

"Shall we take them?"

"I'd hoped you would've chosen a more righteous reason but this'll do," Shard replied and tilted towards the ballistae.

All along the East and Western rises, stood weaponry like crossbows but on a grand scale. Larger than a man, it took three people to even load these things, one to crank back the firing mechanism and lock it in place, while another two carried what could only be described as small trees of death to restock any dwindling ammo.

Though the ones to the west were out of range, two more fired as the ballistae was reloaded. The pointed mass of steel tipped wood sped towards us at a rate that would give Shard a run for his money. It was probably a good start in the way of aerial combat against neighbouring kingdoms known for their Phoenix, but they were forgetting one thing. The Phoenix weren't mindless steeds to be ridden and abandoned as we saw fit. They were intelligent and act on their own free will.

"Thanks," Shard replied. I almost heard him rolling his eyes in my mind. In a barrel roll manoeuvre, Shard swooped past one aerial tree with the other curving harmlessly away.

"You take the ballistae. The scum are mine," I said, eyes following the growing figures.

Shard didn't respond but I felt him smile at the back of my mind. As we dove under the final missile that could be loaded, the enemy evacuated in every direction as Shard sent a sweeping spray of fireballs through the large wooden structures. I laughed as the spindly chunks of wood fell apart on impact.

"My turn." And my eyes grew dark with a snarl of a smile curling my lips. I'd counted 12 men on the hill side. A small outlet for my rage but it would do. Pulling a storm of ice shards behind me, I threaded all my malice and rage into the cracks and crevices filling the ice with hate. They would not be allowed to escape me and I sent forth the rain of terror to slice and carve into the hearts of the enemy.

Screams rendered the air as, once enemy hostiles fled the field, now only bodies of blood and pain were left. I made sure they wouldn't die

311

quickly. They would suffer as I have and as they weaken and their bodies shut down, they will perish. Not one got away without a fatal wound.

"Let's go, Shard," I said, no emotion in my voice.

"We cannot leave them like that."

"Why not? They seek to do that and worse. They were trying to shoot us out of the sky for fuck's sake." My voice was shrill and wily.

"We are not Abacus. We do not torture and seek to cause pain. They fought. They lost. They die a clean death," Shard replied swooping back around.

"Don't you do it, Shard," I said as I felt the build-up of flame. "No, Shard."

As the flames fell down for a merciful kill, I watched in stunned silence. How dare he steal this from me? Slowly, the screams turned to silence upon the hill.

"It is they who seek to torture. They who seek to cause pain. I am just giving them what they desire," I cried.

"Then you are no different," Shard replied, breaching the walls of the capital. He landed in the town square, and I vaulted from his back. All around people made way for the Firebird and its Soul, not sure if we were friend or foe.

"How dare you say that. How dare you say I find pleasure in their torment or seek to deliver a punishment undeserving. I know how harsh people can be. I have been through the fire. They deserve it," I yelled, circling Shard. I was almost to breaking point with how angry I was. A dam holding back a river of lava and I was on the edge of bursting my banks.

"The saddest part is you cannot see the twisted form your soul has taken," Shard said softly, his demeanour as far across the spectrum as it could be to mine. "One man has sowed the seeds of hatred in your soul. You have not given yourself the chance to recover and rip these weeds away. Now, you take it out on all those around you."

"What would you know? You are just an Accipitridae."

I saw the pain that word held carve itself into the very flesh and blood of Shard. He held himself strong and upright, but workings of a terrible nature had begun in his mind.

His glowing eyes dimmed as they lay upon me. "You seek to thread a tapestry of pain in the wake of your own darkness wherever it may stick. I will join the others on the field."

Before I had a chance to react, Shard was off and over the wall. I scowled at the onlookers who decided they preferred the Phoenix over me, taking off down the alleyways. My breathing was ragged and I had difficulty getting it back under control, not to mention the shaking of my muscles after the verbal.

I didn't have long to wait when a young soldier called 'The King" and the square came alive. People were hanging out of upper floor windows and peaking around corners to catch a glimpse of their sovereign while I cursed under my breath. Public speaking and big noting himself is what Baras would have excelled at but I was going to have to make due. All I needed was access to the library. It should be enough the others were helping in this silly, little war.

From the sweeping bend in the main thoroughfare came the King and his guard. He was dressed in a suit of armour flourished with silvers and golds. A crown was welded into the open helm and there was a red cape pinned at the shoulders. It was irksome to see not a dent or a scratch upon the man. If his guardsmen were doing their job, I could understand the kings untouched visage, but they seemed in a similar state. Not a one of them had been to the front lines. All of them were hiding behind the soldiers set to die. Immediately, my temper began to escalate but I held it at bay for I needed this man.

Coming to within a few feet, the King took a moment to slightly nod in my general direction. It was a gesture that was supposed to mean something to the lower classes but was lost on me. This man was nothing if he couldn't even lead his men or even take the time to walk the battlements where there was a possibility for a skerrick of a fight. I may have respected him just that little bit, but not this child living in his walls of steel.

After a moment of me remaining as I was, not returning his bow, the King grimaced. "I thank you, Soul, for your timely attendance. It's been barely six hours since messenger pigeons broke through and already you are on our doorstep. The enemy came out of nowhere and have held us couped up for days. Did you waylay one by chance?"

"We're not here for you. I don't know if you realise it but the rest of your Kingdom has been under attack for months and could have used the reinforcements ourselves," I said, my tone nothing short of reprimanding.

"And leave Talivear unprotected?" His voice became pompous and shrill. "I think not."

It wasn't Talivear he was worried about but himself. Sure, another Kingdom could have invaded and won the realm but without taking care of Abacus, it would have been short lived.

"Oh no, my lord," I said and bowed low. "I would not dare suggest sending all your forces in protection of the people. It would have been

313

wise indeed to keep the King's guard at home with you. Look at them. All that fighting out there and they have yet to even let a mark sully their armour. They must be skilled indeed. I bet you could stand them upon the wall and blind the enemy with their shimmer."

"You seek to mock your King," he said and the guard all stood at the ready. The swish of swords being unsheathed made me smile.

"Oh, settle down, boys. I'm not about to mock my King for anything." The guards took a more relaxed grip on their weapons. "This man isn't my King. I have no King."

Immediately the weapons were focused on me once more but the King had placed a hand on the lead guard in a silent order to stand down. The others followed suit. With narrowed eyes, it was as if the man regarded me for the first time and I could tell he was assessing the attire.

"Normally, those who fly upon the Phoenix are chosen from soldiers and rangers of Telveria. I will say one or two fall through the cracks like Enzo."

My face grew stern but he continued.

"It surprises me to find a Fibonacci amongst the Souls given their history. Any who hail from that tribe had been wiped from Telveria over three hundred years ago. From where do you hail...?" He left an open question asking my name, tucked neatly into the larger question.

"I remember the day well," I said, eyes dark and dangerous. "I need access to your library."

"To what end?" The King asked, unperturbed by my gaze or unconventional answer.

I cocked my head, not understanding how this King couldn't comprehend his position. Then it hit me. There were no threats. This coward thought he could outwit me. Slowly, I let my sabre form in my hand.

"I am not above killing a King and his guard before asking one of the onlookers back there, the way."

Fading into the shadow of his knights the King now addressed me. "There will be no need for violence. Bliven will escort you."

One of the guards looked back sharply at the King who only nodded and gave a shooing motion with his fingers. Sheathing his sword, Bliven started moving across the square begrudgingly.

I was three steps behind when it finally clicked. "Staphin. King Staphin," I said with a laugh. "I'd almost forgotten you called yourself 'King'. I often think of King Spriggan, such strength of spirit. Such kindness. He was a man I did, in time, address as King. Still, I admire how efficiently his successor seized the reigns. Fate seldom moves so

314

decisively without a steady hand to guide it." With that I turned on my heel and followed Bliven.

"What are you implying?" Staphin called. Clearly, I hit a sore spot and it just piled onto my heart. "What are you implying!?"

Ignoring the man, I thought of his father. Spriggan was a caring King and often walked amongst the people who supported him. There was always an extra bowl of broth for someone in need and he would deliver it himself. In battle, he was ferocious. Stalking the battlements, raising the men's morale, and leaping into the thickest of the fighting brandishing that horrifying double winged axe. That man was a born leader.

Even late in his fifties, the man was huge. Long greying hair laying over shoulders that could only have been sculpted from a bull. His chest was bulging and often times too hard to craft capable heavy armour for. It led to his fighting in leathers. The legs were like tree trunks and could carry the man all day at pace if he so wanted. It was the eyes, though, that were most breathtaking. Intuitive, intelligent, strong, and sincere. All his emotions spoke true from his eyes. I couldn't tell you what I would do if I was propositioned staring into those deep blues. It was like staring into the rich ocean, a pastime that could steal a person's heart.

I was two countries away when I heard the news the King of Telveria had been assassinated in his sleep. It rocked a number of nations while others tested the borders with skirmishes and battles. All were repelled with the help of the Phoenix.

I slipped past the borders unseen and made my way to the King's grave in the crypts below the palace. Not a lavish tomb by any means and far too dark. Paying my respects, I spent the next two years hunting the assassin who was hired. I never did get the name of the one who hired the hit as the assassin lay dying. I took my revenge a little too well. It was all too obvious now.

Maybe I assumed the son would be much like the dad. Noble and strong. I assumed too much.

Running face first into Bliven's palm, I shook my head. The guard had stopped in front of me and there was only a general recollection that words were said, but when he could see I wasn't paying attention, he raised a hand.

"What?" I asked.

"Your library is ahead. See the bookkeep if there is something particular you seek." Bliven didn't wait for a response but trundle off to be with his King where he could feel safe again.

The large building was plain in material and structure. It had been built over a thousand years prior for a place to store a previous King's favourite reading scripts. At 20 books, the building included staff quarters for those that could look after them and even read to the King on his visits. The library had grown in time as realisation for the power and value of the written text was recognised. Now, there were hundreds of tomes and scrolls covering the first floor and even spilling into the second. Sure, it wasn't the largest library I'd seen in my lives. Two others had completely filled the second floor of a similar structure. This was just the best I could find quickly.

Pushing through the old, worn wood doors, I was immediately greeted by a musty, almost decaying, smell of paper and bindings. A more subtle woody scent danced in the background and as they mingled it reminded me of a leather clad warrior. The fresh and fragrant leathers drowning in body odour.

Looking around, I couldn't see the bookkeep anywhere.

"Anybody in," I called and there was a loud thump and cry from upstairs.

Taking the stairs two at a time, I rushed to where I pinpointed the sound form. An old man stood with crooked back rubbing his rump. There was a ladder beside him and a flurry of papers all around. I began to piece together what occurred.

The old man adjusted the chained glasses on his face as he looked over me.

"Not Chloe, then," he said.

"I can't say I have ever been given that name before."

"Chloe doesn't like me climbing the ladders. Says I could fall and hurt myself. Doesn't like me doing a lot of things."

"Maybe she has a point but I can see you aren't about to decay away just yet." I smiled softly as I placed the face. "You still giving out the sugar peanuts to the kids in the court, Felix."

A curious expression crossed his face. "Not since I was given this position 30 years hence. I'm sorry but do I know you?"

"Speak plain and true, and you will confuse more nobles than any jester could," I said. I had been bored in court a recent life ago. A child, not yet allowed to sit and mingle with the nobles.

Then a man crunching on sugared peanuts chanced upon me and I devised a plan to outwit the wily Felix and take his treasure. On most nobles, the elaborate and structured plan would have succeeded. On Felix, a man of modest intellect, I was found out quickly. We soon struck up a friendship and I found I could share in the wealth with quiet and simple friendship rather than deception.

There was a moment of deep thought etched into the old man's face as he accessed long forgotten memories, but the look of excitement as realisation dawned was worth it.

"You are Elara's daughter? I heard she lost her life from a cave in. A sad day," Felix said shaking his head.

It could have been so easy to run with the lie but we promised one another only the truth in a society of lies.

"No, my friend, it is still I. Still cursed to live 1000 lives."

"Your mother used to speak like this."

"Felix," I said taking his hand. "I am Elara. I died in Echoes Cave and am reborn."

"Elara?" Felix said with a shake in his voice. His eyes grew bleary as he studied me further. "How have you returned?"

"When I spoke as a child of the Phoenix and the Soul that changed me, it was not some fancy brought forward from the imaginations of the young. We always promised the truth with one another."

"In a society of lies... I'm sorry, Elara. I was so used to the lies that I didn't believe your words. I could forgive you for it wasn't deceit used to get ahead but beautiful intelligence working through imagination. I never considered you spoke truthfully."

"There is few who would believe such a story from a child but now I must ask a favour. I have crossed deserts, and oceans, forests and frozen tundra to ask this of you."

Felix stammered a moment with the magnitude of my lead up. Maybe I didn't cross them personally but rather, flew overhead. A stretch of the truth.

"Ask a. a. anything."

"Do you have any more sugared peanuts?"

A whistle echoed in my mind. *"A heart she still has deep down,"* Shard said.

"A heart guarded fiercely. This is but a reprieve for a friend. Go back to protecting the kingdom."

Felix eyes widened in delight after a moment's pause of confusion. He hurried off to a far corner where his belongings were piled on the table. Collecting a leather bag, he returned and offered it to me.

"You sneaky old man. What would Chloe say?" I pulled a small handful of peanuts from the bag and crammed them into my mouth. The taste was so nostalgic and sweet on the tongue, I couldn't help a small moan. "Mm Mmm. I have missed these."

"Still stuffing your face, I see." Felix said and a blush kissed my cheeks as I snorted.

We both broke into a laughter that warmed the spirits and cradled the heart. One of those laughs that cascades into a second and a third and a fourth before you lose count on the number of times you tried to stop and just let it run its course.

As we had finally began to calm, Felix suddenly stopped, his eyes wide. I followed the line to find a plump middle-aged maid standing in the doorway, hands on hips. She wore a stern look. There was no way I could know but deep in my soul I knew there was no one else it could be.

"Chloe doesn't approve," I said, my voice cracking part way through.

A grinding came from a point part way between Felix's face and nose. Then again, before his face contorted trying to hold back the laughter. We both broke once more, louder than before as Chloe just threw her hands to the sky in an exasperated sigh and stormed off.

It was a small while before we had control of ourselves again. I couldn't believe just how much I needed that and tilted my head to the wonders of life gifting it to me in such an unexpected way. Felix just smiled at me.

"I fully expect you hadn't realised I was still alive and kicking, Elara."

"Ellie is what my friends call me now."

Felix nodded warmly. I could see he was happy that I was living happi... That he believed I was living happily. Still, it was impossible to keep the sadness from my face. It was a flash of a glimpse only but the old man saw straight to the truth of it. His eyes narrowed.

"It was not me you came to see, Ellie. Tell me of your troubles and how I can help."

"I... Can't. There is not the time right now," I stammered.

"The war is outside. Not in here." Felix swept his arm around the room. "You have only the time you give yourself."

A flash of the Lich played behind my eyes and a soft trembling began in my hands. "I don't have any to give. He is everywhere I am."

"Let's start with what you need," Felix said as he tidied his belongings into a bag. "You have entered a library. Is there a topic you would like to research?"

"The Lich," I said softly and Felix paused in placing a mug into the bag, his hand stuck mid-air.

"General curiosity?" Felix asked but there was something deeper in his question. Something I couldn't quite discern.

"I need a way to kill him. I would unmake him so that he never has the chance to bring fear, death and torture to the people of this world again."

There was visible relief written upon the old man's features. "So, you have finally come to undo your terrible mistake?"

"My mistake?!" I asked, incredulous that Abacus's reign of terror could be lumped on my shoulders. "The creature far precedes me by thousands of years."

"You forget you gave me a glimpse into your past. I had believed it was a trick like some jester would perform for the King. Seeing your armour, I realise my mistake. You once gave me a perfect ice rose."

My face remained blank trying to piece everything together. "I remember the act. I just don't see what it has to do with this situation."

"You are..." His brow furrowed. "There isn't anything written in this library that will help in what you seek. Only two tomes mention the terror in passing but nothing substantial and one parchment speaks of a creature that is called Vampyre. They seem too familiar not to be the same."

A heavy weight rested on my shoulders, and they slumped in defeat. This had been my best chance for a quick final battle.

"But..."

I glanced back at Felix.

"You might find it worthwhile entering the catacombs beneath the palace and studying the ancient drawings on the walls within."

"What aren't you telling me?" I asked.

"These answers you need to uncover for yourself. Outside, take the westerly road and head to the small opening left of the palace main gates. It'll take you where you need to go."

The answer had done nothing to quench my curiosity, but I suspect that would be sated in due time. Felix had never steered me wrong before. Stepping in, I wrapped my arms around the old man. "Thanks, Felix. I don't expect I will get to see you again this side of life."

"Then in death, let us toast the good times."

"As long as you bring the sugared peanuts."

He smiled deeply. "Bags of them." Withdrawing from the hug, Felix kissed my forehead. "And Ellie?"

"Hmm?"

"If your path brings you up against a Phoenix. Run. The Firebirds do not like your kind."

I grinned mischievously. "Didn't I tell you? I'm a Phoenix Soul now."

His brow furrowed as confusion set in. "You jest?"

I shook my head slowly. "My friends are currently clearing the fields beyond the wall as we speak. You should climb to the roof and watch the show."

Standing by the door, I bowed low and in a show of flare spectacle, I engulfed myself in a ball of flame and snuck from the room as it dissipated.

"Ha!" The smile that broke on Felix's face was beautiful. "Wonders never cease to amaze."

"Goodbye, my friend," I whispered and headed from the library.

Standing at the end of the street, I looked up at the palace just breaking over the inner wall. Ahead of me was a vast, open cobblestone ground that didn't exist in my last life. At least four houses deep had been torn down to create, what? A killing ground? An open space to know if an assassin was sneaking into the castle? It definitely ain't a muster area for the townsfolk. Only kings who understand assassination and are therefore afraid of how it could also affect them, would do such a thing.

I shook my head and walked out into the emptiness. Two steps, and a crossbow bolt exploded on the stones at my feet.

"Halt! State your business in the palace," A guard shouted from a slitted window. Two more crossbows trained on me.

"Elara ShardSoul, if that means anything to you, dung for brains." I let them murmur amongst themselves a moment. "And I have no dealings in the palace."

"State. Ah, State your business none the less."

I see the name did hold some weight at the Capital. I began walking to the side entrance.

"I have business in the catacombs."

No further bolts were loosed on me and I thought I was home free. No guard would want to risk killing a Phoenix Soul over a visit to the catacombs.

"Kill her! She is a traitor," came the voice of the King. Guess the pigeon had favourable winds. Or my time with Felix was deceptively long.

Two bolts sliced through the air towards me, arcing wickedly at the steep angle. The one about to puncture a hole in my head, I deflected with a gauntlet, but this left me in a precarious position with no way to block the second in time. I needed to rely on the untested armour.

Pursing my lips to help mentally brace for the pain, I clenched my muscles. A thlump of a noise sounded on impact and I looked down to find the bolt was now at a 45-degree angle, partially embedded into the ice armour. The surface of the cuirass had taken the impact and seemed to meld into a consistency much like a gelatinous blob or cube.

Even removing it was hard as I tried to yank it free, getting it on the third attempt. Letting the bolt fall harmlessly to the street, I dusted myself off, smoothing my armour back into place and glanced up at the crossbowmen with a smirk. With a sway in my step, I continued towards my destination passing out of view before they could even get another bolt loaded.

"Open the gates. Take her down," called the King and I heard the iron gates start to grind.

The entry into the catacombs was a long descending stairwell that bottomed out at a light source I noted as flame from the flickering dance of orange. Someone was down there keeping that thing lit for the chance visit of the King or one of his nobles.

Taking the steps casually as I listened for any imminent pursuers. There was activity, but did the foot guard seriously not know I came down this way? I even announced it on my approach. I could just see Staphin pulling his hair out as he tried to direct his men back into the catacombs.

"Sounds like a bit of a ruckus goin' on outside. The fightin' make it to the streets, dit it?"

My mind snapped back to attention but was eased as I noted how the man was casually seated. No guards pursued me and, therefore, I wouldn't come across as a danger to him. Without breaking my stride, I engaged in conversation.

"Seems the King has a traitor in town. Heading to the Catacombs, she was." I smiled sweetly as I watched his eyes bulge almost out of his head. By the time he had some semblance of a weapon in hand and untangled himself from the chair, I was already upon him, ice shard to the throat.

"No need to throw away your life over something so trivial. I'm just going to have a look around and head out again. Promise I won't even attempt anything malicious. Do you understand?"

The man slowly nodded, a small fear lingering behind his eyes. He didn't seem altogether a guardsman with his sweet-smelling perfume lingering in the air. A noble being punished maybe.

I got right up close and in a soft, gentle voice spoke. "Now be so kind as to pass me the keys to the crypt."

The man kept my gaze a moment, sweat beading on his forehead before he glanced at the crypt door. It was quick and I followed his gaze. The door to the crypt was wide open with the keys still lodged inside.

"Good boy," I said patting his cheek. "Your neglect of your job has made this much easier for me."

"No, leave the..."

Standing, I cracked the hilt of my dagger across his head sending the lucky man to the dirt for a sleep and a splitting headache come morning.

As the sound of boots began on the Catacomb steps, I pulled shut the door to the crypt, locking it as I went. The key, I was able to submerge into my armour. I was beginning to like the suit more and more.

A clanging against the barred door behind me, echoed through the dark and empty halls. It was reinforced deep into the rock walls making it harder for thieves to break in and steal those items of value buried with the ancient royalty. I had time to search for what Felix suggested. Torches placed in sconces had been lit to shimmer and play, sending shadows out over the walls that looked like movement in the dark. It wasn't alarming in any way. Having fought the armies of the dead single handed, a few sleepless Kings would be nothing.

A few minutes wandering aimlessly held no success in finding anything unusual. The cave like crypt itself looked as though it was naturally formed and the oldest tombs were found near the front. I could understand crafting the tombs closer to the entryway. It was an easier commute to pray at a grave, but a niggling thought kept resurfacing. If the information I am to find is important it wouldn't be near the front. It would be much further in where royalty could covet it.

The metal clanging coming from the entrance had turned more mechanical now. Someone had retrieved tools to work on the bars, hinges and lock. Maybe I should have used my ice to seal it but I wasn't thinking too far ahead at the time. The caressing embrace of hindsight.

Ignoring the tombs, I pushed further into the crypt. The air wasn't quite as fresh the deeper I went but every now and again I got a whiff of the perfume from the guard. It was Lavendar and Lilac, very similar to the type my mother used to make me where at court.

Rounding a corner, the colour of the walls began to change. The hand of man played its part in crafting it with swirls of a rich and chilly blue not only painted onto the left side but the patterns were etched deep into the stone. I ran my hand along it, marvelling at how smooth the surface was made to be.

On the opposite side of the hall, the colours that twisted and coiled along the walls tended to more oranges and reds. It was sharp and fierce like a raging fire and, with the help of the stone masons, came to life before my eyes. The flickering of the torches only added to the effect.

The patterns disappeared in the darkness of a grand hall opening high above. There were only few torches around the area, one just lying on the ground out of its sconce, but there wasn't light enough to show me what I needed. I knew it would be on the walls above me, I could feel it in my bones, I just couldn't see it and looked around for a way to give me more light.

"You love your ice, Fibonacci, but you are also of the flame. You are the light in the darkness," Shard echoed in my mind.

"I'm still grumpy, stop being so helpful." I pouted feeling silly for not thinking of it.

Shard just laughed in the halls of my mind. *"Humans."*

"In the heart of the square where the old stories dwell," I started to hum before chiding myself. I was going to have that song in my head all day now. Twirling in a circular motion, I brought my hands around, above and in a dramatic motion leaned over to run my hands perpendicular to the ground producing a growing flame like a river.

"A dragon of stone in the cold ceaseless rain." On a whim, I shifted the flame to represent a long and slender dragon running along the stone floor before taking flight to soar around the ceiling raining light across the area.

I stood in wonder assessing the great hall and taking in the large intricate murals painted and carved from floor to ceiling. It would have taken a team of masons and artisans, years to complete this room.

As I began to digest the murals, realised it was telling a story along both walls that came together in a climactic finale on the far wall. And as comprehension dawned, so too did a dread guilt.

The fire side was straight forward, showing a tribe of people, adept in the art of flame wielding. This could only be the BrongTa. If it read correctly, which I had no doubt of, the murals showed the BrongTa bringing forth the Phoenix to this world in a ceremony using a droplet of magma mixed together with a piece of a fallen star. The first three Phoenix are seen rising from ash and flame. It was no wonder, a Phoenix felt akin to the BrongTa and would fight to choose them if they become a Soul.

On the other side was a much sadder scene. A people in the snow with techniques in manipulating and conjuring ice. I looked up at my kin, knowing without looking further just what was about to be revealed. Dark swirls, a black and white tree, and a group séance that seemed to transform a member in the middle into the Lich. It was depressing to think that my ancestry made such a terrible mistake. I understood Felix's halting words.

On the far wall, the two murals collided in an epic battle to last the eons. Phoenix of different hues and intensities of flame, swooping and attacking the armies of the dead.

The left side was a mass of orange tentacles tracing back to a singularity. The controlling body of the Lich.

I tilted my head considering the painting. All the tentacles lead back to the Lich but only one was from behind. My eyes brightened as I considered the implications this line could hold. There wasn't even anything of value on the end of it. Just a small idol type statue looking thing sitting on a pedestal.

The three headed... Could it be the Phyl word Abacus spoke of?

A green shimmer glistened on the walls and my face drained of anything resembling life.

"That is indeed my Phylactery. The essence of our kin in its purest form." the gnarled voice of Abacus filled the room with the help of a cadaver.

I closed my eyes trying to stop the trembling settling into my limbs. "He can't be here," I whispered to myself like a child hiding under the bed as wolves padded through the home.

"It is good that you are researching your family background. It is right you should know the harsh and dangerous reality the Accipitridae hold. We are Fibonacci."

"I am not like you." I spoke with trembling lips. There was focus and meaning within the words but no strength nor volume. It came as but a shallow draft in an already drafty room. Crossing my arms, I squeezed the flesh above my elbows trying to excite any form of courage hidden in my veins.

"The BrongTa fire wielders would label us a danger to creation. They would say we are demons who would freeze whole villages for the pleasure of seeing life in crystal ice and that only they can fight us off with their flame. It isn't a surprise the masses chose warmth over the crisp cool, but they made a huge mistake trusting them. We can right this, Daughter of Fibonacci. You are in a rather unique position to make the world see the threat of the BrongTa."

How do I get out of here. Where can I run to. The words fluttered around in my mind and I couldn't think beyond this. I was beginning to panic.

"It is not courage that pushes a shepherd to protect the flock from threat of mountain lions nor a child to brave the dark in hopes of finding light. It is fear that tempers the heart, melds with desire and brings about cautious movement. Courage is only said to exist after one embraces their fears, not conquers them."

"But I... Help," I whimpered aloud. I couldn't comprehend in that moment that my thoughts were all I required to reach Shard.

"Ah, the Accipitridae speaks. Give me his secrets. Let us defeat them together."

"No," I cried, my arm arcing out and around to produce large spikes of ice that pierced Abacus in the chest, shoulder and random body he carried for speech. Each breath was a terrible struggle through the jittering tremors of my body as I stood half hunched over.

Abacus just looked over the ice as if assessing the nuisance of a mosquito with a sucker in his arm. Slowly the ice began to shrink, being absorbed into Abacus's body without a second thought.

"The Phylactery provides me with all the Fibonacci power I need. You don't need to offer me more. Or did you think ice could harm a creature that was born of it?" Abacus said in a neutral tone.

"But the eye?" I said, thinking of how stabbing Abacus had won my freedom.

"I needed you with the Accipitridae to learn their secrets. We are linked you and I and *I hear everything.*" The last of the sentence spoken straight into my mind. "I was able to awaken the dormant link of our bloodlines when I held you as guest. Soon, I will bridge the gap to your Accipitridae's mind as well."

"You have everything you need, Elara ShardSoul," Shard said. His voice didn't show any signs of fear or worry for what Abacus just said, where I was reeling in terror as my own mind now worked against me.

If not in ice, then in fire. Fire born of the BrongTa flame.

Even as the thought crossed my mind and as I reacted in building the intensity I would need, a green portal was already in the works behind Abacus. A proof in his ability to hear my thoughts. What could I have given away already?

"Keep feeding me information, Daughter of Fibonacci, but to keep you distracted so you do not follow..." Abacus stepped into the portal and before it closed, orange flecked power radiated from him to envelope one of the tombs in the room. The tomb of Spriggan.

Blue flames burst from the very air around me as I released my gathering power, to fly up and dissipate harmlessly against the roof.

I kept watch on both the closing portal and the energy burst. There wasn't a chance this side of life that I would willingly follow into the realm of the Lich once more. Creating a distraction only risked both my safety and gaining that which he wanted to know. Fragments of memory ran through my mind. Fragments of Enzo and of Shard.

"No, no, no." I shook my head, vigorously. Now that I knew what I shouldn't think of, it was even harder to keep it from my mind. I wasn't going to last indefinitely with this hanging over my head... And Shard would know my faults by now. Know the risk I was.

A grinding of stone on stone reverberated around the halls. As the flames running along the roof dimmed back to nothing and all I was left with was the light of the sconces upon the walls, two shimmering, blue eyes rose from the resting place of Spriggan. They were locked to me, dangerous and menacing. The large, solid form looking just as formidable in death as it had in life and my heart began to race. I'd sparred with this man. I knew his form and ability. In life, he was skilled enough to keep me on my toes. A lot of the time it even felt as though he let me win some of the bouts. In death, with a body that wouldn't miss an arm or two, this was going to be a hard battle.

"My friend, are we fated to do battle once more?" I asked, testing if there was any life left in him or if he was wholly taken by the Lich.

The answer though came in the harshest of ways. I couldn't tell just what it was that drew his attention. The soft rubbing of fabric upon stone, a whimper below my ability to hear, the smell of Lilac and Lavendar. All of sudden, Spriggan spun on his heal to tower over his tomb. A terrifying and ear-piercing scream field the cave as I realised the princess had been hiding down here this whole time. The open gate, the perfume, the dropped torch as I entered the cavern. I was so stupid to think I was alone and now I had moments to act as Spriggan lifted a large hunk of stone above his head as if it was nothing intent on smashing the Princess into a smear of her former self.

I lashed out and with a crack, snagged his wrist with the fire branded ice whip I just conjured. It was crude in the shape of the links but the fire made up for it, eating at the flesh and curling skin from the bone.

Wreathing his arm forward I was ripped from my standing position to be sent tumbling through the air and crashing into the rock wall above the Princess. I toppled done upon the frightened girl eliciting a grunt from her before her face began to crumple. I hunkered over her, protecting her with my body.

"Don't you dare start fucking crying," I growled, startling her into submission. I bet no one had ever talked to her in such a way before and that alone was enough to have her instincts kick in, stifling the tears.

"AHHRRGGG!" I groaned, as the stone club pounded into my back. Most of the blow was absorbed by my armour but the strength in this man was enough that I'd be surprised if I didn't instantly bruise. A few more and he'd be breaking bones. I turned back to the Princess and motioned to my armour.

"Take the keys from in there." She didn't move and I swore. "Take them now or I swear to all that is sinister, I'll ram my dagger into your eye socket myself."

With a newfound fear, the Princess reached into my armour and recovered the keys as another blow smashed into me.

"Fucking Bastard," I screamed through the pain. "Get out of her. Make for the entrance. Your dad is there."

The Princess hesitated a moment, mouth quivering.

"Now!"

She finally took off towards the exit wailing all the way. A side swing took me in the rump sending me sprawling across the room. I could see Spriggan about to give chase to the Princess so I set a wall of blue and white flame to block the entrance.

Getting to my feet, I limped along a few metres as Spriggan turned on me. There was a dirty glee in his smile as he began hunting me, and I knew there was nothing of the kind man I once knew left in this husk. King Spriggan would have never raised a weapon to a child, friend or foe, let alone his own blood. The man would have fought his own soldiers in the attempt to protect an enemy child. An unlikely event as his men would have fought beside him tooth and nail. Abacus had a lot to answer for.

Thoughts of the Phoenix nest and looking into the blazing eyes of Shard came unbidden. "Not right now, fuck ya."

Letting the pain of my beaten body fill my senses and clear my mind, I stumbled along in a fighting stance, the whip swapped out for my favoured sabre. The fact I could move my left leg told me it wasn't broken or the hip not dislocated but I couldn't help think a partial dislocation possible. The pain was incredibly intense and I wasn't going to make another swing let alone two if I was unlucky enough to survive the first.

Looking around I noted an odd shaped rock nearby and limped to it, Spriggan slowly stalking me all the while, moments from overtaking me. With a grunt, I dropped my hip onto the rock and felt the ball forced back into place. Screaming in agony, I threw myself aside as the club of stone dashed the floor where my head had just laid.

"Ok, let's dance," I said. I was still limping as the movement in my legs began to sync up once. The pain was still horrible but I couldn't give even a moment to it. I couldn't let anything distract me. Now was serious and I needed to be mentally calm.

Spriggan charged in swinging the club with sweeping strikes, left and right, but I danced around them. Each attack sent wisps of air rolling up my body. If any one blow connected, I was going to be beyond help, but the large weapon made Spriggan slow and predictable. I just had to concentrate.

Another smashing overhead and I dove forward to roll out of the way. A quick off-handed swing caught me off guard, taking me in the ribs. Air burst from my lungs and I gagged trying to find my breath while tumbling sideways. It was only luck that kept my moving. The awkward angle of the blow stealing most of the power.

Skidding along the ground, I caught myself on all fours like a cat. My breath returning in ragged gulps. Tensing my lungs, I sprung away, moving before I fully recovered as Spriggan broke the tomb next to me. The stone shards grazing my scalp.

As a trail of blood traced its way down my forehead to part left and right over my nose, I sent two whistling fire balls into Spriggan. The impact knocking him back a step before he continued his advance. The reprieve granting just enough time to dive past and get to the exit.

Footsteps pounded along the hall and I smiled knowing the princess was safe. 15 armed men entered the room fanning out. There were five crossbowmen and 10 with shield and spear.

Stop in the name of the King. You are charged with high treason and attempting to assassinate the Princess," A Captain said immediately as his eyes found mine.

"The. The. The Dragon King lives."

All eyes turned on the soldier standing with a pale face pointing into the darkness. They then turned to pierce the shadows of the cavern and, indeed, found Spriggan brandishing a club and approaching. He charged the outer crossbowman, shoulder barging him into the rock wall, his body dashed to bits. Spriggan then swung a hard blow taking two of the spearmen at once, sending them hurtling across the cavern with grunts and screams. If luck still survived this crypt, they would live long enough for me to heal them.

"There's your assassin," I said to the Captain as I pointed at the late King. "A Lich has awoken him to do terrible deeds. It was all I could do to get the Princess out of here."

This moment would be the defining moment for the Captain. It was a tough choice to make on the fly as joining me would go against his King's command. It would also be the right decision.

"Telveria to me," the Captain called, facing Spriggan. I smiled knowing he would be a great leader someday, if not today. "Turtle wall."

"Captain. Turtle spring. Get me up there," I said and the Captain's brow furrowed.

"It's an old formation. We aren't sufficiently trained," The Captain admitted.

"I trust your shield."

The Captain locked eyes with me a moment before nodding, accepting the burden. "Turtle Spring," he yelled and I was amazed at how his men fell into place. They built an interlocking wall before Spriggan while the Captain angled his shield for me.

As Spriggan stalked in, the Captain commanded the men to hold. As Spriggan reared back to strike, the Captain commanded to hold.

"Left shoulder," I said and saw a minor adjustment to the angle of his shield. Breaking my sabre down, I morphed it into a dagger of ice and blue flame.

The clash of stone on shield resounded through the hall but I couldn't look up to see the damage.

"Break," the Captain commanded.

Shields separated as I bounced to the centre of the Captain's shield. With a grunt and a push along with my own jump, I was sent soaring through the air, over the soldiers still standing strong, to slide along Spriggan's left shoulder. Using the momentum, I swung around his neck to pierce my knife into the point at the back of Spriggan's head where Riven had an energy line linked to Abacus.

Flames erupted from the late King and he stumbled another two feet before falling face first into the stone floor.

"He won't get up again," I said, glad the theory worked. Spears levelled on me and I smiled.

"I'm sorry, Elara ShardSoul. My orders prevent you from leaving."

"You have not the skill nor the right to waylay a Phoenix Soul."

"I must obey my King."

"And if I offer you life. Can you give me the headstart I need to leave this hall before you obey your King?"

"My life belongs to the King to use in service as he requires."

"Noble but I meant your soldiers," I said, pointing to the three that were downed early in the fight. "They're teetering between life and death."

A look of dark contemplation crossed the man's face and I understood the predicament my choice put him in. Make this deal and twice, rebuke his King's wishes. Let his men die by taking me, and what reason should he hold rank over soldiers if he couldn't save them.

His lips pursed and I saw his knuckles whiten. "I accept." The words sounded as if they burnt like acid all the way out.

Closing my eyes, I drifted across the room in spirit to assess the bodies. One spearman had already passed from the world but the other was fighting on. I poured healing energy over the wounds, mending tissue and reforging broken bones. In moments, his breath had gotten stronger and he was sitting up.

I moved to the crossbowman and to my greatest surprise there was still breath on this man's lips and a pulse so slow, one would be lucky to find it. The man's... Woman's internal organs had been crushed and a rib had pierced the lung. I started reforming the tissue of the lung and using it to reverse the bone shard from the organ before draining it of blood. The blood I had the body reabsorb to remake and reuse elsewhere as was needed. Moving from organ to organ, I revitalised and reversed all the harm that was caused to her before I shifted back a metre to assess the energy lines. Only one line was still dark and I saw that it was from an old injury years before. The eye had shrivelled in the socket and now it sat like a prune, useless, wrinkled and disgusting.

A crossbowman would be at her best with both eyes, so I flooded the prune with healing energy. It was an odd thing to watch the eyeball puff back up, taking on its former shape but I couldn't be sure until she woke whether the healing cured the eye or if there was a deeper issue. I left the gnarled scar on the eyelid in place, a testament to a wound that changed her world.

Returning to my body, the Captain stood by me as the other soldiers patted the spearman on the back. He seemed expectant of more.

"Your second spearman had already passed into the abyss. There was nothing more I could do," I said honestly.

The Captain nodded, contemplating his options. "You offered me the lives of my men and could not fulfill your end of the bargain."

I thought not. Human nature is greed at heart. A small act of kindness, giving everything you can, was never enough when everything more was expected of you. I hadn't wanted to fight them but the Captain will now condemn his men to death.

"Elara ShardSoul, by order of the King, I..."

"I can see!" A cry echoed in the cave. The crossbowman looked around in wonder, tears streaming down her face. "How is this possible?"

The Captain looked at me and I nodded. With fingers pinching the bridge of his nose, the Captain reconsidered himself.

"Go," he said and I raised an eyebrow. "She's my wife's sister. Go, before I change my mind."

I turned to leave.

"And Elara."

I looked back.

"Thank you."

"What's your name?" I asked.

"Col."

"You're a good man, Col. Don't lose that to the cruelty of the crown and its politics."

Standing to attention, Col saluted me with hand on heart. It was a more honourable salute than the simple hand to the forehead. Returning the gesture, I headed for the exit. There was bound to be the King and his lackeys up ahead. Hopefully they make better choices than before.

To my surprise, the open space beyond the castle was empty but for a single figure. Fitz didn't look pleased in the slightest. He actually reminded me of a parent gearing up to reprimand their child, placing themselves in the child's path and waiting to catch them out. I didn't feel guilty, however. There was nothing I had done that was so terrible and, what's more, accomplished our main objective.

"You've caused quite the commotion, Elara."

Oh, using my actual name. I am about to get a lecture. "They'll get over it. I completed our objective and even saved the Princess with my *troublemaking*."

"It's not about what you succeeded in doing, Elara. There is a right and a wrong way of going about getting it done. You put a lot of people in danger and left those we could have helped high and dry. It's only because of the myself, Baras, and Kymberlin's help on the battlefield that I was able to have the King stand down and allow me to escort you from the field."

"So, you're my escort now?"

"I'm your friend, and comrade. Since the moment I met you in the mustering yard for new Souls, I knew you were special."

"You know nothing of me," I spat but Fitz only smiled sadly.

"I see you, Ellie. Broken. A shadow of your previous self. I cannot begin to imagine the pain you went through at the hand of Abacus. I can only see the detriment and depression you've spiralled into."

At the mention of Abacus, the link and thoughts of Enzo and Shard all begun to surface. "No, not now. I can't do this now," I said cradling my head in an effort to keep the memories away.

"We're going to break this open right now," Fitz continued misunderstanding. "You won't heal until you face your demons head on."

"HE'S GOING TO SEE!" I screamed, dropping to my knees and shaking my head from side to side. It was almost impossible to hide from my own memories, especially when I was deliberately not trying to think of them.

Fitz was taken aback by the outburst and my actions not quite understanding what was going on. He tried to comfort me but I was in a repetitive cycle of rolling my head back and forth while whimpering 'no' over and again.

331

"I can't keep them out." I burst into tears as my mind was being stretched in every which direction.

"Then show him and be done with it," came the voice of Shard, soothing the ripples of terror I created in my subconscious.

"I can't give him that information. He'll go on a killing spree, bringing everyone and everything under his control. He could never be stopped."

"He still needs to acquire the essence of life that grants immortality. We will stop him before that happens. Let it go."

"I can't."

"You can. It's as much mine as it is yours. Let the memories free."

"Argh, no." It was becoming painful now to force my mind into submission.

"You turned up in the nesting grounds, Elara."

"Stop it."

"You trapped me."

"Stop it, Shard. Stop it now!"

"You stole from me, Elara."

"It's not what happened. I didn't do it. I didn't..." The pain and turmoil in my mind became too much causing me to slump into a seizure. My mind open to pull out anything locked away in my subconscious.

I met Enzo in the snow-covered woods by our tree...

Chapter 17

He was half an hour late. On most days that wouldn't have worried me as Enzo was probably off with his Phoenix, but today of all days. I was finally going to join him in the skies, gliding along on the clouds upon my own Phoenix. And one day our kids could join us as well. We had a plan. Half an hour late was not part of it.

I traced my fingers over the initials etched into the Fir tree, a symbol of our everlasting love that only grew as the tree did each new season. The number of times we had made love under the needle like coverage or fought beneath the boughs, spilling blood as we traded blow for blow.

Hands covered my eyes and I chided myself for being careless and letting Enzo sneak up on me. The smell of wood and smoke lulling my senses and setting a fire burning in my belly. Maybe another half an hour late might not be such a bad thing.

"Sorry, am I late. I had trouble getting Talon to leave for the battlefront without me?" Enzo asked in that dirty, husky voice of his. A voice that dampened the loins every time I heard it. This man was my perfection.

"Not late, my love," I said, spinning in his arms and wrapping mine around him. "We still have plenty of time to kill."

He pulled my hands back. There was a tenseness in his eyes and it melted my heart to think just how much he wanted today to go right.

"Maybe a bout to loosen up and get prepared for what's to come," Enzo said.

Twirling a finger around his bare chest, I looked up at him with a mischievous smile. "I was thinking something a little more intimate to start the day."

"If we start that, we'll be here all day and lose our chance for you to be my equal. Do you not want to be with me anymore?"

"No," I squealed. "I would never want that. Even if we were separated by space and time. If the whole world had crossed us and we were blinded against one another, promise you would never give up on me. Promise you will keep coming back until I see the light and we are as one again." I looked desperately at him waiting for him to say the words. "Promise me, Enzo."

He smiled gently, kissing my lips and calming my nerves. "I will never let anything, even you, keep us apart for good. We are meant to be together, and I will always keep coming back. You will never be alone, and our love will stretch the course of time. We just need to get through today."

I melted into a puddle in his arms. Barely holding it together enough to remain upright. He was everything I wanted. And now immortality called.

"And this is why we ain't fucking right now, Elara. Get yourself together. The Phoenix are incredibly smart and tactile. One wrong move and we'll not achieve immortality together," Enzo said, a growl in his voice. I took a step back.

"You're right." Bowing my head, I submitted to him. I could never tell this man no nor let him down. "I'm ready to do my part. Are you sure it'll work."

Enzo smiled again, revelling in the power he had over me. "It'll work. We'll make Shard believe I had no part in it so *if* he says no, I can surprise him and we'll take it by force. We will be together, Elara. You just need to not think so much and do as I say."

I nodded. "Let's go then."

"Not just yet." Enzo held a hand up. "We need to give Talon some time to vacate the area so we aren't interrupted. And we need to have this bout. It's all part of the plan."

"How so?" I asked. I wasn't in the mood to fight right now. I could happily just sit with Enzo, his arm around me and wait out the time.

A back hand across the face sent me sprawling to the snow-covered Earth. Holding the cheek, I looked back at him in shock.

"You need to put more trust in me," Enzo said and I immediately felt guilty for doubting him in his plan even when I wasn't sure about it myself. "I'm trying to set up a scenario to trick Shard. I want to show him your strength and how perfect you are to be chosen as a Phoenix Soul. I'm only thinking of you, Elara. Now get to your feet and fight me."

I doubted the man I loved. Why couldn't I just trust he had my best interest at heart. He would never do anything to harm me. I needed to redeem myself in his eyes. Regaining my feet, I crafted ice gauntlets over my hands. When I go out flying with Enzo later, I didn't want my hands to be bruised and sore.

"Good girl," he growled and all my insides purred.

We started slow, going through the routines we practiced and perfected to keep our abilities at their peak. I learned so much along the years in these bouts and on three occasions with bandits and other such miscreants, the skills came in handy. As our muscles loosened and we started to get more into it, the speed and strength of the blows got more intense. Most were blocked, more than even just a year ago but the ones that got through were hard hitting. Lights flashed before my eyes with any head hit and I was starting to fight a growing dizziness but I pushed on. I needed to live up to the image Enzo had of me. I didn't want to let him down again.

Ducking below a lazy right, when I say lazy, I mean the swing was a fraction of a second behind his usually pace, I took full advantage. Smashing a quick left into his kidneys, I followed with a hard right to the face and watched as Enzo stumble back. A new gash had opened beside his left eye with blood streaming down his face. My eyes grew wide and hands came to my mouth in shock. I realised how stupid I was with the gauntlets. How selfish it was to protect myself, not thinking of the damage they could cause Enzo.

"I'm sorry. I'm sorry," I squealed. "I won't ever make such armour again."

Enzo just looked at me with a hard stare. "It's fine. It's time we made our way into the nesting grounds anyway. You head in first. I won't be far behind. It'll show your persistence and commitment."

"O. Okay," I stammered. I wanted to question him again. Really make sure it would be ok for me to enter the nesting grounds. I'd been expressly forbidden on other occasions. I couldn't see how this was going to turn out any different but I couldn't doubt him again. And there was always the backup plan.

"Off you go. We'll be flying together soon. Breathe in frost," Enzo said shooing me along.

"Breathe out fire." Hesitant and worried, I followed Enzo's wishes, making my way down the covered pathway into the nesting grounds. Reaching the entrance to the domed clearing, I peeked inside, scoping out the area. There in the centre of the grounds sat Shard, his orange and yellow flames, shimmering gently over his feathers. They were always a wonder, these birds, the way they carried their flames. It was beautiful.

Taking in a calming breath, I stepped out into the clearing. There was a small movement from Shard as he peered out towards the sound of my footfalls, but immediately upon seeing me, his head came up sharply. I watched as the flames across his body grew in intensity and Shard kept his eyes on me, watching intently.

As I took another step inside, Shard squawked softly, standing and starting to circle, considering me. I could tell he was confused at my presence and knew anyone else unknown by the Phoenix would have already been smouldering as ashes by now.

"It's ok. I'm not here to harm you," I said holding my hands up and taking another step forward.

Shard's squawks grew in intensity and he tilted his head as if he was about to attack.

"I want to join you, Shard. I want to be your eternal Soul."

His eyes narrowed and then he saw Enzo come in. He was bleeding from the head and Enzo just made a motion as if he couldn't stop me. Shard grew dangerous and ignored when Enzo said Shard should forgive my intrusion and that it did show commitment. I was relieved to have Enzo by my side. I don't think I could've confronted Shard without him. I couldn't even understand what Shard was saying, relying only on body language. But Enzo was able to, and he was fighting for me. Fighting to make me a Phoenix Soul and spend untold years together. It chilled my heart in erotically tantalizing ways.

"You must change your plan, Elara. Shard will not accept you," Enzo said nodding gently. I understood immediately that we were changing to plan B. I smiled knowing we were doing this together. "You have moments only."

As Shard expected my departure from the area, I was able to catch him off guard with a quick swish of my hand. Ice grew in a spiralling formation from the ground, much like the shells I found on the ocean shore to the north with Enzo. They bundled Shard up until only his head was clear.

"The others are coming. You need to move him," Enzo said softly to me.

This was the fun part. I had such manipulation over the ice it was almost like a living, moving part. The spiral began to spin from bottom to top in a way that had it careening over the land to the Western entry. Shard was locked in a rolling stasis that only helped to confuse him more and make this easier.

The trees parted as Enzo came close and we were able to make quite a distance before finding another smaller clearing and setting the structure down. Shard's head lolled out like a Terror Hound's tongue, to look up at me with one of his sad eyes. The orange flames inside his iris were less fierce now, as if their very life had been dimmed.

The world darkened around me. Light was not so bright. Smells were not so fresh. The chill in the winter breeze was not so invigorating. I looked at Enzo. The love we shared was not so pure.

What right had I, to lay such a beautiful creature so low. Why did I get to dim the creations of this world to craft a less innocent and magical land. I glanced down at Shard and my heart trembled.

I couldn't do it. I wanted a love that lasted the ages but I now understood that if I pushed forward with the plan, there wouldn't be love anymore. It would be less. One lifetime of true and honest love was more enticing than a lifetime of regret.

"Come on, Elara, the Phoenix will be back soon," Enzo said urging me on.

He couldn't see what I did. He wasn't put into this situation. Talon accepted him as he was. I couldn't believe I was about to do this. I never dreamed I would ever say no to this man and disappoint him so, but it was for the betterment of our relationship. This was the only way we could truly be together.

"I can't do it, Enzo," I said, then took a steadying breath and looked him in the eye. "I won't."

"What do you mean? Don't speak like you don't love me anymore. This is our chance to be together forever." There was a stern expression upon Enzo's face as he approached.

I shook my head. "To force this creature to give up it's free will in deciding its own destiny will dampen this relationship of ours. I wouldn't be able to look at you and not remember this harsh deed."

"You will get over the feeling. I know it might seem a hard choice now but, in time when we have our own family and lives together, it will seem as nothing."

"It's not going to happen, Enzo. We can have all that in this life."

His face just dropped into utter disappointment. I never believed a person could make another feel so bad with a look but there it was.

"You need to harden the fuck up if you want to stay by my side, Elara. I'll take in the slack this time only," Enzo said leaning over Shard. By the time I realised what he was doing the Soul of the current Phoenix Soul was already being ripped from Shard's body.

I tried to stop it, tried to protect Shard, but I was too late. Enzo had already gotten his greedy, little hooks into the Soul essence. As I crafted a dome of ice for protection, I drew Shard into safety, but I was too late as the last of the Soul had been pulled from his body. Enzo smiled as he held the swirling, white green, milky mist in his hand and looked at me. He had no care at all for the status of Shard.

"You need to drink this," Enzo said holding out his hand.

"I can't believe you did that," I cried taking a step back.

"Drink it," he commanded stepping in.

"No!" I screamed and made to run but he was quicker.

Enzo jumped in grabbing me by the hair and yanking me back into himself. Before I had a chance to react, he was forcing the life essence down my throat, choking me as I was forced to swallow.

I struggled to free myself, arms flailing against him as darkness took over. The Soul essence both powerful enough to kill my first incarnation and strong enough to grant my rebirth.

Tears rolled down my face and I slammed a fist into the ground. "Why, Shard? Why would you make me remember that. Why would you give that to him."

"To free your mind of turmoil and allow you to act with purpose. We still have time. Meet me on the wall and let's go end this."

"Ellie, what's going on?" Fitz asked watching my one-sided conversation roll into a seizure that ended with my tears.

"Abacus knows how to become a true immortal. We need to go. He's going to be stalking the Phoenix and Phoenix Souls." I said grabbing the front of his leathers. "We can't let him capture us or the whole world will slowly fall to him."

A grim expression took Fitz's features. "Tell me everything."

He helped me to my feet and as we made our way to the outer wall, I explained everything I had found in the cavern and the memories Shard caused me to unlock. I explained to him just what will happen if a Phoenix Soul was captured again by Abacus. He would rip out their soul and absorb every bit to be used for hundreds of resurrections. If he got more than one, that rate could jump to thousands. He could very well outlast the moon and the stars by the end.

Fitz took it all in his stride, never allowing a single twinge of a nerve or movement of a muscle to let on what he was thinking. As I rounded off my story, he just grimaced and nodded sternly.

"Do we know where his... Thing might be?"

"The phylactery," I provided. "There was a tree I recognised in the murals. A rather uniquely gnarled Oak that was part white and part black. It was said to have been struck by lightning at the first moment time began and the tree froze in place, never allowing even a second to wash over it. This tree was the central feature of Three Pine Village. It is there. I just know it is."

"Then we need to find it, and we need to destroy it. Abacus can't be allowed to rule."

"He'll know we're onto him? He can hear everything from my mind the moment it's thought," I said ashamed by my weakness.

"All the more reason to destroy him. We are going to end him, Ellie, and you'll be able to get a semblance of your life back. I hate seeing you this way."

I smiled weakly. "Thanks." I didn't have the heart to tell him I'd lived long enough already and only sought to end Abacus and Enzo before I allowed my life to be consumed once and for all.

"Kymberlin has left to rally reinforcements."

"Suniel won't lift a finger for us anymore. Not after what we did to his widdle weputation."

I enticed a laugh from Fitz. "You'd be surprised by the resources of Kymberlin... There is one other thing you need to know." Fitz's whole persona shifted to a serious front.

I began to theorise what could be so bad but I needed him to say it. "What?"

"Talon has been informed. This battle is bigger than our in-fighting."

"Fuck," I swore, making my way up the battlements to where Shard waited with Baras, Haze, and Flint.

The sun was kissing the horizon as we landed on the ridgeline of the mountains overlooking the Northern fields. A harsh blizzard was brewing below making it visually impossible to scout the lands surrounding the location of Three Pine. I wasn't even able to pinpoint the tree I needed. I knew it wasn't far off but the blanket of cloud swirling just below the mountains was all consuming.

Making camp against the side of a cliff face sheltering us from the harshest of winds, we settled for a quiet night. It wasn't something we planned for and food was scarce at this time. Flint and Fitz volunteered to hunt in the forests and plains of the southern lands. There were less storms that side and offered the best chance to fill our bellies tonight.

"I'm sorry, Shard," I said scratching his neck as he laid next to me.

"For the memories? Nothing I haven't viewed myself. I know your heart and what you were trying to achieve in the end. I would thank you for that," Shard replied.

There had been some hairy moments between us of late. Mostly, it stemmed from my lack of capacity to deal with my capture, torture, and constant hauntings afterwards. Shard and I were finally starting to get back on track. And he was right. Offering up my memories and not fighting my mind lightened my mood some. We at least know the enemy now and what he wants. The burden is shared by all Phoenix Souls and the Firebirds, and we will all keep each other safe. This is the safest I've felt in a long time.

"No. For what came after the memories. For why I didn't return the next life, or the one after. I could have easily made my way back to the

339

nesting grounds and found you again. Returned what didn't belong to me. I was just afraid... and ashamed. I didn't want to look upon your corpse or face the other Phoenix over what I'd done. I may not have been ready to die. It was selfish and you were forced to wait 300 years until my mind began to degrade."

"I've long since forgiven you for your faults, Ellie. You don't need to apologise to me."

I already knew that. I already understood that. "I guess, I need to apologise to start the process of forgiving myself. A true and honest apology only comes when someone really means it and wants to be better. I'm at that point."

"Let your healing begin."

"Thank you, Shard. I'm glad you were not lost to this world." Kissing the soft feathers on his forehead, I stood and made my way to where Baras had positioned himself. I knew he was giving me some space, not knowing how to handle me of late and I saw him jump as I approached, looking left and right.

"Calm, Baras. Just relax," I said with a genuine smile. He relaxed back to sitting against the rock face and I sat with my back to his side leaning into him. There was hesitation and confusion but after a moment he fell back into the Baras I knew growing up in the keep. Slowly he wrapped his arm around my front, holding me tenderly like he would when watching the stars.

"I think it's that I'm finally finding my way home," I said softly.

"To Three Pine?" Baras asked missing my meaning. He always was very straight when it came to processing information and I giggled.

"Three Pine Village was where I was born, but I cannot call it a home. I meant, when I escaped the Lich's stronghold, a large part of me was left behind. This left me scared, vulnerable, mean, and testy."

"Elara," Baras said, real emotion in his voice but I pushed through.

"I've been trying to protect myself from all outside threats. I couldn't even tell the difference between a friend and a threat at times. And you've been on the end of that. I think the part of me I needed to leave behind to escape Abacus is finally finding me."

"You... You don't need to say this, Ellie. I've been captured, even tortured before. I know your pain. And it is I that may need to apologise to you."

"To what end? You've done nothing, Baras."

"Exactly. I haven't known how to act around you. I've been withheld and awkward. When I was going through what you did, I would have given anything to have someone say that I would be alright. That the actions of others will never define my heart and my strength. Instead, my dad threw me back into the force and I hid from my short comings. It took me such a long time to get past it all. Then, when the same thing happened to you, I still found myself running. Words that I would have wanted to hear caught it my throat. The tender actions that I had craved, stuck in stasis somewhere between thought and action. I found I was still hurting after all this time and didn't believe I could help you, being so broken."

I was stunned watching my dearest friend of this lifetime. He had averted his eyes, almost as if too ashamed to look at me and a lump caught in my throat.

"You dear, old, fool," I said jumping into his arms, holding him tight. My cheeks had started to dampen. "You sat by me while I was lost. If you had been through any semblance of what I had, that took true strength and love. I heard your words even when you couldn't let them free. I just wish I could have been there for you when we were young. I would have taken all the pain away."

"You did, Elara. Even when I kept it to myself, it was you that brought me back. You made life worth living once more."

A shiver ran down my spine as I tensed. Even without seeing I knew he was here.

The clapping of hands sounded across the camp. "How touching. Displaying our emotions like servant girls at court. Are we going to be hugging and crying next..." Enzo said before pausing a moment to note our dampened cheeks. "Too late, I see. Well, you girls get it all out. We have a big battle tomorrow."

"Why do you feel the need to put people down?" I growled turning on him. There was a moment's hesitation in my movement as I saw him. He was dressed in a dark, full body armour designed perfectly for his form. It was surprising it still fit after so many lifetimes but I knew he only wore it when a major battle was to be had. I would guess the armour had started as a silvery steel but the intensity of Enzo's flames had charred it to this devilish colour. He stood with the demonic helmet in his hands. Still, I had never actually seen him fight in this armour. Only head to battle when I was younger.

"Come on, Elara. I was just having a little fun. Don't start spreading your emotions to me," Enzo said, nose twisting in disgust.

I could feel Baras grabbing at my arm, trying to hold me back. I'm sure he didn't want to see me fighting again but I pulled my arm away.

"Sorry, Baras, but I have some things to say to him too. Some emotions to spread," I said.

With a grimace, Baras let my hand go.

"Come to apologise, I see" Enzo said as I approached.

"Excuse me?"

"You gave the Lich exactly what he needed to become immortal. This is why we tried to wipe your kind out. Why the BrongTa attacked Three Pine Village. We knew what was hidden there."

My eyes flared at his brazen words. "My kind. You're the only reason a daughter of the Fibonacci clan lived and three hundred years at that. There was a time you even spoke of love for this daughter of the Fibonacci. You're full of yourself if you think this is all my fault."

"And I still would talk of love for you. That's beside the point."

I scoffed. "Fuck off with your ideas of love. You don't understand the feeling."

"I know what it means to care for someone, to want to hold someone and experience of life's wonders with someone. With you. I still remember what you told me before I helped you gain rebirth. I will always come back for you, wait for you. Even if it takes 1000 years. I know your love is beating somewhere deep inside, longing to resurface and embrace me. I saw it in the forest that night on the way to the Phoenix nest. When you don't have all those nasty thoughts influencing your mind, you still seek me out. Even when you thought I could be a threat."

"You're delusional," I said. It was hard for me to even try and comprehend how someone could have such a twisted view on love and life. "Stepping back and looking at the life we shared, I wasn't in a relationship at all. You were abusive, manipulative and selfish. Everything you did that you say was for me or for us, was only for you. And really? 1000 years? Enzo, this is my last life. My last few days. There will only be ashes for you at the end. Shard made sure of that."

"What the Phoenix has taken, they can return."

My eyes grew dark and my brow furrowed. "Is that a threat?" My fingers flexed and unflexed as if trying to grip a sword I was fighting

342

myself not to craft.

"I will not stand by idle and watch you fade away. There is no threat in that. It is an act of love." Enzo said and I really believe he believed that garbage.

Colour drained from my palms with how tightly I was squeezing my fists. I wanted to stab him. I wanted so badly to rid the world of this cancer growing upon its surface, but I couldn't. We needed him. There was still too few of us and I couldn't rely on Kymberlin stirring the hearts and minds of the Keep to join us in our fight. Suniel would never help me and the soldiers had finally found a reprieve in fighting. No. We nee... We were forced to use Enzo, I corrected.

With great restraint I spun on my heel and almost walked face first into Fitz.

"I suppose you want a fucking deep and meaningful as well. Clear the fucking air between us," I said, piling all my anger and rage onto my friend who deserved anything but.

Wide eyed, Fitz looked around at the situation realising just what was going on. "Umm, no. I, I, ah. I think we got all our issues under control. Nothing you need to say?"

"No," I said stubbornly, holding my façade.

"Good then. Flint caught and roasted a deer. I was going to make a stew with a portion of the meat and some extra herbs and potatoes I picked up. The rest can be eaten as is. Hungry?"

At the mention of food my stomach cried out in agony as I hadn't fed it since yesterday. "No." I remained stubborn.

Fitz just raised an eyebrow and smirked. "That's good. Wasn't enough for you anyway."

I finally smiled. "Looks like a cold night tonight. Hope you don't like that cloak."

"You know I'm not impartial to sharing."

"I think you'll find me too cold now that I've embraced my heritage."

"A shame really. It is actually quite chilly."

"Baras is alone tonight."

Fitz sucked in the top right of his lip as his eyes grew distant. "I couldn't... Well. No... Could I?" Fitz turned. "Hey Baras?"

"Don't even think about it," Baras grunted and my lungs let out such a hearty laugh.

Chapter 18

As the grey predawn light filtered over the land, I sat on the cliff side watching the world wake. A soft, shallow mist sat upon the fields and forests, the taller of the Fir trees sticking above. I could still see the outline of structures through the mist and in some places where it was exceptionally thin, the blanket of snow from last night's storm shimmered. It was beautiful and I was glad I got to witness this on my last day.

As the morning sun bestowed its warmth to the lands and begun to melt the frosts away. Fitz sat beside me. He didn't make to speak or even gesture my way. It was just the silent camaraderie I had come to appreciate from him. A simple gesture of presence meant the world but this morning I would be the one to break the silence.

"There once was a madman that walked the woods speaking of things that he could not know. A child stuck in the well by the cliffs, the wolves were hunting in the Western fields, the village chief had a boil on his inner left thigh that was making it hard to sit or pleasure his woman. So many secrets and pieces of intel he would mumble about the villagers that he was exiled from Three Pine Village to live as a hermit. At times, those who thought his ramblings prophecy, would bring him food to hear about their own futures. Sometimes, good news, but often times, more secrets unrelated to their own questions."

Fitz sat silently listening to my story, decency and an honest upbringing allowing me to finish.

"At times he was asked how he knew what he did, and always he would offer one name. Imil Idrikin, the three faced good of life, death and undeath. People then began to fear his words, for this God was a trickster and loved to gamble with the fates of men. They left him to his hovel and visited no more.

"Fire came from the south in the form of BrongTa. Fire wielders, too afraid of the ice wielders in the North to sleep comfortably in their beds at night. A continent away with nothing of interest between them and they felt the need to bring war upon the Fibonacci 'just in case'. A war that still lasts today in the hearts of those that know it. Hatred runs strong in family bloodlines even when the origin of that hatred was long forgotten.

"It was the madman, Joquil, who put forward the possibility of the Lich. This creature born of ice and death could return our people to the living to continue fighting the BrongTa threat. His soul would be tied to an object of power and therefore could not be killed without first destroying the object. The Fibonacci couldn't lose and very few opposed this idea. The great chief, Abacus, offered himself to become the Lich with eight ruling families sacrificing their leader's lives, strength and intelligence to bolster Abacus and craft this cursed spell. And Joquil himself offered his body to become the Phylactery of Abacus, his form transforming into the three headed statue of Imil Idrikin. As a last act to secure their victory, Joquil wove into the magic a curse on his own statue. A curse that would only allow the children of Fibonacci to touch it or have their lives drained instantly."

"You know where it is, don't you?" Fitz said, hope flaring in his eyes.

"Looking out over this land I had avoided for centuries has brought back memories I didn't know I still had. Riding on dad's shoulders in the first snow fall of winter. Fighting with my brother over who gets to eat the liver of a recent kill. My mum reprimanding me for playing in a dry well."

"They are dangerous. You don't know if there are pockets of water ready to break through or even if the structure is sound after so many years."

"It wasn't that. At the age of 11 you are considered Fibonacci but I was barely 5. At the bottom of the well was the sanctum of Imil Idrikin, hidden away in the forgotten catacombs. If I was to touch the totem before my bloodline awakened, even to feel its texture, my life, my very soul, would have been ripped from my body and my flesh made an instrument of Abacus. Mum didn't want to see that happen."

"They can be protective," Fitz said with a smile. "So, what now. We raid the village ruins, fighting through hordes of the undead to get you to the shrine and destroy the statuette?"

I nodded, rather nonchalant. "The only problem is we don't know if I can touch it."

"How so?" Baras said walking up behind us to stand at my side, arms crossed, looking out over the valley. "You are Fibonacci, are you not?"

"I am in a body with no direct link to my ancestors. My blood didn't awaken at 11 and it was only when I drew on the power of Shard's energy lines, lines drenched in Fibonacci power from draining my ice barrier, that I even conjured ice at all. Only when my mind was fully awakened did I remember the arts of ice completely. It isn't something we can rely on."

"So, what are you saying? You could die the moment you reach the idol?" Fitz asked, concern showing in his features.

"I'll do it," Baras said and we both looked at him. He could really be a dope sometimes.

"You touch it, you definitely die. I am the last direct descendant of the Fibonacci clan... indirectly. I am our only hope of accomplishing this task. The risk of death still high but it isn't absolute like both of you."

Pursing his lips, Baras just let out a soft growl from somewhere in his throat emphasising his unease with the plan.

"We don't do it and Abacus keeps coming back?" Fitz asked.

"Yes," I replied.

"And he will one day achieve what he is after? Either through a single moment of negligence from us or our replacements?"

"Yes," I replied again. It wasn't a matter of if. Abacus didn't need food or sleep. He could hunt us night and day until we dropped from exhaustion if he wanted to.

"Then this is our first option."

"There's more than one?"

"There is. Baras will try after you," Fitz said simply and Baras nodded.

"But..." my brow furrowed.

"Then me, and Kymberlin when she arrives. I won't force him but Enzo can have a go also. It'll starve the Lich of options for stealing souls and when the Phoenix are reborn, they can choose not to bond with another Soul. Once they are released from this world there will be nothing more Abacus can do. He will fail."

"I can live with that win," Baras said.

"Ah, no. You won't, Baras," I told him gently.

"You know what I mean," Baras said. "A last hoorah. To go down fighting knowing it meant something."

"Enzo will never go for it. The whole reason he is still alive today is because he fears death. He is much like the Lich in that respect."

"The only reason we have a chance today is because he fell for the enemy."

My eye twitched. "The only good coincidence that came from that. Don't bring it up again. Though, I want you to both promise me something."

"Anything," Baras and Fitz said in unison.

"If I fall and Enzo won't go next, you find a way to give him a final end before you take your turns."

"I don't know." Baras replied.

"Non-negotiable. It's all for nothing if Enzo won't submit. And don't think I won't slap you in soul form."

"Ok, we agree. Right, Baras?"

Baras just nodded sternly.

"You wouldn't have gone out to scout the lands by chance this morning?" Fitz then asked.

"I can't," I replied shaking my head. "I could possibly perform some close healing in the field but a free spirit tethered to a body is a free spirit up for grabs. Abacus could win in a moment of me flying free. I just can't take that risk."

"Still sends a shiver up my spine every time you talk of becoming a ghost," Baras said with a shudder.

I grinned mischievously. "You should be more worried about whether I have front row seats to yours and Kymmie's show."

"Don't," Baras's finger shot up to stop me in my tracks. "You're going to give me performance anxiety watching over her shoulder all the time."

"Oh, she's on top, is she?"

"Stop, Ellie," Baras said, going red. Fitz was already bawling with laughter.

"Your privacy is safe, Baras. I wouldn't do that to a friend... and then tease them for it."

Fitz's laughter doubled as Baras frowned undecided if that was a good thing or not. And I let my friends mind fester on the possibilities.

"I think it's time we paid a visit to my birthplace. It's been too long."

"Are we flying in?" Baras asked as Fitz was still a mess.

"We'll touchdown there," I pointed at a clearing near a lake. "It's a short trek at that point, but better than being dropped into the middle of an ambush."

"I don't know," Baras said trying to conceal a smile. "What about the Centaurs?"

"Don't." I grinned.

"Agreed then."

"I'll let you tell Enzo we are leaving," I said. I had no desire to talk to the man even vicariously through Shard and Talon. It always left a bitter taste in my mouth I couldn't wash away.

"He already left, a half hour before you came to the cliff side. He's doing large circles of the field," Fitz said, finally recovering. He pointed to a small speck high in the sky to the North.

"Bastard could have let us in," I grumbled. "Not like he can give away our position with Abacus in my head but it's good to know where you allies are."

"Maybe that was the point. That you didn't know, Ellie." Baras replied with one of his rare logical remarks.

"Expect an assault at any point," I replied ignoring the logic, then focused on Shard. *"That goes for you too."*

"Don't come grumbling at me when you don't understand tactics as

well as your comrades," Shard replied with a noise I've decided was definitely some form of bird laugh.

"Hmph," I said aloud and headed for where the Phoenix were roosting.

The flight was short, and I was beginning to get nervous. The enemy knew what we were doing, knew I was going for the one thing that could end Abacus for good. So where was he? I could feel more comfortable sneaking by enemy patrols, but the quiet. Either something big was coming or... No, I can't doubt myself. The idol needs to be here.

"When will you be dropping the armour, Elara? It makes for an uncomfortable flight," Shard said as I dismounted.

I looked down at the ice armour. It was my protection. My heart commenced an array of acrobatics every time I even thought of removing it.

"I. I just can't right now," I stammered weakly.

"You will find that if the world really wanted to harm you, it won't matter how many layers of ice you have around your heart. The pain will still seep through. Your real armour is your friends and the ones who love you. They won't stop the pain, but they will pick you back up and heal you."

I took a deep breath and when I spoke there was sadness in my voice. "I'm not ready."

"I know, Elara ShardSoul, but we are, when you can transition."

I couldn't reply. It was too heartbreaking to think of that kind of strength right now. Instead, I focused on the mission ahead and called for the others to follow. I was right to say Kymberlin wouldn't make it in time. She'd probably still be arguing with Suniel for all his stubbornness.

"Keep your guard up. We can't know what we may be walking into and don't forget, the enemy has the ability to portal in. Green lights give them away."

I started sifting through the trees keeping partially hidden from what laid ahead at all times. It was like seeing an old friend after many moons. The land unfolded before me, and I began to remember every intricate little detail as if it was a living part of me. Some of the trees had changed and grown tall, others were left laying where they had fallen or not there at all should their wood have been harvested. 300 years can change a lot but the soul of the land, that remained beautiful and untouched.

Pushing forward I got down on my belly at the crest of a hill and motioned for the others to do the same. All but Enzo followed the command. He, instead, stood at the base of the rise with arms crossed.

Bastard, I thought to myself but kept shimmying to the edge. The ruins of Three Pine Village were just over the other side. I wanted to remain vigilant right up until I knew for sure we were made.

Peering over the edge, I saw the entrance to the village through the trees. Most of the wall had been destroyed either through fire or decay with the gates not keeping anything out anymore. One was laying upon the frozen earth with the other barely hanging on by a single hinge. I was surprised the weight hadn't torn it away decades ago.

I still couldn't see any movement of the enemy and was beginning to doubt whether we were on the correct path but as Fitz came up beside me, he swore. It was a harsh curse that would only be used on your worst enemies... or Enzo and I scanned the fields before I spotted what he had. My heart sank as two figures stepped out from either side of the ruined walls.

Still dressed in their rangers clothing, hooded and armed, were Caeli and Dustin. Large chunks of flesh were torn away and missing all over their bodies from the Terror Hound attack and their clothing was barely holding together. It was as though Abacus had taken them straight from their deaths to be here before us. It was a sick and twisted act and I wasn't about to let my friends be used this way. Rising from where I lay, I charged over the hill.

"Ellie, wait," Fitz called, reaching out but I was locked in my motions and slipped away too quickly. "Damn it." Fitz grumbled following me, with Baras close behind. He already had his bow out and shot Dustin in the chest. There was no reaction from our friend. I wouldn't expect there to be as the life force of Caeli and Dustin had already been syphoned into the nesting grounds. These were just reanimated hunks of flesh and bone.

As I was coming up on our friends, Fitz had caught up to and overtaken me. Leaping into the air, Fitz speared into Dustin feet first sending them both to the ground while I blocked a savaged cut to my neck with my sabre before all but severing Caeli's left arm. Shreds of her leather armour, the only thing stopping the limb from falling to the ground. Baras stepped around me and lopped her head off in a clean cut.

I turned back to Fitz to find him straddling Dustin with a hand on his chest. At another time, this may have been a pleasant sight but as Dustin's eyeballs began to bubble and smoke started pouring from his ears, I turned away. I hadn't the stomach to watch even the corpse of a friend burn from inside out. A horrid stench struck my nose causing me to immediately empty my stomach at Baras's feet. Stepping back he wiped the vomit away with some fresh snow.

"How can you be so stupid as to run out into enemy territory," Fitz yelled at me for what I think was the first time since we met. I could see he was pained by being forced to destroy his friends.

"I couldn't let them be used by Abacus," I returned but it felt weak to his words.

"And we wouldn't have, but anything could have happened," Fitz said, still some mongrel in his voice. He knelt down beside Caeli, touching each section and melting her away. "You have too much emotion on the field. You don't know how to play it safe. You are our best chance to take out Abacus and if this had of been a trap..."

Green portals began opening around the field and large numbers of the enemy stepped through. Terror Hounds bayed and Chimera roared as more and more of the hoard of undead filled the area. Up in the sky, harpies and winged horses burst into existence to bring the fight to the Phoenix. At least there were no Wyrms this time.

"You gotta be fucking kidding me," Fitz said watching the portals open and let out a deluge of enemies. "This is why we act with caution."

"Sorry," I said, knowing I was the sole reason for walking into this. With a cross slash, I took out a Terror Hound as it raced in ahead of the rest.

"Now isn't the time to apologise. Save it for after the battle. We need to get into the village. Where is the well?"

"North end near the lightning touched tree," I called above the rabble.

Baras, Fitz and I created a small fighting circle and begun the slow push for the catacombs. There was fighting on all fronts and everyone was doing their best with sword, fire and, in my case, ice, but it was hard. Already fatigue felt like it was right around the corner and we'd barely made a few metres.

In the sky, flames of oranges and blues powered through the ranks but as some windows into the sky above began to open, they were instantly sealed again by reinforcements. Nothing so far was going our way.

Then there was that dickhead. As casually as could be, as if out for a morning stroll, Enzo came wandering over the hill. He didn't race to our aid or send rivers of fire to eat at our enemies' heels so as to give us a little traction. No. He walked close to the enemy rear and waited until noticed before engaging in the battle.

Once he did, Enzo set about a flurry of attacks that gouged into the enemy ranks giving no time or manoeuvrability for the enemy to flank him. It created a small buffer for us but it seemed the enemy only started engaging Enzo to keep him from advancing further. He wasn't taking any of this seriously and I actually hoped one of the undead or Chimera could end him.

"I will have that one's soul soon enough," an undead warrior hissed and my eyes went wide.

I understood Abacus could speak through the dead but I believed it only worked on touch. I was a fool to think the use of Riven in communicating wasn't only a psychological battle but Abacus was that twisted. Just like Caeli and Dustin were used to break my mind that little bit more.

Trapping a thrusted spear between arm and side, I dispatched the fighter with a thrust to the throat.

"Very good, *Elllliie*. So nimble," The next undead said and my eyes saw red.

I jumped at him knocking the creature with a half-melted face to the ground.

"Shut up. Shut up. Shut up!" I screamed pounding the decaying face into mush.

What I didn't realise was the gap I made in our defence stepping out of line. It was Baras that took up the slack, killing the undead who charged the hole with a continuous burst of flame while still managing to protect his own quarter.

"Elara, close in," Baras ordered and I was able to catch myself long enough to fall back to the circle.

"Don't let his words control you. He is a coward, hiding in the background," Fitz said and I nodded.

Once I worked out how well ice took down Chimera, they became laughable. Any time one started into a charge, I would pepper it with ice spears from the sky leaving it dead or dying in the path, ready to be feasted upon by the Phoenix. It became so natural to me that when a Chimera that looked to have the body of one of those white, snow bears, and a tongue like a frog, kept coming after my barrage, I froze. It was only a split second to comprehend how the beast peppered with spikes could keep moving but it was enough to allow it to capture me. Its huge stretchy tongue wrapped around my body, pinning my arms at my sides and started to haul me in to its slavering maw. I struggled in getting free noting both Fitz and Baras were too deeply occupied to help. I just couldn't think, watching the sharp teeth inch closer.

"*Incoming,*" Shard announced before he and Flint crafted a corridor of flame straight through the Chimera, ending at the ruins of some stone buildings. The meeting hall and medic house.

Struggling out of the slackening tongue, I still had to cut through it with my first freed arm to make my escape. The tongue was so rubbery it took three hard cuts to get through. Finally, getting the loops of flesh up and over my head, I saw Baras pointing to the flame walls.

351

"They're running round the buildings trying to cut us off. We need to make it through first," he called and without waiting, took off to secure our exit, taking out the two undead stuck within our sanctuary. It was Fitz who snagged the Terror Hound midflight with a dagger. The beast had leapt from the other side of the firewall at Baras, catching fire as he went. When it was killed, it became dead weight and barreled into Baras almost sending him to the dirt but he recovered and continued through. The flames of little consequence

As Baras was about to clear the corner of the buildings, he shouted, "This way," and threw himself through an open door. We barely scraped in ourselves with hordes of the undead cascading around the corner after flashes of green reflected in the surrounding stone. With Baras baring the door using some rotted wood, I reinforced it with solid ice. Immediately, there was banging from outside as they tried to force their way in. Rotting hands and skeletal arms tried reaching through any hole they could find but to no avail. One arm dropped off and dragged itself to where I stood, grabbing my foot with surprising strength. Kicking it, I was able to boot the boney hand high through a hole in the roof and back outside.

"What now?" I asked the others. I hadn't been great with my choices today and needed to clear my head.

Baras shook his too. "Split second decision to keep us safe a little longer. We weren't in a position to defend right away."

"It won't be long before they start teleporting straight in. How far to the well?" Fitz asked.

I thought about it a moment. "The well is set close to here. It was designed to cater for the medic before the feud with the BrongTa. 10, 20 metres at most."

"Think you can get us up there," Fitz asked, pointing to the hole where I'd kicked the groper arm.

"What other choice have we?" I said with a smile.

"Can always wait for your savior, Enzo, to come along and rescue us," Baras said with a laugh.

A shot him a dark glare and without looking, erected a simple staircase to reach the ceiling. I noted the ice on the door had weakened to craft this and knew my mental strength was fading.

"We need to be quick. The ice is fading."

"You're using too much to keep that armour in place," Fitz remarked.

"I'm not removing it," I growled a bit harsher than intended. Regret for my tone ate at me and I tried again in a quieter voice. "I'm not going to remove it."

"I didn't expect you to. We're in the midst of a battle. Lead on."

I could hear the sadness sliding beneath his words. There was a lot I needed to make up for when this was over. Climbing from step to step I reached the top to peer over. Gropey was back and I flicked it from the structure with a quick backhand. Baras and Fitz poked their heads up beside me.

Finding my bearings, I motioned to the well. "Guess it was a little further than I remembered," I said, noting the 30-metre distance still to go.

"It was a fair guess for a three-hundred-year-old memory," Fitz said.

The dead stalked beneath and all focused on our position. There was no way to hide what we were doing against Abacus. It all came down to how we could get to our goal regardless and all I could think of was an ice bridge.

"When we start moving stay close behind. I reckon the platform will only be 2 metres in length and disappearing fast behind us."

"What platform?" Baras asked.

"No questions. Just act. You'll know what to do. I should have just enough energy left to reach the well."

Crafting the first two legs of the bridge, I formed the platform above them. A loud crack boomed as the door gave way and the horde filled the room, coming up quick behind us.

"Let's go," I said and started over the bridge. To my relief, Fitz and Baras heeded my words. Keeping the bridge moving along with legs and platforms, it ate into the back half off it but I didn't turn to watch it melt away. My mind was completely focused on...

"Above," Shard screamed in my mind, an accompanying screech sounding far above.

Looking up my heart sank as hundreds of harpies were speeding straight towards us in a spiraling attack, moments away from colliding. There was nothing we could do but brace ourselves as best we could.

To use an ice shield could very well destroy the structure below us and I didn't trust the use of flame wouldn't do the same, regardless. A flurry of wings and scaley legs rammed us, sending us tumbling from the bridge to the hard snow below. We had no time before the undead began to fall upon us, holding us in place as much as we struggled. Even when we managed to dislodge one, another was ready to take its place.

They didn't want us dead. They only wanted us trapped. That could only mean... I looked around and sure enough a new portal had opened close by. The robed and boney form of the Lich steeping through. A deep ingrained fear spread through my body and I couldn't believe I was

353

about to do this but with a deep breath, I cried out.

"Enzo, help!" The words tasted of acid as they left my mouth and bounced from building to building. I waited only a moment.

"The Phoenix Soul is otherwise occupied, daughter of Fibonacci. He will not be rescuing you." One of the many assailants holding me down spoke for Abacus. The, Lich glided softly over the ground trailing a green, misty aura in his wake. "Have you considered claiming your rightful place with me?"

That would almost be as bad as calling the dickhead for help. He should have taken the battle more seriously. "Go back to the void and decay to nothing," I said looking away.

"So be it, Fibonacci's heir. Your bloodline ends today giving me my final desire."

As the white, shriveled hand reached for my neck, a horn sounded from the woods nearby. It was taken up by another and another until a chorus of horns sounded all around, giving hesitation and confusion to Abacus's actions.

An old fear awoke in me. It was a fear living in my blood and in an instant, I found myself in the town square as a child. The chorus of horns all around as dad scooped me up into his arms.

"No, the ravagers are coming," I began to cry and thrash wildly against my captives.

From the sky, in a fiery blaze, came a trail of flame screaming towards us. At the last moment it turned away and Kymberlin leapt from Ash to smash into the ground sending a shockwave of flame. All the undead within ten metres were launched far across the field and we found ourselves free of our captives.

"Need a hand?" Kymberlin asked but I hadn't the capacity to answer.

From the woods came a battle cry as Korr and hundreds of his Kin raced into Three Pine. The BrongTa had entered the field to kill and ravage once more.

"The ravagers are coming," I repeated over and over again as I held my head, trembling in fear.

"What's her problem?" Kymberlin asked as she kissed Baras after picking him up off the ground. Both he and Fitz shrugged, just as confused. Kymberlin then smiled. "I've been wanting to do this."

Picking me up, Kymberlin slapped me hard across the face, breaking my momentary lapse of sanity. With hand on my chin, I focused on my attacker and found Kymberlin smiling back at me. She was definitely a sight for these sore eyes and I pulled her into a tight embrace.

"Oh, she has really lost it," Kymberlin said, clearly ill at ease with the affection.

"It's so good to see you. I feared Suniel wouldn't send reinforcements." There was still a tremble in my voice but my nerves were settling as I took in some deep breaths.

"The General?" Kymberlin pushed me back. "Ha. I didn't even waste the time going to him."

"Then who...?" I looked around noting the dark complexions and lack of clothing. Many of the fighters were wielding flames as they fought the enemy back with a number of allies surrounding Abacus, keeping him in check. And there in the midst of the heaviest fighting was Korr and his maniacal laugh.

"The BrongTa?" I exclaimed, hand over my mouth. No wonder I was affected so, with the very tribe responsible for my parent's death ascending on Three Pines again. "How?"

"Korr already rallied them to our cause, speaking of the Fibonacci girl trying to put an end to the Lich and its madness. I met them on the road and convinced them to up their timeline. We marched all night and straight into battle."

"You didn't march a single step did you." I raised an eyebrow at Kymberlin who smiled a devilish grin.

"Not at all. I came here riding on the back of Ash. The ride was so easy, I even got myself a few Zs."

"Well, put the sleep to good use protect me on my way to the well yonder."

"Can do," Kymberlin said.

"And Kymmie."

"Hmmm?"

"Don't think that slap was free," I said with fierce eyes edging along a smile. I turned and began a jog to the well

"Just try and get one over me," Kymberlin replied before heading after me, Fitz and Baras, close behind.

All around were fighting and brawls. Mostly the undead were falling to the BrongTa under sword and flame but a few of the allies gave their lives also. It was a sad moment watching people die to the puppets of Abacus. The enemy was already dead and had no right to take a life from those yet to live theirs. I needed to make this quick.

Weaving through the masses, I took to barging and knocking over those that came against me, leaving the dispatching to my friends. It was the quickest way to reach the well but just as I was coming to it, a large scaled beast much like a massive snake encircled the well forcing me to a halt.

The creatures head, swayed this way and that in a hypnotic dance as it watched me. This was going to be close because if it moved like a regular snake, I was going to need to read its intentions and dodge preemptively.

Its neck coiled back and I ran forward diving to the side as the dripping maw overshot me. With a stolen grunt, I rolled hard on my shoulder, coming up alongside its body. Two bursts of fire exploded overhead and I looked up with terrified eyes to find the snake had pulled back above me extremely quick and only the two fireballs from Baras and Kymberlin distracted it from striking.

The recovery speed was unnatural and I had no doubt Abacus had a hand in it. The creature struck again and again as I barely rolled out of reach each time.

Stumbling, I knew I wouldn't be able to move fast enough this time and turned to see needle sharp fangs, venom dripping in great gobs, closing in. The sun darkened and shadows covered my world as the head filled my vision, drowning out the life beyond. Even the smell of its putrid breath was enhanced in these final moments, the smell of death and decay preluding the outcome.

Then a glint of radiant light touched my cheek, filling my sight with promise. The blade of a longsword, swung underhanded, cleaved through scale and flesh, opening the neck of this reptilian beast. And with the strength of the wielder and the weight of the snake, the head was cut through in one fluid movement to roll forwards with the momentum and land harmlessly past my head. It took a moment for the blood to catch up and three pumps of dark fluid splattered my armour.

A dark hand was offered to me and I took it gratefully.

"Swift, Ellie. Victory waiting," Korr said. Of course it was Korr. There was no one else with such perfect timing as he.

"Thank you, Korr, for tidying up the fight. Clearly, I had it under control but your interlude was welcome," I said, a cheeky grin on my face.

Korr just scoffed and moved onto the next battle.

Climbing over the scaly beast, I slid to the entrance of the well and peered inside. Thank the Gods the ladder was still intact, if not a little worse for wear. I tested each wooden rung as I descended and only over stepped one thinking it groaned a bit too much to ever take my weight. It was as easy a climb as it always was and now, I was on the threshold of where I knew I wasn't allowed to be. Mother made sure I understood it was taboo, even smacking me for playing with the other kids near the well.

There were so many memories resurfacing since entering Three Pines.

Strong memories that still made me uneasy entering this place. Fingers trembling, I took hold of the lopped handle and pushed inwards. Hairs on top of my head and down my arms began to rise as a static atmosphere flowed from behind the door. Sparks of electrical atoms pulsed and played within the room, a small area no bigger than the rooms of an inn. In the darkness with the hint of light from above me, I saw the three headed idol of Imil Idrikin. It was a curious hunk of wood with the three phases of life, death and undead, etched around its body. I wasn't exactly sure what to expect of this thing having never seen it myself, but I did believe it was going to be made of stone. Something that would last the ages. To see it had been carved from the wood of the timeless tree was a surprise but actually made a fair amount of sense. It would never decay for time would never touch it.

I reached out intent on taking the idol but recoiled quickly. It was an enlightening moment that even when I wanted the cold slumber of death to take away my pains, deep down, I still wasn't ready to give it all up. There was a part of me locked in the darkness, still fighting to break free.

I sighed deeply. Then I will destroy it here without laying a finger on it. As a wooden statuette, I decided flames would be more than adequate. Low on energy, I focused on a flame between my hands, allowing it to grow with intensity and strength, folding in on itself and becoming denser. When I felt ready, I willed the dark flames of destruction to pour down on the idol to engulf it and rip it's form from existence.

Blood red flames spiraled around the idol encasing it, but at close proximity the heat and destruction was absorbed into the pedestal on which it sat, leaving it safe. Brows furrowed, I tried again changing to ice. Again, the pedestal drew in the raw, magical energy and changed it into a more natural state, feeding the earth.

"Damn it." I said mulling over the conundrum. The setup was designed in such a way that the idol would have to be picked up. Even striking the piece with sword or axe, the idol would still absorb your life force using the weapon as a catalyst.

"Elara, hurry that chunky, fucking arse of yours up. Enzo and the Lich are fighting and Enzo ain't doing too well," Kymberlin called down into the well.

"Shit, fucking dickhead," I said, reaching out and pausing inches from the idol. I tried to remain calm, keep my breathing tempered but my nerves got the better of me and I began to breath at a highly increased pace until there was nothing left in my mind but taking it. On impulse, with my mind running blank, I scooped the Idol up, drawing it to me with both hands.

Immediately, an electrical surge forced its way through flesh and blood. Not a part of me remained untouched and I screamed in agony from the raw power. I tried to let go but my fingers tensed tightly on their own locking the idol in place. Power flowed from me. Energy reserves began to deplete themselves into this chunk of wood and I knew it wasn't my lifeforce it was taking. As my ice armour begun to dissipate, breaking down into raw energy and flowing into the totem piece, I finally understood why it was a Fibonacci could survive such a horrid curse. They would pay with the very essence that made them Fibonacci. My ice, my cold veins, the link to my ancestors, it was all flowing from me and feeding Abacus's strength.

Finally, in my weakened form, the pain but a memory, I found myself crying in the soft earth. One hand still holding the idol, but I began to question if anything even mattered anymore. The one thing that made me who I was, the only thing kept from my original life, had been stripped from me. I laid there in the dirty tunic I'd worn since escaping torture. My armour against the world gone. My soul in tatters. I couldn't even conjure an ice knife to end it all.

"Come to me and I will give you what you seek with my blessings and best wishes," Shard said. *"It will not matter if the idol is not destroyed. And if it is, you will have earned your rest."*

"You would give me death?"

"You need only ask, my Soul, but hurry. Abacus is on the verge of winning. If he does, it would be in his power to bring you back and continue your torment."

The words were frighteningly true. If I ever expected to find real rest, I needed to deal with Abacus first. To see how he treated my friends at the gates and the number of times I'd gone against him, I was sure to have lifetimes of torture ahead should we fail this day.

Pushing myself to unsteady feet, I wobbled a moment trying to get my bearings. The idol had all but drained me and I felt like I'd been binge drinking all day and night. My mouth was dry and my eyes stung, but there was even worse than that. I was cold! The chill draft from the winter world above gave me goosebumps and set a shiver to my muscles. The tunic did little to protect me from that which I had loved since the moment I could call myself Fibonacci.

Thinking of the BrongTa and the way their flames kept them warm even in the harshest of environments, I had to rely on the flame if I could even ignite it.

"I'll provide you energy for everything you need, Elara, Soul of my own," Shard said.

He was being extra nice at the moment but pity can make way for that.

"I do not pity the Ice Maiden her loss. I cry with her in heartache. Your pain is mine also."

I pursed my lips at the sentiment lest I truly do cry again. Focusing on my skin, I ignited the smallest of flame to warm me and protect against the elements I so loved. There was instant relief and after a moment adjusting, I found a temperature suitable to my liking. It would disgrace my family name but this was now about survival and, honestly, the Fibonacci name had been disgraced the moment they conjured Abacus.

"They felt the need for survival too, against the BrongTa and their growing power. The same sentiment but a more terrible outcome. They are responsible but don't cast a stone without knowing they were trying to protect themselves."

Not an argument I wanted to face.

Stumbling along, I grabbed the first rung of the ladder and braced myself to begin the harsh climb. It was strenuous on my already worn muscles, especially juggling the idol. I didn't want to risk putting it down again. I couldn't be sure it would still recognize me if I tried to pick it up a second time. It was a definite this time. I had nothing more to give than my life.

Reaching the top rung, I came upon a harrowing scene. Enzo was being held aloft at the throat by Abacus. He was struggling against the grip of the boney arm but nothing he did made any progress at getting free. With blood draining from my face, Abacus turned to lock eyes onto me.

"I see you have found my hidden totem and feed more power into my lifeforce. I thank thee, daughter, not of my line, but you are too late. Witness the birth of immortality," Abacus said through a random undead.

A green, glowing mist swirled from Enzo's mouth to slowly creep forth towards Abacus. The Lich had his mouth open ready to absorb the lifeforce. I watched it moving almost painfully slow and a niggling feeling gnawed at the back of my mind. I didn't give it heed as I was frozen on the spot trying to decide whether I wanted Abacus to be ultimately stopped, or allow Enzo to die a miserable death. Each had its pros and cons but something just didn't add up.

An eruption of fire, sent undead in every direction as Fitz broke free of the fighting. He raced over the field towards the Lich, sword blazing in a molten coating and then it all clicked. The niggling feeling that I couldn't get past. It wasn't Enzo.

"No, Fitz! Get out of there!" I screamed at him but he didn't hear me already leaping to sever the arm holding Enzo aloft.

Fitz landed softly on his feet, with Enzo toppling to the dirt beside him. The ghostly white arm still holding to Enzo's neck as the green, misty substance reverted back into his mouth. Fitz looked back at me.

"That's not Enzo's soul! RUN!"

I watched in horror as Abacus, not missing a beat, scooped up Fitz with his other arm as if he was nothing. I saw a terrible pain fill Fitz's features. I couldn't get there in time. No one else was coming to his rescue either, all busy containing the fighting.

"A coward am I, hiding in the background?" Abacus said to Fitz with disdain.

I shook my head and screamed for Fitz as I struggled to climb from the well. And when I did, I stumbled upon the snake's body, face planting into the dirt. "This can't be the end. FITZ!"

And then Enzo was back on his feet beside them and I let out a sigh of relief. I watched, waiting for him to return the favour and save Fitz but Enzo just stood there. And Fitz looked like he was choking with arms tense and curled back just off his body.

"Save him, Enzo," I pleaded. "I'll do anything. I'll be yours. Just save him!"

Enzo stood as if in a trance and I shifted to my spirit form. Where Fitz looked like he was choking, a purple aura was draining from his mouth into Abacus. The rich and vibrant purple soul of Fitz had already started to be consumed. Looking to Enzo, my eyes widened in despair as the orange soul of Enzo was harmonising with the Lich. He was one of the Lich's undead lackies and I'm guessing had been for some time.

"Talon doesn't believe it. There's been no death," Shard said, unsure of his own words.

"I'm telling you that's not him. It's all been a ruse since the time Enzo was captured," I shot back with a touch of acid. Dread touched my heart as I watched my friend's soul literally sucked from his body, and I could do nothing to stop it.

A burst of adrenaline coursed through my system as I took control of my body and screaming Fitz's name, I let out a burst of flaming energy more like a pulse wave that sent everyone to the ground.

Abacus floated just above the ground, unphased by my attack. He let the body of Fitz fall to lay beside the toppled Enzo. I began to step towards him. Each footfall a work of malice and hate.

"Why?" It came as a whisper to begin with, as I barely controlled my rage. But as I got closer, my voice grew into a vicious growl full of contempt. "Why do all of this just to get the soul of a Phoenix Soul? You could have taken Enzo's at any time. You could have taken mine just as easily in capacity. Tell me why you are so sick and twisted that you need to put everyone through such pain and destruction."

A wicked smile filled Abacus's face and when he spoke, he spoke with his own booming voice, fluid and clear.

"Since the dawn of time I have longed to be free but the other God's feared my power, my ability. I could not absorb Enzo's soul because I had already killed him before finding out what I needed and I could not absorb yours, Daughter, once of the Fibonacci, because I needed you to freely relinquish your Ancestral energy into the idol. The Soul of flame and the Heart of ice."

The three faced idol started to vibrate in my hands. The tremors grew with such intensity, I couldn't hold it anymore and the Idol flew from my grasp. It shot across the grounds and was absorbed by the timeless tree.

"Now, all I need is but a few moments for my ascension to be complete."

'You won't get it," I said picking up the nearest sword.

But Abacus was already floating towards the tree smiling.

"Don't you run from me. STAY AND FIGHT, ABACUS!"

"No, my dear servant. Not Abacus. I am Imil Idrikin."

The words froze my heart as I realised the weight of everything that was happening. I'd been played by the trickster God and now he was moments from assimilating with the 'Soul' and 'Heart' to become immortal on the physical plain. I struggled to pick up speed across the grounds. Calling for help, no one answered as they were all starting to recover from my pulse attack. Even the Phoenix, as they swooped forward, lost the race. Imil Idrikin touched the timeless tree and merged into the wood. Every trace of him gone from this world.

"No," I ran forward and bashed on the tree. My force only tripling and repelling back into me, smashing me to the ground.

The Phoenix landed in the field, some looking at the tree. Talon assessed Enzo's now still form lying on the ground, and Flint...

A heartbreaking cry rose around the village and I knew Fitz had passed. But it wasn't the time for tears. We needed Flint and every abled fire user to reign destruction down on this tree. We couldn't risk giving the God the time he needed to be able to walk the physical plain indefinitely.

"Flint cries for even the soul of Fitz FlintSoul has left this realm. This will be Flint's final days. We will mourn our sister," Shard said.

"The days of mourning are yet to come," I said loud enough for all to hear as I rose to my feet once more. "The enemy is still alive and a bigger threat than ever. You all have a choice to make. You choose how many loved ones you will mourn this day and the future days to come. Imil Idrikin, the enemy of all life, is still fighting, still becoming stronger. We need to fight back now to preserve what little we have left. What is your choice? Who will lend me their strength in this?"

Many BrongTa and Phoenix stood silent, contemplating their decision. Even my friends who would normally have my back were stuck in silent thought. No one moved and I believed it was all going to be in vain. A Lich? Maybe, but what reason would someone have to go up against a God. Especially one known for his undue torment and pain.

Feathers nuzzled at my hand, and I looked down to find Flint beside me. She looked up at me, her eyes defeated but willing to push forward and a lump formed in my throat.

"For Fitz, the very best of us," I said nodding and Flint chirped.

In that moment, the dam burst and all but a few who were injured took up the call and stepped forward. Phoenix, friends, past enemies turned ally. We were all ready to fight. I was thankful that none of the undead had become animated again since Imil Idrikin left the field.

We circled the tree, with focus and determination, the Phoenix taking up positions North, South, East, and West. I looked around to find Talon missing from the bunch. He was still back, hanging over Enzo. About to call to him, I was interrupted by Shard.

"Leave Talon be. He won't be of any help at this time. Imil Idrikin has detached and the

pain has started to set in. His choices are to begin resurrecting Enzo now in his existing body as it was untouched and viable or become crippled by the pain until he starves to death, in what could be weeks, or days if someone takes pity, before they are both reborn."

I let out a sigh as glowing embers appeared, as if separating from Talon, to float down upon Enzo bringing warmth and life. It was out of my hands, and I turned back to the main issue.

"Everyone, focus your strongest attacks on the trunk. One or two of us may not be enough to break through but together I know we will," I called. The belief was false, but the hope was high. The group just needed faith.

Flames of many different hues and colours, strength and heat, converged on the trunk of the timeless tree. Some came in streams while others rained down fireballs or erupted streams of flame up the tree's trunk. One exceptional BrongTa even wielded fire wrapped in lightning, and it was this that destroyed the first fragments of the tree.

A great cheer went up, and the group continued with renewed vigour and force. From within the tree, the hues of whites and blacks started to take on a deeper glow of orange and yellow. It shone from within as if a sword on a blacksmiths forge, slowly gaining in heat and intensity. I could feel, the burning aura scorching and biting at my skin but I pushed forward. I gave it everything I had and when I felt I could do no more, dug even deeper, my mind swimming with exhaustion.

No one had been prepared for the explosion. A loud boom that coursed through mind and body, stealing hearing and causing more than one person to physically be sick on the field. Coloured lights of every colour danced and shifted and changed, darting and playing up into the sky to drift away on the four winds. The tree itself had been ripped apart with chunks of wood splinters scattered across the field. Apart from the split and charred trunk no higher than my knee, there was not a piece I couldn't wrap my fingers around.

It was a few long minutes before the chiming, ringing tone in my head subsided and the bright blinding light on my eyes faded away. Everyone seemed worse for wear but there was a consensus of smiles and relief. We were alive and that was all that mattered.

"You idiots. You've all been fooled and manipulated to one final purpose. The entirety of the Fibonacci clan's power that was already inside and a large mass of the BrongTa Clan's power reinforced by the stolen Phoenix Soul have come together to destroy the Timeless tree. The very shield that locked Imil Idrikin away. The war between BrongTa and Fibonacci was sparked by leaders of both clans so that there would never come a time when we would work together and free the Terrible God. Hate was supposed to win out," Enzo's voice broke through the cheers. He was leaning heavily against Talon with a grim expression. "I suggest running."

A dark laughter filled the field, chilling everyone to the bone. My shoulders sank as I watched the dark, misty form of Imil Idrikin growing into the sky to block out the sun and steal the light. Cries and screams of anguish filled the onlookers at a terrible rate and everyone fell into despair. The God's great and haunting eyes were overwhelming as they looked down into the very depths of all souls that gazed upon them.

"What's your plan?" Shard asked.

"Not falling into despair like the rest? Why are you still fighting?" I replied hopelessly.

"Why not? I've been listening to your depressive and self-abusive mind for days now. I have not the care to enhance the state by adding to it. What is your plan?"

"Leave me alone. Just let me pass from this world. It's lost anyway."

"Only when everyone gives up. I will fight."

"Then you will die."

"I know your heart, Ellie. You still have yet to give in. Your mind and your instincts are your deepest curse right now."

"You don't know."

"You didn't want to die in the well, and even now you felt a sudden sadness to even say I would die. You're still there, Elara. Fan the embers. Rekindle your flame."

Before I even had a chance to reply, Imil Idrikin began an assault. His great arm arcing through the atmosphere, destroying the top of the nearby cliffs and sending rocks and boulders in all directions on its way to pummel the massed group. People started running in every direction trying to get away from something that could flatten the entirety of Three Pine Village in moments. I stood my ground, more for the loss of where to run than any feelings of courage. Only one risked everything.

In a scorch of blue flame, Shard sped towards the incoming hand. Such a small creature against a God. I couldn't watch... I couldn't look away. A deep white glow manifested around him growing quickly. As Shard was about to hit the God's hand, he stalled mid-flight and spread his wings. A full circular rainbow encased the white light in a massive shield that burst in a brilliant arc of raw energy as the two powers collided.

The arm, all the way back above the elbow, disintegrated in dark wispy clouds and Imil Idrikin let out a bellowing cry that would have shaken the entire continent.

Like a shooting star, Shard was shot back along the course he'd flown to slam into the earth, gouging away the dirt.

It was then I noticed I'd been crying, and raced across to lift his head in my arms. I was dazzled by his transition. The deep blues I had come to know and love in his feathers had changed to a magnificent white, the flames almost burning clear.

With a weak shudder, Shard turned his head to me and let out a soft whistle. His body was spent and his eyes barely held mine.

"Why did you do that? Why did you have to attack him?"

His eyes closed a moment, and I thought he was gone from this world, but his head began to gently roll back and forwards.

"I did not attack him... Ellie. I protected... The ones I... Love." Shard's voice trembled in effort.

"Why for me? It should be me dying for you. I was the one that had a debt to make up for. I was the one that wanted to protect you." I bashed the ground as fallen tears sizzled on his feathers.

"Forgive yourself…" His breathing shuddered and there was a terrible rasp. He tried to speak again but it was garbled.

I glanced back at Imil Idrikin who, even now, was repairing his busted arm. The pieces floating back together in a dark mist.

"Forgive yourself the debt. It was repaid long ago. As you love me, I too hold you dear. You are worth protecting, Elara." Even his thoughts were dim.

"I'm nothing."

"You are everything and more. The path you have walked has been abusive and neglectful. You have been abandoned and lonely for a long time and every time you have tried to walk the right path it has backfired. That doesn't mean there will always be darkness. Take a moment to step back and settle your light. You can choose to walk away from any path and start again. You will find light again. All you need do is look. You are strong, Elara."

"And how do I walk away from a God?"

"You don't. You destroy it utterly."

I blanched. "With what? My flames are all but gone. My ice was stolen. Even your strength with the ascended white flames could barely wound it."

"A physical fight between a God and a human can be very one sided. But a Drifter… Those abilities are something even he could not have accounted for," Shard said and a last final breath shuddered through his beak.

"What abilities, Shard?" I asked but his head limped lifelessly to the side. Tears blurred my vision as I gently shook him. "What abilities?" Suddenly, there was cold once more. My breath turning to mist before me.

"You have no abilities now," Enzo said, coldly from behind. "Did Shard return to you what you need to be reborn before he died?"

Ignoring him, I placed Shard gently to the earth as his body had begun to return to ash. I looked around. Baras was tending to Kymberlin, a gash upon her leg, and Korr was talking to Flint quietly. Flint? But where was Fitz then? I looked around frantically before spying the body lying where he fell. The memories of the moment came flooding back in to weigh ever more on my heart then Shard alone.

I stumbled across to him shivering and trying to rub warmth into my arms. "I know you'll forgive me, dear friend, but I will be stealing this after all. No daggers in the night. Right?"

I gave a soft, sad chuckle and wiped a single tear away, as I removed his cloak and draped it around me. It blocked out the harshness of the wind and the beginnings of sleet. It wasn't going to keep me warm indefinitely but I'd been through worse. It'd do for now.

"Thank you, Fitzroy," I said, hand on his chest before turning to face the giant form of Imil Idrikin, hanging over the valley. He was almost completely mended.

A hard hand grabbed my wrist, turning me back. "Did Shard give to you, what you need to be reborn?" Enzo growled. He was becoming annoyed with me.

"The battle isn't over." I replied simply. I had nothing in me for him anymore. No love, no hate, no indifference. He was just another person of this world. Twisted and imperfect.

"If you can't be reborn, I won't let you go into battle. There is still a chance with Flint now that he has no Soul."

Maybe I did feel something dark towards Enzo. He had such a way with words that moved me. My stare became fierce. "You cannot stop me," I said, my voice dripping with venom.

Before he had a chance to reply, I shifted into my spirit form and grinned as he went out of his mind trying to wake me. "Serves you right."

"You have such great courage."

My heart stopped.

"Coming into battle without knowing the abilities I spoke of."

"Shard?" I finally whispered. Turning, I found him sitting tall in a blaze of white light. "Shard! I thought I'd never see you again." I ran to him and jumped into his chest for a warm embrace before scratching his neck. Even in spirit he was reacting with shivers of glee.

"We have a small amount of time left. I will be here until the suns final rays when I am born again within an egg to await your final death and be reborn. You though, will only have a short time before you soul is lost to the Aether. If that happens, we both die. You must defeat Imil Idrikin quickly."

"When this is all over you will not have to wait lon…"

"Do not make me your excuse to cut your life short. You will live a full and happy life like you always deserved. I will not accept your soul to awaken me should you end it quickly. Live in every way I want you to so that I may see it upon your death. You deserve life."

"I…"

Shard just tilted his head sternly and my shoulders sagged.

"I will live, Shard," I said, but could I live happily being guilted into it.

"When you find it, you will be able to."

"Find what?"

Shard gave an awkward, bird smile with the beak opening to a weird angle and tilting his head but remained quiet.

"Your hopeless," I said, the smile contagious. Turning, we faced the God together.

He was surprisingly small in this form, a shadow of himself was cast about him in the giant we all saw in the physical. A deep purple light shone within the God's chest. Fitz's spirit still fighting the assimilation.

Without taking my eyes from the God and my friend, I spoke to Shard. "What can I do?"

"You can do anything in spirit. Just know the bigger you go the quicker you'll drain away."

I smiled. "I don't need anything too big," I said before conjuring my ice sabre and armour. It wasn't true Fibonacci but rather a droplet of my own soul in the shape of my former items. "Keep him guessing, ok Shard?"

Shard let out a joyous whistle and took off into the air to circle above while I closed the distance between the God and I.

"Surprised you are still wanting to face me. Especially here in my realm," Imil Idrikin said, spreading his arms in a wide arc. He suddenly grunted and dove sideways as a ball of white flame sped through the point he stood moments before.

"Put that Accipitridae on a leash. This fights between you and I," Imil Idrikin growled.

"Shard is free of my influence. You saw to that," I replied. "If you're going to fight me, come on then. Quite with the blah blah blahdy blah." I made the mouth movements with my hand just to emphasise a little more and maybe get him worked up. It wasn't likely though.

When Imil Idrikin did come, he was fluid and in control. As he conjured a spear, I couldn't help but see the similarities to Riven's and knew to watch for the possibility of it splitting.

I allowed him his way with the first attack. There was a need to gauge his ability, knowing it was likely he would hold back at the start. When it came, I almost missed it. A purple flash along his arm causing me to move by instinct and I just tilted my head enough for the tip to graze my cheek. He brought it back to a two-handed stance and thrusted left and right in a flurry of moves before trying to sweep my legs. Each movement ate away a little more of Fitz's soul as he used the energy for strength and speed. It was useful for Imil Idrikin but he didn't realise yet. The slight flashes gave me just enough warning to get out of the way.

Another purple spark just above his knee and I jumped back expecting a kick. Nothing happened as Imil Idrikin just watch me closely for what I might do.

"Go left," Shard said and I dove right choosing Shard's left. Imil Idrikin, with his back to Shard, chose left and straight into a fire ball knocking him past me. I slashed at his back as a purple spark came into light right where I was aiming for. I hadn't the time to change tactics but the attack got through with no movement on the God's behalf.

Imil Idrikin doubled backwards in pain and I smiled remembering how Fitz used to show me where to attack and how to attack when he was teaching me, along with the dramatics of it all. After this attack came a simple neck slice. My breath caught in my throat as I saw a purple flash across Imil Idrikin's neck.

Hesitating too long, I lost my chance to attack as Imil Idrikin recovered and spun to face me once more. He was enraged now and danced through a number of manoeuvres that would have laid me low had I been unaware but I wasn't unaware. Fitz was helping me through it. He was showing me Imil Idrikin's intentions then highlighting the places for me to attack just like in our training sessions. He wasn't being used by the God. He was still fighting. A deep shame came over me for almost giving up before. He didn't even have a body and he was still fighting.

I danced along in the heated battle, swaying left and right always holding the upper hand. Even when Imil Idrikin got faster and more precise, Fitz just upped his timing to suit. Finally, I spotted an opening and funnelling spiritual energy through the sabre, sliced Imil Idrikin through his tendons on the right arm above the elbow. His wrist went limp and I stepped past him seeing another purple spot over his ankle. With a spinning cut, I clove through the Achilles tendons and Imil Idrikin, fell flat.

The light of Fitz had started to dim within Imil Idrikin. "That's enough my friend. Save some energy," I said and the purple all but vanished.

"I am not your friend," Imil Idrikin growled dangerously. "Even with one arm, I am still dangerous." I smiled realising he didn't have a clue where my advantage had come from.

He floated back upright, but Shard had been waiting for that. Diving in with claw's stretched out front, Shard sunk his talons deep into shoulder and stomach. A guttural cry arose from the God as Shard tried to tear him apart.

"No. Rip open his chest." I called.

Shard considered me a moment but trusted me to no end. Pinning the God, Shard tore through Imil Idrikin's rib cage.

"Perfect. Hold him a second."

"What are you doing?" Imil Idrikin cried as I thrust an arm in his chest.

"No. Don't do that. Leave me alone."

Pulling my hand away, I held it close to my chest and found I was beginning to go see through. "He's all yours, Shard. I need to head back. I'll speak to you on the cliff top."

Shard let out a brilliant twittering song and tore into the God. Destroying him utterly. I couldn't even remember my concerns going into the battle but with my friends, even going against a God was nothing.

Shifting back to my body I found a delicate scene unfolding. Enzo had Flint cornered demanding that she give me the essence that could make me immortal once more. Talon was shifting about around the outside of the confrontation but I could tell he was too frightened to get any closer. Enzo had a terrible hold over the Phoenix.

"Even if she accepts, how do you know I will?" I said and Enzo swung on me with fire in his eyes. "I mean, I was a pushover when I was younger and I still denied you. I am a completely different person now."

"You're forgetting it was I that made you drink the life essence."

"I see there is no way around it then. You always get what you want in the end. At least stop scaring her and let me talk her around this time."

"It didn't work so well last time."

"Last time, I was seen as an invader. You made sure of that. You twisted the situation entirely. Right now, Flint and I are on even ground."

With pursed lips, Enzo took two steps back but kept his eyes on Flint, still adding that extra layer of intimidation.

"Would you like to bond with me, Flint?" I asked gently holding out my cupped hands in front of me.

Her eyes were terrified, jumping from Enzo to me and back again. I knew it was the last thing she wanted having only just lost her bonded soul.

"Don't worry about Enzo. Flint, just look at me." Waiting until I had her full attention, I continued. "I have lost Shard and you have lost *Fitz*." I motioned with my eyes at the misty purple, glowing ball in my hands and Flint finally noticed Fitz's soul. I held a hand up as she began to get excited. "We could have a good life together and allow our fallen friends the long rest they deserve. If you would like to bond with me and give yourself another chance at rebirth, please come to me now and bow your head."

Slowly, Flint skimmed around the outside of Enzo, his eyes following her movements, and came to me. Hope filled her eyes in that moment and it was so beautiful and warm to behold. She bowed her head low and I hugged into her, gentle and innocent while allowing her to absorb the Soul of Fitz once more. It wasn't everything he was but he would be there with her now and she could take him with her through her next rebirth.

"Make sure to get out of her quickly, ok," I whispered in her ear. "It's about to get messy."

With a chirp, Flint took off into the sky and in moments, was far from the field.

"What is this?" Enzo demanded.

"I returned Fitz's soul to her. She is whole again," I said happily.

"You did what?" literal flames began to pour from his armour as Enzo started on me with sword in hand. "How dare you. After everything I've done to secure this for you."

"I promised Shard I would live a full life but it seems my time will be at an end sooner than we both planned. At least he doesn't need to wait too long."

"Shard? The lice ridden parrot will not see another life. I will destroy his egg long before his resurrection."

Talon actually hissed into a low reverberating chirp.

"I always knew you were a threat to the Phoenix. That you wouldn't hesitate to take one down if need be."

"Oh, I don't need to but if it would spite you... A pity you won't get to witness the act." Lifting his sword Enzo made to strike when three large talons burst through his chest in a spray of blood that stained my cloak and hair.

Enzo turned with disbelief to find Talon was the one to end him.

"Why?" he uttered before falling over in death.

"I'm sorry it had to be this way, Aethalion. May you know peace in your next life."

There was a look in his eyes that echoed freedom and he chirped a final melodic song before laying upon the earth. His body began to instantly transition into ash.

I was confused, knowing Talon held no wound.

Korr came up beside me and rested a hand on my shoulder. "When Phoenix kill own Soul, none return."

"What?" my eyes blazed.

"Phoenix block path to rebirth. Both final death."

"Talon will never be reborn because he destroyed Enzo, his Soul?"

Korr just nodded once.

My breath trembled in my lungs as I found out new depths to Talon's act... but then smiled. He knew what would happen and he did it anyway. That, final look of freedom. Talon had wanted this. Needed this.

"I hope you find the freedom you were looking for, Aethalion."

Chapter 19

It was more crowded than expected on the cliff top overlooking North and South. The BrongTa could move quickly when they wanted to, moving the great distance in only half a day to beat the sun. I could have sworn some form of magic was involved but I didn't broach the subject. The tribe was allowed its secrets. I was happy that they could join us for the farewell of Fitz and Talon along with the awakening of Shard. As ancestors of those who brought the Phoenix into existence, they held this privilege.

The sun was beginning to get low and I knew it wouldn't be long now. Focusing, I closed my eyes, to transition into spirit. I wanted to say my last goodbyes knowing Shard would be circling, but a hand touched my shoulder and I turned to find Korr standing by me with an elder of the BrongTa.

"I am sorry to encroach on your grieving but I wanted to broach a subject with you," the elder said. He had a greater grasp of the northern accent than Korr did.

"I am sorry..." I looked to Korr in silent question of the man's name.

"Gurradingabubbulundiagunhabeneha..." A hand rested on Korr's arm.

"She is occupied right now. Let us return afterwards."

I realised Korr had been stopped half way through. "Wait, there was more?"

Korr nodded and the Elder smiled.

"We will see you after, Elara ShardSoul." The elder turned and walked back into the crowd with Korr close behind.

I settled back, sitting on the cliffs edge and transitioned. Startled, I burst into laughter finding Shard sitting beside me. The white feathers really suited him.

"Thought you may have been flying," I said as I settled.

"There is nowhere else I want to be."

I got up and wrapped my arms around his neck. "I'm going to miss you, Shard. You knew my every thought and memory intimately and you never judged me once. Even when I went off the rails. It is you that is needed in this world."

"And I will return in time but it is not me. It is just simple kindness. When you go out into the world, think of me and do one kind thing each day on my behalf. You'll find that kindness grows."

My lip began to quiver as I held back tears. "I don't want to lose you, Shard. I don't know how to go on without you."

"You will find the way forward in time. Life is full of loss and regret but there is also joy and happiness mixed in too. Come on, the sun is sinking now. You need to go back and sing the hymn."

As I watched the sun get ever closer to the horizon, I held to Shard tighter sneaking in a final neck scratch.

"Rest well, my friend," I said and shifted quickly to my body lest I stay with Shard forever. Tears filled my eyes and I walked over to stand beside Flint. "I welcome your words into my heart and mind to sing for our lost friends and kin."

Flint nodded and I placed a hand on her neck slowly scratching as I would have Shard. As Korr had before me, I allowed the words of Flint to flow through me, using my voice to sing the Hymn of the Phoenix. Even as the words reverberated in my mind, I still couldn't understand what I was saying.

The ashes of Shard gathered in a dancing sphere above our heads, seemingly brought in on the four winds. Raising my arms as I sang, I let go of the blue and white flames that resided within me to surge up on blazing wings and merge with the gathering ash. I watched as they grew and merged, shrank and dimmed, all the while drinking in the final rays of sunlight.

A smile touched my lips witnessing the brilliant explosion that formed the Phoenix of Shard. Trails of flames were left in his wake as he, first, circled me in tight form warming the skin and, then, heading off into the distance where the nesting grounds lay. His essence safe until my own could mix in with him.

Tilting my head back, I closed my eyes and let the tears flow free. I knew it was going to be hard. I was just happy I didn't collapse into a heap on the rock shelf. It was dark when I could allow myself to move once more, the stars riding the night sky in a beautiful display.

Then my eyes widened. I was surprised to find the Phoenix and Korr along with the Elder, Kymberlin and Baras, had remained behind.

"Sorry, were you waiting on me?" I asked, a touch of guilt crossing my mind as my cheeks reddened.

"It is beautiful, the true emotion felt for friends. We carry them always in our hearts and minds. We were happy to wait," The Elder said.

My blush deepened. "You wanted to talk to me before. I am sorry but I will not be able to remember your name with any ounce of clarity but could we have the discussion now."

"Gurra will be fine," Gurra said and I nodded. "What I wanted to discuss involves everyone here."

I looked around seeing the tightknit group. "It seems serious."

"What I ask involves sacrifice and more loss for those that remain."

"Then don't ask it," I said. "I don't want to know."

"It won't be your choice in the end. You are here because you deserve to be involved," Gurra said.

"I don't want to know," I said turning to walk away.

"The Phoenix deserve to give birth to real chicks again."

I froze in my stride. Of all the things I had expected to come from his mouth. There was a deep sigh as my shoulders sagged in defeat. I would never hold this back from the Phoenix. Walking to where Baras sat, I sat beside him for comfort and leaned my head against his shoulder. "I will listen and accept whatever the Phoenix decide."

The Elder nodded and stepped forward to address the group. "The BrongTa can shift the magic of the Phoenix. We can draw the essence and life force of one to open the pathways for creating life in another. Two Phoenix would choose this life as their last, giving everything to restore the reproductive abilities in Shard and Ember. It will only work on Phoenix within their eggs. And the Phoenix that gain this ability will lose the path to rebirth."

Shit, I thought to myself, hitting my head upon Baras until I felt his hand in my hair. He gently cradled my head to be still, showing me love.

"So, we are not only choosing to sacrifice two Phoenix but to make the choice for Shard and Ember whether they have one or many lives more?" Kymberlin asked, her face set in a frown.

"It is why we have all been chosen to be here. You know Shard and Ember best. What they may want."

"Stop," I said, standing. We aren't going to go back and forth about who wants what and why. It is not up to us. If there are two Phoenix who choose to sacrifice themselves then do so. Nothing lives forever. Talon is an example of this. This way the Phoenix may have a chance to thrive again. Shard and Ember will get what they get. They could get angry or upset either way."

"Agreed," Baras said beside me. Korr and Kymberlin made no objection.

"Gurra. I understand you want to breach this subject tenderly but, in the end, we all could say yes and two Phoenix no. It is a straight forward question. Are they willing to give their lives for the future of their species."

Baras took a quick shuddering breath. "They are all willing but two are already chosen."

I pouted but kept my chin up. "And who will I be saying goodbye to."

Flint stepped forward and a lump started in my throat. I nodded my understanding. She lost her Soul. She was in the depths of pain. "You are quite sure?"

Baras looked sharply at Haze as if talking. "She is the only female left. Her energy will syphon into Ember."

"Not much of a choice then but I see you still face it with strength and love." I embraced Flint as I had Shard. "I will make sure to protect the eggs of the nest."

Flint backed off and whistled a soft melody before taking flight for the nesting grounds. Flames of yellow and orange lighting the night sky in her wake.

"And the male?"

Baras seemed to be in a deep discussion with Haze. Emotions playing all over his face in the voiceless conversation. In the end, Kymberlin wrapped her arms around his waist, holding Baras from behind.

"It's ok, my love. Ash and I have chosen this. It is best. You love the field and have held the dream of being a Phoenix Soul since young. Your legacy will be the last Phoenix Soul."

"But I don't want to take this from you, Honeypot," Baras said and a sudden unexpected grinding noise sounded from my throat as I tried to hold in the laughter.

Kymberlin shot me a dirty look before turning back to Baras. So much love and caring for the man shone in her eyes. "I will not be long for the field, Baras." She said, stepping back, holding her belly.

"Are you dying?" Baras asked suddenly concerned.

Kymberlin just raised an eyebrow. The opposite nostril also lifting at his density.

"Oh my god, you're with child, Kymmie. Baras you're going to be a dad," I said to help the man along. There was real emotion in my voice as something beautiful and happy was occurring for once.

It took a few moments for the words to register with Baras but as they did, his eyes grew wide.

"A child?"

Kymberlin just nodded and Baras teared up moving to take Kymberlin's hands. He was excited, over the moon even and completely lost for words but Kymberlin, myself, and even Korr all cried tears of joy.

I allowed Baras and Kymberlin their special moment. Walking to where Ash was roosting, I sat beside him.

"We haven't had too many fond memories together. You always seemed a little shy and held back. Maybe you were just weary of me because I was Fibonacci."

Ash let out a soft whistle.

"Today you are doing something amazing. It takes a certain beautiful and loving soul to make the sacrifice you are today. I will look after the nest... And keep an eye on Baras, the child, and your Honeypot."

Ash gave the same awkward and crooked smile that Shard did.

"Farewell, Ash."

Getting to my feet I walked to the edge of the cliff. The rim of the moon was just peaking over the horizon. A soft mist lay upon the peaceful land below.

Taking in a deep breath, I screamed with all the force my lungs could give, out over the land.

Epilogue

I sat by the eggs stroking Shard's hard shell. My hand was now wrinkled with darks spots echoing the eighty years of this life. My hair had greyed almost thirty years ago, about the time Calan had passed from this world. Father of my children and a good natured and honest man. I knew it wasn't quite what I had with Riven but I loved him non the less.

My youngest, the cheeky sod, had married Asha, joining Baras, Kymberlin and my families together. There was a great celebration over this but none of us parents could see how their love grew with an age gap of 12 years. Asha had always been indifferent around boys and then suddenly, she and my son announced their engagement. They've given me the most grandkids, though, so I can't complain too much.

I couldn't say what happened to Korr. I could feel his energy swirling within the egg of Ember but I'd lost touch with the big man. He spent years at a time learning BrongTa secrets and perfecting the White Ash Flame. The last time I saw him, two years after the great battle, His hair had turned pure white. He told me it was from awakening the White Ash Flame, but I believe he was reverting back to some form of goat. I smiled at my inner monologue.

And now it was just me in the wilderness. My life hanging by a thread, at the mercy of some terrible sickness, the healers say. I laughed merrily. Those healers couldn't understand even the simplest of ailments. Drink the blood of a moose. Bathe naked in the light of a full moon. Put myrtle in a jar with your own piss under the bed for a week while you sleep.

Pfft. I don't know what witch woman had trained them but they were a joke. With my Drifter abilities I was able to see right to the heart of the problem and cure it with my own energy. This time however, it was my energy that was running out. Organs had begun to fail and there was nothing more I could do. The only sickness I suffered from was old age.

"So, I lived a full life, Shard, and, yes, there was heartache and turmoil and pain. But there was also love and purity and endless memories of such perfect joy. I learned to smile again. I learned to view the world without negativity. I learned what it meant to truly live a life. Thank you, Shard, for calling me out and showing me there is more than the hardships. I hope your life and that of your chicklings are just as wonderful.

"Farewell, Vashardiel."

There was no fear of what I was about to do. No worries for what was to come. I couldn't tell if Shard had heard my ramblings or not but at

377

least when my life energy transfers to him, he will experience it and will know I was happy.

Placing a hand atop Shard's egg, I allowed my life force to flow from my body and into his, providing the energy he needed for hatching and his early days. The world started to dim as shadows filled my vision. When the light fled me completely, I could barely hold myself aware. My head rested on the soft earth beside Shard, and everything started to fold in on itself. Then, a voice in the darkness.

"Rest well, my friend."

Thank you for your time. If you like what you've read? A review on Amazon goes a long way. I hope to hear from you.
Or if you just want to chat, find me on Facebook.

~

www.ingramcontent.com/pod-product-compliance
Lightning Source LLC
Chambersburg PA
CBHW050534260626
47157CB00002B/297